The Veiled Soul

Abbie Chandler

Front cover art creative attribution to
www.CoverDesignStudio.com and Kasia.

Back cover art creative attribution to
www.CoverDesignStudio.com and Mike Bailey-Gates.

For my father, who always thought I could do anything. I wish you could have seen this, and I miss you every day.

Chapter One

There exists an ancient race that predates humanity. They hide in the shadows, weighing the actions and intentions of the soul and passing judgment on the damned. They are the hidden backbone of humanity, balancing life and death, creation and destruction, good and evil. I do not know their history, their story, or their motivation. I am not meant to. I am merely a tool, a small speck of dust no longer allowed to understand the world.

I am a reaper.

I live in a parallel realm controlled by judges, serving my punishment for sins against humanity. I pass between the two worlds, ferrying souls to their final resting place. I am nothing more than a shell, deprived of my soul and my memories. I watch, and I am watched. Only the split of time between life and death allows me to touch anything real.

But walls collapse. Boundaries tear. And the oddest chain of events can leave a bloodied trail to the unexpected.

1943
Just outside the Auschwitz gates

The drops of blood in the snow hypnotized her as they spread outwards, contaminating the purity of frozen innocence. White to red. One single drop forever changed the ground beneath. The blood expanded as it marked her path of guilt, leading from her blade to the man with the twisted cross upon his uniform. She had witnessed the cruelty of his actions and was responsible for the lifeless eyes that now stared upwards.

She glanced at the path she had made, her gaze landing on the corpse. The thoughts in her head were dancing to the accelerated beat of her heart, but only one thought stood out.

He is coming.

Her grip on the handle of her dagger tightened as she scrambled for a memory. He was coming. He would take her back, but who was he? And where could she hide?

He is coming!

A wave of emotion fell over her. She shoved the dagger in her pocket and ran, struggling through the deep snow, desperate to put as much distance between herself and the proof of her sin.

Crunch. Crunch. Crunch.

The stolen boots on her feet were too large, and she stumbled as she entered a deeply wooded area. She pulled herself up, running, gasping. The trees clawed at her face, but a sense of urgency and an explicit memory of the prison that awaited her fueled her.

The temperature dropped in the most unnatural way, seeping into her bones. She struggled against it, but it wrapped around her, trapping her, paralyzing her. She managed to crawl up to a tree and slip her hands into her pockets before she froze to the point of immobility.

As she stared ahead, she was struck by the irony of the vision before her. Here she was, in a world of color, but only able to stare at the white of the snow and the gray of the trees. There was no sun to warm her skin, only the clothes on her back and the blood of another.

It was hardly a change for her.

Starting as a small dot and spreading outwards into a portal, a mask of gray shaded the snow and trees. It was just a small area, enough for two men to emerge from the gray world, themselves still visions of black and white.

Her eyes locked with the man on the left. He was her enemy, but she didn't know why. He was tall, well over six-feet, tucked away in gloves and a trench coat. As the colors melted into him, she saw his piercing blue eyes. She struggled to sear the color into her brain.

Remember him.

She spoke, struggling against the paralysis. "He was hurting people. I watched him first; he was killing them! You cannot hold that against me!"

He shook his head. In a monotone voice, he began to speak. "Annalia Sophia Asim, you are charged with crimes..."

"He was a murderer," she whispered.

"And you are not a judge of souls!" he burst out. His blue eyes flashed with anger. "It is always you, and you don't even realize it!"

Her eyebrows drew together in puzzlement of his words, but in favor of her survival, she instead focused on his passion. He had anger. He had humanity. He could be weakened.

"I am sorry," she whispered. The words slipped out of her mouth, surprising even her as a plan formed in her mind.

He lifted his hand upward, controlling her, forcing her body to obey him. She flew into the air in one fluid, unnatural motion. He floated her body closer to him, stopping her only inches from his own. "Are you really sorry?"

She said nothing in return, and after shaking his head at her silence, he put one hand against her chest. "Annalia Sophia Asim, you are charged with crimes against mankind. You will serve your sentence stripped of your humanity."

He put a second hand on her head, and she tried to struggle against the essence flowing out of her. Her memories were fading. Her will was failing her.

She closed her eyes and focused. She concentrated on the energy within her and with one burst of power, she momentarily freed herself from his control. With the last of her strength, she buried her blade in his side, but it was too late. Even as he fell away, the last of her memories and the essence of her soul left her.

She floated across the boundary of realms, nothing more than a human shell, gripping her blade, able to see and listen but not process. She existed but only as a shadow of who she once was. She watched him stumble and struggle. She saw his partner disappear as the gray world surrounded her and her captor. She watched his panic as the blood flowed out of him.

Put it back.

The words surrounded them, echoes of the wind. She fell to the ground unable to react to the impact.

Even as he stepped towards her to obey the wind, she could not move, could not understand her surroundings. She cared for nothing.

Put it back.

Present Day

It was the last job of the day, and it was by far the messiest. Lia watched as a fountain of dark red spurted out of the chest of one pale man. Figures worked frantically to try to stop the gushing of blood, but it was futile. The hospital machines whined in the background. It was faint, dulled by the fog that surrounded every part of Lia's life.

Aware that time was at hand, she stepped forward. Splotches of blood stood out on her discolored clothes, and as soon as she leaned forward, it painted almost every inch of fabric on her body. She took a moment to gaze down at the color, so unused to seeing herself in such a vibrant manner. The appreciation only lasted a moment as she reached out her hand, still changing from the hues of gray of her world to a chalky white, and placed it on the chest of the dying man.

It was a sensation that she experienced multiple times a day, and yet still she could not explain it. Calling for the soul, navigating it, and excavating it was an intuition.

She felt it brush up against her hand and gave it a tug. In an instant, she was controlling a ball of blues and greens swirling around, hovering just above the palm of her hand. It was calm, ready, and for that, Lia was grateful.

She backed into the corner of the room, watching with muted interest as the doctors continued to work on the man, her presence obviously unnoticed. After a moment, the room fell into a deathly silence; even the machines had quieted to observe the passing of time that was both natural and feared. The colors and the people faded, leaving Lia alone with the soul in a silent world. Only the soul held its color.

Lia sat it down and watched as it manifested itself in its natural form, a black and gray version of the body that was now dead on the other side of the boundary.

He was an elderly gentleman with withered skin and calm eyes; his hair still held onto its roots in tufts and curls, standing in whichever manner the strand chose. He wore tattered jeans and a t-shirt still shredded and spattered with blood.

"Are you an angel?" the soul asked.

Angels were always the first conclusion that souls jumped too. "No, I am just a reaper."

Clearly disappointed, the man nodded. "Am I going to heaven?"

Lia turned her back on him and faced the wall. "Where you are going is not for me to know. I am only here to open the entrance."

The man looked at himself in dismay. "Is this how I have to look when I meet my maker?"

Lia shrugged. She placed the palm of her hand on the wall of the hospital, and light shot out from the touch, eroding away the physical form of the wall. She looked at the gentleman. "All you have to do is step through."

The man walked forward before hesitating. He turned to her. "You know, I often wondered how this would be. I was always prepared to die. I even looked forward to it after my wife passed, but you were not at all what I imagined."

Lia wavered for a moment. It was not uncommon for souls to

stall the inevitable, talk about their life, or plead for just a few more days, but she felt an odd spark of interest in what this man had to say. "What did you imagine?"

He smiled sadly. "Oh, many things. Angels with trumpets, my wife throwing me a welcome home party, even a line at the pearly gates."

"Maybe that is what awaits you on the other side."

"Are you sad that you are guiding souls, and yet you don't know what it is you are guiding them to?"

Lia thought for a moment. "No."

He put his hand up and played with the tendrils of light that curled around his fingers. They seem to beckon at him seductively. "Then why do you do it?"

Lia cocked her head. "It is not a choice. It is a punishment."

The man stopped playing and stared at her. "How long have you being doing this?"

"Decades I suppose. I do not know."

"What is your crime?"

Lia's hand wavered slightly, and the light dimmed considerably. "I do not know. I have no memories of anything except this."

"How long will you be punished?"

Lia smiled bitterly. "Until they decide I have served my sentence."

"And who are they?"

Lia pushed her hand against the wall and the light brightened and spread wider until it hid everything except the two figures talking. "The judges that weigh your soul. Please, it is your time."

The man pushed his hand through and looked at Lia. "I suppose I'll have my answers on the other side. Perhaps you will as well." With that, he walked through the light, and it swallowed him whole, leaving Lia alone. When she removed her hand, the lights faded, leaving her alone in the gray hospital room.

She looked down at her shirt. The blood had faded to black

and gray, but she could still feel the stickiness of it as it pressed down on her body. Blood always weighed the heaviest when it belonged to someone else.

Her jobs completed, she faced another quiet and dull evening of being alone. She had only a few years of memories to entertain her and no soul to allow regrets or excitement. She made her way home, hopping on the empty buses and cars driven by the phantom chills of the physical world. Lia stepped through the walls of the house she inhabited and laid down on the bed. She was not tired, but she would still sleep to pass the time.

She would not dream.

The alarm on Lia's iPhone jangled noisily several hours before her first reap the next morning. An unscheduled event usually meant a reaper had finished their sentence and was allowed to move on. A message accompanied her alarm. Her month-long stay at the house was almost up. She would need to find a new place to squat.

She stretched languidly on her bed and rolled herself off, careless as her feet hit the hardwood floor. Perhaps earlier in her career she would have winced in anticipation of a cold floor, but it was always cold. Everything was cold.

The reaper realm existed on top of the physical world, and everything was intact except for the actual people. She saw animals, buildings, even planes, but there were no loud noises like laughter or crying.

There was no color.

While reapers go about their lives unseen from the living, they were only allowed to crash at a single place for one month at a time because their ghostly footprints remained. Whether it was a cup someone didn't remember leaving out or a desperate search for the remote, more than a few weeks of unexplained occurrences could leave nasty lasting effects on the physical world. The judges didn't like cleaning up.

Still, it unsettled Lia to move all the time. It was easy enough to slip through the wall to the next apartment to see if it was livable, but sometimes she wanted to find something different.

Her phone vibrated again. Her reaper unit's messenger wanted her to join him for dinner. Paul was a reaper, but he was always oddly eager for company and still desired to feel the connection of companionship. Lia enjoyed his company from time to time as a way to break away from the mundane.

Her phone listed the rooms and times of her reaps. Her day's work would consist mostly of hospital patients, a comfortable job for a reaper. The new reapers in her unit were forced to run around town, hopping different modes of transportation to make reap times. There was little of that for her.

Lia started a pot of coffee. Her stay in the empty hotel room offered her indulgences that other places did not. Although she didn't need the caffeine, she indulged in what she could only imagine were habits. She still jogged to keep in shape although her body weight never changed. She still ate even though her body didn't need nourishing. These were little things that she rarely thought twice about. Many of the reapers still went through the motions of the living.

She gazed out the window. This place offered a view that pleased her. Though she rarely saw color, even the reaper realm could not hide the mountains. She had heard that Colorado was a sunny and beautiful place, but every day was hazy and gray to her. Still, the mountains rose in the distance, and when she looked at them, she felt a connection to the world.

The effects of the weather still occasionally slipped through the veil. The dampness of the rain and the frigidness of the snow sometimes nipped at her skin. If she focused, she could feel the warmth of the sun on her face. These were cracks within the boundary. Just the other day, a brilliant yellow butterfly fluttered past her face, vivid against the hazy gray sky. It was haunting and beautiful.

She lived for the days where her reaps occurred outside. Her few minutes in the physical world allowed her skin to kiss the sun and bask in the glow of the moon. Today she could feel the cold seeping in from the windowsills and knew the haze that hugged the mountains wasn't all from the reaper realm.

Lia poured herself the cup of coffee and inadvertently passed a mirror on the wall. She stopped, a rare occurrence, to stare at her reflection in despair. Her dark hair hung limply down her back, and her lips were nearly as pale as her skin. Her eyes bothered her the most. As years passed, they seemed to die a little more, becoming more dull and lifeless. Some days her irises were so dark they were black. Maybe she was becoming death itself.

She didn't know how reapers died. They no longer possessed souls to reap. She entertained the idea that maybe the body and soul rejoined briefly before forever separated and set free. Or maybe it was just a rumor. Maybe reapers were merely reassigned and never moved on. In any case, she had a feeling she was not supposed to dwell on these ideas.

Drops of coffee dotted the counter, and Lia used the sleeve of her sweatshirt to wipe up after herself. She was a good reaper, well trained or perhaps just well programmed. She never really knew the difference.

As she passed through the wall to the outside world, a thick fog greeted her. It took a moment for her eyes to adjust. An eerie silence blanketed the streets, but it was no different than any other day. Her unit of reapers consisted of one master, one messenger, and less than a hundred reapers. It was rare to cross paths with another on the street.

Lia liked the solitude. She wandered along the streets occasionally walking through the shadow of a living soul across the parallel world. It was a freezing numb sensation that raised goose bumps on her arms, and she often wondered if the living felt the same.

After about twenty minutes of strolling, she found a cute street of houses and slipped through a particularly charming two-story. The television was on The History Channel, and Lia joined her invisible companion. It was a documentary on World War I, and Lia listened briefly. She had taught herself to navigate the computer and reveled in knowledge of the past. She was wired to feel detached, uninterested from such notions, and sometimes the knowledge quickly evaporated from her mind, but the initial spark to learn was always there. The channels changed rapidly, ending with the news. Lia cocked her head and listened to the story. People were fascinating sometimes.

"Yesterday a young bartender showed up for his shift dressed in a Batman costume, insisting on doling out justice for crimes against restaurant workers," the news anchor announced. A video started playing on the screen as a young man with a boy-band haircut swooped around the bar dressed in a black mask and cape.

"I am the hero this restaurant deserves, but not the one it needs right now," he said menacingly to a table, his voice low and raspy.

"The man was eventually arrested for disturbing the peace. In other news, the hunt is still on for a young girl missing in Colorado. Audrey has the update. Audrey?"

After a moment, Lia got up and wandered around. She scouted the place with vague interest. The bathroom alone told her she was in the presence of an elderly man who was dying. His medicine cabinet contained pills meant to ease his passing. There was a sweet herbal aroma that lingered even in her nostrils across the barrier. She expected his name and address would appear to some reaper's phone within the next few months.

His little house was filled with pictures that told a story of a wonderfully fulfilling life. Half of them were of him and a beautiful woman with dark hair that eventually turned to a snowy white in the later years of her life

Lia studied the growth of their children, grandchildren, and great-grandchildren. She reached up and touched one of the pictures, and for the strangest moment, hoped that his passing would be gentle.

There were no dogs to bark at her, a world of books, and a guest bedroom. After a moment of consideration, Lia decided this would do for the next few weeks. There was never any need to notify anyone of the new address. The judges always knew where to find her, and so the master was always aware of the new location.

Her phone broke the silence, and she glanced at it. She had one hour until her first reap at the hospital. It was time to get moving.

Alex Karkov was only a semester and a half into his first year at the University of Colorado at Boulder. He was a lazy worker at the coffee shop on campus, and lazier still when it came to school. He came from money and was only doing what it took to meet the bare requirements set by his father to take over the family business.

In fact, Alex would probably make a terrible CEO of Karkov Industries, the manufacturing company for skiing and snowboarding equipment. That was okay because Alex Karkov was not going to survive to see the sunset.

The two things Alex did excel at were drinking and snowboarding. Unfortunately, Alex was not great at doing both at the same time. At the moment, Lia was watching a myriad of doctors attempting to save the life of this adventuring alcoholic after he, in an early morning drunken stupor, tried to snowboard off the roof of a house.

She could see bones jutting out in places they should not be visible and knew he was bleeding out internally.

Craning her neck to get a better look, she thought dispassionately about how such a lovely face was wasted on such a stupid boy. The doctors worked on what they knew would soon be nothing more than a corpse. They exchanged looks over the body, their eyes resting on the numbers that were rapidly falling.

It was time.

Lia stepped forward, invisible in the world of the living, and pressed her hand to his chest. His soul immediately curled up in her hand, and she slipped it out, quietly stepping back as the body began its final phase into death. The color and the people melted away leaving Lia alone with the soul.

It was swirling in a transparent angry ball of reds and yellows. She placed it on the floor, her face cold as it expanded, faded in color, and formed into the likeness of the dead Alex Karkov.

"What the hell is this?" he demanded, even in death a cocky young man.

Lia tried to be gentle, but compassion never came naturally to her.

"Alex, your time has come," she began.

"Time for fucking what?" he interrupted.

Patience was also not her strong suit. "You are dead," she said flatly.

"Wait, what? I'm only eighteen!" He turned desperately to her. "Put me back, I know you can do it! Please, I'm not ready to die."

"I can put you back if that is truly what you want, but your body is dead. You would only be trapped in a rotting shell. I cannot imagine that would be fun," she pointed out.

His eyes fixed on her. "You can't talk to me that way."

"I will try to make this as easy as possible, so do not fight it." She reached her hand up and placed it palm first on the wall. Once again, the scene faded into the bright lights that radiated from her touch.

"This is your final destination. All you have to do is step through."

Alex didn't move. He asked the age-old question. "What's beyond there?"

"I do not know," Lia said. There was no trace of impatience

in her voice. By now the question no longer irritated her. It was simply another part of her job, and the answer was always automatic.

"What if I don't go? Will I just stay here on earth? Will I be able to haunt people?"

It was also another wildly popular theory. "Your soul is not meant to roam free. Without a shell, a body, it will eventually wither away."

"What about ghosts? They stick around. Are they not souls?"

"Ghosts do not exist. In the end, you will fade away to nothing because you are not meant for this place anymore."

Alex nodded slowly. "I could just run, right now, if I wanted too?"

Lia removed her hand, and the lights faded. She reached her arms out towards him, gripped her fists around an invisible rope, and yanked them back, watching as he jerked and fell to the floor. "Now that I have touched your soul, I am linked to you. For a small amount of time, I will feel what you feel, and I can control you. I can force you through to the other side. I have done it before."

She reached down and helped him off the floor. "I know you are scared. Everyone is. But you are an adventurist, and this is nothing more than a new adventure."

It was obvious that his pride was hurt, but he was broken. "You know, I never did anything with my life. I was such a disappointment to my parents. I just wanted to have fun in college, the life that you see in the movies, but then I was going to settle down and be the best damn CEO Karkov Industries had ever seen. I wanted to impress my father. Now they'll never remember me as anything but a fuck up."

"That is not true. Grieving families always remember the good. You are so young. You have not had time to fuck up your life. Consider it a blessing." She reached over and opened the portal again. "It is time."

Alex smiled sheepishly and took another tentative step forward. "I don't think I can do this."

Lia nodded, hoping to look sympathetic. "Well, that is what I am here for," she said with a sigh. "Good luck in the next life, Alex Karkov." She pushed him in. He shrieked, and plunged forward, disappearing in the portal.

Lia removed her hand, and the lights dissipated. She rolled her head back and forth, stretching out the muscles in her neck. Keeping that portal open for so long had drained quite a bit of energy out of her. She hated the chatty ones.

Unfortunately, her phone was already sounding another alarm. Thirty minutes until her next reap a few hallways over.

People were always dying.

It was eight o'clock when Lia finished with her shift.

She met with Paul and a few other reapers at a local diner. Paul was already behind the line in the kitchen whipping up dinner for the group. "Hey, Lia! Whatcha feel like tonight?"

With his bubbly personality, Paul was annoying. Privately, Lia suspected he was an experiment for the judges. Maybe it had something to do with the lack of customer service in the reaping business. Most reapers had lost their sense of soul long before their collection, long before they lost their actual soul. Lia had a feeling she was no different. Paul, however, stood out with his social tendencies and had become a messenger shortly after joining the unit.

Reaping had begun using smartphones a few years ago. Before that, messengers were used to pass along reaping assignments via paper. Now they were the middlemen for the master and the reapers, conducting meetings on their behalf. The reaper realm ran like Lia suspected a corporate business did.

She made an order for her usual BLT sandwich and chips, a meal she had an affinity for after discovering it several years ago, and took a seat next to a perpetually cracked out looking blonde teenager. "Deirdre," Lia greeted coldly. She didn't particularly like Deirdre, finding her to be crude.

"Enjoy another day of dead people?" Deirdre asked sourly, making it apparent, as usual, that she didn't like Lia either.

Lia ignored her. Her eyes passed over the group. She was familiar with all the faces, all except one. He was a middle-aged man with salt and peppered hair and wrinkles around his strained eyes.

"Transfer or new?" she asked. There was far too much turmoil on the man's face, and she suspected that he was new.

She was right. "My first day out of training actually," he said after clearing his throat. He stuck out his hand. "Allen."

He had a hint of an accent, and Lia liked that. She searched the few years of memories that she did possess, but she couldn't place it. Reapers could be transferred, and so each unit was made up of accents from all over the world. It was one of the few personal qualities that a reaper kept. She liked that Allen was polite, even if his eyes were still full of pain from whatever he had experienced in life.

"Lia. Welcome to hell," she said quietly, reaching out to shake his hand. She felt some interest stirring inside her. With his fit and trim body, the new man looked as though he would make a great escape from her routine.

Paul joined their table, carrying plates of food. "Okay! So this is not an official meeting, but I've just gotten word that we have a new master."

This caused no apparent reaction in anyone. Privately, Lia was unsettled. Jackson had been a fair master, kept to himself, and left her alone. She didn't like the idea of change.

Paul surveyed their lack of energy on the subject. "Right. Okay, moving on. It's my dead day!" he declared joyously.

"Paul, you don't know when your dead day is," Deirdre muttered.

"I know. I'm making it up," Paul said ignoring her nasty

attitude. He leaned over and pressed a wet kiss to Lia's cheek. She immediately slapped him.

"No touching," she said automatically. Paul rubbed his cheek and smiled.

"I love it when you play rough," he teased. "I hope everyone has met Allen. We've set him up in the place next to Jackson's for the next few weeks if anyone wants to stop by and harass him."

Introductions were shuffled around the room, and Lia munched on her sandwich. Although she could barely distinguish taste, she recognized textures and enjoyed the satisfying crunch of the meal. She hated these social hours, but for some reason, they all gathered together from time to time. And, much like tonight, most of them never said a word. They only went through the motions of eating, content with being close to someone else.

Hours later, Paul automatically stretched and rolled out of Lia's bed. He no longer had to be told when he wasn't welcome anymore, and Lia knew that he didn't mind. Whether their few moments together was out of some fundamental desire or out of habit, she knew that neither one of them got any sense of real pleasure out of it.

She couldn't remember how their trysts had started, and it was never a scheduled moment or a time of passion. Usually, every few weeks, one of them would simply show up, and, after a bit, they would leave.

It was one of the rare moments where Paul was quiet. There was no idle chatter or annoying comments. Lia wondered if he felt anything at all while he was with her. She would never ask, and she doubted he would ever say.

She watched as he pulled on his pants. With a glance over his shoulder, accompanied with a small smile, he sauntered back through the wall. She rolled over in bed and faced the opposite side.

There were so many things about the reaper world that she

didn't understand. Part of her felt isolated and craved contact, and part of her relished the silence of the world. She didn't think she was supposed to feel anything, but she knew that even the muted moments with Paul left her beyond frustrated.

She wanted to touch something real.

When she reaped souls, she relished the moments where she could touch a body. For just a few seconds, when the worlds collided, the skin would be warm under her fingers, and she would feel the heartbeat subside as she guided the soul out of the body.

Then the physical world would melt away, and she was left empty.

She wasn't tired. She was never tired, but she still closed her eyes and willed her body into a restful mode. There was nothing left to do for the day, and she wanted some peace from her overactive mind.

Chapter Two

Hunter Logan stepped back after exhausting all possibilities. "Time of death, ten forty-seven am," he called out, slipping his mask off his face. The young man's blood covered his surgical scrubs, and Hunter's neck was cramped from the awkward way he'd angled his head for a better view. He tried to avoid looking at his scrubs. He'd come to abhor the sight of blood.

After announcing the time of death, the other doctors and nurses bowed their heads in a moment of respectful silence. One of the nurses turned off the machines, amplifying the sounds of the sobs heard from outside the room. The acoustics in the hospital bounced off everything and could be heard from corridors away. It echoed the heartbreak and pain.

The worst part of his job was talking to the family. He'd long ago felt that he'd lost the compassion he needed. There were days where he felt like nothing more than a simple shell.

The Karkov family was highly influential in all parts of Colorado, and the hospital was no exception. The loss of their son within the walls of the facility would reduce their money flow to the hospital, and that meant his work here would be put under great scrutiny from the hospital administration.

He despised hospital bureaucracy. The board members focused on money, reputation, and politics first and let the real priority of the health of the patients fall by the wayside. The death of Alex Karkov would be high on their radar.

"Mr. and Mrs. Karkov, I'm Dr. Logan, a general surgeon here at St. Antony Central Hospital. I'm sorry to tell you that Alex suffered multiple internal injuries during his fall. As a result, he bled out faster than we could repair the damage. I'm sorry for your loss," he said, clasping his hands in prayer form as he talked.

"We are going to sue you for everything you have!" Alicia Karkov had not come from money, and thus flaunted and threatened with her newfound influence.

Her husband, however, was far more level-headed and wrapped his arms around his wife to avoid any violent confrontation. "Alicia, I'm sure the doctor did everything he could for Alex. Let's just concentrate on where we go from here," he said quietly, tears running down his face.

"The nurses will assist you with the procedure from here. They will also have all the paperwork, and you can call the hospital at any time if you need any more information on the details. Once again, I'm sorry for your loss. We did do everything we could for as long as we could." The automatic words poured out, but they were no less true. Hunter always did his best. To lose a life always seemed to strip another layer from his soul.

"Thank you, Doctor," Mr. Karkov said quietly.

"You are welcome to go in and say your goodbyes. Take as much time as you need." Hunter remained where he was until they were around the corner before letting out a small sigh of relief. The confrontation hadn't gone as badly as he first imagined.

Still, he knew that as soon as he was out of his scrubs and gearing up to go home, his boss would be waiting for him.

He had been called in on his day off to help with a car crash that had entered the ER six hours ago, and the Karkov boy landed on his table just as he was trying to change out of his scrubs. It had been a long and trying night. He did not want to deal with any board members. The loss of life was bad enough.

Hunter made his way to join the other doctors cleaning up. "Helluva mess," one doctor muttered to him.

"No kidding. I'm sure McCarthy is going to chew us out as soon as we're done here," another chimed in.

"Gentlemen, ladies, we did the best we could, and that's all anyone can ask of us," Hunter said, wearily. These days, he was making an effort to turn things around. His therapist had recommended an optimistic front whenever possible, even if he didn't feel it inside.

"It's just a waste of youth," one nurse said sadly, shaking her head. "He couldn't be more than twenty, drinking and partying his way to an early death. Parents just don't teach their kids any common sense anymore. I mean, how are we supposed to save a kid from six internal injuries? It would have taken a miracle."

Hunter turned from his washing station and stopped suddenly. For a moment, the temperature dropped, sending a massive cold chill up his spine and raising the hairs on his neck. A nurse narrowed her eyes as she watched him shudder. "Dr. Logan? Are you okay?"

He looked around and noticed that none of the other staff had reacted. "Just a cold chill," he said mildly, thinking about how he had never experienced one with such intensity.

Corinne, Hunter's favorite nurse, popped her head in the door. "Dr. Glassery, you're needed in room 227. There is a young woman with injuries from multiple stab wounds. They're saying she may be a victim of the Phoenix. I don't think she's going to make it through the night, but they are asking for all hands on deck. Dr. Logan, they're saying you can head home. The Chief is too busy with the police right now to deal with the Karkov family, so if you slip out now, you'll probably miss him."

"Thanks, Corinne. Have a good night," Hunter said as she hurried out. He turned to Glassery. "A live victim? This place is probably crawling with police."

Glassery shook his balding head. "I hate going into a room knowing I'm probably going to lose," he said sadly. "I hope they catch that son of a bitch soon."

Hunter nodded, but his mind was already on other things.

Hunter's home was about twenty miles north of the hospital. Because of its size, he shared it with his brother Aaron and Lauren, Aaron's girlfriend. The arrangement suited him. The dark green house was large with four bedrooms, two living areas, a huge spacious basement, and a large fenced in yard. It sat two streets away from a large park where the rolling green hills, fishing ponds, tennis courts, and playgrounds spanned several blocks. Hunter had originally bought it thinking of his future family living there. That was before he proposed to his ex, before he left for his first tour in Iraq.

Now it seemed to have very little personality. Hunter, particular about cleanliness, kept it neat and orderly but furnished it with a large flat screen television, several bland pieces of sitting furniture, a coffee table, and a bar. Occasionally Lauren would sneak in a throw pillow here and there, but the dog usually turned it into a chew toy. Lauren always accused Hunter of teaching him that trick. The truth was that Hunter cared very little for whatever changes she and Aaron made to the house. He was gone so often that he felt like a stranger in his own home.

Jacks, his three-year-old golden retriever, met him at the door. The dog was a source of joy and frustration. His family had adopted him after several months of Hunter moving back. They were concerned when he came back different, disconnected. After receiving the fur ball wrapped in a red bow, Hunter immediately tried to give the dog back. There was no way he'd be responsible for another life. Unfortunately, something had happened on that trip back to the humane society. He'd made a connection with the dog's warm brown eyes and made a u-turn back home. He had simultaneously regretted and loved the decision ever since. Jacks was a loving and loyal companion, but his curiosity was always a source of trouble. It never failed to surprise Hunter the kind of trouble that damn dog could get into.

"Hey boy, did you miss me?" Hunter asked taking a moment to scratch behind the dog's ears. Together, they crossed the house.

The dog's nails clicking across the hardwood floor until they reached the back door where Jacks bounded out happily to relieve himself.

When Hunter went upstairs, he noticed a trail of dirty clothes leading from the hall to his bedroom. "Jacks," Hunter growled. He flipped the light on in his room and saw where the retriever had knocked the dirty hamper over and spilled his clothes.

"Jacks!" Hunter bellowed. His dog came bounding up the stairs but on seeing the mess he had made, immediately tucked his tail between his legs and lowered his head. He whined pitifully.

"What is this?" Hunter said, trying to ignore the sad look on the dog's face. He reached down and picked up a shirt, shaking it in Jacks' direction. "Did you do this?"

The dog whined again and slunk slowly out of the room. Hunter shook his head and gathered the dirty clothes back in his hamper. He stripped his clothes off and fell face down on the bed.

Jacks jumped up and cuddled next to him. Hunter reached down and scratched the dog's head. Soon they were both fast asleep.

That evening Hunter was joined by a blind date. His coworker had set him up with the beautiful blonde hoping they would hit it off. Hunter kissed her lightly on the cheek, resting his hand at the small of her back as they followed the hostess through the restaurant to their table. His date seemed both surprised and flattered when he pulled out her chair, and she giggled nervously.

As he took his seat, he thanked the hostess, a cute blonde who looked right out of high school, and noticed his date shoot her a second look of inspection.

"Kat, what do you think your drink preference will be this evening?" he asked as he opened the menu.

She was a beauty in a simple blue sweater dress that contrasted against her soft curls. His co-workers had explained that Kat was having a hard time adjusting to Colorado after a life in New York and was looking to meet new people.

"A nice oaky glass of chardonnay would be wonderful," she responded thoughtfully, glancing over the wine menu.

Hunter nodded absently, looking over the beer list and wishing he could have one. A young woman stopped by their table, leaning over to place a cocktail napkin down "Welcome to Alfino's! I hope we're all having a good evening. My name is Alicia, and I'll be taking care of you tonight."

"We are doing well, how about yourself?" Hunter asked politely, glancing up from the menus. Kat kept her eyes down.

"I'm having a great evening. Would you like...."

"We'll start with a bottle of your oldest St. Supery Chardonnay, and two glasses of water," Kat interrupted the waitress abruptly. Hunter frowned at the rudeness.

"Actually, I'll just have a tea, please," Hunter said quickly. He ignored the look on Kat's face.

"Okay, just a glass for me then," she said slowly.

The server nodded with a smile frozen on her face. "Excellent choice. I'll give you a moment to look over the appetizer menu while I get your beverages ready."

As soon as she left, Kat's face brightened. "Those servers are trained to go on and on if you let them," she said. "Better to nip it in the bud before you let them get too far into their speech. The roses they have as their centerpiece are gorgeous. I would have, of course, gone with some Bleeding Hearts, but those are my favorite. They're just not something you see every day. Every girl loves a rose though, so I suppose that's why they chose it. The upkeep on fresh flowers must be exhausting though," Kat mused, glancing up coyly from her menu.

Hunter nodded absentmindedly, trying to look interested. "The bruschetta seems like a good choice," Hunter said, bringing the focus back to the menu.

"Darling, I don't think so. The calamari or scallops would be a much better choice," Kat said laughing. Hunter shifted uncomfortably in his seat.

"I'm not a huge fan of seafood," he responded quietly.

"At this place, you won't even know it's seafood. You simply must try it," she said, finalizing their plan.

Hunter sat back quietly throughout the meal, picking at the seafood that made his stomach turn. He could not have been more grateful when his date allowed him to order his pasta the way he wanted it, and shoveled it down as she prattled on about her favorite type of jewelry and clothing brands. He nearly choked when she told him she would never dream of having children. When she mentioned that football was a vulgar sport, he decided that the date would be over as soon as she took her last bite.

She barely touched her meal and the minutes ticked on endlessly. She complained about the bikers, and the mountains, and the hippies, and the students. She insulted campers, fishers, hunters, and tree huggers. She insisted that outdoor living was unhealthy, and ticks would most certainly be the death to all of Colorado. Finally, Hunter couldn't take it anymore.

"If you hate it here so damn much, why did you transfer?" he demanded irritatedly.

She looked up from her dinner in surprise. "The transfer secures me a position back in New York as CEO of our headhunting unit. There are two potentials here in Colorado that would be perfect for our clients, and if I secure those deals, I'll be at the top of the firm. Six months from now, I'll be back in New York with the job I deserved years ago. This bitch snatched it from under me, but now she's going on maternity leave, and once I have her position, they'll realize they won't even need her to come back. She could not have gotten knocked up at a more convenient time."

A slow, malicious smile spread over Kat's face as she studied the chiseled features of her date. "You know, you would love it in New York," she said seductively.

Later that evening, as he unlocked the front door, he blamed it on the bad day at the hospital. There were times where he desperately needed to feel something. As he led her up the stairs, he had a feeling Kat would understand why he wouldn't be seeing her again.

"Lauren mentioned that you came home with someone last night," Aaron reached up and sunk his basketball through the hoop, giving an immediate macho victory whooping noise, followed by an awkward dance.

"Lauren needs to mind her own business," Hunter muttered as he watched his brother's antics.

Aaron jogged to the side of the driveway to retrieve the ball. "So. Was she hot? Blind dates always suck when they're not hot." He passed the ball to Hunter.

"She was beautiful. Perfect body, gorgeous face, long blonde hair. She's financially stable and puts on a classy front. Unfortunately, she's emotionally unstable and a classic bitch," Hunter dribbled past his brother and went for the shot. It bounced off the rim. He snagged it and tried again.

It swooshed through the net, but Hunter had no victory dance. Aaron slapped his brother on the back. "So are you going to call her again?"

This irked his ego. "No." His tone was hard, and the ball dropped unmanned between the two of them.

"Look, man, I just want you to be happy. Mom's worried about you and is constantly badgering me to check up on you."

Hunter sighed and wiped his hand across his sweaty brow. Once again, he'd lost his temper over nothing. "It's fine. I'm just a bit edgy today."

Aaron retrieved the ball. "Sounds like you need another one night stand," he said laughingly and easily maneuvered around his brother. Although Hunter had taught him everything he knew about basketball, Aaron had easily surpassed his brother in skill years ago.

Hunter growled and focused on the game. After a few minutes, Aaron stopped, gasping for breath. "I think I'm ready to propose to Lauren."

Hunter stopped mid lay-up and turned to stare at his brother. "Did you do that on purpose?" he accused.

Aaron laughed. "No man. I was kicking your ass anyways. I've been trying to find the right time to talk to you about it. It just came out."

Hunter wanted to go and hug his brother, but he was covered in sweat. "You've been dating for a while now. I like her. The family likes her. She's good for you." He nodded as he thought it through. "Congratulations Aaron. I think it's great! Have you gotten her a ring?"

"I went to look at rings, but they all looked the same to me. I was going to ask Mom and Steph to go with me next time. I've saved up quite a bit of money living with you, so it shouldn't be too hard." He took another deep breath. "I've also saved up for a down payment on a house. Lauren and I have gone several times to look at one in Westminster. I think I might make an offer," he said tentatively.

Hunter stared at his brother. He would be living alone again, but he'd been talking more openly with his therapist, and he felt like he was doing better. It should be fine. "Sounds like everything is lining up for you, bro. Let me know if you need anything. Except moving of course. You're on your own for that."

"Boys, will you give your daddy some help on the grill? You know your father, if someone isn't watching him, he's likely to set the whole damn yard on fire." Hunter looked up to see their mother calling from the window.

"Sure thing Mom. There is no way Hunter's going to rebound from this ass kicking anyways," Aaron called out.

"Watch your language young man!"

"Sorry Mom," Aaron said with a grin.

They made their way around the house to the backyard where their brother and sister were setting up the picnic tables, and their father was firing up the grill. Physically, all the Logan kids looked the same with the same blonde hair and blue eyes. Stephanie, the only girl, liked to streak her hair a different color every month, but other than that, no one would ever mistake the Logan's for anything other than siblings.

Steph was the baby of the family, and because of the family's tendencies to be overprotective, she was certainly the most wayward and naïve. She worked as an intern at Google while she finished up her degree in public relations at the University of Colorado. Just to drive her three older brother's insane, she dated guys like she changed her hair color. There was a new one every month.

"You two are sweaty," she said with a wrinkled nose as she endured the wet hugs her brothers gave her.

"That's what happens when you do actual work," Aaron teased. "You get a little sweaty."

"Shut-up, I do actual work!" Stephanie protested, pushing her brother away.

"What, sitting at your cushy desk in the air conditioning, pushing papers around? That's real work right there," Hunter chimed in.

Trent, the youngest son, tried to come to his sister's aid. "Leave her alone, guys. She's good at what she does." Trent, who did sit at a desk and push papers around with his Ph.D. in history, was always a little embarrassed that he was not as hands on as his brothers. Aaron was an engineer at the Purina Puppy Chow plant in Denver, and it was a toss up between him and Hunter on who had the most physically demanding job.

Mindy Logan was a retired high school math teacher who now helped Brett Logan out at the family bookstore, Logan's Books. They were supportive of their children's careers, pushing them to pursue what they loved to do most.

Their family home was small. Hunter could remember sharing a room with Aaron and Trent until his parents could afford to finish the basement. Hunter, as the oldest, got to move into the new room, but Aaron and Trent went all the way through high school sharing a room. Steph got her own space. It was crowded, and they squabbled all the time, but Hunter could not have imagined a better childhood. Despite their differences, the Logan's were a close family and got together at least once a month for a family dinner or a barbecue. There were very few instances where the entire family was not present at their monthly dinners.

Their mother brought out the steaks, and the Logan boys all crowded around the grill for their usual ongoing argument on the best ways to season and cook a steak. Jacks bounded around the yard with Lola, the family cocker spaniel. Lola was on her last leg, but she always managed to find the energy to keep up with the young retriever when he came to visit.

"Lauren said you went on a date last night, Hunter. How did that go?" his mother asked.

Hunter gritted his teeth. He and Lauren were going to have to have a talk. "It was just a date, Mom. I probably won't be seeing her again."

"Well, I'm just glad that you're dating again. It has been so long, honey. I would like Carol to be history," she said casually.

Hunter ignored the remark about his ex-fiancée and instead mentioned that he'd seen Steph out with another guy. That provoked an argument that the whole family managed to get behind.

By the time the evening was over, Hunter was exhausted, and Jacks was coated in mud. They showered together and hit the sack, ready to pass out.

Hunter thought about his date the other night and considered giving her a call and a second chance but quickly rejected the idea. She was just not his type, and no matter how many chances she had, she would probably just drive him crazy.

Jacks' quiet snores eventually lulled Hunter to sleep. He dreamed all night long about ghosts, but the dreams faded away by morning.

Chapter Three

There was a knock on Lia's door early in the morning. She sat up and blinked for a moment.

"Come in," she called out, alert and focused.

As a man slipped through the wall, Lia stared. There was a jolt in her mind, but it instantly disappeared. She stood up wearily. Her guest commanded attention, dressed in a black trench coat, his dark hair curling at the nape of his neck and around the collar. He looked like he was in his thirties, but, of course, looks were deceiving with reapers. His skin was far tanner than most reapers, and his eyes were captivating. They were icy blue. For a moment, all she could do was stare. Color. She was astounded. After a moment, they faded to gray, and Lia blinked. Was she imagining things?

He pulled off his gloves as he looked around her place. As she waited awkwardly, she felt as though he belonged there, and she was intruding on his home. Finally, he stuck out his hand in greeting. "I am Westin, the new master of the area." He spoke with an accent similar to Allen's.

She touched his hand gently, uncomfortable with the tension that settled between them. "Lia," she said shortly.

He held her hand for a moment too long. "You're trembling."

"Too much caffeine I expect. It is a habit I indulge in far too frequently. Are house calls going to be a common occurrence for you?" she asked as she pulled away.

"No, no of course not. I intend to respect the privacy of those in my unit. One of the messengers mentioned that I might speak to you on a private matter."

"Have I caused trouble?"

Westin strolled around the room. "It's odd isn't it, the things that leak through from their world to ours? For example, your home reeks of a substance known as marijuana and there is a barrier block for aromas." He stared at her intently.

"Master, if there is..."

"Westin," he interrupted.

"What?"

He moved closer to her. "Please do not refer to me as Master. While I am the new master, and I will expect the respect and obedience associated with the title, I do not want the title used."

Lia began again. There was no uncertainty in her voice, only impatience. "Very well. Westin, is there something in particular you wanted to discuss with me? Or are you simply here to inspect my temporary shelter?"

A wry smile crossed his face. "I do believe I mentioned respect."

Silence followed his comment, and he continued. "I am here because the report from your old master mentions trouble with the new reaper, Allen. He has finished his induction and training, and yet he struggles with controlling a soul. There is mention that the transition was unusually difficult for him. You are the oldest reaper in this unit. He will shadow you for a few days on your reaps or until I feel he is comfortable enough to be on his own."

Lia balked. "I am not a trainer. I am sure Paul is far more suitable..."

"Obedience," Westin interrupted. Lia quieted. "Respect and obedience, Lia. There were no reports that you were trouble for Jackson. Are you going to be trouble for me?"

Lia felt an awkwardness that she couldn't explain or identify. It was not something she was sure she felt before. She was uncomfortable with Westin, but she was trained to listen and obey the master. "I am not used to the responsibility of another reaper," she said quietly.

She met his gaze through the silence that followed. The look in his eyes held her attention. He seemed to be searching for something from her.

"I will change your schedule to accommodate the extra workload. I will expect an oral report at the conclusion of each session. In return, if you would like a day off, that could be arranged."

Lia cocked her head. "What would I do with a day off?"

He didn't answer. After he had stepped back through her door, Lia sat back on the bed, oddly shaken by the visit. Jackson had always kept his distance from her, allowing her free reign of places to live and space during her down time. Westin seemed to distrust her. Lia feared things were about to change drastically.

Westin paused on the other side. The shock of seeing her name on the roster was nothing compared to seeing her face-to-face. He couldn't deny the moment of confusion in her face when she saw him, but she had clearly not made a connection. Having the two of them so close together would be dangerous.

He lifted his shirt and gazed at the jagged scar that ran down his side. Something was wrong, and he was right in the middle of it.

Allen was clearly uncomfortable with his new companion. Lia didn't know if it was because she was a stranger, a reaper, or a woman, but she could see the violent reactions in his eyes every time she brushed up against him.

It was amusing, so she did it often.

They had hitched a ride on the bus and were heading to the hospital. He had barely spoken a word that morning, and she had been happy with the silence. When curiosity got the best of her, she decided to try and break the ice.

"You are British."

"And you're very old."

The statement caught her off guard, and she whipped her head around to stare at him. "What did you just say?"

He seemed startled by her sudden demand and cleared his throat. "I assume, from your mannerisms and status in this unit, that you are very old."

Lia narrowed her eyes. "I had never really thought about it." She stared out the window, suddenly wishing she hadn't opened this line of communication. Outside the window was nothing but dense fog with the faint outline of passing buildings. There was nothing to look at, nothing to distract her.

"Look, Allen, I know it is probably frustrating that you can not remember anything about yourself, but you will drive yourself insane if you try to figure it out. Our memories will never extend past a few years, and there is no reason to bother yourself with history. Being undead is like being reborn. We no longer have souls. We are different people now, and you need to focus on the new you. What is at your disposal that can entertain you now? How will you pass the time between reaps? These are the questions you need to be asking."

Allen cocked his head. "That's interesting," he muttered.

"What is interesting?"

"You seem upset, but I'm not asking questions about me. I'm speculating about you."

Lia gave him a hard look. "I do not care about my past. Furthermore, I do not like that you are shadowing me. So the quicker we can assimilate you, the happier I will be." she said coldly.

Allen smiled. "People that don't care don't react," he said simply.

"You are a frustrating man, are you not?" Lia asked as she settled back to looking at the misty morning.

"I'm curious, which tells me a great deal about myself. I seem to like knowing how things work, how people work, how they react. I know that I have this heavy feeling in the pit of my stomach, and I associate that with guilt. I understand that reapers are chosen because of something they've done wrong, something evil, but I feel like an exception. I feel like whatever I did, I knew it was wrong, and I wished I hadn't done it."

"That is not how it works," Lia pointed out. "This is a punishment, but it is rare that a reaper would care much for the why and the who. We are chosen based on the sole fact that we fit a type that can do this job without becoming emotional or hard to handle. People that feel regret or any remorse are not chosen. What you are feeling right now is a desperate need to hold on to some living feeling. I have seen it before. It has nothing to do with reaping and everything to do with being dead."

"So I am dead."

Lia shrugged. "No, but since you no longer walk among the living, you might as well be dead. Truthfully, you are immortal. You are still alive, and you will remain that way as long as the judges choose."

"How does this work? Jackson explained how I do my job, but how does this work and make sense?"

"It is all a behind-the-curtains operation, and most of it will remain a mystery. I know that there are judges that determine who reaps whom. I do not know if they maintain life and death, but I know they have an immense amount of power. "

"Have you ever seen a judge?"

"I do not even think masters have seen judges."

Allen was coming out of his shell a little. "And you're okay working in such a cloak and dagger operation?"

"It is a punishment, Allen. It does not require my approval."

Lia found the idea of ghost towns amusing. She thought of herself as the walking dead, and essentially, the hospital was her domain. There were too many deaths for her to act as the only reaper in the hospital but to spend more than a few minutes with another reaper, during work, was rare.

Having Allen tag along was creepy. Normally, until her world merged with the living at the time of death, the only sounds that echoed in the halls were her own footsteps. Occasional cries of mourning or pain were strong enough to reach into her world, but, for the most part, the hospital was silent and still. Even listening to Allen breathe was distracting.

"How do you get used to walking through walls?" he asked suddenly.

Lia shrugged. "I do not know. It is the same way you learn to walk like an infant. I mean, we still knock as a courtesy to other reapers, but it is not like it would do us any good. If the only thing on the other side resided in the living world, who would answer? You have to think of this whole place as a different kind of world, one that is manipulated by death. You are essentially part of death, and this world caters to you. It resembles the world you used to know because it makes it easier for us to merge paths when we reap souls, but we cannot be a part of it. Instead, we are made so that we can walk through walls. It makes more sense than having to deal with locked doors and such."

"And the lack of color? It's so depressing."

Lia stopped suddenly at a coke machine and reached through it, stealing a can of coke. "I agree with you. I suppose whoever created this world did not have time to deal with color." She held up the can. "It is my favorite drink. I cannot taste it, but I like the bubbles. Someone told me that the can was red. I did not know for sure until I held it during a reap. That was a real conversation starter."

"You like seeing color when you reap?"

Lia smiled. "Do not tell anyone, but seeing the colors in the soul? I find it beautiful."

Allen reached out and touched her. It was the first time he had initiated a touch, and she didn't like it. She was not here to make friends. "You will get used to this life. I know you do not remember your past life, but you still remember having one, and soon that will fade. The days will turn to months, and the months will turn to years. Decades will pass, but you will not know. If you let go of whatever it is that you are holding on to, it will make the adjustment easier."

"I don't even know what I'm holding. I just feel alone and abandoned," he said softly.

Lia took a step back. "You have to get over that. We are soulless, Allen. No one will comfort you here. You will need to find ways to comfort yourself.

She pulled out her phone and checked the time and location again. "Brace yourself," she said. "It is time."

Merging worlds was intense, creating a rush of adrenaline. The sudden pounding in her chest, the trembling of her hands, the inflation of her lungs, it was exactly like being alive.

It was reanimating the dead.

The colors rushed down the hall as if chased by demons, slamming into them like a wall of water, drenching them in life. Sometimes she was standing in the wrong place and could feel a sudden presence of someone else or something else. She watched as a gurney slammed into Allen. It melted right through him, but it still threw him off balance, and he toppled onto the floor.

She reached down and pulled him back on his feet. "You get used to it," she said quietly. She took a deep breath and shivered.

"I can always feel its presence," she said softly. "But I never see, or smell, or hear anything else to indicate it is real."

"Whose presence?"

"Death."

They watched the bubble of life before them. There was a middle-aged woman on the gurney, a doctor straddling her from above performing CPR. Even now, Lia could see the life flickering in and out of the woman.

Lia stepped forward and lightly hovered her hand over the body. It was drenched in water, and for a moment Lia could feel the weight of the waterlogged lungs. If her talents impressed Allen, he did not let on. "She is drowning still, even on land," she muttered.

She lifted the soul out, watching the soul transform from yellow to blue to green to yellow.

"It is confused. It does not know what is going on. You have to watch these; they are the most unpredictable, and often they run."

"What do you mean run? I thought they couldn't escape you."

Lia sat the soul down. "They cannot, but once you reap a soul, you are connected to them, like a ball and chain. If they run, you will feel it, pulling at you. If they are angry, you will feel that anger, or sadness, or excitement. You are linked with that soul, and the sooner it moves on, the better."

The demands from the doctor for the woman to live were ignored, and soon the soul morphed. The colors rushed away, and they were facing an angry and confused dead woman.

"What is this? It can't be my time! I have a child," she said frantically. "Put me back. You need to put me back!" She climbed back on the gurney.

Lia closed her eyes to ward off the intense emotions of betrayal. She honestly didn't care if this woman calmed down or not, but her emotions were wild and off the charts, and Lia needed the link between them to disappear.

"Everything is happening as it was meant too. There is no reason to fight it," she said calmly.

The woman collapsed in a ball of sobs. "I just wanted to take her tubing. She just wanted to go tubing for her birthday," the woman gasped.

It was normal for souls to completely ignore the situation. They treat reapers as normal fixtures to deny that anything abnormal or supernatural was happening. Lia knew it was important to remind them of reality.

"My name is Lia, and I am your guide. I am going to help you move on," she said calmly. "I just need you to trust me, and I promise a smooth journey for you," she lied easily.

She touched the wall, absorbing the flow of energy as she once again opened the portal to the afterlife. The woman was immediately distracted as the light surrounding her. "Oh," she breathed. "It's beautiful."

"All you have to do is walk through," Lia said beckoning.

"What's on the other side?"

"Your destiny," Lia answered.

The woman climbed off the gurney and reached out, grasping Lia's hand. "Are you coming with me?"

"No," Lia said.

The woman frowned. "I don't want to go alone," she said backing away slowly.

Lia looked at Allen. "When this happens, just pull. Or push. Or whatever you need to do."

"Pull or push what?" She woman grew hysterical. "No, I can't do this. You can't make me!" She pulled against the hold Lia had on her. "You're a demon! Let me go!"

"Good luck," Lia said, and pushed the woman through the portal.

"What the hell?" Allen demanded as the world melted away leaving them alone in the hallway. "You scared her half to death."

"The biggest reaction to death is denial. Your job is to get them through that portal no matter what. I am fairly certain that this bridge between life and death that you represent will pale in comparison to what is on that side. It does not matter how you act or who you pretend to be. You just need to get them through."

Allen shook his head. "It's not right."

"The results are always going to be the same. It is your only job. If you want to handle it differently, that is fine. So long as the job gets done." Lia leaned against the wall. Opening the gateway drained her, and she took a deep breath.

Barely speaking, Allen kept his distance from her the rest of the afternoon. There was only one reap left on her schedule, but it was far from the hospital. It was not odd for her to have a reap away from her domain, but this one was so remote that it required GPS coordinates that would take her to the mountainside of the canyon in Boulder. The prospect of fresh air and perhaps some sunshine excited her, so the remote destination did not bother her. Not that it mattered. She was not allowed to refuse a reap.

They took a bus to the entrance of the trails at the base of a mountain. The haze of the realm clung to the mountain, and, as they walked, it was hard to see the path. The brush was dense and nearly impossible to clear, and Lia saw that they were both bleeding a little from the thicket, but, of course, neither could feel the thorns.

"Allen, I know this is not easy. And maybe you will be the kind of reaper that will take his time with the souls and hold their hand, but eventually you will see this as time management. The faster it gets done, the better it is for everyone. Some souls are eager, some do not care, but most are going to be angry and difficult. You do not have time to coddle them."

Allen took a moment to look out at the dust. "I know. I understand, I just don't know what to say about all of this. I don't think I can do this."

"You don't have a choice." She looked at her watch. "We have about ten minutes until the actual reap time. You should take some time, walk around, explore a little, and clear your head."

"I'd just get lost," He glanced at the dense fog. Suddenly he frowned. "That's odd."

Lia peered around him and froze.

The mist was dissipating, and the sky was opening up in patches, and the color started to bleed towards them, melting into greens and browns. "Something is not right," Lia said backing slowly away. "I can smell the earth. It is too soon."

"Could the time have changed?" Allen asked, panic rising in his voice.

"Reap times do not change. Normally it is like a collision, but we are melting into them, literally. This is a mistake, a tear in the worlds." She started backing up.

"I found you."

Lia spun around at the new voice. It was gravelly and heavy, and it came from a figure dressed in all dark.

"Oh dear God," Allen whispered.

The figure was still in splotches of black and white, but he hunched over a small figure of color. It was a little girl. Lia instantly recognized her as the soul that needed reaping.

"I've been looking for you for a long time," the figure whispered. He pulled out a knife and pressed the edge of it to the girl's cheek, watching as the blood ran down her face. The little girl was quiet, but the fear was obvious on her face. Her eyes darted around wildly, but his were trained on Lia.

Lia's mind was racing. "How is it that you see me?" she muttered.

The girl started whimpering in pain, and he moved the blade to her neck. "Take her soul. I want to see it before I kill her."

"Do something," Allen pleaded, frozen in place.

"Shut-up, just let me think," Lia demanded. She started to shake. She'd never heard of the living witnessing a reap, but he seemed so comfortable, so familiar with the situation. She could not refuse a reap. None of it made any sense. She looked around; the colors were still melting everywhere, shifting, making her dizzy. She took a deep breath.

"You have a job. Do your job," the man demanded.

Lia shook her head. "I do not understand..."

The little girl started to scream. She couldn't have been more than six. "Now look what you did. Tell me, does it affect you at all? Does it bother you to watch someone die? To watch a child die? Does it feel any different than when you murder someone?" the man asked intensely. He moved the knife, scraping it against the little girl's arm. "I wonder what would happen if I just plunged the knife in before you had a chance to remove her soul. Would it trap it so that she could never escape her body? Would it just rot away in the corpse?"

"How do you know so much?" she asked. Her heart was pounding in her chest. Was she afraid? She was untouchable; nothing could harm her. Why was she scared? The man smiled. "You know, I never actually thought I would find you. And if I did, I was unsure of what I would do. But, I feel now, that there is only one thing I can do."

He tossed the girl aside, like a rag doll, and before Lia could react, he changed his grip on the blade and plunged it in Lia's midsection.

Lia doubled over, not in pain, but in an immediate defense reaction. She reached up and slammed her hand on his chest. She could feel his healthy beating heart. The man let out his breath and grunted in pain.

His soul butted up against her hand, and Lia's eyes widened in surprise.

Where most souls were malleable, his was solid.

Suddenly, Lia felt the ground shift beneath her. Her hand still on the man's body, she watched as the sky split in half and fell around her. A feeling that she had never experienced before filled every nerve ending in her body, and Lia released the soul. She watched as the man was practically thrown away from her. She watched Allen race towards her, but he was rapidly fading, and he disappeared before he reached her. She began to crumple to the ground.

The earth shifted beneath her. The grass and dirt disappeared, and, as she fell, concrete slammed into her body. She watched in horror as the blood turned from gray to red, spilling out onto the sidewalk.

Her blood.

There were screams around her, and Lia looked up. People were racing towards her. She could see the familiar doors of the hospital. She was being touched; someone was pushing on her stomach. A child was crying.

"What?" she muttered, her vision swimming.

Pain hit her like a brick wall. It was more than the gash of her midsection but also the weight of everything pushing her down. Gravity. The hands that were touching her, the wind whipping her face, the gravel beneath her body, was too much to bear.

So much pain.

She bowed her back and screamed with all the air in her lungs

Everything went black.

Chapter Four

Beep.

"I need an O.R. room cleared stat! Young female with a stab wound to the left abdomen."

Beep. Beep.

"We'll have to check the security tapes. She lost a lot of blood. She may not regain consciousness."

Beep. Beep. Beep.

"The security cameras must be broken. It looks like she just appeared in the parking lot with the little girl."

Beep. Beep. Beep. Beep.

"The child is in shock. She says she was in the mountains, and then she just appeared here. She's never seen this woman before."

Hunter finished stitching the woman's wound and stepped back as the nurses took over the bandaging. He stripped off his gloves and went to wash up at the sink. He knew the FBI agents were standing outside the room, waiting to hear from him.

They finally had a survivor.

The unconscious woman had been rolled into his room while the rumors were flying. She was outside the parking lot with a little girl and no identification. The child was hysterical and unable to say anything logical. She insisted they were on a mountain and the woman appeared out of nowhere before the bad man stabbed her, and then they were whisked magically away to the hospital.

The survivor looked severely malnourished. She was too thin, and there was little color to her skin. Her dark hair was limp and straggly. Her clothes were soaked in blood.

As soon as he'd touched her, he felt a cold chill like he'd never experienced before. It was enough to make him pause, but he knew he had to work quickly. If he could stop the blood flow, she would probably survive.

There was no injury to her head and no immediate indication of her comatose state. Hunter ordered a few more tests to make sure there was nothing he was missing.

He watched her now through the window. There was something about her that he couldn't quite put his finger on, but it didn't matter. He needed to speak to the FBI quickly before the media stormed the hospital doors.

The temperature dropped, and Lia shivered. She dug her toes into the gravel and looked around. She stood on a beautiful riverbank where the waters moved gently on the shoreline. Several lush green trees swayed gently in the breeze, but there was no sound. She couldn't hear the water or the leaves rustling or any birds singing. The area was deafeningly silent.

She was not alone. To her left, a figure struggled in the calm waters. It fought against the serene river but made no cries for help. In front of her, on the bank also watching the struggling figure, stood a tall, looming, dark, blurry figure of a man.

The more she stared at him, the blurrier he became. A strange whine began in her ears. "Who are you?" she called to the man.

"Careful, Annalia. You have but a few precious moments here," he responded in a thousand voices. They all echoed in perfect unison seemingly made up of all accents and both genders. They bounced off invisible walls.

Lia stepped forward. The river stones were smooth against her feet. "Why do you call me that?"

"That is your name."

She glanced around. She felt an odd sense of falsehood in the river before her. She tried to focus on the man. "You know who I am?"

"Yes."

"Tell me," she demanded urgently.

"You are Annalia." His tone was patient.

She glanced over at the drowning figure. "That person needs help."

"Yes," he said amused.

"Are you going to help them?" Lia asked.

"Are you?"

She scowled. "I just got here."

The figure moved closer. "You are here now."

Lia didn't move. The whine grew louder, and the river began to blur. The colors were so vibrant.

"You have killed so many, Annalia. Why not simply leave this one to die." He reached out and touched her forehead. Her vision darkened, and she cried out as she fell.

Other than the whirr and beeps of the machines, the room was quiet when Lia opened her eyes. She whimpered as the lights flooded her mind. The pain was intense. Gravity was weighing her down, pushing on every bone in her body. She could feel the expansion of her lungs. Every breath was deafening.

She stared at the blue outline of her hospital gown, running a finger over it gingerly.

Color.

Pain.

This wasn't right. Crying out, she pushed herself up. Her hand pressed up against her gown and felt the bandage underneath. A wave of nausea hit her. She should be here for souls, not here as a patient. It didn't make sense. She jerked the wires and tubes off her body and tried to get to her feet. Stumbling, she caught herself on the wall, hitting her head.

Solid.

With a moan, she slapped her hand against the wall again, but she couldn't get though. The door swung open next to her, and three nurses and a doctor ran in. Lia backed up quickly, tripping over the IV stand and falling to the floor. She grabbed her side again as the pain lanced through her, but she kept silent and stared at the audience before her.

The doctor held up his hand and spoke quietly. "Corinne, if you could stay with me to help see to this young woman, the other two are welcome to alert the agents that she is awake. She is not to be disturbed until I give the go ahead." He locked eyes with Lia and spread his hands out. "I am Dr. Logan, and this is Nurse Corinne. You were attacked two days ago, and you are at Saint Antony Central Hospital. There is no need to be frightened. You are going to be just fine." He held out his hand. "Let's get you back in bed so we can talk."

Lia tried to block out the pain and focus on her options. There was only one goal in her mind. Survival. She nodded to the doctor who leaned over and helped lift her gently from the floor. She tried to stifle her cry of pain, but a quiet moan slipped past her lips.

Even when she leaned back on the hospital bed, she felt sluggish. Lia shrank into the pillows, defeated.

"I'd like to ask you a few questions if that is all right," Hunter asked in a quiet voice.

Lia felt calmer as the pain eased. She nodded.

"Let's start with your name."

"Lia," she responded automatically. As the word slipped her lips, she tensed. How was she going to answer any questions? How was she going to explain her presence here? She didn't even know how to explain it to herself.

"Good. Lia. I like that name. Do you have a last name?"

Lia thought hard. She didn't know much about the time period, but her smartphone, computers, and television told her that this was an advanced time in technology. Not advanced enough to know about reapers, but advanced enough to catch her in a lie. To say that she didn't even know her last name would be ludicrous, but to give a false last name could be even worse.

The doctor mistook her silence as stress. "Lia, it's okay if you don't remember. Just tell me what you do remember about yourself. Age? Family? Address?"

When she didn't answer, Hunter nodded. "Okay Lia. Sometimes traumatic experiences can cause retrograde amnesia. It may take some time for those memories to return. Usually, something you'd never suspect like a word, or smell, or a sound will trigger a memory. When that happens, you just need to relax and let it come to you. I know it's scary, but you're not alone."

She tried to respond, but her throat burned. Her words caught in the sandpapered walls, and she winced. Lia glanced over at the nurse. "Could I have some water?" she rasped. The nurse nodded and left the room.

"When she comes back with your water, we'll take a look at your injury. The good news is that the blade missed all the major organs. The bad news is that you did lose a significant amount of blood, so while your body recovers, you're going to feel very weak. You'll stay here at the hospital for a few days while we monitor for infections, but I don't see any reason why you won't be able to go home after that. Right now, we're giving you some drugs for the pain. They'll make you groggy and feel a bit out of it, but they should help you sleep."

The nurse returned with the water, and Lia gulped down so quickly she choked a little. Alarmed, the nurse took the cup away from her. "Easy now," she said soothingly.

Lia had never felt such a need for the substance. Her throat was achingly dry. The water washed it all away, refreshing her, and giving her a bit more confidence. After the spasms had calmed down, she reached down and pulled up her dressing gown. All she could see was a bandage. "Can I see it?"

Hunter nodded, and the nurse reached over and helped unwrap the bandages. She winced as the sticky tape ripped off her skin, but she was too stunned at what was underneath to react.

The wound ran just a few inches across the side of her abdomen. Stitched up in black, it was an angry blistery red line, puffy and white around the edges. Lia ran her fingers over it. Any injury that occurred as a reaper healed instantly with very limited bloodshed and no scarring, but here she was now, her skin being held together by materials unknown to her, keeping her from bleeding out.

She noticed on the other side of her injury was a slight protrusion of her skin. It was similar to her new wound but had healed over, noticeable now only by the pale ridge of her skin. She touched it, observing the tighter feel of it to the rest of her skin. In a world of black and white, the difference would have been unnoticeable. Lia wondered how long she'd had the scar.

Hunter saw the bewilderment on her face. "From the looks of the scar, I'd have to go with childhood injury. I'd also have to say that you were lucky that the cut wasn't very deep."

Feeling her cheeks warm, Lia tugged her dressing gown down. "Do you know who attacked me?"

"That's something for the police to discuss with you. They would like to have a word if you are feeling up to it?"

Lia seemed to shrink further back in the bed. "The police?"

The doctor's eyes narrowed. "Yes. You and the little girl are the first two known survivors of the serial killer terrorizing the state. They're hoping you'll be the nail in his coffin."

The drugs were clouding up her mind, and she struggled to stay sharp. She could not let the police or the doctor become suspicious of her. "Little girl? I do not know anything about her or any serial killer."

"If you feel that talking to the police is too stressful right now, I can delay them until tomorrow."

Lia shook her head. It would be best to get it over with, and maybe they could give her some information on the man who could see reapers. "No. I think I want to try and help if I can."

"Okay. I'll let them know that you're ready. If, at any point, you feel that you are too stressed, you can tell them to stop. The FBI means well, but they can be a little pushy. Just touch the alert button on the side if you need help, okay?" He pointed to the remote at her side.

Lia nodded. Corinne patted her leg comfortingly. "Just do the best you can, sweetheart."

As they exited the room, Lia tried to gather her thoughts together. If she stuck with the amnesia story that her doctor had so willingly handed to her, she could get through this. Once out of the hospital, she'd be able to find some answers.

Outside in the hall, Agent Mark O'Ryan tapped his foot impatiently against the linoleum. He and his two partners were the only ones in the small waiting area, and they had been there for several hours, waiting for the patient to wake up.

Agents O'Ryan, Mallich, and Lichton had been tracking the killer, nicknamed the Phoenix by the media, for several years. They suspected he'd been killing across the country for far longer, but it had taken many painstaking months to make the few connections they had. There was even evidence that he was killing all over the world, but that was even harder to prove.

The killer had been active in Colorado for six months, racking up a total of ten victims. The agents had moved out here only a few weeks ago after the ninth death. They were hopeful when the tenth victim had made it to the hospital still alive, but the young woman had died before the doctor could even examine her.

The agents rose as Hunter approached. O'Ryan was head of the small task force. He was the youngest of the three agents, but leadership came with ease, and there seemed to be no tension between him and his older associates. "Doctor, the nurse told me the young woman was awake. We would like to ask her a few questions."

"I'm afraid the patient is suffering from what appears to be retrograde amnesia, possibly stemming from post-traumatic stress disorder. Physically, she seems to be mending from her wound well, but she doesn't remember much of anything about her life. She says her name is Lia, but that's all I could get out of her."

Lichton raised his eyebrows. "She doesn't remember her identity?" His deep voice matched his large frame. The oldest of the three, Mohammad Lichton was physically intimidating. Well over six feet tall, he was broad with dark skin and no hair. His manner was always patient and calm. Even in interrogation, O'Ryan had never seen Lichton lose his temper. "Is that normal?"

Hunter held out his hands. "It is very common for victims of violence to block painful memories. It is less common, but certainly not unheard of, for these memories to extend further. In most cases, the memories do return, but we can't judge the amount of time it takes. For now, I would strongly suggest that you do nothing to cause her stress. If she tries to force the memories, she may only end up regressing. The best thing for her is to feel safe, comfortable, and trust in her instincts."

"How long will you be keeping her?" O'Ryan asked.

"Right now we're simply monitoring the wound. She needs to rest while her body recovers from the blood loss. As long as there are no complications like infection, we should be able to release her in a couple of days. From there we'll ask that she make an appointment in a couple of weeks for us to remove the stitches."

Mallich exchanged a look with her agents. She was a tall woman, slender and plain. O'Ryan suspected she could be very beautiful, but she never wore any make-up and always wore her blonde hair pulled back in a severe ponytail or bun. She was stern and always professional. It was one of the very reasons O'Ryan had picked her for the team. He also suspected that she had developed a physical relationship with Lichton, but they never made it obvious, and he never pried. "What sort of tests can you perform on her memory loss?"

"There aren't any tests. We usually send these patients to see a therapist, but it can be a slow process. There's no cure for amnesia. Just working through the traumatic experience. I'm hoping that you can put her someplace safe while she recovers. I imagine that if she is a living victim, she's in danger."

"I'm sure there will be a missing person's report soon for her. Once we get her identity, we can go from there. We would like to speak to her," Mallich responded briskly.

Hunter nodded. "Right this way." He led them back into Lia's room. O'Ryan and Lichton stepped to the side, hugging the wall. O'Ryan didn't want anyone to scare the woman. She sat in bed, her eyes alert but filled with fear. There was little color in her lips and even less in her cheeks. Her hair hung limply, tangled around her shoulder and brushing against her elbows. The hospital gown hung limply on her small frame. O'Ryan frowned. The victim looked as though she had been kidnapped and held hostage for months.

Mallich was the only one to approach Lia's bed. The doctor hung back and made the introductions.

"Lia, these are Agents O'Ryan, Mallich, and Lichton. They are from the FBI. They just want to ask you a few questions. I'll be right outside in the hallway. Remember what I said. If you start to feel upset or stressed in any way, you may ask to continue the questioning at another point. Is that okay?"

Lia nodded. "I am not sure what is going on here," she began.

"It's okay, Lia. I understand that you're having trouble accessing your memories. We just want you to tell us the last thing you remember," Mallich said quietly in an uncharacteristically smooth voice.

"I woke up in a hospital a while ago with machines attached to me and my skin stitched together," Lia responded.

"Do you know how you got your wound?" O'Ryan asked.

"I am told that there was a serial killer and a little girl," Lia said slowly.

"You were found with the girl in the parking lot of the hospital. We're not sure how you got there. The child, Amanda, was kidnapped two days ago. The kidnapping fits the MO, the pattern, of a serial killer in the area. The media is calling him the Phoenix. You were both found together, but Amanda is unclear on how she got to the hospital, or why she was with you. She says that she was in the woods in the mountains. Does that sound familiar?" Lichton's voice was deep and raspy.

"Why is he called the Phoenix?" Lia asked, ignoring the question.

"He leaves a bag of ash next to his victim," Mallich responded. The blank look stayed on Lia's face.

"The Phoenix is a bird that can rise from the ashes of his dead body. Our killer leaves ash at the crime scenes. We can account for similar crimes lasting over a decade," Lichton recounted.

Lia nodded. "I have no memories of a mountain or a child or a bird. I do not even know my last name."

"It's a mythological bird. It's not real," Mallich explained. "We would like to take your fingerprints. It's a long shot, but it's possible that we could find a match. Would that be okay?"

Lia's brow furrowed. "Okay," she said slowly.

O'Ryan pulled out some paper and an ink pad. "It's a little old-school, but it works." He held the inkpad out to her. Lia stared at it. Time seemed to slow in the awkward moment. She reached out and tried to take the ink.

Lichton came to her rescue. O'Ryan studied Lia as the large man stepped by her bed. She didn't react as though she were scared. Lichton took her hand, extended her index finger, and rolled it in the ink. Next, he rolled it on the paper. She stared at the imprint. "This can identify me?"

The agents exchanged looks. It was as if they were dealing with a child. Mallich handed her a wipe for her fingers. "No two fingerprints are alike. If you are in the system, our computers will make a match."

"We've also identified multiple blood types on your clothes.

Since there were no injuries to Amanda, we believe the blood belongs to you and the unsub, unknown subject. This is incredible news. It will be the first DNA sample we've had to attach to him. With your permission, we'd like to obtain a sample of your DNA to isolate his," O'Ryan asked.

She nodded again and allowed them to take a cotton swab to the inside of her mouth. She immediately coughed and reached for her water.

"We are monitoring all missing reports for someone that matches your description. Chances are good that someone will claim you soon, and we'll be able to put the pieces together. In the meantime, we are keeping your circumstance quiet. The unsub has never left a live victim before. It's possible he believes you are dead. For your safety, we'd like to keep it that way. That also means we can't make a public broadcast about you, but that's okay. We're confident that someone will be reporting you missing soon," O'Ryan said, capping the cheek swab.

"What if no one is looking for me? What am I supposed to do?" she asked.

O'Ryan smiled. "I'm sure it won't come to that, but we'll keep you protected until we know something."

She frowned. "I think I would like to go to sleep now," she muttered.

The agents nodded. "We'll be in touch shortly, hopefully with good news. There will be an officer posted outside your door, and only a few people will be allowed to see you. We don't want you to be scared," Lichton said as he followed the others out the door.

They closed the door behind them and stopped a moment to stare at each other. The doctor stepped forward. "Everything okay?"

"She seems confused with basic concepts. Is that normal for an amnesia patient?" O'Ryan asked.

The doctor shrugged. "The brain is still a mystery to us. Every patient is different. Sometimes the patient remembers everything except personal details, and sometimes simple facts have escaped them."

"Is she healthy? She looks malnourished," Mallich pointed out.

"She's lost a lot of blood, and she could stand to put on a few pounds. We'll watch her eating habits while she's here, but I don't think there is anything to worry about. You think she may have been kidnapped first?"

"It's too soon to tell. Once we get some background information on her, we'll be able to go from there. Thank you for your help, Dr. Logan." O'Ryan reached out and shook the man's hand. "We'll be in touch."

Lia sighed with relief as the agents exited, and the door closed. Her hands reached for her stomach, but instead of fingering at the bandages, they ran aimlessly over the old scar she had discovered. As she looked around the room, she took note of everything she was feeling. She felt certain contentment with colors, wonderment with sounds, excitement with touch, but there were other emotions she was having trouble identifying. They loomed large in the pit of her stomach.

Very little of what the agents had said made any sense to her. She didn't understand the terminology or the process, but she could tell from the look in their eyes that they knew something was different about her. What would they do when they found that she had no home?

The pain was intolerable. The bright lights, the piercing noises, the scratching of the material on her skin, even her breath was difficult to process. Every minute that went by proved more wretched than the last.

Her body wasn't just recovering from blood loss. It was recovering from reanimation.

It terrified her.

O'Ryan sat back in his chair and massaged his temples. Lichton and Mallich had gone back to their hotel rooms earlier that evening and had encouraged him to do the same. The last thing he wanted to be was alone right now. Even though there was no one around him at the moment, he had the pictures of the dead to keep him company. He told himself he could not rest until their killer was found.

That was only part of the truth. The other part rested on his silent cell phone. For three weeks now, he had not been able to pick up the phone and call his wife of four years. Clearly, she felt the same. He had flown home for a few days to surprise her on her birthday to find her with another man. Harsh words fell on angry ears, and now, away from the fighting, he could see the truth in them. His job had always been more important than her.

He stared at the board of photos. Maybe he should abandon them. After all, he had been pursuing the killer for months with no new evidence. The ash left behind was human, but none of the victims had been burned to death, and there was no DNA to link it to anyone. The victims came from different backgrounds, different locations, different ages and genders. There seemed to be nothing to suggest a pattern except for the deliberations to not create a pattern.

In the center of the board were the two newest pictures. He stared at the woman with no memory and the little girl whose words made no sense. Why were they left alive? Where did they come from?

He clicked his pen over and over again, ignoring the echoes off the walls. There was something nagging at him. Something was staring him right in the face, but he simply couldn't see it.

His eyes roamed over the photos of victims and, after a moment, he got up. Flipping the board over, he looked at some of the older pictures.

In the corner was one of the first victims in Colorado. She had been found vacationing in a cabin in the mountains with her husband. She had been stabbed once, but her blood was smeared in a message on the wall behind her.

Set me free.

The message was bizarre, and it had been the only message found. The body was cleaned up and positioned on the floor; her feet crossed at the ankle, and her arms crossed over her chest. Her hair had been dyed black. She had looked almost angelic when the husband had found her. There was nothing to link her to the serial killer. There was no ash, but the stab wound was in the right spot, and there was a string of murders in the same year following the unsub's pattern, so O'Ryan had kept the file. The husband had been cleared on an airtight alibi, and the agent knew in his gut that the husband wasn't involved.

He stared now at the picture. It was unmistakable. He ripped the picture off the wall and flipped the board again. In the space next to the picture of Lia, he placed the first victim.

They could have been twins.

Chapter Five

Allen sat cross-legged on the floor of Westin's home. Westin, to the confusion of everyone, had taken up residence in a library. He paced anxiously across the floor before turning back to the new reaper.

"Allen, are you sure that he not only saw Lia, but recognized her? Did he use her name? Did she recognize him?"

Allen shook his head. "Yes and no and no. But he said he'd been searching for her. He stabbed her, and suddenly I was back in the reaper realm alone. No Lia. No soul. Nothing. She was bleeding. And she was reacting to pain. I don't understand. Is she dead? Is this how we die? Some bloody unnatural thing jumps between realms and murders us?"

Westin stopped pacing. "No. That's not how you die." There was a source of frustration in his voice. He tried to calm himself down. The situation wasn't good, but there was no need to alarm the young reaper. "Could he see you?

Allen thought carefully. "I think so, but he never addressed me. It doesn't make sense to me. Does the system not work?"

This was a dangerous conversation, but Westin was going to drain Allen's memory, so he might as well be honest. "Not always. Have you discussed this with anyone else?" The reaper shook his head, and Westin nodded. With a little pity, he reached out and touched Allen's head. The man stilled, his eyes glazed over, and the expression on his face went slack. It took some doing, but Westin managed to extract only the memories of Lia's last reap. When life flooded back into Allen's eyes, Westin straightened.

"Allen, I regret to inform you that Lia will be transferring units. Paul will be working with you from now on. Do you feel that you're making progress?"

Allen nodded. "Lia seems a little different in her ways, but the message is the same. I think I'm getting the hang of it."

Westin wanted to drill Allen a little more on Lia's unorthodox ways, but he felt he shouldn't press the subject. He dismissed Allen and walked through the reference section to the library office. Once Allen shut the door, Westin closed his eyes and directed his thoughts outward.

His answer was immediate.

We need her.

The most unnatural breeze carried the message. Westin focused his request.

It denied him.

You are no longer bound to her.

Westin shook his head angrily.

You are no longer bound to her.

Angrily, Westin reached over, shoved all the papers off the desk, and slammed his fist down. Rage filled him, and he no longer kept silent.

"Bloody hell, she gets stronger every time. It'll be a massacre! This has to end!"

There was a moment of silence, and it stretched so long that Westin began to think he'd been abandoned. He slid to the floor in regret and knocked his head against the desk. He hadn't felt this powerless in four hundred years.

It took a few minutes before another small breeze finally got his attention. It was a message of uncertainty.

You may watch her, but you may not interfere. We need her.

The library quieted once more. Westin held his breath for a beat, waiting for them to change their minds. No other messages followed. Shaken, he stood and ran his hands through his hair. He hadn't thought it through. He'd been freed from her only a few years ago, after centuries of punishment, and in one frustrated moment, he'd ruined it.

He felt the imaginary weight of shackles press against his soul.

He bound himself to her once more.

Lia had slept the night before with true exhaustion. The drugs had helped her sleep, but she dreamed. They were odd moments twisted together, strangers who claimed to be friends, reapers who claimed to be lovers, and children who said she could fly. The scenes in her head moved fluidly, but nothing made sense.

She woke knowing she wasn't alone.

At the end of her bed stood the young girl from the mountain. Amanda. She was much cleaner, the bruises were fading, and her long blonde hair shone under the lights. The girl watched her curiously; her blue eyes examined her intensely. Lia struggled to sit up. For the first time, Lia wondered about the girl's fate. She was supposed to have died on that mountain. What would become of her now?

After a moment of silence, the girl thrust out a small miniature stuffed bear. "I'm Amanda. Everybody says you saved me from the bad man," she said softly. She climbed on the bed and placed the bear in Lia's lap.

Lia took it gently, her eyes weary on the little girl. She kept quiet.

"I didn't tell them that you were invisible or that you could move us with super lightning speed. Superheroes must keep their identity secret. I'm sorry that you're broken now."

Lia's eyes widened with surprise. "How do you know I was invisible? Maybe I just was not there."

"I saw him talking to you. I saw him hurt you. There was all this blood, but I couldn't see you. Not until you were broken. You just appeared, and then you transported us here! But your secret is safe with me. I didn't tell them anything," she whispered.

Lia held the bear up. "Why are you giving me a toy?"

Amanda's smile brightened. "It's my teddy bear. His name is Gregory. He's my friend when I'm lonely. I thought you might be lonely now that you're broken. Maybe Gregory can be your friend now."

Lia frowned. "Does he talk?"

Amanda giggled. "No silly!" She quieted. "When I'm sad I make believe that he talks. He was a present from my mommy before she went away. I think my mommy gave him to me because she knew I'd be sad that she was gone."

Lia cocked her head. "Are you still sad?"

Amanda shrugged. "It was a long time ago. I have a step mommy now, and she's nice. She makes me less sad."

Lia nodded. She looked at the child and realized this was the most honest conversation she'd had since the incident, and it was with a child. "Amanda, do you know anything about the man who hurt me?"

Amanda nodded. She spoke slowly as if reading a script in her head. "Sometimes he talked a lot, and sometimes he was really quiet. He said young souls would make them desperate, and he said he was sorry, but he had to do what needed to be done. He's really old, like you."

Lia raised her eyebrows. "What makes you think he is old?"

"He told me he was old."

"What makes you think I am old?"

Amanda smiled. "He said you were older."

Lia frowned. This man seemed to know a good deal about her. "Did he say anything else about me?"

The little girl twisted her mouth in concentration. "He said that you were special. He had never felt so powerful before, and he wanted more power. Is he your archenemy?"

"I am not sure."

"He said he had to break the chains. Did you chain him?"

Lia shook her head. "I do not think so. My memory is not

like yours. I forget things. They make me forget because I once was a bad person."

"Are you still a bad person?"

Lia was quiet for a moment. It was the first time anyone had asked her that question. "I do not know. I do not think people can change."

Amanda crawled further up, climbing over into her lap. Lia frowned and backed into her pillows, but there was no escape. The little girl threw her arms around Lia's neck and hugged her. "To me, you're not a bad person," she whispered into her ear.

Lia gently disengaged herself from the girl. "Thank you for your present," she said softly.

Amanda nodded. "I have to go. My daddy doesn't know that I am here, and the man at the door said I couldn't stay long. I hope that, when you get your powers back, you catch the bad man."

Lia nodded and watched Amanda leave the room. She stared at the teddy bear for a long time, gazing into its blank glassy eyes. It was just a thing, and yet Lia felt a connection with the toy. It was just a shell like she had once been.

A thought hit her. She gasped and doubled over as if she had been stabbed again.

She was alive with no soul.

A shell.

She leaned across the bed and retched.

Hunter noticed the teddy bear that was now constantly at Lia's side, but he made no comment about it. She tended to grip it like a shield, and if it comforted her, Hunter wasn't about to ask questions.

Despite the fact that his services were no longer needed, he continued to check in on her regularly. She was the first patient he saw when he started his shift and the last one he checked on before he left. Every time their eyes met, he saw a little less fear in hers.

She was healing quickly. The truth was that Hunter had never seen anyone heal as quickly as she did, but when he made a comment, she shrunk farther away from him. He kept his thoughts to himself now. Color was slowly returning to her cheeks, and although she was still underweight, Hunter couldn't deny that she was attractive. Her black hair was tangles and scraggly, and her lips were still pale, but every day that passed seemed to bring new light into her eyes. It was fascinating to watch. It was like she was coming back alive.

There was something odd and different about her, and Hunter couldn't quite put his finger on it. It was disconcerting, but he felt protective of her.

She had the knowledge of a child but was still intellectually sharp. She learned things quickly, and if she was alarmed by her lack of knowledge, she didn't show it. Instead, she asked questions about every new topic he introduced her to and listened intently.

She seemed oddly at ease with her lack of identity, and although the agents were getting frustrated that no one had come forward, she acted unconcerned. Hunter had the oddest notion that she wasn't expecting anyone to claim her.

Today was one of her last days at the hospital, and she seemed a little more guarded with him. Her thoughts appeared to be elsewhere as he tried to talk to her. "Lia? Lia, are you listening?"

She turned her head and focused on him. "I was just thinking about what was going to happen to me now. You are releasing me?"

"I am releasing you to the agents' care. They should be here shortly to go over the procedure with you. I'd like to talk to you about that stab wound."

Lia nodded. "I heard you. Do not get the stitches wet. Do not exert myself and make them tear. Do not try and take them out myself. You want me to come back in two weeks, and you will remove them yourself."

Apparently she was listening. "That's exactly right," Hunter smiled. "Showering will be tricky. I suggest that you wrap some plastic around the area and try to seal it with some tape as best as you can. You can sponge around the area outside the shower. It may still get wet, but you want to make sure you don't soak the area. Dab it lightly with some rubbing alcohol, and if it tears or starts to look discolored, you need to come back immediately."

Lia nodded. She pulled the bear closer to her chest. Hunter frowned. Tomorrow would not be easy for her. The agents would escort her out into the world, and she would be alone.

She voiced no questions, and Hunter left her to her thoughts and made his way to the cafeteria for lunch. He found it odd that such an attractive woman's disappearance had gone unnoticed. More than once his eyes had strayed to her left hand, looking for signs of a ring. He found none.

"Hey Logan, how's your mystery woman?" Hunter looked over to see Glassery matching pace with him as they entered the cafeteria.

"She's doing well. She'll be released in the morning," Hunter responded guardedly.

"Oh yeah? Someone claim her?"

"No, I don't believe so."

Glassery clapped him on the back. "Well, I suggest you make your move before someone else does! With no memories, she should be an easy catch!"

Hunter shot him a look. "I'm just a concerned doctor," he said in a low voice.

Glassery barked out in laughter and pushed his glasses up on his nose. "You didn't even visit your mother this often when she was in last year. Who do you think you're fooling?" His face clouded over. "We're all having to sign waivers stating that we're to keep our mouths shut about her. Do you think she's in danger?"

"They think the killer doesn't know she's alive. I think they're going to feed false details about her death to the press. I guess she'll be in real danger if the killer realizes that he left a witness."

They made their way through the dining hall and grabbed trays at the cafeteria line. "McCarthey is cracking down. Most people here even believe she's dead. The rest of us are signing our life away," he whispered to his friend.

"Her life might depend on it," Hunter responded.

They dropped the subject when others joined them, and although Hunter tried to focus on the group, Lia consumed his thoughts. Of course, tomorrow she would be gone, and his attention would be needed elsewhere.

He was certain that once she got her life back in order, she would never think of him again. After all, she had far bigger problems.

The sweatshirt and sweatpants were comfortable, but they hung on her frame loosely. Lia constantly tugged them up. Hunter watched her fidget and pace around the room and seemed amused by her antics. She was oddly self-conscious about what she was wearing and how she looked. It was absurd considering that she'd been in a hospital gown this whole time. Still, she hugged the teddy bear close to her chest and wandered.

This had been her home for days, but this morning, as she was getting ready to leave, she realized she hadn't looked around. She had felt that this was her prison, but now that she was being freed, she was curious about how the hospital looked from this side, the side of the living.

There were few colors to speak of, and they were washed out by the harsh luminescent lights. The voided colors dominated the room. White covered the walls, the machines, and her bed. There was no window to the outside world, and the chill of the hospital rattled her bones. Visually, there was little difference from what she used to see to what she saw now.

Her clothes had gone with the police, and her only possessions now were the sweats on her back and the toy clutched under her arm. It didn't bother her much; she was used to being without possessions.

"Go over it one more time," Hunter said softly, distracting her.

"No over exerting myself, no exercises that could tear my stitches. Do not get the stitches wet, and change the bandage twice a day or as needed. Come back in two weeks to have the stitches removed," Lia recited tonelessly.

"And you have your pain prescription..." he pointed out.

"I will not be filling it," Lia interrupted. She hated the groggy haze the hospital drugs gave her. She was adjusting to the pain.

"Don't be alarmed if you have any memory flashes. It may take some time, but you should start regaining your memory, and it's going to be confusing. You should keep a notebook to write down what you see and how you feel. It should help you work through any anxiety you might experience," he advised.

Mallich walked in at that moment, her heels clicking on the tiled floor. Lia could see her gun peeking out from under her gray blazer. She stared at it. "Are you ready to go?" Mallich asked crisply, breaking up Lia's thoughts.

Lia nodded. "Yes."

"Very well. Dr. Logan, thank you for your services. I'm sure we'll be in touch. Ms. Lia, it's time to go."

Hunter shook Mallich's hand and reached out for Lia's. "I'll see you in two weeks, Lia. Take care," he said warmly.

Lia nodded, trying to remember the proper procedure. She had watched the doctors, nurses, and agents interact with each other. She tried to mimic their sincerity. "Thank you, Dr. Logan," she repeated hesitantly. Hunter smiled.

As Mallich led Lia down the hall, she provided a little more explanation in a low voice. "As I've mentioned before, this is a temporary home. You will be provided with security in case the killer is watching. You are not to mention to anyone the circumstances of your situation. This is a loose version of witness protection. We will provide you with a cover, a job, and a stipend until you regain your memories, and then we will go from there."

As they pushed their way through the double doors, Lia froze in the sun's glare. Even during reaps, a thin layer of the reaper realm had shielded her, but here she was, vulnerable to its complete wrath. She gasped and immediately threw up her hands to protect herself. Mallich stopped. "What's wrong?"

Lia lowered her hands. "It is nothing. The sun...it is bright," she said softly. After a moment, she allowed herself to be enveloped it its warmth. The first seconds of false wrath turned pleasant and inviting. She smiled, and a sound of laughter escaped her lips. It was comforting.

If Mallich thought her actions were odd, she didn't let on. Her face remained blank as she gave Lia a few moments to adjust to the outside before leading her to the car.

Heat rolled out of the car as the door opened, and Lia embraced it. "Buckle up. It's not a far ride," Mallich announced, starting the car.

Lia was silent the whole way. She felt an odd sensation as she looked out the window. It was less extreme than fear, but it still seemed to take over her body, making her tense.

Lia was concerned about the days ahead of her.

Chapter Six

Mallich had little to say as they drove from the hospital. She sat stiff in the driver seat and barely cast a glance Lia's way. Lia was too involved with looking out the window to pay attention to the female agent. She could see the snow peaks of the mountains in the distance, an odd contrast to the summer skies, and Lia was pleased with the stark distinction between seasons. She gripped Gregory, butted her head against the cool glass and watched as they drove past the pedestrians and cyclists, drivers and shops.

The agent slowed as she turned into a paved drive. A black iron fence outlined the perimeter of houses and yards. The flower beds were meticulously manicured and still bloomed in the late summer months. Her hands shook with delight at the pinks and reds that lined the gate.

"Pretty," she said softly.

As Mallich pulled up to punch in her key code, Lia stared in wonder at the delicate petals. She was no stranger to flowers, but she couldn't ever remember having seen so many in one place. They bloomed in pinks and yellows, blues and reds, captivating her imagination and spreading a feeling of joy inside her. She smiled.

"The code through the gates is 3752. I'll write it down for you when we get inside. You are not to give this code to anyone. The agent must approve guests and will personally buzz them in. This is a minimal security safe house. It's meant to blend in and give you a chance at a normal life, but that doesn't mean you need to take any unnecessary chances," Mallich explained as they pulled through the gates. "You will be given an extensive handbook to read the rules. You will be expected to follow these guidelines."

Mallich's stern voice pulled Lia out of wonderland and into reality, where she was both bait and prisoner. It was still early in the day, and most people were at work. There was little activity in the neighborhood, but they still passed the occasional dog walker and lawn mower. She bit her lip at the thought of dogs. Would they still behave the same way around her, acting as if she were a ghost?

"Here we go." Mallich pulled up to a two-story brick building with black trim. It was small in comparison to the other houses, but the yard was well kept. Lia was pleased to see a splash of color amongst the flowers in the front, and she was eager to get out and smell them.

"We have an agent who poses as a frequently traveling business man. He only stays here when he's in town. This provides a cover story for short-term renters. We have you all set up with a new ID inside." Mallich opened the door and stepped out. When Lia hesitated to follow suit, Mallich leaned over and tried to smile gently. It came out more like a grimace.

"I know it's a lot to digest, but the sooner you get out of the car, the sooner you'll settle into your new temporary home," she pointed out.

Lia tried to return the smile and stepped out. The agent kept referring to this place as temporary, but Lia knew that this would be the most permanent home she'd had in a long time. It unsettled her to think of a place like home rather than a crash pad.

The air was fresh, and the flowers provided a pleasant fragrance on her way up the walk. Lia reached out to touch the delicate petals, marveling at how soft and silky they were. She could have pulled it off the stem with an easy twist of her fingers and crushed it.

She released the petal. Mallich was already up the walk and holding the door open for her. Lia picked up her pace and, as they passed the door, she pressed her hand against it.

Still solid.

"The first floor contains the kitchen, a dining area that we converted into an office, and a living room. Upstairs you'll find two bedrooms and two separate bathrooms. There is a nice sized porch out back leading into the backyard. It's fenced in for privacy. Both the front and back entrances are monitored with cameras. The feed is sent to our temporary offices at the station. It won't be monitored twenty-four hours a day, but if anyone knocks or rings the doorbell, the sound will alert the station. Also, the tape is recorded so we'll always have a record," Mallich droned on, pointing her fingers in all directions as if she were a flight attendant.

"Are there cameras inside as well?" Lia asked.

"No. You will have as much privacy within these walls as possible with a roommate. There is a male agent trained to work with people in your position. Of course, if you are more comfortable with a female agent being here, I'm sure that can be arranged as well." The woman frowned suddenly. "Although, come to think of it, I don't believe there is a female agent that has had the same training."

Lia frowned at the thought of a roommate, at the thought of being watched. How would she get any answers if she were constantly under surveillance? On the other hand, she knew nothing about how to survive, so the idea of having someone here to help guide her might not be a bad thing. "I am sure it will be fine," she said finally.

Mallich closed the door behind her. "Feel free to walk around while I get your paperwork together. I'll need your signature."

Lia nodded and took her cue to leave. Out of habit, she surveyed the new place as if she were still a reaper. The place was minimally furnished with no decorative accents. A beige couch and navy chair faced a small flat screen on the wall of the living room. A side table with a blue lamp stood in one corner, and a silver corner lamp let off a soft glow on the opposite side. A sturdy wooden coffee table provided a center, but there were no magazines or coasters to make it feel like a home. In the reaper realm, it would have been perfect.

This, however, was a different world, and she wasn't invisible. Here she could touch more, and affect the things around her. The blue curtains on the windows were closed making the room feel small and stuffy. Lia wanted to see the sun, so she opened the curtain and cracked the blinds. The sun streamed in, and she felt seeped in energy.

The bland taste of the living room followed throughout the house. There were just enough furniture and appliances to make it livable, but nothing to suggest that anyone lived there. As a reaper who had lived for minimal space, Lia was pleased with the furnishings. She just wished there was a little more space.

Mallich had already closed the blinds and the curtains in the living room as Lia made her way back down. "Once Agent Caxton is here, you can open them back up again. I don't want anyone to see all this paperwork." She had spread out the papers on the coffee table. "Have a seat," she commanded, pointing to the couch.

Mallich settled in the chair across from her, crossed her legs, and folded her hands in her lap. Lia could sense tension radiating from the woman.

"Lia, your situation calls for some blending of programs. For instance, we want to protect you, but we don't have enough of a reason to put you in witness protection. For your safety, we are telling the public, and hopefully your attacker, that you and the little girl were found dead. We are not giving them any details because, frankly, we don't know what those details might be, and we don't want your assailant to pick up on that little tidbit.

"Your amnesia places you in the Marks Program. This is what I am detailing for you now. It's a program that will run up to a year, giving you a place in society while you recover your memories. We set you up with a home in which all bills will be paid. We will also pay a small stipend for groceries, toiletries, a small wardrobe, etc. Finally, we have a job set up for you which will allow you to make and save some money."

Lia's eyes widened. "Why would you do all this?"

"The program is named for a woman who worked specifically with trauma victims. There were multiple cases where amnesia victims would get their memories back in a few months but had fallen behind on their expenses. Marks spent years rallying for a system to help these victims. The Marks Program is designed to make sure that when you return to your normal life, you won't find it so difficult to catch up."

Lia wasn't in a position to point out that her situation was a little different, so she kept her mouth shut. Mallich continued. "You will see an appointed therapist at the hospital who will help you with memory recovery, post-traumatic stress, and issues that pop up as you try to fit back into society. After she believes you are suitable for work, we will talk about your job." She leaned over and pointed to the first packet of information.

"This outlines what we just discussed. Also, it goes into detail about dollar amounts. Read it over and sign the bottom. Your first name will do, followed by an X for your last name."

Lia skimmed it over. She had very little concept of money, so the amounts meant nothing to her. At the bottom, she signed Lia X.

"Moving on. This next packet contains the guidelines for your protection. It gives you information on the rights the agents have while guarding you as well as a rulebook for your behavior. Read that over and sign the last page. You'll get to keep the handbook as a reminder."

Lia raised her eyebrows as she skimmed over the paperwork. She was to use only the name on her ID and the background information given. She was never to have guests over without permission from her agent, and she had to check-in via cellphone every hour. She looked up. "I do not have my phone." Her eyes widened suddenly in panic. What had happened to her cell phone?

Mallich raised her eyebrows. "You remember having a phone?" she asked curiously.

Lia bit her lip hesitantly. Now was not the time to slip up. "I feel like I should have a phone," she said slowly.

The agent nodded. "You did have a phone, but it has been damaged beyond repair. We can't even trace the serial number on it, so it's likely a knockoff iPhone. It was a dead end. I'm sorry. We will provide you with a new phone. It is equipped with GPS location and abilities to call and text."

Lia nodded. After a few minutes, she signed again. Lia X. Mallich ripped off the back page and handed the packet to her. "This is your bible. I would recommend looking at it every morning. We have no reason to believe that you are in danger, but that doesn't mean that you are not. Understood?"

Once again, Lia nodded. She was starting to feel like one of the bobble heads she'd seen on the dashboard of so many cars.

Mallich reached over and handed her a wallet. When Lia flipped it open, she found some cash, a bank card, a few grocery cards, and her new identification. She frowned at the image. "When did you take this?" she asked.

"Pretty good isn't it? It's the picture we used from the hospital to scan you in the system. It has been altered to look like a DMV picture." Mallich seemed proud of the work.

Lia had spent so much time absorbing her surroundings that she had forgotten to look at herself. The picture was not flattering. Her hair was limp and greasy, her eyes flat, and her skin was past pale. Lia shoved the picture in her wallet. The image made her oddly uncomfortable.

"We felt that use of your first name might be dangerous, but in the end, we were told that keeping a link to that memory could be useful. Lia Briggs just moved from Vermont with her brother.

They are looking to start their new lives in Colorado. Don't try to provide details. The more lies you tell, the more you'll have to remember. No names, no locations, no stories. Keep it simple. If someone presses, you simply hide behind the excuse that you don't want to talk about it. Memorize your date of birth, your age, your phone number, and your address. Do you understand?"

Lia Briggs. That sounded nothing like the truth. "Yes, I understand."

Behind her, she could hear a car pull up in the drive. "Agent Caxton will be working with you. He will be playing your brother, so you'll need to learn his information as well. Caxton can also provide transportation. You will be protected at all times until we catch the unsub. You should feel safe. If, for any reason, you are unsatisfied with his actions, you can contact us, and Agent O'Ryan will assign you with someone from the local police." Mallich smiled. "Ready to meet Agent Caxton?"

The idea of having someone live with her made Lia's stomach turn. She couldn't even fake a smile. They both stood as the key entered the door.

When he walked into the room, Lia pressed a hand to her stomach. Her eyes widened, and a strange feeling spread through her. Panic? Fear? Surprise? "Lia Briggs, meet Agent Westin Caxton. Caxton, Lia."

He wasn't wearing his trench coat and gloves, but why would he? On this side of the veil, the sun was intense. Westin's eyes held a warning as he stuck out his hand. "Miss Briggs. Pleasure."

Lia's hands trembled as she touched him.

Lia couldn't even nod or meet his eyes. Westin withdrew his hand and turned to Mallich. "Is everything in order?" he asked quietly.

"All of the paperwork is signed. I've left an appointment sheet for you in the kitchen. I think her first meeting with the therapist is this Wednesday. Hopefully, she'll be able to start her job by next week. The kitchen isn't stocked, so you may need to run a few errands. There is a list of things she should pick up as well," Mallich instructed. Lia could hear the woman, but her focus was on Westin. She moved, slowly backing into the corner of the living room.

"Lia? Is everything okay?" Mallich asked.

Lia's eyes flitted over Westin. "Everything is fine," she said tonelessly.

Mallich's eyes narrowed. "If you want me to stay tonight, I'm sure Agent Caxton wouldn't mind coming back tomorrow."

The idea of spending the night with Mallich snapped Lia out of her stupor. She forced a smile. "It is just so much information," she said. "I will be fine. I think I just need to look over all this paperwork again. Maybe a trip to the marketplace will make me feel better."

Mallich smiled. "The marketplace?" she asked.

Lia laughed nervously. "The grocery."

"All right. Your phone is in your room with all of our direct numbers. We'll be in touch. Enjoy the rest of the day. The weather is beautiful." Mallich nodded at Caxton.

"Thank you, Agent Mallich. I'll handle it from here." He walked her to the door, and they kept their heads together talking closely. As soon as he had ushered her out and closed the door, he turned to face Lia. She had backed up into the wall.

"Lia..." he began slowly.

"Do you know who I am?" she burst out.

"Yes. I know who you are. Well, I vaguely know who you are."

"What the hell does that mean?" she asked tightly. She was testing him.

"I was your master for a day. I didn't really get to know you," he pointed out. He watched as Lia visibly relaxed, half collapsing against the wall.

"How can you suddenly be an FBI agent? A week ago you were a running a unit of reapers, and now you're standing in front of me like a normal human being!" She was startled by her sudden burst of frustration and tried to calm herself down.

He gestured towards her. "You're not exactly walking through walls either. Besides, I have more power than you do. After word got out about what happened, I asked permission to follow you through the veil."

Lia started pacing around the room. Her relief at knowing that Westin was on her side was short lived. He wasn't here to take her back, but she wasn't even sure if she wanted to go back. She wasn't sure of anything yet. "Why am I here? How am I here?"

Westin ran a hand through his hair. "I don't have any answers for you, Lia. I'm sorry."

"Do not say that. Apologizing does not get anything done. I am walking around in the physical world without a soul. I was nearly murdered by a human who could see me. I am now human and mortal and soulless, and you were sent here because they do not know what is going on? Or maybe they just do not want to tell you what is going on. Or maybe they do not care!" The more Lia talked and paced, the more her words ran together. Reality was being cruel to her, and she wanted Westin to know it.

Westin tried to put up his hand to stop her, but she was on a roll. "I have no idea who I am. I have no idea what year I am in." Pulling up her shirt, she ripped off the bandage. "My skin is being held together by a thread, and there is a little girl out there who thinks I have the power of invisibility and instant transportation. I do not know how to live, but I have to convince a doctor that I am normal so that the police aren't breathing down my neck."

She finally stopped and slid down on the couch.

"Feel better?" he asked sardonically.

"Yes," she said coldly. After a breath, she tried to tape the patch back against her skin. It stung where she had ripped it off. A lump caught in her throat, and she tugged her shirt back into place.

"Good. That is the last time I want to see you melt down. Your theory about the judges knowing what's going on and providing no information is probably correct. I'm sure once they believe you need to know, they'll find a way to tell you. In the meantime, we do have to blend in. That means following the orders of the police. My infiltration should make things far easier for you."

Her eyes narrowed. "How are you able to infiltrate?"

He smirked. "That's a secret that I might reveal in time. As both agent and master, the rules still apply. You will listen and obey me. Understood?"

She considered his words. Technically, she was a free reaper. No longer under the thumb of the judges, she was free to make her own decision and retain her memories. This world complicated though, and Lia feared she would not adjust well. She was programmed to obey her master, but more importantly, Lia suspected she needed Westin. He was her link to the reaper realm and humanity. "Yes," she said quietly answering him.

"Good," he clapped his hands together and rubbed them. "It's still early. I suggest we do some shopping and see how you can handle the public." He surveyed her. "Any requests on where we go first?"

She pulled herself off the couch. "I need coffee."

Chapter Seven

Lia gripped her coffee cup as though it were her only hold on life. It spread warmth through her fingers and reminded her that she could feel. When she drank it, the liquid slid down her throat and warmed her belly, reminding her that she now required sustenance. Energy spiked through her nervous system, shaking her fingers, reminding her that she was alive.

She studied Westin as he navigated through the rush hour traffic to a nearby strip mall. He looked so at ease with the mechanisms and laws associated with driving. He checked his rear view mirrors and applied the brake effortlessly. He used his turn signals and never got upset with the other drivers. She wondered how it was possible that he knew such things.

"How old are you?" she asked.

He raised his eyebrows. "Why do you ask?"

She pointed to the steering wheel. "You know how to drive."

He shrugged. "It's a recent talent I picked up. It has nothing to do with my age."

"Will you teach me how to drive?"

He glanced over at her briefly with a puzzled look on his face. "Why do you want to learn?"

Lia mulled the question over. "I think that I should learn at every opportunity. How often does a reaper get a second chance at life?"

Westin snorted. "What's the point if you just have to go back to reaping? You'll forget everything. There are no guarantees that this second chance is a done deal."

"That is not the point," she said softly. "Even if I do not remember, I will be able to enjoy the experience now."

Westin turned into the parking lot. "I guess that's true. Of course, teaching you to drive could just be sending you to an early grave."

Lia wondered if that was an insult, but her attention was promptly diverted to the store in front of them. "Target," she read slowly. "I have seen this before. I have passed it on my way to the hospital. What does it have inside?"

Westin navigated the car into a parking spot. "A little bit of everything, which is why we are here. We can pick up some clothes for you, groceries, toiletries, that kind of thing."

Lia nodded. She was unsure what a toiletry was, but she had a list from Agent Mallich. The first word she recognized was aspirin."

"Can we pick up the aspirin first? The pain is unpleasant," she explained.

Westin had his hand on the door handle, but her request seemed to stop him. "What do you feel? Just pain from your stab wound?"

"My head hurts almost constantly. My skin hurts sometimes, and my neck aches. I did not realize there was so much pain associated with living."

He eyed her silently. "You'll get used to the elements and the physical pain will lessen. If you are here long enough, I think you'll find that pain is one of the quintessential parts of living. Without it, you'll have no way of judging the pleasant side of life."

There seemed to be an underlying sadness in Westin's tone, but Lia didn't know why. It occurred to her that she trusted a stranger with her life. The thought didn't sit well in her stomach.

As she exited the car, she froze. A new feeling was creeping over her. It was slow, cold, but as she concentrated on it, she felt it getting stronger. It iced over her very core. She gasped and grabbed the car. Westin came around and stared at her. "What's the matter with you?"

Lia grabbed at her chest. "I feel different. Stronger and

excited," she said slowly, trying to identify everything happening in her. She breathed in deeply. It was a feeling that she had felt before, but with less intensity. It happened when she reaped a soul, and it lingered before moving on. "It is him. I tried to reap his soul. I think I am tied to him." She whipped her head around the parking lot, searching.

Westin's face went dark. "Him who? The man who attacked you? You touched his soul?"

"Only for a moment." Lia swallowed at the memory. "It was a reaction to his blade. His soul was solid, and I was so taken aback that I released it." She looked at Westin. "How long will I be able to feel him?"

There was a moment where Lia thought Westin would start yelling at her. His face clouded over, and he seemed dangerously angry. After a moment, he just shook his head. "I don't know. It's not a big concern for now. Let's get our things," he said coldly.

As he turned his back to her, Lia bit her lip. Though she suspected that Westin disliked her, she felt his hatred towards her now. She wished she knew what she had done to offend him, but asking would probably make it worse.

The alien feelings subsided, and she looked around the store in anticipation. This was her first opportunity to touch and explore without the confines of walls. While the agents had been stifling, Westin was content to let her roam as he led her through the store.

"Clothes are the biggest task we need to tackle. I have a wardrobe, but you'll need to pick a few things. Keep it simple, just as you did as a reaper. You'll want the basics, something comfortable and maneuverable."

Lia tried to be practical. She started out well enough with pants and shorts, but she was constantly distracted by colors. Westin moved behind her, patiently and quietly while she whipped her head back and forth at the selection. As soon as her hands hovered over one, a different color would catch her eye.

She fingered the materials of a green dress on the first rack. It shimmered subtly against her skin and flowed like liquid as it dropped from her fingers. Lia had never worn anything except jeans and sweats. Her breath caught as she thought of the possibilities. She was like a kid in a candy store.

A giggle escaped her, and she twirled, drunk on excitement. It was the first moment since she'd crossed the veil, the first moment she could ever remember, that she felt happy. The choices were a little overwhelming, and Lia was determined to branch out. She knew nothing about fashion and had no one to dress for, but she wanted to look pretty. The feeling was odd and alien, but she embraced it and dove head first into the challenge before her.

She could see Westin frowning as he watched her, but she ignored him. In the end, she had piled almost half the store selection in the cart, including a few dresses she doubted she would ever wear. She bit her lip and raised her eyes to Westin for permission.

He eyeballed the cart and looked at her. "Do you need all of this?"

"No," she said honestly.

He sighed. "Narrow it down to enough tops for a couple of weeks," he said.

"Can I keep the dresses," she asked hopefully.

He started to shake his head but stopped. "Two dresses," he muttered. She smiled and went about narrowing her selection. Lia felt an urge to try everything on, but she knew it wasn't necessary. She'd been the same size for as long as she could remember.

"Try to do better when it comes to shoes," he said quietly as they made their way to the selection.

It turned out that shoes were a particular weakness for Lia, and she internally struggled. She made a few practical choices, and tossed them in the basket. After a moment, she slipped a pair of heels off the shelf and stepped into them.

Her legs wobbled a bit as she shuffled to the mirror. How did women walk in these? Why did they torture themselves? When she reached the mirror, she understood. Her legs looked long and shapely. Her posture was straight, her breasts perky, and the heels drew her body up to a lengthy height. The change was amazing. She took another step forward and nearly fell. She put her arms out like she was walking a tightrope and tried again. Her balance had improved, but she wondered if she was supposed to bounce so much.

With regret, she put the blue stilettos back on the shelf and reached for a shoe with a smaller heel. The effect wasn't so dramatic, but her legs looked good and her step was safer and more comfortable.

There were strappy heels that laced all the way up to mid-calf, but Lia couldn't figure out how to buckle them at the top. She muttered with frustration for a moment before tossing them off her feet. There were wedges, and while Lia was unsure how she liked them, they were comfortable and gave her the height the stilettos did, so she tossed those in the cart as well. Some of the shoes scrunched her toes at the tip and others flopped too much at the heel. Others had so many straps that she wasn't sure where her toes were supposed to go.

People strolling by were starting to stare, but Lia defiantly met their gaze, and they quickly averted their gaze. By the end, she had tried on almost every pair of shoes the store had offered. There were far more in her basket than those she had put back.

Westin had wandered away, and when he returned, he shook his head. "You have more shoes in the cart than outfits. Put some back."

Lia tapped her hand on the cart. She couldn't make up her mind. Finally Westin stepped in, pulling boxes out. She frowned but didn't intervene. He left her with a pair of sandals, flip-flops, tennis shoes, heels, and wedges.

Lia decided to push her luck. "Do you think I could get a couple of books and a notebook?"

Westin whipped his head around. "Why do you need a notebook?" he asked tersely.

Lia thought quickly. She knew he would shut her down if she couldn't think of a reasonable excuse. There was no need for a notebook. If she were collected again, she would not be able to retain any of her memories or anything from today's purchases, but she felt a need to record everything she could. "The doctor told me to keep a journal to help with my memories. It might be suspicious if I do not follow through."

Westin considered her thought process. "Two books and one notebook. And then we concentrate on goods and supplies. Got it?"

"Thank you," she said impulsively.

Westin raised his eyebrows. "Did you just thank me?" he asked.

"It is common courtesy to thank someone when they are kind towards you," Lia said absently.

"So is saying you're sorry when you do something to upset someone," he pointed out.

"Apologies are misleading. They are bandages on the surface of larger problems, and people say them without meaning. I am genuinely thankful for my purchases today, but I do not believe you or myself are sorry for anything that we have done. If we were sorry, we would not continue to do the things that we must apologize for. You said it yourself; life is full of pain. If I know anything about being alive, it is that we are always doing things knowing full well the consequences. Apologizing merely provides false comfort," Lia retorted.

"Pick out your damn books. Meet me in the grocery section when you're done, and don't get lost," Westin said, suddenly angry. He grabbed the cart and left her alone with the shoes.

Lia hiked her sweat pants up and fidgeted nervously. She had no idea what she had said to upset him. She considered following him for a moment but decided to leave him be. With a small smile, she followed the signs to the books. Running a hand over the metal bookcases, she studied the titles and pictures. It was a rare occasion that her crash pads contained books, but she always studied them with unexplained energy. She'd read the Bible, the most common book found, multiple times and poured over a series involving a wizard and owls. One household contained books with whips and chains, and another had a multitude of books for dummies. Now was her chance to choose her own reading material.

She became absorbed in the summaries on the back. When she thought she'd found something she liked, she would sit it aside. Soon other customers were stepping over the pile of books she had in the center. Afterward, she sat in the middle and wondered how she was going to pick.

"Ahem."

Lia looked up, startled. Westin was staring at her over a full cart. "Are you still looking at books?"

"It has only been a few minutes," she objected.

"It's been an hour, Lia. I've picked up all our supplies and a damn notebook for you. I thought you were lost."

"Oh," Lia said quietly. She looked at her books. "I am not sure which ones I want."

With a sigh, Westin squatted down. He studied her pile. Leaning over, he tossed a few books into her lap. "Those are good. Start with those."

Lia's eyes widened. "You just gave me five books," she said quietly.

"Remember that next time I ask you to do something you don't want to do. Now pick up the rest, and let's be on our way," he muttered gruffly.

Lia moved quickly to straighten the books and put her purchases into the cart. She pulled out the notebook that Westin had picked out for her.

It was simple with a black fake leather binding and far more pages than she thought she would need. Westin ignored her smile, and she placed it quietly back in the cart. Maybe he didn't hate her as much as she thought.

At the counter, she watched the transaction, fascinated. He inserted a plastic card into a machine, and the machine sucked it inside only to spit it out a second later. Her eyes rounded in wonder, and she examined the machine as he walked away.

"Lia," he called. She pulled herself away from the counter and jogged after him. He tossed the bottle of aspirin at her before they returned to the car. "Don't take too many or they'll mess up your stomach," he warned.

She tried to swallow them dry and ended up crouching and dry heaving outside the car. Westin shook his head and ducked inside the car. Lia followed suit, a rare flush on her face.

They rode back in silence.

The temperature dropped, and Lia shivered. She dug her toes into the gravel. They bit into her skin, and she winced. In the silence of the false scene before her, something tugged at her memory. She had been here before. She looked left to the figure struggling in the calm waters. In front of her stood the tall blurry man.

"You!" She cried out. "I remember you. I remember this. Why could I not remember it before?"

"Sometimes, to see the truth, you must forget," he answered in his thousand voices.

She stepped forward, the rocks still digging into her skin. "Who are you?" she demanded.

"It is unwise to ask questions to which you already know the answer."

"What are you doing here?" she asked frustrated with his riddles.

"I am watching."

She looked at the dying figure again. "Why are you watching?"

"To understand the future, you must understand the past."

"And that person?" She pointed out into the river. "What is their future?"

He moved closer and the river grew blurry. She struggled to regain focus. He didn't make a sound as he reached out and touched her forehead. Darkness swept over her, and she cried out as she fell. In the void, she heard him speak.

"It is possible they will die by your hand."

When her vision returned, she was standing close to a fenced in area with small huts and shovels and wheelbarrows scattered about. Men in uniform moved around the area, talking in a language she didn't understand. She tried to hide behind the posts, but, as men passed her, it became clear that no one could see her.

"It is a dream," she whispered. It would only be the second dream that she could ever remember having. Unlike her first dream, she was in control of her actions. She strode confidently around the perimeter.

As she rounded the corner, she saw one of the male guards bending over a thin young woman, her dress hiked up around her waist. As he shoved himself inside her, tears ran down her face. Lia frowned in confusion. If the woman was upset, why didn't she scream?

Movement from around the corner caught her eye. Lia squinted her eyes. A woman was crouched down in the corner of one of the buildings. The woman moved quietly around the edge until she was just behind the man. In a flash, she jumped, one hand covering his mouth, the other bringing a blade into his chest. He grunted and slumped. The woman let him fall dead to the ground. She turned to the young woman, put a finger to her lips, and pointed for her to leave. The woman didn't even seem to care that the man was dead. She pulled down her dress and dragged herself around the corner of the building and out of Lia's sight.

Surprise and fear stabbed into Lia as the woman's face came into clear view. Shaking a little, she moved closer to the scene. She watched as the woman clipped the wires and snuck through the fence. Her knife was still dripping with blood.

Lia was watching herself.

She focused on the other version of herself and began to sense different emotions. Although she was in a different body, she could feel what her dream-

self was feeling. She could feel confusion and fear. She was relieved that she had killed, terrified of her future, and confused with her present. Her other self began to run.

Lia narrowed her eyes. Instead of following, she walked over to the dead body. The symbol on his uniform was familiar, but she couldn't place it. She reached down and dipped a finger in his blood. It was still warm and thick. An energy still lingered in the air. It radiated from the power of taking a life. She started to hear her own blood roar in her ears. Time slowed as she stared at the life flowing out of the man. It was beautiful. Taking this man's life felt so necessary and so right.

This was a memory. This was her first kill: the crime that started it all.

In a flash, Lia jumped to her feet. Adrenaline pumped through her veins as she started to run, to chase the memory version of her herself. When she reached the end of her tracks, she froze.

Westin stood in front of her other self. Everything was blurry around him. There was an energy pouring out of her memory, rushing from her body into Westin's. Lia watched as her memory pulled out a blade and stabbed Westin.

Lia stumbled back in shock and began to fall...down.....down.

With a start, Lia jackknifed upwards in bed. Her chest was heavy, and she struggled to breathe. Her hands tingled, and her palms were sweaty, soaking the sheets.

Lia threw back her comforter and raced out of bed, pulled open her door, and rushed down the hall to Westin's room. She shoved open his door, flicked on the light and was on him before he even had a chance to rollover.

"What the hell?" Westin muttered. He struggled against her, but Lia straddled him, pushed him down and raised the hem of his shirt. She stared at his side.

Westin froze as Lia ran a finger down his scar. Her mouth was set.

"You are not a master," she accused.

Westin carefully pushed her off him and pulled down his

shirt. "I am a master, but it's a relatively recent development," he muttered roughly. Rubbing a hand over the scruff on his face, he pushed himself off the bed and faced her.

"You were a collector. You were my collector," she scrambled off the bed and backed into the opposite corner. "Did you not think that I needed to know this?"

"Why does it matter? You knew that you were collected. Why do you care whether or not it was me?"

"I thought you were here to protect me," she said heatedly.

"I'm not here to protect you! I'm here to protect everybody else!" Westin shouted. Silence thickened the air, and he started to pace.

"How did you get your memory?" he asked finally.

"It was a dream."

"What exactly did you see?"

"I saw myself killing someone. Then I saw you taking something from me. I think it was my memory. Everything seems fuzzy now." Lia frowned. The more she tried to remember, the less she could see of the dream. The feelings remained though. She looked at her hands. She could still feel the phantom weight of the man's blood on her hands. She wiped them on her clothes.

"Who did you kill?" Lia frowned, and Westin strode over to her and grabbed her. "I need you to remember Lia. Who was it?"

Lia pulled free. "Like you do not know," she accused. She bit her lip. "My head is fuzzy. There was a symbol on his shoulder, a twisted cross. I cannot remember much more than that."

Westin nodded. "The concentration camp," he said softly.

"When was it?" Lia asked softly.

"Nineteen forties," Westin said absently.

She did the math in her head. "I look to be in my late twenties. That war was seventy years ago. That puts me somewhere between ninety and a hundred years old." She looked up at Westin, disappointed. "I guess Allen was wrong. I am not so very old after all." She frowned. "Why did I have that dream?"

Westin perched on the edge of the bed. "You wouldn't have it unless the judges released it on purpose. They want you to remember."

"Why?"

Westin shook his head. "I guess we'll know soon enough."

"Will I have more memories? Memories of my life before I became a reaper?"

Westin's eyes hardened. "I don't know. Go back to bed," he said coldly.

Lia felt the anger in his words. She straightened. "You hate me," she accused. He didn't answer. "Would you like to tell me why?"

"Go to bed Lia. It's not a request," Westin said, his mouth set.

Lia clenched her teeth but walked silently out of the room. In bed, she pulled the covers up tight to her chin and tried to sleep, but she tossed and turned. The memory of her dream twisted around in her mind. It ran faster and faster until all Lia could see was the weapon and blood. She could hear the dead man's blood pumping and the slash of the knife. In her mind, she could hear his heart stop, and the blood pour out into the snow.

It sounded like home.

Chapter Eight

The rooms in the rancher were empty except for the couch and television in the living room, and a chair and mirror in the bedroom. The closet was locked at all times. The place smelled of mildew and dust but was otherwise clean.

Charlie sat on the floor, his back against the couch, and stared at the blank television. In his mind, the screen was filled with memories of the past few days. Dried and cracked bloody bandages were tossed carelessly next to him, and he ran a finger over the handmade stitches that crossed his abdomen.

His plan had not worked at all.

All along he had thought that killing Lia would free him, but now he could see the flaws in his plan. He could feel her now. He sensed her pain and her confusion. There was a mixture of fear, but mostly there was strength. With every breath that Charlie took, he could feel her feeding that strength to him.

Despite the unexpected blood loss, this was the strongest he had felt in decades. Now that she had crossed the veil, he could not let her go back. He had to plan, to strategize. Finding her had taken so very long, and the idea of killing her had been easy. Now he had to gain her trust. He needed to know what they had planned for her. He needed to know what was expected of her. He needed to remind her of herself.

He smiled. He'd had the most pleasant dream last night, a dream of blood and snow. He felt an urge to see it again. He leaped to his feet with ease and made his way to the full-length mirror in the bedroom.

It had been a few years since he had last crossed the veil and age was catching up with him. Where he had once resembled a twenty-year old, he was now creeping into his thirties. It didn't bother him. He wasn't doing this for vanity or eternal youth. Still, he would need a vacation when this was all over. Despite the strength, he could feel his empty half weighing him down. He would need to refuel soon.

He grabbed a marker from the top of the mirror and closed his eyes. The image was crystal clear in his head. He began to write descriptions on the mirror. At the very bottom, larger than all the other words, were his main points.

Blood.

Snow.

He wanted to see them again.

The house was silent that morning. Listening to see if Lia would have more dreams, Westin had slept in fits for the rest of the night, but her room had been silent. He beat the eggs a little too hard and had to remind himself to calm down.

He knew she thought that the guard was her first and only kill. What would be her reaction when she realized that the dreams were going backwards? He poured the eggs on the stovetop and whisked them, unaware that Lia had quietly come down and was watching him.

"What are you making?" she asked softly.

Westin nearly jumped out of his skin. "Scrambled eggs, bacon, and toast," he answered tersely. "Pour us some orange juice and sit down. It's almost ready." He watched her out of the corner of his eye. "Did you have any more dreams?"

She shook her head before sitting at the table. She looked small and harmless as she examined the room. Her expression changed with every new sight and smell. For a moment, Westin wished that things could have been different. If they had met on different grounds, he might have been able to help her. Now all he could do was hope they reached the end with as little bloodshed as possible.

He piled eggs on top of her plate. "You'll need to focus on your eating habits. As a person, in this world, your fuel comes from food alone. You may feel strong coming from the reaper plane, but you are underweight, and soon you'll feel the effects of malnourishment."

He grabbed his plate and sat down to join her. She ate in silence, and he watched as a small smile started on her face. She liked the eggs.

"Tomorrow you'll have your first visit with a therapist. You've done all right so far with hiding your identity, but therapists are trained to detect abnormalities. You can hide well behind amnesia, but you still have to act like a normal person. Does this make sense?"

Lia nodded. "What will they want to ask me?"

Westin shrugged. "I don't know. I imagine their main concern will be dealing with the trauma and trying to recover your memories."

Lia put her fork down. "Speaking of trauma, you have not said much about this serial killer. He saw me, Westin, and he acted as though he knew me. He used my name."

Westin nodded. "Allen said the same thing. I don't have any answers for you."

"Amanda said he needed to break the chains. Does that mean anything to you?"

Hiding his reaction, he chugged his orange juice. "I have no idea what that could mean," he lied.

"Did he know that the judges would pull me through the veil? Is that why he tried to kill me?"

"Again, I don't know. I'm just here to make sure things don't get more complicated."

Lia frowned. "Are you here as a master or a collector?"

Westin rubbed the stubble on his cheek. "For me to blend in with society, I have to possess certain talents. These talents only come from collectors."

Lia swallowed. "Will you be collecting me when this is over?"

"Unless I am tasked to collect you, I am only here to watch. As long as you don't kill anyone, they cannot task me or anyone else to collect you."

She nodded. "I could do that."

Westin saw her grip the fork so tightly that her knuckles turned white. She couldn't even lie to herself.

After a moment, Lia stilled. "Should I be worried that he will try again? Could that happen?"

"You still have reaper strength. The energy from the plane immortalizes you, but that will wear off the more you are human. As of right now, you could probably easily overpower him and heal from anything that isn't instantly fatal. That's not always going to be the case though. You should be worried," he said quietly.

"If I kill him, will I go back?"

"Do not kill him," Westin said sharply. He took a deep breath. "What I mean is, right now I'm unclear on what the judges want," he lied. "Until then, you are not to harm him or anyone."

A look of disappointment passed Lia's face, but she resumed eating. After breakfast, they cleared the plates on the table, and Westin motioned her into the living room.

Westin pointed to the chair. "Sit," he said gruffly. He settled on the couch while Lia tried to make herself comfortable. There was an odd tension in the air.

"You still need to pass yourself off as human when you face the therapist," he said quietly.

Lia stared at him. "I am human."

"I know. That's not what I meant. You need to be normal. You need to convey the appropriate emotions. You've been out of practice," Westin said slowly.

"Because I do not have a soul?" she asked blankly.

He shook his head. "You just need some practice. You're a smart woman, but you can't do and say what feels natural. You have to act as they require you."

"I will do the best I can."

"How do you feel about not being claimed?"

Lia snapped her head up. "What?"

"No one has come forward to identify you. That implies that you have no family or friends who care about you. How does that make you feel?"

"Sad," she responded without a beat.

"It's complicated, Lia. Sad is not complicated. Try again."

She sighed and glanced at the wall. This was a ridiculous exercise. Why should she care what other people thought of her? "Sad and angry," she muttered half-heartedly.

"No," Westin said angrily. "You're not putting any thought into this."

"I am supposed to sound natural. It is not supposed to require any thought," she pointed out.

"There is a serial killer out there who knows your name and who you really are, but he is not the biggest danger. What if the agents stop looking at you like a victim and start looking at you like a suspect because you can't appropriate your emotions? Do you understand what that means?"

The sunlight streamed through the windows and reflected in her glass of water. A rainbow danced on the opposite wall, three or four colors fading into one another. She stared at it for a moment. What would happen if she were imprisoned on this side of the veil? What would happen if she were forced back to the other side? There would be no sun to warm her skin and no rainbows to make her smile. She focused on the question at hand.

No one had stepped forward to claim her. Any real family she had would have died a long time ago. She had no one to call a friend. In truth, her life was no different than the lie she was hiding behind.

"It makes me wonder what kind of person I was to find myself in this position. I am scared of what I cannot remember and of what I do not know," she said quietly.

Westin raised his eyebrows. "Good. Have you had any dreams?" he asked, still playing the part of her therapist.

"My dreams are jumbled and confusing. They are meshed and twisted scenes with people I have met and things I have said. None of it makes any sense," Lia replied slowly, recounting her dreams that were not memories.

Westin leaned back and crossed his legs. "There is a serial killer who may still be after you. How do you feel about that?"

"He will not get away a second time," Lia said coldly. Westin raised his eyebrows. "I mean, I am scared. I trust in the protection of the agents and try not to think about it."

"That one needs work," he said softly. "How do you plan on facing the future?"

"One day at a time," she said honestly.

"Do you want your memories back?"

Lia inhaled sharply. "I want to know who I am," she said quietly.

Westin leaned over staring straight into her eyes. She pressed back into the couch but met his gaze. "How will knowing who you are change your actions in the future?"

"Are you asking as my therapist or as my master?" she asked, swallowing hard.

After a moment, he leaned back. "As your therapist."

She nodded. "I suppose I will not know until I get my memories back."

Westin nodded. "She won't find it odd if you take your time with your answers. She knows this is a tough and confusing time for you. Do not go with your gut reaction. Think about what she wants to hear." He got up and turned his back on her. "Tread lightly, Lia. I'm afraid there is more at stake here than you or I realize."

She exhaled slowly after he had gone and stared at the rainbow on the wall.

Knock knock knock. Knock knock knock.

"Connor! Connor!"

Connor winced. His head was pounding, and somewhere in his dreams, a little man was screaming his name. He had an enormous hammer and kept banging on his temple.

"Connor! Connor!"

"Connor! Open the focking door! Your mum will have our balls if you don't move your arse. Open the focking door!"

What? His mom was here?

With a groan, Connor rolled over and promptly fell on the floor. He groaned. "What? What?"

"You're going to be late. Open the focking door!"

Connor opened his eyes. The hotel room was blurry, and his mouth tasted like something had crawled in and died. He groaned again and tried to climb back on the bed. His eyes fell on the red numbers on the clock.

Nine twenty-seven.

Nine twenty-seven?

"Fock!" He bolted upwards and stumbled to the door, dragging his sheet with him. He opened it up to find two of his friends hanging on the frame. "I'm late."

His friends laughed. "No worries mate. We set your clock wrong last night to make sure we weren't late. Now where is the lovely lass you took home last night? We were hoping to get a good look at those tits!"

"Lass?" Connor ran his hands through his hair and looked around. "Yea, I remember her. I do not think she's here."

His friends started to whistle. "What is that?"

"What is what?" Connor looked behind him. His friends were staring at his side. He dropped the sheet, baring his pale naked ass to the hall and looked at his side. "What the fock is that?"

He raced to the mirror and stared. Marking his slightly freckled skin was a dark black tattoo, still slightly raised, contrasting against the angry red, irritated skin. His mouth dropped open. "It hurts. Why did I do this? When did I do this? Who did this? What is it?"

His friends moved in and closed the door. "We didn't get in until well after the tat shops were closed. How did ya get into one?"

Connor fingered the area and winced. "I need some aspirin. Do any of ya idiots have some aspirin?"

His friend shook his head. "Look, mate, we have to get ready. Ya aren't late yet, but ya will be, and your mum will kill us. Forget the tattoo. Actually, praise the tattoo. Do ya know what those American girls are going to think of your Irish accent and your mysterious tattoo? Ya are going to get so much tail."

"Girls. That girl. Ya didn't see her leave?" Connor asked. He struggled to remember something about her. Long red hair, pale creamy skin, perfect hips, and didn't she have a freckle in that one spot? One blue and one green eye. Wait, did that even make sense?

"Sorry, mate. No girl. I still don't know why she went home with ya. Come on, we'll pick ya up some aspirin, tat cream, and bandages on the way." His friend bent down and grabbed the sheet, putting it back on the bed. "Either ya were bleeding pretty bad from the tattoo or the girl was a virgin."

"What?" Connor stood by his friend and stared at the bloody sheet. "Do ya think I'll have to pay for that?"

His friend shook his head. "Doesn't matter. Ya have to get dressed. We'll pack your stuff while ya get ready." He leaned in and sniffed Connor. "Ya need to shower. Ya smell like alcohol and pussy."

Connor grumbled, still staring at the blood. What the hell happened last night? He turned on the water, waiting for it to heat up. After a moment, he climbed in.

The hot water hit the side, the pressure searing onto the tender skin. Connor crumpled to the floor.

"Fock!" he screamed.

For whatever reason, the Denver Police Station was nearly empty when Westin walked through. Those that were present either nodded in acknowledgment or called to him by name. The headaches didn't bother him anymore, and he responded with ease as each name popped into his brain. Officer Tyler Morgan. Officer David Jackels. Detective Erin Meyers. Even though he had never set foot in the office, everyone who worked there believed he had arrived with the FBI agents, and those agents believed he'd been in the unit for years. When he did finally depart for the other side, every memory of him would be erased.

When he first started out as a collector, the alterations of memories concerned him. He was careful not to affect anyone's life too much, and often he was hesitant that the memory trick would even work. He would try and touch them in some way, to confirm that his memory was passing into them. After time, he was confident enough that his mere presence or even the mention of his name would solidify a new memory. The headaches were always the same though, as each new memory of someone would evolve into his head so did the pain.

Westin reached the conference room where the agents were set up and knocked quietly before entering. He had already stolen their memories about the Phoenix killer, and he could swipe new material from them if he wanted, but he liked being a part of the investigation. He also wanted to make sure they weren't showing too much interest in Lia.

As it turned out, that was exactly the case. In the middle of the board, Westin could see Lia's picture placed next to a woman with a similar physical appearance. He frowned at the phrase behind the woman's body. *Break the chains.*

"Caxton, I'm glad you could join us. How is Lia settling in?"

Ryan asked, extending his hand.

Westin smiled. It was rare that he heard his real name, but it was always a pleasure. It reminded him of who he was. Up until a few hundred years ago, collectors were able to keep their memories, and Westin had never been without his. It always occurred to him that it would be easier if they would just take it from him.

"She's a bit uncertain and troubled, but she seems well," he acknowledged. He took his seat at the table and faced the bulletin board.

O'Ryan nodded and tapped the board with his finger. "Excellent. We were just about to try to talk out these anomalies. We have a killer who followed a pretty steady pattern until now. We have a victim far younger than the others and in pretty decent shape. We can't even say for sure that the killer is the one who left all those bruises on her. Is it possible that she's a victim of domestic abuse?"

"There were pictures posted to social media before the kidnapping. There aren't any marks on her. She has to be connected. The videotapes show her in the parking lot with Lia. That can't be a coincidence," Lichton pointed out. His voice echoed in the room.

"Is there any proof that either one of them is connected with the serial killer?" Westin asked casually. If he could separate Lia from the case, the whole mess would be less complicated. In fact, if he could alter their memories to forget her altogether, it would be far easier to clean up. But the judges had their reasons for keeping both Westin and Lia in the loop. He had a feeling they knew more about the situation than they were letting on.

But then again, so did he.

"It's true, but her wound matches, and there is ash all over the girl. Is it possible that it's a copy-cat?" Ryan asked his group.

"I think we need to stop questioning the connection between the girl and the killer and start questioning the relationship between Lia and the killer," Mallich finally said.

Westin turned to her sharply. This would not be good.

"You think there's a personal tie between the two?" Ryan asked.

"I think there are far too many things that don't add up." Mallich stood and walked to the front, her heels clicking on the floor. "We have all seen amnesia patients before, but Lia is different. She doesn't understand basic concepts. She seems very unconcerned about the fact that no one has claimed her. There is very little fear in her and much curiosity. I wouldn't hesitate to say that she acts like a woman reared in a secluded community."

"I thought the doctor said that amnesia was different in every case, and her mannerisms aren't that unusual," Westin asked, reading O'Ryan's thoughts.

"We shouldn't overlook the possibility that it stems from something else. Someone should have stepped forward by now to claim her. A secluded community provides a plausible explanation," the woman pointed out.

"Like a cult?" Lichton asked.

"Exactly like a cult," Mallich nodded.

O'Ryan looked at the board. "It doesn't fit the pattern. All the victims were taken from tight-knit communities and loving homes. Why would he snatch someone from seclusion?"

"I think, because of that very reason, we need to look at Lia as someone who has personal ties with our unsub. Perhaps they grew up in the same cult together. Maybe she is family."

Westin closed his eyes. Things were getting worse. "He travels all over the country. Why would he tote a female with him? You've seen Lia. She's a beautiful woman, hardly someone who blends in. I think it's more probable that she just reminds him of someone. What if Amanda was the intended victim, and Lia simply interrupted? It's possible she wasn't even involved with the killer to begin with."

"So you think she escaped a cult of some sort and just

happened to witness an attempted murder?" O'Ryan asked.

Lichton joined in. "I buy into that. She's uncomfortable around the police. That could be a trait ingrained in her as a child. She's unused to the world; she may not even have a last name. Whether she ran away or she was tossed out, it makes sense. Maybe our killer found her, saw something in her that reminded him of someone he once knew, and he took out his rage on her."

"One stab wound that perfectly fits his MO is not rage," O'Ryan pointed out. "That's methodical. It's more likely that he stalked her or held her against her will. Also, Lia looks strikingly similar to one of the victims. It could be a coincidence, but I think we need to investigate all angles. Still, I like where this is going. It's possible that her background could give us clues to his identity. Caxton, can you get close to her? Find out what she's remembering? Find out what goes on in those therapy sessions?"

Westin nodded. "Sure. I could try. But like you have already pointed out, she's not very trusting."

"She'll trust you," O'Ryan assured him. "All right, next question. How did a young girl and a woman bleeding to death travel miles to the hospital without anyone seeing or reporting them? There are no blood trails to assume that they walked, so someone drove them. Do we think the killer left them alive for a reason?"

There was no immediate answer. Finally, Lichton spoke up. "The idea that someone found this woman and a little girl and anonymously dropped them off is ludicrous, but I think that the idea that the Phoenix dropped them off is even more farfetched." He shook his head. "Maybe who ever found them has something they want to hide from the police."

O'Ryan nodded. "Coordinate with the local police. We can discuss a plea deal for the driver if they fear facing lesser charges for a crime. We need them to come forward. What about her phone? It was fried from the inside out. Tech has been unable to recover any data from it. Do we believe that the killer torched the phone on purpose?"

"What if the phone never belonged to her to begin with," Westin suggested. "She could have found it."

"Why would she carry a damaged phone around? It's not like it could be repaired," Lichton pointed out.

"So what, you think she kept her own torched phone to turn it in to an insurance agency?" Westin responded dryly. "It was a knockoff iPhone. It's not like she would have gotten any amount of money for it."

"Maybe she didn't know it was a knock off," Mallich pointed out. A moment of silence settled over the room as they tried to figure out what their next lead might be.

O'Ryan studied the board. "Let's talk about this woman here." He pointed the woman pictured next to Lia. "She was found not far from here in the mountains."

Westin frowned. "I thought you were ruling that one out as one of his victims. There was no ash left at the scene, and the message doesn't fit the MO." Westin could look at the picture and see Lia. Both women had small, delicate facial features, dark eyes, and pale skin. The victim was even underweight and similar to Lia's body type. He had no doubt that this was his killer, but it would link Lia to Charlie. He couldn't let that happen.

It was easy for Westin to bundle Charlie and the Phoenix in one nameless serial killer, but he needed to face the truth. Charlie had a name, and he needed to be stopped.

The agents prattled on, trying to decide what was a connection and what was mere coincidence. Westin had tuned out. Mallich had already planted a seed of doubt in their minds and soon they would be looking at Lia with a far more critical eye. He needed to get her out as quickly as possible, but even more so, he needed to stop Charlie.

His responsibility to her and his responsibility to all of Charlie's future victims weighed on his mind. He would have to choose between them.

There was a knock at the door, and an officer entered. "There's a package for Agent Caxton and the files from forensics are finished."

The three agents looked at Westin with inquiring looks. "Left a few things behind," he explained as he grabbed the package. "Thanks, officer," he nodded to the young man. He passed the files onto O'Ryan.

After glancing at the papers, a look of surprise crossed his face. "This is the DNA result from Lia's clothing. Some of it does belong to her, but there are traces of blood from at least seven other people here." He looked up. "They don't match anyone in the system."

Westin pulled himself up to his full height. This was information that would link Lia to the dead. No matter what his orders were, he couldn't risk it. Protecting the reaper system was always a priority. He reached into the minds of the agents and lifted the information out. For a moment, he was tempted to erase all of the information of Lia away, but even this small disobedience could cost him. He stepped out of their minds and watched as they took a few seconds to collect themselves. He took an additional second to put a memory trace on the file so that anyone who looked at it would only see a reference to Lia and the killer.

"I should probably head back to the victim. Call me if anything comes up."

The agents nodded with dazed looks on their faces, and Westin exited the building. In his hand were the files he'd requested using his newly acquired agency connections. While the real agents inside had files that lasted a decade, Westin now had information that went back over half a century.

He needed to know exactly what Charlie was up to.

Chapter Nine

Connor had been in the states for a little over two weeks now and had finally settled into a small rental in the industrial section of Denver. He had wanted to be in Boulder where he would be a full-time graduate student, but money was tight until he could secure a part time job.

His bedroom window overlooked his neighbor. From what he could tell, most of the houses on his street stood vacant, waiting to be rented. The man next door was his only adjacent neighbor. He seemed to live alone. There was no evidence of a wife or a family, and there were never any visitors. He looked older, somewhere in his thirties, but Connor was unable to pin down an age. The man had a full set of dark hair, and his skin didn't look aged or weathered. He sported no glasses or showed any outward physical signs of age. If Connor had to guess, he imagined the man took great pains to keep himself in shape.

Connor decided the best way to get to know Colorado was to properly introduce himself to the man next door. He was a social person by nature, and this was the first time he'd ever lived by himself. He wanted a friend. And he thought someone with good eating habits might be a good influence on him.

He waited for the car to pull in the drive and raced out to intercept him with a six-pack of beer. "Bout ye?!" Connor called out. The man paused at the door and turned. He was neither taller nor bigger than Connor, but for some reason, Connor felt a shiver run down his spine. He shrugged it off.

"Right. I hope I didn't startle ya. Name's Connor. I moved in next door a few weeks ago." He stuck out his hand. The man shook it with a firm grip and constant eye contact. Connor's eyes widened at the power behind it. The man silently released his grip.

"I'm getting ready to attend CU in a few weeks. It's my first time in the states, and I don't know too many folks," Connor continued. "Actually, I don't know anyone."

He held out the pack of beer. "This is for ya. It's an invitation to pop on by if ya ever want to blather."

His neighbor took the beer and nodded, a slightly puzzled look on his face. Connor frowned. "I never got your name."

"It's Charlie."

A lopsided goofy smile crossed Connor's face. "Pleasure to meet you, Charlie!"

Lia bit her lip as Westin pulled up to the hospital entrance. Westin was trying to remind her how to behave. "Her name is Miranda Teston. Call her Dr. Teston and show her as much courtesy as you can. It's okay to play the shy card. Be vague but pretend you're honest. Be agreeable and positive about what she has to say. Do as we practiced, and you'll be fine."

"I do not understand. If you can alter memories, why do you not just alter hers and make her think that we have already met?" Lia asked crossly. She was not looking forward to a meeting with a therapist.

"I could, but I have orders. Right now I'm only allowed to monitor the situation," Westin responded patiently as if Lia were a child.

Lia rolled her eyes, careful to hide her reaction from Westin. He had told her about the multiple DNA results, and she knew the actions he had taken. Clearly, he wasn't above breaking a few rules now and again. She reached over and pulled open the car door. As she walked to the hospital, she tried to remind herself that she was a confident woman with nothing to hide.

She'd dressed in a pair of jeans and a bright blue tank top with a white cardigan. After running a brush through her hair, she felt she almost passed for the living. She tugged on her purse, unused to carrying such a bulky item, and she swayed a bit on her matching heels.

When Westin had asked her if the shoes were necessary, she'd answered honestly. They made her feel pretty, and that made her feel confident.

She stopped by the front desk to ask for directions. The woman glared at her and pointed to the elevator, telling her to get off on the third floor. As she moved to the elevators, she felt an odd sensation pass over her. Someone was watching her. She looked over her shoulder and saw a familiar face. "Dr. Logan," she murmured as he joined her next to the elevators.

"Ms. Lia, you're back earlier that I expected," Hunter said.

The elevator dinged, and she jumped a little. "I am here to see an appointed therapist," she explained moving into the elevator. She felt a little self-conscious being in such a small space with him.

"I see. What floor do you need to be on?"

Lia's mind went blank. She flushed. "Three," she finally blurted out.

Hunter pushed three and leaned casually back against the wall. "You look pretty today. It's nice to see a little color back in your cheeks."

Lia flushed even brighter. She straightened as her skin tingled a little bit. "Thank you. Everything is from a place called Target," she rambled.

Hunter raised his eyebrows and smiled. "I liked Target before, but now I'm an even bigger fan," he teased quietly.

She smiled and tried to collect her thoughts. She sounded like an idiot. There was an awkward silence while she tried to think of something to say. Hunter came to the rescue. "Have you had any memory flashes?"

"I do not believe so," she said, glancing at the floor.

"How are those stitches?"

"Good," she said quickly. She took another breath. "I am doing everything you told me. There is an agent staying with me, and he is making sure I follow directions."

"A bodyguard, huh? That's pretty cool."

"Yes, cool," she said lamely.

"You seem nervous about the therapist," Hunter observed as the door opened.

"I think everything makes me nervous," Lia admitted. "I am not sure what to expect at the meeting. Afterward, she is going to decide whether or not I am fit for a job. I am not sure what kind of job I will be getting, or how well I will perform at this job." She stepped out the elevator.

He reached out and touched her arm. "Don't get stressed. Everything is going to work out. The doctor is not going to okay you for anything you aren't ready for, and maybe trying to move on will help you recover a little faster."

She pulled away from his touch. "Thank you," she said softly. She was unused to someone being nice and so positive to her. Showing appreciation seemed to be in order.

"I see a therapist too," he said casually. The doors attempted to close. They shuddered as they were forced open again.

Her eyes widened as she stared at him. "Why?" she blurted out.

He laughed. "For the record, it's not usually okay to ask why someone is in therapy. I spent some time overseas in the military. It hasn't been easy adjusting to civilian life."

"You were in the military?' she asked. He didn't seem like the war type, but then, she knew very little about the military.

"I was still a doctor, but it was an entirely different atmosphere." The doors attempted to close again. "I'll see you in a couple weeks, okay?"

She frowned. "What happens in a couple of weeks?"

A wry smile crossed his face. "You're supposed to come back so I can take those stitches out."

"Right," she lowered her eyes and fidgeted. When the doors tried to close again, she backed out quickly, happy to put an end to the humiliating conversation. "Okay. Thank you again Dr. Logan" she called out.

"Call me Hunter." He stepped back and allowed the doors to start closing.

"Okay, Hunter," she said awkwardly but the doors were closed, and he couldn't hear her. She rubbed her hands up and down her arms. There was an attraction to him that she easily recognized, but the desire to be close to him was a little overwhelming and unexpected.

"Get yourself together," she muttered to herself as she tried to straighten up.

Her heels clicked down the empty hall as she searched the rooms. She slowed at each door to read the sign, stopping when she reached the office of Dr. Teston. She fidgeted a little before finally pulling the door open. To her relief, the waiting room was empty. She made her way to the receptionist.

A young woman looked up from the book she was reading. She had short spiky brown hair with a few blonde streaks in the front. She wore heavy makeup, but Lia suspected she was a natural beauty beneath the orangey lipstick and brown eye shadow. The woman stared at Lia, waiting for her to say something.

"I am here to speak to Dr. Teston," Lia said after clearing her throat.

"Name?"

"Lia."

"Last name?" the receptionist asked, clearly irritated.

"Um...Lia X? I do not have a last name," Lia said, lowering her voice.

"Fill out this paperwork," the woman said, clearly not

interested.

Lia took the clipboard and glanced over the paperwork. She had no idea what she had done to make the woman so unpleasant. The receptionist rapped her knuckles on the counter, jerking her attention away from the paper. "Ma'am. You can sit down and do that," the woman said pointing to the empty waiting area.

Lia glanced behind her. "Right," she muttered and took a seat.

The papers demanded information that she didn't have. She filled out her first name and drew an X through the last name. She peeked at her driver's license for her address and bit her lip as she tried to remember her phone number. Her hands started to shake when it asked her birth date and medical history, and she abruptly stood when she got to the insurance portion of the paper.

"I do not know any of this information," she said angrily to the receptionist. "That is why I am here to begin with," she shoved the clipboard back at the young woman.

A door on the side swung open, and a tall, slender woman stepped through. "Ms. Lia, I apologize for the delay. Is everything okay?"

"There is all this paperwork I am supposed to fill out, and I do not know the information." Lia fumbled in her purse for her wallet. "I put down this fake information, but I do not know if that is okay."

The woman stepped forward. "It's okay Lia. I'm sure that will be fine. The police have already submitted some information to us, so your identification card will be just fine. Jane will copy it for you, and we will give it back to you as you leave. Will that be alright?"

Lia nodded and handed Jane the fake license. The woman forced a smile as she took it. "My office is right through here if you want to get started," Dr. Teston said quietly.

Wanting to say a bit more to the flippant woman at the desk,

Lia narrowed her eyes at Jane but decided instead to quietly follow the doctor through the door. Westin demanded she keep a low profile, and growling at the receptionist was probably not a good idea.

The office was tidy. The green carpeting matched the green and white tiles out in the halls. There were two khaki chairs in the middle of the room and a desk in the corner. The green reminded Lia of the color of calm souls and for a moment, she was soothed.

"Have a seat Lia. I want you to feel comfortable during these sessions." Dr. Teston sat in the chair opposite of Lia. "I went to the University of California for both my masters and doctorate. I've been working here at the hospital for almost ten years now. Amnesia is most common for head injuries and post-traumatic stress disorders. In your case, we are looking at the latter. I don't want you to be scared or think that it's a hopeless case. Blocking memories is a coping mechanism for the brain. There are cases where just the stressful memories are blocked, but, in this case, your amnesia is more severe. I don't want you to feel anxious about it or about these sessions. I just want to talk to you about what you do know, how you feel, what your options are, and some coping strategies. Let's start with your name."

Lia shifted in her seat. The cushion was oddly comfortable. She fidgeted to buy some time. "I am not sure. When the doctor asked me my name, Lia popped into my head."

"Think back. Was it a sound or a visual word that you saw in your mind?"

"A sound?"

The doctor nodded encouragingly. "That's good. It's more likely that Lia is a sound your brain remembers hearing over and over rather than a word you recently saw. How do you feel when someone says your name?"

Lia furrowed her brow. "I am not sure what you mean. I feel like someone is calling my name."

Dr. Teston smiled. "Good. Is it an automatic reaction? It

doesn't take time for you to process that someone might be calling your name?"

Lia nodded. "Yes."

Dr. Teston made some notes. "Excellent. What's your last name, Lia?"

"I do not know," Lia said sharply. What kind of doctor was this?

"Okay. I'm going to be throwing out questions like this occasionally. Sometimes the brain will answer automatically when you aren't thinking so hard about it. There shouldn't be any stress involved. Either you can answer or you can't. When you can't, we'll simply move on. Is that okay?"

Lia was sinking farther into the chair, and the air was getting warmer. Despite the doubt in her mind, she was feeling comfortable. She nodded her head.

"Let's start with the events that have occurred since the incidence. Act like you're telling me a story. Generalize the parts that you feel are unimportant and go over details you think are important. Tell me what stands out to you and how it made you feel?"

Lia focused. "I was disoriented when I woke up. I did not know that I was in a hospital until the doctor came in. I think I was scared. I felt like things were a blur because there were so many questions in my mind, but the doctor was nice. He made me feel like I was important, and the FBI agents also made me feel important, but they are a little stifling. When we went to the safe house..."

"Back up a moment, Lia," Dr. Teston interrupted. "How did you feel when you found out what happened to you?"

Lia fell silent. She became engrossed in her thoughts and couldn't remember what Weston and instructed her to say. In her mind, she could see the killer with the blade, talking to her even as he slid the blade inside her. She thought of his soul, the weight of it when it bumped against her hand. Her fists tightened.

"Lia? This is a safe place. No one is going to harm you while you are here," Dr. Teston said softly.

"I do not understand why me. I do not know why he would seek me out. Why would he think that I was special?" Lia said honestly. As she said it out loud, she felt exposed and relieved at the same time. She straightened up and looked at the doctor. "There are many things that I do not know about myself, but I believe that I am just a part of a system. There is nothing special about me."

The doctor smiled softly. "I think maybe you are getting in touch with your true self, and I hope that when this is all over, you'll understand how unique you are. Your strength is evident." She slid her glasses off and leaned forward. "Lia, your amnesia may stem from your belief that you are not strong enough to deal with the truth. You need to trust yourself."

For the first time in a long while, Lia genuinely wanted to laugh. The idea of trusting herself was absurd. The judges of the world had sent a warden to protect people from her. Trusting her was the last thing anyone should do.

It was enough to reel her back to reality. There was no room here for honesty. She straightened up in her chair and shoved her feelings aside. She was a shell.

"I am rambling. I hope they catch the bastard, and when they do, I want to look him in the eye and tell him that leaving me alive is the biggest mistake he has ever and will ever make." Lia looked straight into Dr. Teston's eyes, daring her to comment. The very thought rose a lust for blood in Lia that was overpowering. For a moment, the silence in the room rushed outward, and Lia could hear the heartbeat of the doctor. She narrowed her eyes. The feeling was familiar, and it called to her, sought control of her.

"Let's talk about what you were thinking when you were shopping," the doctor said, unknowingly breaking a spell.

Lia blinked, and her hearing returned to normal. She shook

her head a little. "I liked shopping. I thought the bright colors were nice, but they were a bit much on me. I wanted books and shoes. Westin, I mean Agent Caxton, had a list, and he did most of the shopping for me, but he allowed me some books and probably more shoes than I need."

Dr. Teston smiled. "There is nothing wrong with books and shoes. I am a shoe girl myself. How old are you?"

In my nineties, Lia thought. She paused before shaking her head. "I do not know."

The doctor made some more notes on her clipboard. "What are you writing?" Lia asked.

"I am making notes now so I can compare them to your progress later. Think about your new home. Is there anything you feel is missing or anything you feel shouldn't be there? Sometimes you might be making comparisons to your own home but you don't realize it."

This wasn't a question Lia was prepared for, but she thought back to some of the crash pads she had before. "I think the coffee maker is nice, but it seems a bit too fancy. I do not have a need to adjust the strength or set a timer. There are not enough pictures around, but then, I guess there would not be. The rooms are small. When the blinds are closed, the walls feel like they are closing in on me." She stopped and took a deep breath. "I think the flowers are pretty out front. I like to smell them. I like that there are not many trees. The sun on my skin is pleasant, and the neighbors are friendly. They wave when we are driving around. I do not think I am used to that."

It seemed to take forever for the session to end. Dr. Teston would ask a question, and Lia would try and formulate a normal answer. When the doctor asked her about her dreams, she told a half-truth, saying that she couldn't remember her dreams. In all honestly, all she could remember were fuzzy details, blood, and slated satisfaction. Finally, the session came to a close.

"Well Lia, I think this went well. It's important that you be honest with me. Keep that notebook close and document every dream and every feeling that you have. Feel free to bring it with you when you come in case you need to reference it during our session. It's okay to evaluate everything. In the end, the most important thing is that you believe in your strength to come to terms with what happens to you. "

Dr. Teston flipped through her notes. "I want to see you once a week for the next few weeks. The agency has agreed to sessions for six months or until your memory returns, whichever comes first. How do you feel about working?"

Lia bit her lip. She didn't want to work. Dr. Teston read the expression on her face. "I know that it's scary, but I think immersing you in society is a good idea. The job would be low in stress level and high in people interaction. It's a good way to get you comfortable with others. Unless you have a strong objection to it, I'm going to recommend that you start next week."

Westin had said that her working would be fine, and Lia couldn't think of a strong objection. She nodded silently.

"Excellent. Well, we are done for today. I'm going to see you on Friday. The same time is fine if that's okay with you?"

Lia nodded. It wasn't like she had anything else to do.

"Okay. Don't forget to pick up your ID from Jane on your way out. Have a good day."

Lia got up and realized that her legs were wobbly. The doctor held out her hand, and Lia shook it awkwardly, walked out of the office, and picked her ID up from the stony-faced receptionist.

Despite her nerves, she found herself keeping an eye out for Hunter. Seeing him would have brightened her walk to the front, but she wasn't so lucky.

Westin was waiting for her when she broke through the doors. The sun hit her skin, warming her. He silently handed her some Advil when she got in the car, and she swallowed them easily.

Whether he read the look on her face or whether he simply enjoyed the silence, he kept quiet on the way home, allowing her to stew in her thoughts. As she stared out the window, she felt a new feeling emerge. An alien excitement overwhelmed her, and she sucked in her breath.

Somewhere out there, a killer was very happy.

Chapter Ten

The top of the mountain was closed, but not before tourists had gotten a look at the gruesome scene. The blood meandered from the gaping wound on the man's midsection until it pooled in a small puddle a few feet from the body. The victim was propped against a tree dressed in an American military uniform. A crudely drawn swastika was pinned to the shoulder of his jacket.

O'Ryan stared at the pile of ash next to the body. "Please tell me that he's not military," he said tightly.

"He's not military," Lichton confirmed. "Vic's name is Jason Norris. He works as a mechanic for the ski lifts." He pointed to the swastika. "What the hell is that supposed to be?"

"Something new," Mallich said quietly. She looked at O'Ryan. "Copy-cat?"

"I don't know. This is oddly detailed. It's unusual that a copycat would add such an elaborate spin on things. Whoever killed this man is sending a message. I think it's more likely that our killer is evolving. The question is what is he evolving into?" O'Ryan stepped aside as the local coroner came through.

"What's different now that causes such a drastic change?" Mallich asked.

"She is what is different. This may have nothing to do with him, and everything to do with her," Lichton pointed out.

O'Ryan didn't need to ask which victim they were referring too. Amanda and her family tidied up nicely, but the amnesia victim left nothing but loose ends. All three of them stared at the patch on the corpse.

The new development didn't sit well with them.

The temperature dropped, and Lia shivered. She dug her toes into the gravel. They bit into her skin, and she winced. In the silence of the false scene before her, something tugged at her memory. She had been here before. She looked to the left at the figure struggling in the choppy waters. In front of her stood the tall blurry man.

She gripped her head as her memory returned. The murder. The collection. Pain ripped through her skull, but she ignored it. What was she doing here? "How is it dying by my hand? I am not holding it in the water," she asked through gritted teeth, staring at the drowning body.

"This is the beginning," the voices echoed.

Lia stepped forward, and the river rocks cut deeply into her feet. The blood trickled through the dirt.

"Why do you keep bringing me here?"

"You must remember who you are."

"I already know what I have done."

"You must remember who you are."

"Now who is being repetitive?" she grumbled. Frustrations surged through her. "You are the reason I cannot remember!" she shouted. Her words bounced off the waters creating several small waves that crashed along the bank. She glanced at the figure in the water. "What do you want from me?"

He moved closer. "To surrender to who you are." He touched her forehead. The darkness swept over her and pain surged through her body. She fell.

When she opened her eyes, she surged forward, stumbling into a wall. She tried to think back to the riverbank, but the more she wanted to retain the memory, the more she forgot. It simply didn't make sense.

Her fingers grazed the boxes, and the wood jabbed at her skin. She jerked her hand away. All around her, boxes were stacked up to the high ceilings. Dirt and loose gravel were stamped on the floor, and wood beams supported the roof. She turned slowly. The place was expansive. She knocked on a box. It was solid all the way through.

In the distance, she could hear a scuffle. In an instant, Lia was on her feet and ducking behind the boxes that scattered farther along the wall. Just as she moved out of a sight, a door opened, and sunlight spilled in. She could hear shouting.

As she looked up, she saw a tall young blonde woman running through the warehouse. Behind her, chasing her, was another version of Lia.

The memory of Lia launched herself up and forward tackling the blonde woman. As they tumbled to the floor, Lia could see a glint of light reflecting off metal.

Her eyes widened as she watched her past self raise the blade and bring it down. The blonde woman twisted at the last second, and the knife harmlessly hit the ground. The woman struggled now, trying to use her height to overcome Lia and throw her off, but it was useless. Her scream echoed off the bare walls as the knife slid in.

Instant gratification slammed into her, and she fell to the floor. A wave of relief and pleasure swarmed through her, and she clutched her chest. She felt dazed and happy, drunk on the death of another.

The feelings slowly dissipated, and silence fell. Lia stood and walked over to the body where past Lia was staring. They were mirror images of each other as the blood stretched out on the concrete floor, running around Lia's feet and between her toes.

Her heart began to beat with excitement as she reached out and tried to touch the other version of herself. She was ignored. The other Lia's eyes widened as they stared ahead. Lia turned to see the portal between the planes open.

Westin stepped through.

"What?" Lia whispered to herself, shocked.

"Annalia Sophia Asim, you have been charged with crimes against mankind. You will serve your sentence stripped of your humanity." Westin's voice cut through the silence, searing into Lia's brain.

Annalia Sophia Asim.

As she reached out to touch Westin, the ground disappeared beneath her. Once again, she was falling...

Lia sat up and promptly fell off the couch where she'd been napping. Her heart was racing, and she could barely catch her breath. Trembling, she pushed herself to her feet and raced upstairs to her bedroom. She fumbled for the notebook that she kept by her bed, knocking the pen off the table. It rolled under.

"No," she cried. Without any further thought, she shoved the table aside. The lamp crashed to the floor. Grabbing the pen, she opened the notebook on the bed and started to scribble everything she could remember, starting with her name. Lia. Annalia. Sophie. Asim. Asim. Asim. She growled in frustration as the memory slipped away. Westin. Collector. Twice. She wrote it over and over again.

The sound alerted Westin, who charged into her room. "What the fuck is going on?"

"You tell me," Lia said tightly. The details were fading. She looked up from the notebook. "You seem to be my very own personal collector, so you tell me how it is possible that I killed two people in two different time periods."

Westin relaxed and leaned against the doorframe. There was no surprise on his face. "I'm not your personal collector. I've collected other reapers too," he said easily.

Anger rose in Lia's chest. "How many times have you collected me?"

"Seventeen."

Lia gripped the notebook so hard that one of the pages tore out. "Seventeen? I was set free seventeen times?"

"No. You escaped seventeen times." Westin's eyes moved over Lia. His expression darkened. "You have killed nineteen people. I would think that would upset you more."

Lia met his stare. Even as she thought about it, the memory of the blade sliding into flesh reawakened in her. Excitement flushed her cheeks, but she didn't back down. "How is it possible that a reaper escapes? Does this kind of thing happen often?"

"No." Westin crossed his arms. "You seem to have a greater desire to escape than all the other reapers. And by escape, I mean kill."

Lia looked down at her hands. Twice she was faced with her crimes, and still she felt no regret. "That is not normal," she said quietly.

"Who did you kill? In your dream?" Westin asked.

Lia closed her eyes, struggling to remember her dream. The lust for blood dominated her memories, but as she focused, she could see the victim on the floor. "She was blonde, close to my age but much taller. It was a warehouse. I do not remember what I was wearing." Lia looked up.

"That would be your eighteenth victim. I believe that was Africa, somewhere around the turn of the twentieth century. You lasted four hours before killing her."

"Eighteenth victim?" Lia stood up. "My dreams are moving backwards?"

Westin nodded. "It appears so."

"Why the dreams? Why do you not just tell me who I have killed?"

"It's against orders. I am only here to observe," Westin said, shrugging his shoulders.

"And to prevent me from killing someone," Lia pointed out.

"Actually, no. That's against my orders as well," Westin said before turning and walking down the hall. He paused before he reached his room. "I can't physically stop you if your urge to murder number twenty strikes, but I can always listen if you need to talk."

"What is the longest I have gone without killing someone?" Lia asked quietly.

"Three months." He didn't even turn around. "And then you killed three people before I could even make it through the portal."

He went back into his room and shut the door quietly.

Lia sat on the bed and stared at the notebook. There were few details written. As the memories blurred in her mind, she was only left with the feeling of satisfaction, the satisfaction of taking a life.

She tried to push the thought out of her mind, but it lingered. She moved in front of the mirror and stared at herself. Despite the flush in her cheeks, she still closely resembled death. Abruptly, she decided she needed a change of scenery. She wanted to feel alive. She wanted to look alive.

She moved quietly down the hall and knocked softly on Westin's door. "What?" he growled.

"I need a favor," she said softly.

It was comforting in a way that Lia could not describe as a stranger ran her hands through Lia's hair. The woman fluffed it and smoothed it and sprayed it and teased it. At first, Lia had felt at odds with the situation, but now her eyes were drifting shut in euphoria.

"You asked me to bring you to the mall, and as soon as I turn my back, you disappear." Westin's amused voice flitted through her peaceful state, and her eyes flew open. She could see his reflection in the mirror, arms crossed, eyes searching for an explanation.

She pursed her lips and stared at him. The woman standing behind her seemed uncomfortable as she unsnapped the plastic cape around Lia's neck and whipped it off. She reached over and ran her hand through Lia's hair one more time. "Girl needed a haircut," she drawled in a thick southern twang, picking up a hand mirror. She turned Lia around in the chair, positioning her right in front of Westin. Holding up the mirror, she gave Lia the opportunity to see the back of her hair in the reflection.

Lia shifted her focus to the hand mirror. Instead of falling limply, her hair flowed over her shoulders in soft curls. It shined under the lights and beckoned to be touched. Lia complied, running her fingers through the soft tresses. "It looks nice," she said wondrously.

Westin shook his head. "This is your response to your new

found knowledge? You go and get your hair done?"

Lia handed the mirror back to her hairdresser. "I start my new job tomorrow. I thought I should look more fitting for the part." She stood in the chair. "You do not want me to bring unwanted attention to myself, do you?"

Westin rolled his eyes. "You were far more invisible before you decided to doll yourself up."

"Who wants to be invisible?" the hairdresser interrupted. "Now your girl will make every woman want to be her and every man want her. Isn't that every guy's dream?"

"She's not my girl," Westin said frowning. "Pay the woman, and let's go. We can discuss this further over dinner."

Lia smiled at the woman. "I have this card. I hope it will do," Lia said pulling out her credit card. The woman gave Lia a strange look and pointed to the credit card machine.

"Just swipe it here, darling."

Lia's eyes lit up. Excited, she slid the card down the slot.

Nothing happened. Westin reached over and flipped the card. "It has to swipe the magnetic strip on the back," he said tersely.

"Right. I know that" Lia lied as she swiped the card again.

"Okay," the woman said curiously. She handed Lia the receipt. "Total and sign here, darling."

Westin leaned in Lia's ear. "You need to leave a tip. I'd say ten dollars. Write that on the first line. Then add the tip with the number above it and write it on the second line. Sign your name at the bottom."

Lia nodded and did as she was told. At the bottom, she signed Lia X.

Westin leaned in again. "What's your last name?"

Frustrated, Lia crossed out the signature. She signed again, Lia Asim.

"Your other last name," Westin said in a low tight voice.

Bearing down on the pen, Lia crossed out Lia Asim. It ripped a hole in the paper. She took a deep breath and tried again. Lia Briggs. She gave Westin a side-glance, and he nodded.

She handed the woman the receipt and ignored the raised eyebrows. "Have a good day, darling," the woman said awkwardly.

Lia nodded and joined Westin. "I think I would like to pay with cash from now on," she said quietly.

"I think I can arrange that," Westin said as they entered the mall. Pushing through the crowds, he led her to the food court. From the moment she had stepped in the mall, she had been overwhelmed by the sheer number of people that walked passed her. They carried shopping bags under their arms, talked on their phones, and yelled at their kids. They had children in strollers, in odd straps on their backs, and on leashes. The younger generation pressed themselves into the dark corners and locked lips while the older generation toddled slowly across the tile on their canes. Lia marveled at how different everyone was.

"We can have dinner here. Pick a place," Westin ordered.

Lia turned in circles as she watched all the people stand in lines and walk away with trays of food. "I do not think I understand this," she said biting her lip in concentration.

Westin grabbed her by the shoulders and turned her again. "All of these places serve different types of food. This one has burgers." He turned her again. "Chicken." Another rotation. "Hotdogs, Chinese food, Italian food, and questionable tacos," he listed as he spun Lia around.

She looked up at Westin. "I like eggs and the way a BLT looks. Do any of them serve eggs and BLTs?"

"Something new then," Westin said in amusement. He steered her around again and pushed her towards one of the food joints. "Bad Chinese food," he randomly chose.

After spending a few minutes looking at the menu, she declared she wanted to try everything. Westin shook his head and placed an order for her. She carried her tray of chicken lo mein and crab rangoon to an empty table.

"This does not look clean," she said surveying the crumbs on the table.

Westin brushed it off with his hand. "That's the joy of eating in a food court," he explained as he sat down.

"Eating at a dirty table is a joy?" Lia asked slowly, pulling out her chair.

He ignored her. "We have a small problem," Westin said as he tore open a soy sauce packet. Lia watched in fascination as he soaked his rice in the brown sauce. She bit tentatively in her star-shaped, crab-filled shell. It wasn't bad.

"Try the sweet and sour sauce with it," Westin suggested. She picked up the container with the syrupy red sauce and was about to pour it over her food when Westin stopped her. "Just dunk it, like a dip," he instructed.

She dunked her rangoon in the sauce and touched it to her tongue. Her eyes lit up with delight as she bit into it. "That is wonderful," she said, her mouth full of food.

"Pay attention. There was a new body discovered this morning next to a pile of ash," Westin said, searching her face. "The victim was dressed in a military uniform with a homemade swastika patch on his shoulder. He was dumped at a ski resort in the snow."

Lia narrowed her eyes. "Blood and snow. Are you suggesting I killed him?"

"If you had killed him, I would have an order to collect you. I think you should be concerned with the implications."

She shoved some noodles in her mouth and nodded. "The link is strong," she swallowing. "He shares my dreams. I did not know that was possible, but then, there is clearly a lot I am not aware of. Do you think I will share his dreams?"

"That isn't the issue right now. We need to distance you as much as possible from your memories. You have to write false dreams in your notebook and keep no written record of your memories. If the agents suspect there is a link, they are going to start looking a little harder at you."

"It is hard for me to remember the details," Lia objected. "I need to write them down."

"You are not going to remember them anyways," Westin argued.

"Only if I continue my pattern. You are here, telling me not to kill anyone. I feel that I can do that. The dreams leave me unsettled. Focusing on the details could help me focus on other aspects of life."

"What unsettling feelings do you have?" Westin asked slowly.

She didn't want to answer. "I want to know who I was before."

Westin shook his head. "They're not going to show you that. Keep a false notebook. It's an order," he said softly.

Lia pursed her lips but kept quiet. It was so confusing. The judges were giving her memories of blood. It was as if they wanted her to go back, but they had given her this chance. Was it a test?

"You start your job in the morning. It's to integrate you into society, but you need to keep a low profile. Go in, do your job, try not to socialize, and get out. Keep to yourself and hopefully people will leave you alone."

Lia pushed her food away and stared at the people bustling around them. "Can you see the people marked for collection? I mean, when you look around, do they stand out to you?"

"I try not to look for evil," Westin said. "It blends in. This society is numb. Every time they watch a violent movie or television show, every time they read a violent book, every time they glance over the news and look dispassionately at the dead, they give camouflage to predators, and they don't even know it."

Lia looked at Westin. "Why do you think I kill people? I do not feel the need to hunt. Do I just wake up one day and decide to take a life?"

"I don't know, Lia. This is the first time I've ever had to monitor you. Usually, I am alerted when you slip through, and then I am given a collection order."

"You think I am going to fail."

He looked her dead in the eye.

"I don't think you'll last the week."

Chapter Eleven

Hunter stared at the television screen without comprehending. His mind flitted from the different points of his week, but they always came back to the woman. Lia. It was an interesting name for an interesting woman. It had been a long time since he'd reacted to a woman in such a way, and, of course, it was a woman he couldn't have. Not so long as she was his patient. Not so long as she had no memory. Not while she struggled to figure out her identity.

With a sigh, he grabbed the remote and turned off the television. Jacks whined softly at his side with a tennis ball in his mouth.

"Come on boy, let's go outside," he muttered, snatching the tennis ball out of the dog's mouth. Jacks turned in circles before racing to the door and barking at Hunter, urging him to hurry.

Hunter went through the motions of playing fetch, but his heart wasn't into it. After a few tosses, the ball rolled unnoticed to his feet. Jacks caught him off guard and jumped up, trying in vain to lick him in the face.

"Okay, okay," he laughed, scratching the dogs ears. "I'm sorry, boy. I guess my mind isn't here." Jacks whined and abandoned the ball in favor of chasing a squirrel.

Hunter's phone buzzed in his pocket, and he pulled it out. It was a text from a friend.

Haven't seen you in a while. Come have dinner?

Are you bartending? He texted back

Yup.

I'll be there, he responded.

Should you be drinking?

Hunter frowned. There were some questions better left unanswered.

As he put his phone away, he heard a rustling noise. He looked up, already knowing what he would find.

Jacks was digging into the flowerbeds again and looking for the bone he had hidden there a few months ago.

"Jacks! No," Hunter called out. He ran over to retrieve the dog. Dirt few out from underneath the shrubs and crumbled on his pants as he reached down.

"Jacks! Come here!"

The digging stopped and, after a moment, Jacks crawled out from the shrubs, bone in his mouth.

"Bad dog," Hunter said loudly.

Jacks wagged his tail, dropped the bone at Hunter's feet, and bowed his head, giving him his best sorrowful look. Hunter caved. "Come on, boy. Let's get you some dinner." The dog's ears perked up at the word dinner, and he raced back to the house.

He fed Jacks and grabbed his keys, heading for the restaurant.

His friend Karen Owen used to be his neighbor when they were growing up. She and her husband opened Owen's Tavern together in the next town over. They struggled through the first couple of years before the restaurant finally took off, getting the attention of both locals and tourists alike. Despite owning the place, Karen liked to bartend a few nights a month, and her husband, Andy, loved to jump in the kitchen and cook occasionally. When Hunter worked at the clinic next to the restaurant, he and his co-workers used to stop by for drinks on a daily basis. Then he'd been called away, called to serve his country, to stitch the wounded and heal his fellow patriots. Instead, he caused more death, seen too much death, and couldn't save enough souls to heal himself. When he'd returned and started at the clinic again, he'd visited the tavern too often, drank too much, and lost himself in the numbing effects. After a few therapy sessions, he kept himself from the tavern, away from alcohol.

That was months ago. Now seemed a good time as any for him to see his friend. Promising to refuse him alcohol, Karen and Andy had both begged him to return.

Though it was late, there were still plenty of cars in the parking lot. He pulled in, took a deep breath, and made his way to the bar.

The double doors opened into a small room lined with wine bottles and menu posters. Behind the host stand, the room opened into an expansive bar. Dark green booths lined the wall, and high-top tables sat in the middle before the bar opened up, oval in shape and lit with faded lights. Two televisions hung on the walls at either end and Karen stood behind the bar, polishing wine glasses.

He smiled in anticipation as he walked through the doors of the tavern and because he usually walked straight to the bar, he almost missed the woman standing at the hostess stand.

"Dr. Logan."

Hunter stopped at the familiar sound and turned to see Lia standing there, dressed in black pants and a black shirt. Noting the change in her hair and the flush on her cheeks, he stared for a moment. He wanted to memorize her new look and drink her in. Finally, he leaned against the podium and smiled. "I thought I told you to call me Hunter," he said teasingly as he tried to keep the atmosphere light. Even in his head, it sounded like flirting. He cringed inwardly.

She fidgeted. "You did. I forgot. Hunter." She looked around. "Would you like a table?"

Hunter cocked his head before logic finally settled in. She was in work attire, standing behind a podium. "You have a job here?" he asked, cursing his bad luck.

Lia nodded. "Yes. I walk people to tables. It seems like an easy job, but the servers tend to get upset with me, so I do not think I do the job well. I am not sure what I am doing wrong though. They get upset if I do not seat them and if I seat them too much. It is confusing."

Hunter smiled. "How long have you been working here? I just saw you last week."

"A few days. Today is my first day by myself. The trainer irritates me, so I am happy to be away from her. Do you enjoy coming here?"

"Karen is a friend from when I was a kid. I used to come here all the time. Do you like it?"

Lia shook her head. "The owners are nice, but I dislike much of the staff. It is nice to have something to do, to feel like part of society. Are you meeting anyone?"

Hunter shook his head. "No. I'm just here to talk to Karen." He looked at his watch. "What time do you get off?"

"The dining room closes in twenty-one minutes," she said quickly.

He laughed. "Counting down the minutes?"

Lia shrugged.

"Would you like to stay and have a drink with me? The bar stays open for another hour, right?" The words were out of his mouth before he could stop them. He inhaled sharply as he waited for her reply. She intrigued him. Even if he couldn't touch her, he had to get to know her better.

"I have to ask Westin for permission," she said. "But if he says it is okay, I think I would enjoy spending time with you."

Hunter looked around. "Who is Westin?"

"The agent watching me."

Hunter raised his eyebrows. "Your bodyguard? Is he here?"

Lia pointed in the bar at the stool directly facing the door. "That is him. I will go ask."

He waited while she approached a very tall, stern man. Westin looked up and ran his eyes over Hunter before nodding to Lia. They exchanged a few words.

She walked back. He liked the confidence in her step. She didn't seem afraid to make eye contact with anyone. "He says it is okay."

Hunter smiled. He felt the tension unfurl from his chest. "Good. I'll go introduce myself and have a drink while I wait. Good luck with the rest of your shift."

Lia was already looking past him as a server made a beeline for her. "I will try," she said softly.

Hunter found it odd that the agent hadn't been to the hospital with the others, but perhaps taking care of witnesses outside the hospital was a more specialized job. He was anxious to hear more about the case.

"Agent Westin? I'm Hunter Logan." Hunter stuck out his hand.

"It's Agent Caxton. Westin is my first name. You're the doctor?" the agent asked as he reached out his hand. Hunter studied him carefully. There was a strange air about the man. Physically, he looked the same age as Hunter, but he seemed much older. He shook hands with the pretense of authority and confidence. Hunter found himself admiring this man even though he knew nothing about him. And yet, he found himself wishing he could better hide his secrets, that he was too exposed. It was a strange sensation.

"Yes, I treated Lia when she first arrived at the hospital. I don't recognize you from the first meeting," he responded slowly.

"I was called in when the woman was found," Westin said smoothly, and Hunter immediately felt at ease. "You understand Lia's position here? Discrepancy is important right now. Please keep that in mind when you converse with others," he said in a low voice.

Hunter nodded. "Of course. Can I buy you a drink?"

The agent shook his head. "I wish, but I am just nursing this one to blend in." He pointed across the bar to a seat at the corner. "Sit over there please so I can keep an eye on both entrances."

Hunter shook his hand again. "Sure thing." He wanted to ask more questions, but the agent clearly wasn't going to talk about anything in public. He moved to his seat, and Karen smiled warmly at him.

"Hunter, you are looking good. If I wasn't married," Karen said with a smile as Hunter sat down.

"You'd still pick Andy because you're a smart woman," Hunter responded with a wry grin.

"Very true," she conceded with a smile. She put down her wine glass and leaned over the bar to give Hunter a kiss on the cheek. "Too busy to come see an old friend now that you work at that fancy hospital of yours?"

"It's a tough gig, but that's no excuse," Hunter said bowing his head. "It has been too long. I'm sorry Karen." He cleared his throat. "I don't think I've apologized for my behavior in the past. You've been a good friend. Thank you for that."

Karen smiled. "Darling, after what you've seen, no one expects anything from you. I was more worried when you dropped out of sight than when you were passed out drunk on the counter tops. I understand if you need space, but I like to know what's going on in that head of yours."

He nodded, sufficiently chagrined. He wanted to say more. He owed Karen that, but he just couldn't discuss it now. He looked around. The bar was empty, but it was late. "Place looks great!"

Pride swept across her face. "We have our down moments, but things have been good. We have been very lucky. I am afraid that, at any minute, we are going to see the effects of the recession and find ourselves penniless." She sat a glass of soda in front of him. "How is the family?"

He eyed the soda before closing a fist around it. "Excellent. Mom has retired and spends her days annoying Dad at the shop. Aaron might be getting engaged, but that is not to escape your lips. Trent just got promoted, and Steph has purple hair and three boyfriends."

Karen leaned across the bar. "Is it okay? I don't want to make any assumptions," she asked eyeing the drink.

He nodded. "It's fine. I'm still adjusting, so a no-alcohol policy is good." He smiled at her as he took his first sip. Karen watched him intently as he put the glass down.

"How is your love life? You're staying far away from Carol I hope?"

Hunter glared at her. "We don't talk about her."

She laughed. "You may not talk about her, but I will say I told you so until I am blue in the face. I told you she was cheating on you, and you put a ring on her finger."

His looked hardened. "I'm warning you, Karen..."

She paused. "Do you miss her?" she said quietly.

"I still think about her from time to time, but I don't feel anything except extreme stupidity. Everyone could see it but me. I trusted her completely." He shook his head thinking about the woman he had loved so much. "But," he said, his tone lighter, "it is a lesson learned and an event I have put far behind me."

"Good!" She swept a towel across the bar. "I take it that means no new dates recently?"

Hunter scrunched up his face. "No good ones anyhow." He glanced over his shoulder at Lia, who was talking to some late night guests.

Karen followed his gaze. "You know her?"

"I treated her at Saint Antony's. You do this kind of thing often?"

Karen pulled out a few liquor bottles and began wiping them off. "Andy's dad retired from the police force not too long ago. At his request, we took in a few parolees when we opened. Word just got out. She is the first amnesiac we've had though. She's an odd thing."

Hunter nodded. "It's amazing to spend time with her. It's like the world has never even touched her. I've never seen anything like it."

Karen stopped and stared. "You like her."

"I think she's interesting," Hunter said mildly, trying to deflect her curiosity.

Karen smiled and glanced over at Lia again. "Beautiful black hair, dark eyes, creamy skin, and perfectly perky tits. That adds up to more than interesting," she said dryly.

"How's Andy?" Hunter said changing the subject.

She chuckled. "He's good. He thinks we should hire another manager and take a little time off. Maybe try for a baby," she said casually.

"Karen! That's great news!"

She waved her hand. "We'll see. I hate to get comfortable. We could fail at any moment," she said looking around. "But business has been steady, and we're slammed on the weekends. Fingers crossed we keep going."

They chatted a little more, and Hunter sipped at his soda, privately wishing it were a beer. He found himself glancing at the clock and counting down the minutes.

The last customers of the night walked in just as Lia was about to lock the doors. She put on her well-practiced smile and nodded to them. "Two?" she said mechanically.

Dr. Teston and Westin both thought this job would be a good idea, but Lia quickly realized that neither one of them had ever held a restaurant job before. At no point in her training or tonight did she think that this job would keep her from killing people.

At first she couldn't believe her only job would be to walk people from the door to a table. She thought it would be easy up until the moment she realized that people were stupid.

This last couple was no exception. After Lia led them to a table in the last open section of the restaurant, the man stopped in front of the table. "Can we have a booth?" he asked.

"What is wrong with the table?" Lia asked.

"A booth would be more comfortable," the man said, his fat belly jiggling as he looked about the restaurant.

"Okay." Lia wanted to point out that the restaurant closed in two minutes and comfort should be the last thing he wanted, but she instead moved them across the section to a booth. The server had already instructed her to not seat the booths as they had already been cleaned for the night, but Lia didn't mind. She didn't particularly care for the server.

"Actually, can we have that booth over by the window?" the woman said pointing to the other side of the restaurant.

"That section is closed for the night," Lia said not moving.

"But our dog is in the car and we'd like to keep an eye on him."

"So, when you walked in, you knew that you wanted a booth by the window. However, you refrained from telling me until I walked you in the opposite direction. Is that correct?" Lia asked crossly.

Her boss, Karen, was watching from the bar and quickly intervened. "Lia, thank you so much. I will make sure that booth by the window is ready, and we can seat our guests over there," she said in a patient but sharp voice.

Lia handed over the menus silently and went back to finish locking the door. Karen came over to meet her. "Lia, I know this job highlights the stupidity of the human race, but we try not to point that out to them," she said mildly. She smiled. "I believe you have a date waiting for you in the bar. Go ahead and clock out. I'll pour you a drink. What would you like?"

Lia frowned. She wasn't sure she was supposed to be drinking, but Westin had encouraged her to blend in. And Hunter had invited her.

Lia bit her lip. "Surprise me," she quietly, unsure of what she should be drinking or even what the different types of drinks were. She took a step to the bar and then stopped. "Karen, you called

Hunter my date. Is that because we are going to be social?"

Karen smiled. "It's because he likes you. Don't be nervous."

Lia nodded. She glanced over at Westin, who was still nursing his beer. Hunter was watching her.

She walked over to Westin and leaned in. "Is this okay?" she asked.

"I would have let you know if it wasn't." Westin studied her. "It's not quite what I had in mind," he said mildly, he eyes flickering over the doctor.

She shifted uncomfortably. "It is nothing. I am being friendly. You told me to be friendly," she pointed out.

He nodded. "Be careful, Lia."

She clenched her teeth. "If you do not think I can handle a simple social call, just say so. You still have the right to forbid me," she pointed out.

He sipped his beer. "I could," he said simply. "Do you want me too?"

She narrowed her eyes and moved away from the table. Her feelings were none of Westin's concern, and she was tired of playing games. She approached the doctor cautiously. "How is your beverage?" she asked Hunter as she moved into the barstool. She found that it spun, and so she moved herself from side to side as she ran her hands over the grain of the bar's wood. It was smooth beneath her fingertips. She continued stroking it.

"It's fine. It's just soda. How was the rest of your shift?"

She stopped rocking. "People are stupid," she muttered. His smile lit up his face, and she found herself smiling as well. "They are far too comfortable with their lazy and gluttonous ways," she said softly. "I am not sure what I might like to drink. Do you have any suggestions?"

"I know I asked you for a drink, but as your doctor, I should actually caution you against it. Are you taking your pain pills?" he asked. Lia shook her head. "In that case, I'll let Karen be the expert. She makes some mean drinks."

Karen poured a few juices and spirits into a mixer and started shaking. "This is one of my favorite drinks. It makes me feel like I'm in paradise," she said, pouring the yellow concoction.

Lia stared at the neon yellow drink. "It is very bright and happy," she said as she pulled the glass closer to her. She leaned over and took her first sip. It was the perfect mixture of sweet and tangy.

"This is delicious!" she said delightedly. She took a few big gulps.

Hunter grabbed the glass. "Easy," he said alarmed. "That thing has enough alcohol to land you on your ass if you are not too careful."

Lia tried to remember if she had ever had alcohol before, but no memories came to mind. She spun the drink around. "Why do you drink alcohol if it lands you on your ass?" she asked.

"In moderation it can be relaxing. It helps you unwind after a long day. Too much can be harmful. I would be lying if I said that too much didn't sometimes lead to a good time, but I think baby steps are necessary."

She looked him directly in the eye. She may have forgotten the effects of alcohol, but she didn't forget how to talk to a man. "Are you here as my doctor?"

A slow smile spread across his face. "No, I suppose I'm not."

Lia took another sip. "Good." She felt her cheeks heat, and she hid her face before her glass. What was wrong with her? "How was your day?" She tried to remember all the phrases she and Westin had practiced.

"It was long. I feel the same way about my patients as you do your customers. They do stupid things to injure themselves, and then they don't listen to you when they leave, and there is all this paperwork where you have to justify every action you take. I'm not saying that doctors shouldn't be accountable for their actions. That part is certainly necessary, but it does drag a day out."

"Do you specialize in stitching people back together?" Lia

asked, finishing her drink.

"There is a lot of that," he said laughingly. "I mostly deal with general and trauma surgery in the emergency room. Unless it's something specific to the brain or heart, I can usually patch it. It's hectic, but I do love the rush."

"Lia, do you want another one? It's on the house after working today without finishing your training," Karen offered.

Lia hadn't even realized that she'd finished her drink. She glanced over at Westin, who nodded. "Yes, please. I enjoyed it."

Karen started shaking up another cocktail, and Hunter glanced at Westin. "How do you like Agent Caxton?" he asked curiously.

"He is helping me to merge back into society, which is helpful and frustrating," Lia said slowly. "I appreciate the services offered, but sometimes I want to stab him," she said, smiling at the irony.

"Fair enough. How is everything going with that?"

Her eyes widened. "Oh, I have not stabbed anyone yet."

His smile spread slowly across his face. "I meant merging into society, but that's good to know as well," he said laughingly.

"It is exhausting, but life is exhausting. Westin, Agent Caxton, says I drink too much coffee, but I feel sleepy all the time. I like reading and watching the television. The show with the zombies is particularly entertaining, but I feel that the characters are not very smart. Then I watched this other show about reapers where they change identity but are still alive. That one I find entertaining and funny. Maybe that is how it should work," Lia said hurriedly. The more she drank, the faster she talked.

Hunter held up his hand. "All right, take a breath. I suppose a fresh perspective makes things very interesting."

Lia drained some more of her drink and leaned in close. "What about you, Hunter? What do you find exciting in life?"

He leaned back and cleared his throat. "I think the connections you make are important," he said slowly. He stopped and stared at her as if he wanted to say more.

After an awkward moment of silence, Hunter continued, but Lia's vision was unfocused. She narrowed her eyes and leaned closer, trying to clear it. Her vision only blurred more. She gripped the bar and slid off her stool, standing on shaky feet. Hunter grabbed her, asked her what was wrong, but his voice was distant and muted. She opened her mouth to cry for help, but the restaurant was already fading. She blacked out.

The temperature dropped, and Lia shivered. She dug her toes into the gravel. They bit into her skin, and she winced. In the silence of the false scene before her, something tugged at her memory. She had been here before. She looked to the left at the figure struggling in the violent waters. The wind bent trees and broke branches. The tall blurry man stood in front of her.

The pain returned with her memories, and she saw the struggling figure in the water, heard the accusations of the man. More than anything, she wanted to prove that she was not responsible for that person's death. Their death, whoever they were, would not be another on her head. She would save them. Lia raced to the waters, adrenaline pumping. She barely felt the sharp edges of the pebbles at her feet. When her toes touched the waters, she was flung back on the riverbank. The blurry figure stood before her.

"I can save them," she whispered.

"Neither you or I can change the past," the voices answered.

The blood from her torn skin trickled to his feet. "Bad blood," she whispered. She looked up. "Why am I here?"

"To remember."

She looked at him crossly. "Not here. Physical. Human. Alive. Why am I alive?"

"We need you."

"To remember who I am?"

"To remember who you are."

"I know who I am," she said bitterly. "I crave life, but I want to watch it pour out. I want to touch it. I want to understand it."

He bent down, his arm outstretched. "You crave life but cater to death."

She scrambled away, trailing blood. "I want to wake up. I do not wish to see you anymore!"

"You must see to wake up." He reached out and touched her forehead. The pain ripped through her body, and she fell into the darkness.

"I will not, I will not, I will not." A bar replaced the river, but it was not Owen's Tavern. She was drifting through another memory. The floor was dirty, and the tables were crudely carved and barely stood on their own. She couldn't see anyone in the room, but she could hear a chanting on the other side of the bar. Even as Lia stepped around to get a good view, she knew the voice was her own.

Lia's memory was dressed in an old-fashioned dress. Buttons ran from the top of her throat to her waist where her dress seemed to billow out endlessly. She rocked back and forth next to a man on the floor who was unconscious but still breathing.

The vision of Lia gripped a knife in her hand. Why was it always a knife? "I will not, I will not. I do not want to go back," she cried out. She raised her eyes in Lia's direction. Afraid she could be seen, Lia stumbled back against the wall. The reflection just stared. Her hands were shaking. "I do not want to go back," she whispered. She leaned forward and put her ear on the man's chest.

"I can hear the blood pumping through your veins. I know it is wrong, but I want to see it. Why? Why!" She screamed at the man and raised her knife, plunging it into his heart. She collapsed on the floor next to him, drawing her fingers in and out of the blood. "Bad blood," she whispered. "You have bad blood."

Lia turned and stumbled out the door. She knew that Westin would be coming soon to collect the memory that still lay on the floor, making no attempt at escape. She just wanted to go back, back to her date with Hunter. She wanted to be as far away from the body, from herself, as she could get. She couldn't escape. The lust for blood knocked her down, and as she hit the floor, everything slowed. She could hear the beating of her own heart. She wanted to turn back, to see the beauty in the blood spilling on the floor. She gripped the floor and shook her head. After a moment, she pushed herself up and reached the door.

It disappeared, trapping her. Instinctively, she tried to walk through the wall. It was solid against her body. She slapped her hand on the wall. "Let me out," she said through gritted teeth.

The scene dissolved around her, and she slumped to the ground.

Suddenly she was back in Owen's Tavern, leaning against the bar. Westin, Hunter, and Karen were all standing around her.

"Are you okay Lia?" Hunter asked, now in doctor mode.

Lia shuddered uncontrollably. The vision was fading, but she could see the bartender on the floor, his life pouring out of him. She tried to block the vision. When she caught her breath, she attempted to smile. "I think perhaps that is enough alcohol for me," she said shakily.

Karen laughed. "Don't worry girl. Working around here with me will help you build up a tolerance. I thought you were going to pass out."

Hunter frowned. "Lia, it's possible that could be experiencing flashbacks of your past. They could come unexpectedly. Do you remember anything? It's possible that if you remember your trauma, you may also experience some post-traumatic stress."

Lia stared at him. His intensity shook her even more. "I'm fine," she said softly. "I'm not sure what happened. I don't remember anything though," she lied.

He frowned at her. "Lia," he said softly but fell silent when Karen put a hand on his shoulder.

Lia shook her head, trying to escape the memories she didn't even know she had. "I did not mean to scare anyone." She smiled at Hunter. "I would like to continue, but I think I need to lie down for a bit."

Hunter nodded. "Yes. I should have thought this through a bit better," he muttered.

Westin took her by the arm. "Time to go," he said in a low voice. She said goodbye to Hunter and walked slowly out the car. Westin let her buckle up before pouncing.

"What the hell was that?" he demanded.

"It was a memory," she muttered tiredly.

"What did you see?"

Already the memory was fading. "Blood. I saw my lust for blood."

Chapter Twelve

Charlie sat on the empty stool of the small bar. He was the last patron in the place, and he watched as the bartender, the only employee, cleaned up. Despite the ban on indoor smoking, the place reeked of cigarettes. It mingled with the aroma of spilled alcohol. Taking a deep whiff, Charlie smiled. It smelled like sin.

Theo was a small middle-aged man who said he had always dreamed of being his own boss. Charlie sat and listened as the man regaled stories of when he was a younger bartender and experienced the thrill of taking over the place when the previous owner retired. It was a reversal of the normal cliché as Charlie remained quiet, listening to Theo go on and on about the good old days.

"All right Charlie, it's been a great night, but I gotta get some sleep. The older I get, the harder it is for me to work these late hours. My wife keeps telling me to switch to the afternoon shift, but then I miss all the action, you know? You need me to call you a cab?"

Charlie shook his head. "Thank you, Theo. I can honestly say you were the perfect bartender tonight. I didn't like the mixed feelings that she had, and I need to reassert myself in this relationship. I need to remind her who she is."

Theo leaned against the bar across from him. "You got an old lady at home who is giving you trouble, huh?"

Charlie gripped his pint glass. "She's a little confused. I just need to set her straight." He pulled his arm back, leaned forward, and smashed the glass against the bartender's head.

Theo stumbled back, crashing against the liquor bottles. Charlie leaped across the bar. He winced as he landed hard.

"Theo, I am feeling my age tonight buddy." He straightened up and walked over to him. "Look, I didn't get all the details, so I'm making up this part as I go along. Just relax. I think, so far, you're the luckiest of them."

Confusion and fear were written all over the bartender's face. Charlie narrowed his eyes. The bartender from the dream had been unconscious. He grabbed the liquor bottle and smashed it against Theo's head, knocking him out. As the bartender fell to the ground, Charlie looked at the floor, trying to decipher the fuzzy images of the vision he'd had the night before. "Too much glass," he muttered. "There wasn't any glass." He turned about to survey the area. Spying the broom and dustpan in the corner, he started to clean up the mess.

"Don't worry Theo, I'm going to leave it spotless for you," he muttered as he worked. After he cleaned up the glass, he positioned the body face up and sat next to him.

"See here's the thing. She had a living body in front of her, still breathing, and not giving her any trouble. Like you, right now. And then, rather than finishing the job, she starts to freak out. Kill him. Don't kill him. Why kill him? The whole thing was giving me a headache."

He leaned over and gripped Theo's head. "I can feel what is inside her. I know that it calls to her, demands life, yearns for blood. Theo, it is powerful. It's like a drug, and satisfying that need is a feeling that rocks you to the core. She is the luckiest woman in the world, but she can't appreciate it!" Charlie dropped his head and leaned back. "With every death, she becomes more alive, but she just doesn't understand."

Theo began to stir, moaning. Charlie slipped his knife out. "I need to make her understand. Theo, you are going to help me make her understand." As the bartender tried to roll over, Charlie swiftly brought the knife down.

When the reaper came to take the old man's soul, Charlie pretended to be oblivious. There were times when he messed with the reapers for fun. Now that Lia was on his side, he couldn't allow the other side to meddle with his plan. As the portal closed again, he went to work, wiping up his fingerprints and discarding the glass. Finally, he emptied his small bag of ash next to Theo. "Just a personal touch, Lia. I'm sure you understand," he whispered into the silence. He stared at the body and ash, willing to feel what she felt during a kill. He wanted to be a part of the rush.

It was always there in small doses. Until the visions and dreams, he didn't even realize how good it could be. Now, more than ever, he wanted to connect with her, touch her, feel her.

His desire for her was making him more powerful than ever.

Lia sank deeper into the cold water. After the odd rush of adrenaline she'd felt hours before, she decided to try her first warm bath. The water and bubbles covered her, weighed her down, and made her feel as if nothing real could touch her. Long after the heat had left, Lia still tried to sink deeper into the secrets of the water, afraid to get out.

Her bathroom door opened, and Westin walked in. There was no awkwardness in the room, and Lia didn't bother to cover herself. "You've been in here for hours."

She held up her fingers. "I am withering in the water. I think perhaps I am like the witch in the movie about Kansas and Oz and the little dog. If I stay long enough, I might wither away to nothing."

"Is that what you want?"

"How do you distinguish between good and bad?" she asked, ignoring his question.

He hopped up on the bathroom counter and leaned against the wall. "You just learn. The more you live, the more you see and experience things. You learn the difference, and you make a choice."

She leaned her head back and stared at the ceiling. "I

watched The History Channel. I wanted to know about World War Two. Then I wanted to know about other wars. So many people die. People slaughter so others may learn a lesson. They lust for blood and vengeance. Why is it so different that I lust as well?"

"You've been here a few weeks now, Lia. Soon you'll surpass your record. Why haven't you killed anyone?"

"You told me not to," Lia said quietly. "I follow you because you are my master. You are also my collector though. You could save a life by taking me in."

"Do you want to go back?"

Lia shook her head violently. "No."

"Is that why you haven't killed anyone?"

She turned her head and met his stare. "I told you why."

Westin laughed. "Lia, you don't follow orders. You do what you want. Do you think taking a life is wrong?"

Lia shrugged. "Some deserve to die." She smiled at him. "You follow orders."

Westin nodded. "I try to, yes."

"You blindly follow orders for a system that does not work."

His raised his eyebrows. "What makes you think that the system doesn't work?"

Lia chuckled. "I am proof that the system does not work. You collect reapers to protect the population, yet the judges allow the soulless to walk the earth. There is no better prison than the reaper plane, and yet how many times do I escape? That is proof that the system doesn't work." She shivered and pulled the plug, running her toe along the edge of the drain.

After the water had drained, she lay in the tub, feeling the hard porcelain press against her skin. The air weighed her down. "The water protects you," she muttered. She turned to stare at Westin.

"What do you want?" Westin finally asked.

Lia stood up and reached for her towel. Wrapping herself in

it, she relished the soft touch of it on her skin. She looked down at Westin. "I would like to eat. I am hungry."

Westin shook his head and stood, towering over her. He leaned in close, staring down at the top of her head. "I do not know how you feel about yourself or the world. I collect you after the fact, so I can't comment on what happens during your kills. I don't know what you think of good and evil, and I don't care what you think about me. What I do know is that death calls to you, and for as long as possible, I'm going to make sure you don't answer," he warned in a low voice.

She lifted her head. "There is a hole inside of me. I just want to fill it."

"Fill it with life," he said. "You have to get out. You have to leave for work in twenty minutes."

She frowned. "I am not scheduled to work tonight."

Westin smiled. "Your boss called and asked if you could pick up a shift this evening. I told her you weren't busy."

She tried to glare at him, but it was halfhearted. "Asshole," she muttered.

He raised his eyebrows. "What was that?"

She blew out her breath. "Nothing," she muttered. "This job alone will drive me to murder."

She watched him get out of the car and run his hand over his chest, taking a moment as if unsure he should walk into the restaurant. Safely behind the tinted windows of the restaurant, she studied him. He gave her a fluttering feeling in her stomach every time she saw him. There was an ease about him that made her envious, a confidence that she couldn't recreate, but there was also a sadness about him that made her curious. Certainly the handsome doctor didn't have any dark secrets. He saved lives. He gave her flutters.

Hunter made her nervous.

She stood up straighter and had a bright smile waiting for

him, a smile Karen had taught her, and tried to look and feel as normal as possible. "Dr. Logan, what a pleasant surprise," she greeted.

She studied him carefully. He did not look surprised to see her. An easy smile broke out across his face. "Lia, what have I told you about calling me Dr. Logan?"

Hunter. The name rattled in her head. It didn't suit him at all. Wasn't she the hunter? "Hunter," she amended out loud. "Going to the bar?"

He leaned against the podium, making her catch her breath. Since when did someone standing near her affect her so? She felt her pulse jump and her hands shake. "It depends," he said easily. "Will you be joining me afterward?"

She bit her bottom lip. Westin had not stayed. He would be picking her up soon, and he would probably be angry if she stayed late. She was split. Part of her demanded that she be loyal. Part of her wanted to spend time with the man who made her feel alive.

It wasn't like she was going anywhere private with him. "Maybe for a few minutes," she said quietly. "Agent Caxton will be picking me up soon."

He smiled. "I can work with a few minutes. See you soon," he said quietly, pushing himself off the podium and strolling back towards the bar. Lia's heart skipped a beat, and she swallowed hard. The sensation was not unpleasant, but it didn't sit well with her. He made her feel out of control, and she wasn't altogether sure she disliked it.

"Hunter!" she called out. He turned, and she swallowed hard. "Are you here to see Karen?"

He smiled. "Among other people," he casually said as he turned his back and made his way to the bar. Lia let out her breath slowly. There was something about that man.

Hunter was the last customer. At closing time, she felt her hands shake a bit as she locked the doors. After a moment of debating, she pulled out her cellphone and called Westin.

"What?" he growled.

She hesitated a beat. "Lia, what is it?" he muttered.

"Dr. Logan is here. I would like a few extra minutes to stay and speak with him," she said finally. She tapped her finger against the podium waiting for him to respond. "Westin?"

"I can give you twenty minutes," he said finally. She could hear a few voices in the background.

"Who are you with?" she asked.

"If I thought it was something you needed to know, I would tell you," he said tersely.

She frowned and hung up the phone. After a second, she bit her lip, pulled out her cell phone and texted a quick thank you. She ran her hand through her hair and over her blood red blouse and black skirt. She suddenly wished she had put on something different, more girlie and less bold.

Karen was back behind the bar talking to Hunter. She handed Lia an envelope. "You keep forgetting to pick up your tips," she chastised. "They're available the next day, okay?"

Lia nodded. Her eyes were on Hunter. He was staring at her intently, and she realized she was holding her breath. After a minute, his face broke out into that slow easy smile that made her so envious. He gestured to the stool next to him. "Drink?" he asked.

"I think I will just stick with coke," she said quietly, sliding into the barstool. Karen poured her the soda and smiled. "I'll be in the office doing some paperwork if you need me."

They weren't alone. A few servers were still cleaning up their sections, but with Karen gone, it felt as though they were the only ones in the world. Her heart beat quickly, and the air felt thick. Lia stared at her coke, struggling to think of something to say. She settled on the tried and true. "How was your day?"

"I had the day off from work," Hunter replied. "It was nice."

She tapped her nails on the wood nervously. "What do you

do on your days off?" she asked curiously. The more she thought about it, the more she realized she knew nothing about him. It bothered her. She'd never needed small talk or personal information about someone she was interested in before. She conveyed interest, and they usually complied. This was far more difficult.

"My parents own a bookstore. I went to help with the inventory."

"Tell me about your family."

Hunter sat back and regaled her with stories about his childhood. She stared in curiosity at the light in his eyes when he talked about his family, and wondered about her own family. Did she have a sister who had at one point driven her mad? Did she have a brother who always beat her at everything? Did her parents love her?

Did she kill them too?

"What else did you do?" she asked suddenly, trying to switch gears in her mind.

"I took my dog to the park, made dinner, and caught up on some of my shows."

"You have a dog?" she asked, suddenly alarmed. Would the dog still sense something different about her?

"I do. He's a golden retriever named Jacks. Do you like dogs?"

She shook her head. "I am not sure," she said slowly.

He winced. "I'm sorry. That was insensitive," he muttered. She watched him carefully. He seemed honestly apologetic.

"So, on your days off, you work with your parents. You do not like to relax, sit down, enjoy the day?" she asked, changing the subject.

"I like to keep busy. I guess that's why I entered med school to begin with. I love the chaos." He talked idly for a few minutes about his job. She was amazed by the stories he told and recognized several of the patients. She had reaped their souls. It reminded her of how different they were. He tried to save lives and when she wasn't killing people, she was ferrying their souls to the other side.

"You keep asking me questions. I think it's time I asked you a few," he said teasingly.

She looked down. "I would not know how to answer them," she said quietly.

"There I go again, putting my foot in my mouth. I'm sorry, Lia."

"You do not have to apologize. You should not have to treat me any differently because I am unsure of myself," she said quietly.

He hid behind his soda for a moment. "Actually, I do. You are still technically a patient of mine. There are boundaries that I shouldn't cross."

She cocked her head. "What kind of boundaries?"

He sighed. "You are a beautiful woman. You turn heads wherever you go. It's hard to not be attracted to you, but you are still my patient, and that means that I can't do anything about that attraction," he said finally.

She swallowed hard. "And when I am not your patient? What happens then?"

His features hardened. "Just because you don't remember your past doesn't mean you don't have one," he said suddenly cold.

A wave of sudden anger washed over her. She didn't know where it had come from, and she narrowed her eyes and clenched her jaw. "You asked me for a drink," she said suddenly. "If you do not want to be around me, then you can stop requesting my company," she said angrily. "I work here. I do not have a choice about being here, but you do. If you do not want to see me, you can stop coming in. Karen can tell you the nights that I am not working. We could very easily go back to a professional relationship!" She pushed herself up and turned towards the door.

"Shit. Lia, wait," he said hoarsely. He reached out and grabbed her hand. Lia spun around to remove his hand, but his other came up to her waist to stop her, and the shock of his touch on her body stilled her. She watched Hunter's Adam's apple work furiously as he swallowed. He pulled her closer.

A sound startled them. Hunter immediately dropped his arms and stepped back. She frowned before realizing that the sound was coming from her. It was her cellphone. Embarrassment flushed her face. What was going on with her?

She dug her phone out. It was Westin. "What?" she snapped.

"Having a bad night?" he responded coolly into her ear.

She eyed Hunter. "Are you here to pick me up?" she asked trying to regain control of her temper.

"Yes," he said quietly. "I suggest you regain your composure before coming out."

She took a deep breath. He wanted an apology. She would not give one. "I appreciate everything you have done for me," she said finally. "I will be out in a minute."

She disconnected the call. "That was Westin," she said.

Hunter stepped back, a mask of cool slipping over his face. "Westin, huh?" he said casually. He nodded. "You probably shouldn't keep him waiting."

She narrowed her eyes. How could a person be so hot one minute and so cold the next? "My stitches itch. I have an appointment with the therapist the day after tomorrow. Could I get someone to take them out?"

"Someone?" he asked.

"Yes," she maintained stoically. "Someone."

His features softened. "I'm working. I'll take a look at them."

"Fine. Good night." She turned and stalked out the door. For good measure, she swung her hips a bit more than usual.

Westin was watching her from the car. "Is that show for me?" he asked as she swung into the passenger seat.

"Do not be ridiculous," she snapped.

He laughed. "I take it things didn't go well."

"Could you please just drive" she muttered.

His laughter stopped abruptly. "You are not staying, Lia. Keep that in mind. Whatever emotion you are investing in this man could turn out to be very dangerous."

She turned the face him. "I am not investing any emotion in anyone." She turned the stare out the window. "It does not matter. He does not trust me."

"And you think he should?"

"No. I suppose he should not."

Chapter Thirteen

Connor took a break from his textbook and stretched. He was only a few weeks into the semester, and already he felt behind. It had been a few years since his undergraduate studies, and he was out of practice.

He moved across the house and gazed out his bedroom window. Charlie kept his blinds drawn at all times, but Connor could see the lights were on. His neighbor kept to himself, but Connor decided company and beer were just what he needed. He grabbed a couple of bottles from the fridge and headed over.

He knocked firmly on the door, telling himself he wouldn't take no for an answer. Charlie looked pale and disheveled when he responded to the knock. He stepped out on the porch and closed the door behind him.

Connor held out the beer. "Pint?"

A strangely maniacal grin crossed Charlie's face. "Sure. Why not?" Connor smiled with pleasure. He had expected more of a fight. His neighbor's demeanor had almost completely changed, and Connor suspected something had made the man jubilant.

They popped their bottle caps and settled on the patio steps. "So Charlie, what do ya do?" Connor asked conversationally.

Charlie sipped his beer slowly. "I do set designs for scenes," he said after a moment.

"For plays and shite?" Connor asked surprised. The man didn't seem like the theatrical type. In fact, the more Connor thought about it, the more he realized that Charlie didn't seem a type for anything. He was shadowed somehow, like a man who didn't quite fit together. It made Connor want to know more about him.

"For whatever needs doing. You're from Ireland?"

"Norn Iron. I grew up in Belfast, but I've spent some time in Cork and a few years in England," Connor replied.

Charlie cocked his head. "I spent a few years in Ireland," he said casually.

"What part?"

Charlie shrugged. "It was a long time ago. All over I suppose. Tourist sites," he muttered vaguely.

Connor frowned. "Ya spent a few years visiting tourist sites? Your job must pay well!"

"I did some work while I was out there," he answered before quickly changing the subject. "Why are you in America?"

Connor tapped his finger against the glass. "I'm working on my graduate degree in history."

Charlie raised his eyebrows. "That's right. CU. So you chose to study in the country that has the least amount of history?"

Connor grinned and swallowed the last of his beer. "America is the land of opportunity."

The glasses clinked as Charlie sat his empty bottle next to Connor's. "So I have found," he replied.

Connor shook his head. There was something odd about his new friend.

Tension smothered the air as the agents stared at the three new pictures on the board. None of them had anything to say. The muted sounds from behind the glass walls slipped under the door as they tried to figure out what to do next. The stale breadcrumbs of the Phoenix were replaced with a grotesque masquerade of deaths that were even more disturbing and no less enlightening.

Starting at the corner, they had placed a picture of the ski lift operator, dressed in a military uniform with the odd doodled swastika. Below him was the woman they found the next day in a warehouse, complete with a set of early twentieth-century weapons and no background linking her to them. Now they stared at the bar owner who was left with a message. *Embrace the gifts bestowed upon you.*

All of them were laid out next to a pile of ash.

Westin fidgeted in the back of the room. He had seen these victims before, but they were blurred memories, backdrops for Lia, who always stood front and center. Although Lia was vague about the details of her visions and dreams, Westin could remember enough to link the murders.

Charlie was sending a message.

"So what do we think of this message?"

O'Ryan's words startled Westin as they mimicked his thoughts. The young man tapped his fingers on the desk. "A ski lift operator dressed as a Nazi, weapons from nearly a century ago on a woman who sells life insurance, and a business owner with a message. Our killer is changing the pattern. Why? He has our attention. What does he want?" He turned to Westin. "Anything new to report with Lia?"

Westin unfolded his legs and leaned forward. "She acts as I would suspect her too. She seems fearful for her life. She's troubled no one has claimed her. She is frustrated by her lack of knowledge and our own. She hasn't done or said anything to raise suspicions. "

O'Ryan stood and paced for a moment, staring at the board. "Mallich, go back through all the crime scenes. Try to find a connection to these gifts he's referring too. See if there is a literary or pop culture reference to the message as well. We need something to explain this new behavior."

He looked at Westin. "I don't like the lack of information we have on this woman, but I can't question her any further without a reason. Drop hints about some of these new developments, Nazi's and gifts and so forth. Look for a reaction. Go through her notebooks if you have to. I just feel like she's hiding something or we're missing something. If nothing else, there must be something in her memories. We need to dig them out."

Lichton stood. "These themes that he's portraying can't be random. There has to be a connection. I'll see what I can find out."

Westin watched as they all fell into a routine, typing on the computer, making phone calls, scratching in their notebooks. No one seemed to notice that he hadn't left yet.

His fingers itched to reach inside their minds and erase all knowledge of Lia. He closed his eyes and reached out, gingerly asking for entry. It was so easy. People were always so preoccupied with what was going on with everyone else that they never even imagined that someone could touch their inner thoughts.

He could see Lia in their minds. She was a shadow of doubt, a forming obsession, and he knew that she would haunt them until there was something real that they could grasp and explain her oddness.

All it would take was one planted thought in O'Ryan's mind, and it would spread like a disease to the others.

O'Ryan reached up and pressed a finger to his temple, massaging it. After a moment, he reached into his computer case and pulled out a bottle of aspirin. The painkiller was a reminder of the single moment Westin disobeyed orders, a reminder of the severe consequences. He pulled away and settled back into his own mind, leaving the others to whittle away at their growing suspicions.

Lia stared at Karen. "You want me to do what?" she asked again, still not sure she understood.

"I know it's an odd request, but the truth is that with Ariel going to Europe for two months and Willy cutting back his hours for school, I'm desperate for a new server. I never really needed a new hostess. So, instead of going through the hell of sifting through applications, I would rather just throw you on the floor. You're quick to pick up on new things, and you have already learned the menu. Your customer service skills are a little lacking, but we can work on that. Please, Lia, you've got to help me out here."

Westin had dropped Lia off a little early to that he could check on the agents. Karen had pounced on her with a server's apron and training menu.

"It's a lot more money," Karen said in a tantalizing voice, still holding the items in front of her.

Lia reached up hesitantly and took them. "I am not sure I will be good with people for such long periods of time," she said quietly.

"I'm too desperate to worry about that now," Karen said, clapping her hands enthusiastically. "Now, you'll need to pick up some non-slip shoes, but for today, just be careful in the back. I've got a black shirt you can have. I'll start you out with two tables until you get the hang of things. If you have any questions, ask anyone except Cheryl. She can be a real bitch when she wants to be."

Lia imagined the horror that would cross Westin's face when he realized what her new job would entail. The image alone made her smile. "I will try," she said, laughing inside.

"Thank you so much! You're the best," Karen said happily. She made her way back to the office, and Lia stared at the menu. Waiting tables couldn't be too difficult, she mused. Perhaps she wouldn't be so bored.

She moved to the restroom and tried on her new shirt. She was gaining some weight with Westin's cooking, and the shirt was a little tight. She frowned and tried tugging on it a little bit. It had a high collar but clung to her breasts and stomach. After a few moments, she simply gave up. She'd seen some of the girls wear even tighter shirts, so she supposed this one was fine.

The lunch shift was busy, and she struggled with her first

round of tables. She knew very little about the food. No, she couldn't recommend anything. No, she didn't know the side items. No, she didn't know if the meal was dairy free or gluten free. She didn't even know what gluten was. She spent most of her time asking questions, and not everyone was patient with her.

On the plus side, there was always something to do, and she found herself able to integrate herself into the wait staff with ease. It wasn't until the shift started to slow down that she found her patience waning.

Two businessmen sat at the table, and for a few minutes, they were deep in conversation with each other. Lia knew it was rude to interrupt, but after a bit, she was too frustrated to wait anymore. She approached the table.

"Hello," she tried to say politely. They continued to talk, not even looking up. She gave it a few more seconds before trying again. "Hello," she said a little louder.

One of them finally looked up. "We're not ready, can you come back?" he asked clearly irritated.

"You are not going to be ready if you do not look at the menu," Lia pointed out.

The man's face tightened in anger. "Excuse me?"

"This is a place of business. You are supposed to come in and order food and eat. You cannot do that if you do not look at the menu," she said again.

"We're customers. If we want to sit here and talk before ordering, we're going to do that," the man snarled.

"Do customers come to your place of work and talk idly with themselves before doing business with you?" she asked.

"What the hell are you talking about? Where is your manager?"

"I am going to guess that they do not. That is why we expect that when you come to our place of business, you conduct yourself to our standards. Customers that come into our establishment order food. They talk before their food gets here, they talk while they eat, and for a bit, they talk after they eat. Presumably they need their food to settle before they move because they have eaten so much. The process should start relatively quickly so that the restaurant can continue doing business. That way it makes money, and I make money. I am sure there is a similar process for whatever it is that you do." Lia smiled at the men.

A few of the tables surrounding Lia had grown silent.

The men looked at each for a moment and looked at Lia. "I'll take a sweet tea," one of the mumbled.

Lia nodded. "One sweet tea. And for you, sir?"

The man mumbled his request for water. "I will bring your beverages out for you while you look over the menu. Thank you," she said, her tone still even, and she walked away.

Karen cut her off in the wait station. She stared at Lia for a moment. "Lia," she said warningly.

"Have I done something wrong?" Lia asked.

"You can't talk to customers that way. You have to let them do what they want to do."

"That is ridiculous. They should adhere to certain standards just as we do. How can I take care of them if all they do is sit there and talk to each other?" Lia pointed out crossly.

"I know it's hard to understand. If there is another problem, come talk to me about it before you talk to them. Okay?" Karen asked sighing.

Lia nodded. She wasn't entirely sure what had happened, but her table gave her no more issues. The other servers crowded around her to hear the story, and they all sighed with jealousy. Lia smiled, unsure why they were so envious of her but enjoyed the attention.

At the end of the shift, Karen handed her tip money. "I want to be clear on something. I own half this restaurant. In any other place, you would have been fired for what you said to those men. This is an industry where the customer is always right and gets everything they want. As a result, the servers here get treated like doormats."

"I am not sure what I did that was wrong or right. I see a mutual benefit in this place for everyone involved. When things go smoothly, everyone is happy. If someone upsets the balance, no one is happy. Should we not make sure that the balance is kept?" Lia argued.

"It makes sense, doesn't it? You don't think like everyone else, do you?" Karen looked at Lia quizzically.

Lia shifted from one foot to the other. "I do not know how everyone else thinks," she said softly. "I could pretend to think like everyone else if you would like."

Karen shook her head. "No. Unless people start walking out in droves, I want you to think like you. Did you like waiting tables today?"

"It was less boring than walking people to tables," she admitted.

"Good. Get some non-slip shoes tonight. I'll see you here tomorrow night. Lia?"

"Yes?"

Karen reached around and closed the door behind them. Lia inhaled, feeling the small office close in around her. Her chest tightened.

"How are things going? Do you need anything?"

"I am fine." She gripped her server book tightly and glanced around. Logically, she knew the walls were not closing in on her, but she found it hard to catch her breath.

Karen nodded. "All right. I just wanted you to know that I'd like to help in any way I can. I know I am your employer, but I can also be your friend if you'd like."

Her words distracted Lia from the small space. "What?"

"A friend. I'd like to be your friend."

Lia wasn't sure she'd ever had a friend before. "Okay," she said slowly. She thought back to when she socialized with reapers.

They talked idly about reaps, but she had never considered any of them friends. It required a connection that simply couldn't be made without a soul.

Karen smiled and reached around, opening the door. "Have a good night, Lia."

Lia ambled out to meet Westin. Her thoughts were preoccupied with connections and souls. It would never come naturally to her, but maybe, just maybe, she could learn.

The temperature dropped, and Lia shivered. She dug her toes into the gravel. They bit into her skin, and she winced. In the silence of the false scene before her, something tugged at her memory. She had been here before. She looked to the left at the figure struggling in the violent waters. The wind bent the trees and broke branches. She ignored the pain pounding in her head as memories came flooding in. She focused on her surroundings. She was determined not to forget again.

"This is getting tedious," she called out to the blurry figure.

"It is necessary," the voices responded. He moved towards her. She tried to step back, but her ankle twisted on a rock, and she fell. The rocks stabbed deep in the palms of her hand, and the blood flowed freely.

"I have not harmed anyone," she said through clenched teeth. "Leave me in peace!"

"I cannot do that." He stood over her. "You must not resist."

As he reached down for her, she fought against the pain and crawled away. "Why could he see me?" she asked quickly. "The Phoenix. He could see me when I was a reaper. How could he do that?"

"I do not know."

"Do not lie to me," she hissed.

"I cannot lie. I am not omniscient, Annalia. Your Phoenix eludes even me."

"Do you want me to kill him?"

His hand hovered over her. "Do you want to kill him?"

*She eyed his hand. She could not escape. "I want to be free. Free of him,"
she swallowed hard. "And free of you." She reached up with her bloodied hand*

and grabbed his. Immediately, the pain cut deep into her, and she fell in the darkness screaming.

By the time she had straightened, she was standing in the middle of a bedroom. It was small, a simple twin sized bed with a desk in the corner and a set of drawers along the wall. As she walked over to the window, she realized she was in a small inn.

There were horses and carriages below, but the moonlight showed no people. Still, Lia knew that someone lurked in the shadows.

The door opened, but she didn't even turn around. She knew that she would only see herself sauntering in, with a man or perhaps even a woman, luring them to their final moment.

She closed her eyes and leaned her forehead against the window. She could feel her heartbeat accelerating with the excitement of the seduction and the thrill of deceit. Her hands began to shake, and chills broke out along her skin. She felt that nothing would ever compare to the power that beckoned her now, the power of death.

Behind her, she could hear muted noises. The smell of alcohol mingled in the air, mixing with the musk of desire. Heavy breathing and whispers reached her ears.

"I saw what you did to her."

Lia's voice echoed softly against the sudden tension of panic. Desire changed to confusion. Lia felt an invisible tug on her arm. Powerless, she turned and watched as her memory quietly and easily sunk her knife into the fat belly of the surprised drunk. "I'll take from you what you desperately wanted to take from her," her reflection whispered.

The memory took a moment to clean her blade before standing up. "I know you are there," she announced to Lia.

Lia leaned against the window, her eyes wide.

"You want to know more about me, I can feel it. Come find out," the memory taunted, walking closer to her. She didn't stop until they were face to face. "Come find out who I am," she whispered.

Grey began to bleed out from the center of the room until Westin stepped through. Lia's memory turned to face him. "Come find out who I am," she said shakily as the knife dropped from her hand.

Westin reached out and beckoned the now frozen memory. She floated to him. "I already know who you are," he answered softly.

"Then tell me," Lia screamed at the figures, beating her first against the window behind her. "Stop playing these games and tell me!"

The glass broke, and she fell backwards through the air, to her death, down, down, down...

Westin stood over her as Lia opened her eyes. Her body was tensed, ready for impact, but her body was curled up in her bed. She kept her eyes on Westin, searching his face for the truth. Sunlight streamed through the windows.

"What are you not telling me," she asked softly.

Westin tossed some clothes on the bed and turned his back. "Hurry up, you're going to be late for your doctor's appointment."

Chapter Fourteen

"Welcome back Miss X."

Lia glared at Jane. She'd been standing at the desk for nearly two minutes while the young woman typed at the keyboard, openly ignoring her.

"You are not very good at your job," Lia pointed out.

Jane shrugged. "That's probably true. Still, the doc could fire me if she wants. I think she believes she can help me in some way." She passed the papers. "Remember enough to fill these out?"

"Why do I need to fill out more paperwork? I have been coming here for two weeks."

"Yeah, I never got around to putting in your information, and then I lost your paperwork. It doesn't matter. It's not like any of the information you provide is true, right?" The woman smiled at Lia. "Go on then," she said, pointing her long acrylic blue fingernails towards the chair.

Lia slammed the clipboard on the desk and leaned over. "You annoy me," she said in a low voice.

Jane rolled her chair back. "Perhaps we should talk to the doctor about some anger management classes," she said, her voice trembling just a little.

The fear in Jane's eyes sent a chill through Lia's body. She felt a surge of power and leaned in to drink in the essence. Jane suddenly narrowed her eyes.

"Personal space," she snapped angrily.

Lia straightened. The mood was broken, and all that was left was irritation. She snatched the clipboard from the table and stalked to the chair at the end of the waiting room. She bore down on the pen so hard that the paper tore when she tried to write her name. She clenched her teeth but refused to get up and ask for a new form.

She hadn't been sleeping well. When she wasn't having dreams about her past, she was having odd, twisted dreams about the present. They were different from her visions and memories. Instead of being present and watching the action happen, she would be watching from some unseen place, like an omniscient figure judging the actions of others. While they were not real, she still felt tired and awkward when she woke.

These were the dreams that she documented in her notebook, although she did record her memories in various ways. She never came out and directly wrote what was happening, but she included them in her odd mix. Lia wanted to talk about them with someone who wasn't Westin, with someone who wasn't going to punish her for the things she had done.

Having completed the information forms, she stomped over to the desk and slammed them down. "Sorry," she said with a smile. "They slipped." Her voice was deadpan, but she felt an odd satisfaction to the blatant lie. She felt that Westin would be proud of her passive aggressive actions towards Jane.

Jane eyeballed the forms. "They're ripped," she pointed out.

Lia leaned closer, wanting to feel that power again. "I am sure you can still read them. I suggest you do whatever you need to do with this information because I can assure you, I will not be filling them out again."

The young woman reached over and snatched the clipboard. "Whatever. You can go on back. The doctor's been waiting on you for a few minutes."

Lia walked away without a word and let herself into the office. Dr. Teston was still behind her desk, shuffling through some paperwork. She looked up with a genuine smile.

"Lia! Have a seat. I'm eager to hear how things are going." The woman stood and came around the desk, sitting in one of the chairs. As usual, Lia sunk right in to her seat, feeling warm and comfortable.

"Doctor," she said nodding in acknowledgment. "How is the office?" she asked awkwardly. She never really knew what kind of small talk to make with the therapist.

"My patients are rarely dull," the doctor said. Lia relaxed. The therapist had a way of making her feel at home despite the odd circumstances surrounding their visits. The entire office was enveloped in a sense of trust that Lia never felt anywhere else. "Let's start with the obvious questions. Any memory flashes or feelings of familiarity towards anything?"

"Odd dreams, but I do not think they mean anything. I think I am a little bit claustrophobic, and I do not like pickles."

The therapist laughed. "I'm not a fan of pickles myself. Tell me about this claustrophobia you experienced."

Lia looked out the window. It was not an experience she wanted to relive. "It was nothing big. The office at work is small. The owner wished to have a word with me, and when she closed the door, I felt it get hot and tight. It was hard to breathe." Lia took a deep breath.

Dr. Teston smiled gently. "That does sound like a classic case of claustrophobia. In this case, it's probably mild. I'd avoid elevators and closets. That's something that would most likely carry over, despite your memory loss, rather than show itself as a new symptom."

"I do not feel claustrophobic when I am in the elevator," Lia pointed out.

The doctor made a note on her paper. "What was going on when you had these feelings?"

Lia thought back. "I was talking to my manager. She was asking how things were going and if she could help me in any way."

"Maybe your feelings had nothing to do with your surroundings but your reaction to your manager. Creating new relationships can be a complicated process. How is work going?"

"I am waiting tables now, although I do not think I am doing it right. Karen told me to be careful with what I say, but she thinks my honesty is refreshing."

"Is she talking about things you say to employees or customers?"

"Both, I guess."

The therapist made some notes in her notebook. "Give me an example."

Lia shrugged. "Yesterday my table asked me a question and then did not listen to the answer. I had to repeat myself to each individual at the table. I told them that if they had listened to me the first time, it would have saved them time and saved me trouble."

"Serving tables can be a thankless job. I remember my years of serving through school. There are times when you are going to feel unappreciated. Are you sure it wouldn't be easier for you to stick with the hosting position?"

Lia shook her head. "I do not believe it has to be a hard job. I am sure I can handle it."

"How do you feel interacting with people?"

Lia thought back to Jane. "Some are easier than others. I went on a date. Well, I suppose it was not a date. It was more like a social interaction."

"What made you say date to begin with?"

Lia squirmed. "Others qualified it as a date," she said.

"You did not want to qualify it as a date?" the doctor asked patiently.

"Dates are specific social constructs, and they seem to be deliberate, but he has not inquired about or labeled it a date." Not to mention he hadn't come in to see her since that night.

"Do you feel you are in a position to date?"

"Do you think that it is not safe for me to date?" Lia asked. "Do you think I am being watched?"

"That's not my area of expertise. I'm more concerned there might be something in your past that can prevent you from being available for this man."

Lia knew there were no attachments in her past. She was, however, concerned about the attachments she had in the present. "I do not think that is the biggest danger."

"You are afraid of the man who stabbed you."

Lia frowned. "I try not to think about it much." The truth was that Lia did think about it. Every morning when she woke up, she felt a little bit weaker, a little bit closer to death. It had never occurred to her to consider her immortality. How close was she to death?

"Do you want to talk about your date?"

Dr. Teston interrupted Lia's thoughts, and she blinked. After a moment of consideration, she shook her head. "No." She leaned forward. "I want to talk about my dreams. They are surreal. I watch myself doing things, and I cannot interfere. I feel what she feels, and I desire what she desires, but I cannot act as she acts. She has a freedom that I do not. Why is that?"

"Well, our dreams can stem from a number of reasons. In some ways, they are odd variations of whatever preoccupies our mind when we sleep, and sometimes they arise from a deeper part of our subconscious. What actions does she portray?"

Unable to say murder, Lia chose to be vague. "Intimate and morally questionable actions. I do not want to be specific."

The therapist nodded. "There are cases where the things we want manifest themselves on a large, sometimes grotesque, scale in our dreams. It doesn't mean that you necessarily desire what you see but that you want the freedom that is associated with it."

Lia stared aimlessly out the window. "I think I want it all," she muttered.

"What was that Lia?"

She turned her head and smiled. "I said that is all, thank you. I should get going. I have an appointment to get my stitches removed."

Dr. Teston frowned and looked at the clock. "We still have some time if you want to discuss this or any other topics a little further."

"No. The past few days have been less than eventful. I am sure I will have more topics to discuss at our next meeting. Thank you, Dr. Teston." She reached out and shook her therapist's hand.

"You won't get away so easily next time, Lia," the therapist warned as she released Lia.

Lia's mind was already on a different subject. She felt her body betraying her as she thought about seeing Hunter, but she reminded herself that he was not interested in her and did not trust her. And she was in no position to prove him wrong.

As she waited nearly half an hour in the waiting room and even longer in the exam room, she began to get nervous. How would he react when she was no longer his patient? How would she react when she saw him again? What was it about him that made her so emotional, so irrational? When he finally entered, she felt the air escape her lungs. His face betrayed nothing. "I'm sorry if you had to wait long. There are always unexpected instances at the hospital," he said as he closed the door. "If you give me a minute, I'll get a nurse. She should be present while I look at your wound."

She narrowed her eyes. She would not make it that easy. "No, this is fine. I do not want to wait any longer," she replied in a clipped voice.

He frowned at her. "I think..." he began.

"Dr. Logan, I would like to get this over with," she interrupted.

Something flashed in his eyes. Sadness? But it was quickly gone. He nodded, and his professional demeanor was back in place. He reached over to lift her gown. "So how are the meetings going?" he asked conversationally, his hands skimming across her abdomen.

She felt her breath hitch, but if he could be professional, so could she. "General emotions? The meeting was enlightening. I think, perhaps, I am finding a little more about myself with her help." Lia bit her lip. Saying it out loud made her realize that it was true, and it suddenly occurred to her that the truth might reveal itself in time.

"That's good." He pushed on her wound. "Any pain, swelling, or unusual discoloration?

She shook her head. "I did get them wet the other evening. I took a bath. I like the way the bubbles feel on my skin," she said quietly. She smiled inwardly as she felt his fingers tremble. He pulled the tape and gauze off gently. She felt the goose bumps prickle on her skin and an excited chill ran through her body. Annoyed at her reaction, she pulled away a little.

"I'm sorry, did the tape pull your skin? These things can be a bitch. Everything looks good, so I see no reason we can't remove the stitches and get rid of the tape once and for all." His voice was even, but Lia saw his pupils dilating slightly, darkening his gaze. It relaxed her, knowing that he was having the same reaction she was.

He cleared his throat, apparently nervous. "This is going to be cold," he said softly as he wiped some disinfectant on her skin. She trembled with the chill but didn't pull away. She kept her gaze on him, watching as he swallowed hard before touching her again, feeling his hands shake slightly.

There was a slight pull as he cut each of her stitches. Any noise that occurred outside the door faded away, and only their heavy breaths remained. The air thickened with tension.

The more she concentrated on him, the more she was aware of his heartbeat. It seemed impossible, but she could see his pulse on his neck. She could hear the roar of his blood in her ears, or maybe in was her own blood. Her hands started to shake, and peripheral vision blurred.

Lia closed her eyes, wanted to block it out, but all it did was create flashes of images in her head. She saw the life retreat from his eyes, the blood spilling from his body, and the horror on his face when he realized what she had done.

"All finished," he announced, shattering the images. She lost control. Without a second thought, she grabbed his shirt, pulled him closer, and kissed him, desperate to erase the thoughts from her mind.

The darkness receded at the touch of his lips, leaving only her desire for him, alive and inside her. It was nothing like kissing Paul. Hunter growled, leaned in, and demanded more from her. It shocked her nerves and made the hairs on her neck stand up. It took her breath away.

Resting his forehead on hers, he finally spoke. "What was that for," he whispered.

She pulled away. "I wanted to know what it would feel like," she said evenly.

He rested his thumb on her scar, brushing it back and forth. "It should fade soon." With a sigh, he tugged her gown down.

Lia shook her head. "It is a reminder. I do not mind it."

"You're angry with me about the other evening," he said quietly.

"Yes, but you were right. You should not trust me. You have no idea who I am," she said. She turned away and stripped her gown off, exchanging it for her shirt. When she turned back, he'd turned his back to her.

"I want to get to know you," he said, his words bouncing off the wall.

"You may turn around. I am dressed." When he faced her, she took a deep breath. This was the moment. Westin told her to step away, and she had bigger things to focus on. She did not have time for this attraction. "You were cold with me."

"You can be cold too," he said softly. She tapped her fingers on her legs. Why was he looking at her like that? What was she trying to say? She shook her head. He stepped closer. "Don't deny it. You walked in here today intending to be indifferent, but you kissed me. So what do you want, Lia?"

"You kissed me back," she muttered. What did she want?

"I did. You should know what I want, but you hold all the cards here. I won't do anything you don't want me to. After you walk out of here, you're no longer my patient. So what do you want, Lia?"

The closer he moved, the more helpless she felt. "You," she whispered finally.

He put a finger under her chin and nudged her face towards his. "Then I will trust you. And we'll see where this goes. It'll be complicated, and it could end in disaster. But until then, let's enjoy it." He brought his lips down to hers again. She sighed contently and surrendered to him. He moved his hands down to encircle her waist again, and she reached out to run her hands along his chest. He was so solid, so warm, so real.

He broke away. "I've got another patient to see," he murmured. "But I'll be in touch."

She nodded and stepped away from him. The cold air rushed between them, and she took a deep breath.

Westin would not be pleased, but she really didn't care.

Hunter watched her walk down the hall and shook his head at himself. The woman was a mystery. There was so much energy locked away in her small body, but she was at odds with it.

He ducked into a supply closet and took a few deep breaths to clear his head. Her desire for him was apparent, but it seemed mixed with something. He'd seen sadness in her eyes and, at one point, even fear. Was there something she wasn't telling him?

After his breathing and heartbeat had returned to normal, he slipped back out and tried to blend back in with the hospital staff.

As he took a turn, he bumped into another man. When their skin touched, he felt an intense chill. The man turned and smiled apologetically. "I'm so sorry, Dr. Logan. I should watch where I'm going."

Hunter frowned and tried to place the face with a name. "No worries. Is there something I can help you with?"

"No, my other half was just here. I was just observing the developments," the man said with an odd smile. "I have got to say, you never know what's going to happen in a hospital, right?"

"I hope things turn out well for you," Hunter said awkwardly. The man seemed to look right through him. "Have we met before? Your name has escaped me."

"Oh no, I've just seen you around. I've heard of your work. You have a reputation for patching people up. I find that fascinating. One moment an individual is broken, and the next they are whole and new again, all because of you."

"Just part of the job," Hunter responded awkwardly.

"Well, I can see I am keeping you. I'm sure you're off to save someone's life. Good luck to you, Dr. Logan."

"And to you. I hope you get good news about your significant other." Hunter was backing away, and as he turned, he could have sworn he heard the man laugh.

Chapter Fifteen

Smoke filled the air, and a loud noise pierced her ears. Lia threw herself to the ground. Crouching in the corner, she cried out.

"What the fuck is going on?" Westin raced through the kitchen to the stove. He turned off the knobs, opened the windows, grabbed a towel, and fanned it under the smoke alarm. The noise stopped, and eventually the smoke dissipated. Lia stayed in the corner, finding herself oddly miserable.

"I was defeated by meat," she said quietly.

Westin dropped his arms and came over to inspect the frying pan. "I don't think that's meat anymore. Were you trying to cook?"

Lia stood but pressed herself against the counter. She felt defensive and embarrassed. "I have been watching you. I awoke early this morning, and so I decided to try to cook. I followed your every step verbatim." She peered into the pan. "It does not look like bacon and sausage anymore."

With a sigh, Westin ran the burnt meat under cold water, causing it to sizzle and steam. Once cooled, he tossed it into the trashcan. "Why didn't you just wait?"

Lia crossed her arms. "I told you. I wanted to cook."

"Okay. Why didn't you ask me to teach you?"

"You are never in a teaching mood. Besides, I did not realize it would be difficult! Not everything is supposed to be so hard!" She banged her fists down on the counter in frustration.

Westin held up his hands. "Okay, okay, settle down." He turned on the water and started scrubbing at the pan. "Did you have a dream?"

"Yes, but it was not a memory. It was disturbing, and I woke up, but when I fell back asleep again, the dream started right back up again." She rubbed the back of her neck. "I am tired. It is not a fun feeling." She eyed Westin. She'd been waiting for a moment to discuss the next chapter of her life, but the timing never felt right. Taking a deep breath, she decided just to throw it out there.

"I have decided to pursue a relationship with Hunter Logan."

Westin stilled for the moment. "Are you asking permission?"

"No," Lia said frowning. "I am telling you that I am going to pursue a relationship with Hunter."

"And if I forbid it?"

Lia raised her eyebrows. "You have no hold on me here. I can do as I please."

"And if you kill him?"

"I am not going to kill anyone," Lia snapped. She hadn't told Westin about the episode at the hospital. She had controlled herself, and it wasn't any of his business.

Westin laughed dryly. "This shouldn't be a conversation that I have to have with a person. But I do. I have to have this conversation with you because it's only a matter of time."

"It does not help that I have to witness myself killing people. Is it supposed to disgust or arouse me?"

Her argument was met by silence. "What do you want from me?" Westin finally asked. "If it's trust, it's not there."

She rubbed her arms and wrapped them tightly around herself. "I just want a chance to live this life as much as possible before the judges decide what to do with me. I could be gone tomorrow."

"It's not like you'd remember any of it," he pointed out.

"But it makes a difference now. It makes a difference to me."

Westin sighed. He tossed down the towel and leaned against the counter, his face closed in concentration. "I'll skip the office today. We'll go out. You and me. Maybe if you appreciate life, you won't be so inclined to take it. This doesn't mean that I agree with your decision. It just means that we're going to take it one day at a time. Okay?"

She leaned against the wall and stared at him. She didn't want to spend the day with him. She wanted him to tell her the truth. He knew more than he was letting on.

"I am supposed to kill the Phoenix. That is why I have the memories. They are reminding me of who I am and what I am capable of," Lia said softly.

"We've already talked about this. Killing him gets you collected again. Without a direct order, you are not killing anyone," Westin muttered.

"If I follow orders, maybe I will not be collected," Lia pointed out.

Westin put the spatula down. "Do you want to kill?"

Lia shrank back into the counter. "I did not say that. I am merely pointing out the obvious."

"You don't have to say it. It's written all over your face. What drives you?"

"He is a killer. He deserves it."

"This is not an eye for an eye society. You can't take the lives of everyone you think deserves it. Answer my question. What drives you to kill someone?"

Lia took a deep breath, expanding her chest. He wanted the truth. She walked over to him and put a hand on his chest. "It is unnatural. I feel as though I can hear your heart beating." She moved her hand up, trailing a finger to his throat. "I see your pulse quiver at your throat. I imagine all the blood running through your veins. It is a rich bluish purple color that screams for oxygen." She took his hand and placed it on her chest. "As I imagine stopping your heart, my own picks up pace. Adrenaline shoots through me, and I feel chills and heat all at the same time. My hands shake and my skin crawls with the need to end your breath. I want to be the last person you ever see. I want to be the final touch on your skin. I need to see that moment when life escapes you."

Her hands dropped, and she stepped back. "Sometimes the need is like oxygen. To live, others must die. Sometimes it is just a passing fancy. I feel so torn. I know it is wrong, and I want to stop myself, but I simply cannot. I do not understand why I feel this way, but I am fighting it. I am trying to overcome it."

Westin swallowed hard. "We're going to spend the day people watching, starting with breakfast. Get dressed."

Westin could feel Lia staring at him over their empty plates. The local breakfast diner was crowded that morning, and the noise level had forced Westin to change his tactics. Rather than trying to have a private conversation screamed across the table, he had asked her to observe the place in silence. At first, she glared at the fellow diners. He tried to imagine what she thought as they waited for their food.

All he could see were the changes throughout the generations. As a collector, he had been able to move in and out of the veil for centuries. Collecting reapers was not a busy job. To be collected, there were a list of standards so long that not even he was aware of all the restrictions. Add that to the long serving sentence of reapers, and you have a recipe for a slow business.

He wasn't entirely sure how many collectors existed at a time. In truth, he'd only ever met one, and there were extenuating circumstances. Being bound to the one reaper who managed to escape the veil meant he saw more of the world than most collectors. He had the odd cleanup jobs that were given to him and the occasional collections between Lia's kills, but, for the most part, he drifted through life.

Time passed at odd intervals. Sometimes it moved so quickly that he felt that he was collecting Lia several times a year, and sometimes it was so slow that he felt that centuries passed before he was collecting anything at all. Somewhere along the way, it occurred to him that the judges had altered his ability to judge the passing of time. In many ways, it was a blessing.

Today, as he searched to find ways to connect Lia to life, he realized how unconnected he was himself. He couldn't remember the last time he had an honest conversation with someone. There was no one he could call a friend or even an acquaintance. Lia was his only companion, and he lied to her on a daily basis.

His abilities made it easy to enter someone's life without the effort of awkward introductions and exit someone's life without the pain of goodbye. In truth, he felt he was the worst person to teach Lia what it meant to be a person.

Still, he watched. He observed people in the passing of time. He wondered about their lives, dissected their actions, and studied their emotions. The core of humanity was the one thing that had not changed throughout the years. People strived to love and be loved. They wanted to protect and nurture, and they needed to feel important.

It was the way they went about it that had changed. Things that had once been taboo were now standard lies that passed through everyone's lips. Desperation left more and more marks as generations passed. Time was marching on, and still no one knew their purpose in life.

While Lia could only observe the masks of the customers, Westin was able to touch their minds. At first he was gentle. On the surface was a flurry of activity. They stressed over daily activities, suffered financial concerns, felt guilt over past events and anxiety over the future. The deeper he went, the less activity he found. The core was all the same. Were they doing the right things? Were they loved? Were they making a difference?

He pulled away from them and studied Lia. He wanted to touch her mind, to see what was at the core. His time with her was brief. Collections took only minutes. He was told of her motivations before and knew of details after, but the physical connection was short. Now there were no restrictions holding him back. He knew there would be no consequences if he delved into her mind, but fear held him back. He'd touched minds that were dark. Part of him was afraid that Lia's mind would leave him gasping for breath. She was different. He could already tell that there was a darkness inside of her that was unknown to anyone else.

Except Charlie. He, no doubt, understood Lia's darkness.

After breakfast, they broke through the madness and walked outside. Safely inside the privacy of the car, he rolled down the windows but made no move to put the car into drive.

"What did you see?" he asked her quietly.

"People eating," she answered simply. She had turned her head, and he could not read her face.

"Go deeper. Tell me what you saw when you looked at them. If their lives mean so little to you, there must be a reason."

"I saw chaos. I saw gluttony. I saw selfish desires and self-loathing. There is no discipline in people and even less respect for others. I sat in a crowded restaurant with people practically in my lap, and I do not think the first person saw me. They do not see predators. They do not see victims. They see only themselves."

She did not turn her head or raise her voice. Westin turned the key. "Where are we going now?" she asked.

"Somewhere where you can visit naked human emotion."

Westin drove the twenty minutes to their destination in silence. Lia's face showed no emotion until after they entered the building. Even then, it was only skepticism.

"An art museum? You want me to look at pretty pictures?"

He took her by the elbow and led her to an empty corner. "Art is a physical form of human emotion. Its creators use canvas and clay and any materials on hand to mold their feelings. You're not supposed to look at it and see a pretty picture. You're expected to look at it and examine how it moves you. I want you to look at it and wonder what inspired the artist to create the pieces. It's a place of internal reflection, so evaluate in silence. We'll talk after the tour. Okay?"

She gave him a dubious look but kept silent as she began the tour. Having little interest in the pieces himself, Westin let his mind wander as he strolled through the crowd. He thought back to his predicament with Charlie. He knew she wouldn't take the news lightly. He'd spent weeks lying to her, but he'd spent years lying to himself.

He would have to tell her the truth soon. There was no way around it. Charlie would soon be reaching out, and if Lia killed him, the consequences would be final. It was no longer the question of how Westin would tell her, but when. He owed her the truth.

He felt a tug in his brain. The judges were reaching out.

The threat is still not neutralized. We require immediate action.

Perhaps it was a blessing that they were not omniscient. He formed the answer with his mind. *The threat has not shown itself. We need more information.*

Make sure she is ready.

This angered Westin. *Ready her to kill so that you can collect her?*

Do you pity her, collector?

Westin shook his head in frustration. *She is not to be pitied, but this is not entirely her fault.*

She is your fault.

But you can set her free.

There was no answer in return, only the throbbing of his head. Communicating with the judges drained him. He took a moment to slump against the wall while he regained his equilibrium.

Lia was already a few displays ahead of him, and she didn't notice his setback. He watched her a few moments while his energy returned. Finally, he pushed himself off the wall to catch up with her. She turned to face him. "I have seen everything that I need to see. I would like to go now."

Westin massaged his temples. "I need some fresh air. We can talk at the park."

"I am hungry."

He stared at her. "You just had breakfast a few hours ago," he pointed out.

She shrugged. "Trying to understand humanity is exhausting."

He nodded. She spoke the truth. "I'll pick you up something from a vendor. Let's go."

Westin purchased two hot dogs and walked over to the bench where Lia was watching everyone. A breeze swayed the trees and ruffled his hair. Many had come out to try and fly kites, picnic, read, and throw Frisbees. People of all ages were out strolling, holding hands, and playing. No one looked twice at them, which is exactly why Westin picked it.

"It's a hot dog," he explained as he handed her the item. "You probably don't want to know what is inside, but it tastes good."

She watched as he took his first bite and mimicked him. Her face lit up with delight. "It is delicious," she said, her mouth full.

He sat down and watched her for a moment. "What did you see in the art museum?"

"Pain and suffering." She swallowed her mouthful. She pointed to the people around her. "Look around us. These people are not involved in anything except the minuscule square footage around them. That museum held nothing but the inner scars of people. They have nothing to live for, so why should they live?"

Westin leaned his head back. Part of him agreed with her, but it wasn't the message he was trying to teach. He needed to change tactics.

"Why do you not kill people," he asked.

She took another bite of her hotdog. "What?" she asked, muffled.

"When you are with Hunter, alone, what makes you pass up the opportunity? You certainly decide to not kill people more than you decide to kill people. What makes you choose between who lives and dies?"

She thought for a moment. "Part of me feels like a judge. I see the evil in people; I see their selfish lives or actions, and I know that I must put an end to it. It is not the most important part, but it is how I see the difference between life and death. I feel that I need to kill, and I look for those who deserve it."

"You are not a judge of souls," he reminded her. "Besides, you have killed people who didn't deserve it."

She whipped her head around. "I do not know what you want from me. I am trying to be a good person."

"It doesn't matter what you try to be. It only matters what you are. If I let you go out in the world and be alone with people, I don't want you to try to not kill them. I want you to not kill them. It's a big difference."

"There are people I like," she said softly.

"That's not the point. You don't know anything about connections. I need you to understand your own humanity so that you can connect with others."

She studied him, those dark eyes piercing into him. "You think there is humanity left in me?"

"The tug that you feel between good and evil, the butterflies in your stomach before you see Hunter, the desire to learn new things are proof of the humanity in you."

"Humanity without a soul?"

Westin looked away for a moment. "Humanity is not all about your soul. Your soul may dictate your desires, but your will dictates your strength. If your will is strong, it can overcome anything. If your will is weak, it becomes submissive to your soul, or your lack of soul."

She touched her chest. "I feel incomplete."

"You need to be strong. You may never be complete again," he said honestly.

What he didn't mention was that it was his fault. If she did not become whole again soon, she would die.

Chapter Sixteen

The tavern had closed an hour and a half ago. After finishing her work, Lia tapped her feet in frustration as her last table still sat. Her mind wandered from the emotionally draining day with Westin to the upcoming events of this weekend. Hunter had invited her to the state fair.

She had told herself that a few hours alone with Hunter would be easy, but as the time drew near, she felt a stronger pull towards something she still couldn't explain. While at the art museum, she had seen an obsession with death and life. Her cravings didn't seem so odd after the insane ride through the core of humanity. The only difference was they fantasized while she followed through, but she couldn't tell Westin.

Each day that passed pulled her deeper and deeper into a twisted past life that centered on her lust for blood. Each hour pulled her closer to the cravings of a killer, and each moment made her weaker. She wasn't even sure that she could keep her hands clean this weekend, but her desire to see a different part of life was stronger than her common sense.

With her mind made up, she glanced at the clock. The table had finished eating and paid their tab a while ago. Enough was enough. "Is there something else you wanted?" she blatantly asked.

"We're fine, thank you," the man said.

Lia's eyes narrowed. "Good. We have been closed for thirty minutes. If there is nothing else you need, kindly exit the building." She was taking pains to be more polite to the guests per

Karen's request.

She watched as their jaws dropped. "You were aware that we were closed, no?"

"Yes, but we aren't finished. We'll be leaving in a few moments," the woman responded. She had sharp features that tightened in anger at the implication Lia was imposing on her.

"I have no doubt that you can finish up your conversation at a later point, or on the telephone, or perhaps through email. Your desire to communicate face to face is admirable in this age of technology, but this venue is closed. We would appreciate it if you no longer wasted our time by forcing us to stay here while you finish your conversation. I am sure you have a life to carry on. Please do not forget that we do as well." Lia remained calm, trying to keep her temper in check.

"We would like to speak to your manager," she woman said frostily.

Lia nodded. "Would you like to waste his time as well? I will be right back."

As she went to fetch Andy, she could hear the guests talking about her nerve. She found him in the office frowning over the money on the desk. She knocked lightly on the door before opening it.

"Andy? There is a table that would like to speak to you."

He sighed and rubbed the bridge of his nose. "What did you say to them, Lia?"

"I asked them if they needed anything. They said no. They have finished eating, and they have paid. I asked them to leave."

He nodded. "What were your exact words?"

"I told them they should continue their conversation elsewhere and stop wasting our time."

His jaw hung open just a bit, but then he just shrugged. "I was polite," Lia pointed out. "I used words like kindly and appreciate."

"I am sure you did, Lia. I'll go talk to them." He frowned at this money. "I could use a break." He left the office, locking the door behind him. Lia followed along behind.

"Good evening. I hope your food was to your liking," he started, but the guests cut him off.

"Your waitress is practically kicking us out the door. I demand an explanation for hiring such rude wait staff," the woman said.

"I apologize if she sounded brash. I would be more than happy to offer a complimentary drink on your next visit," Andy said, bowing slightly.

"Rest assured, I will not be coming back to this establishment if you insist on hiring such rude servers."

"Ma'am, I believe Lia was merely pointing out that we have provided you with as much service as we can for the day. Our business hours are over," Andy said.

An angry red blotched the woman's cheeks. "Excuse me? I am a paying customer! I will stay as long as I see fit! I would like the contact information of the owner."

"I am the owner. Andy Owens, at your service." He reached into his pocket and handed her a business card. "Once again, I apologize if my server seemed rude. I am sorry that you have decided not to come back, but if that is the case, you are no longer a patron of this establishment, and I would like you to leave. While I put customers first, my employment staff needs to be treated with respect. Respecting our business hours respects her and me. Any questions?"

Lia smiled inwardly. Andy and Karen were far more protective of their staff than they were of their reputation. In turn, this usually produced clientele that were pleasant and respectful. They had a few conversations with Lia about her blunt nature, although she still wasn't sure what that meant, but they seemed to appreciate her logic.

"Of all the nerve," the woman jumped up from the table. "You better believe that not a single pleasant word will leave my mouth about this restaurant," she threatened and stalked off.

Her companion stood as well. "I am sorry that we were here so late. I'm also sorry about my associate's outburst. I enjoyed the food and the service. Thank you," he muttered, obviously embarrassed, and raced after her.

Andy turned to Lia. "Finish cleaning the table and head home. You have the weekend off, correct?"

Lia nodded. "Hunter is taking me to the state fair," she said, surprised about the excitement in her voice.

Andy smiled. "We'll see you on Monday."

As she cleaned the table, she found herself daydreaming about the events to come. When she made her way to Westin's waiting car, her vision blurred. She tried to focus on putting one foot in front of the other, but her stance began to wobble. She became disoriented, dizzy, and as she fought to find her balance, she dropped to the pavement, unconscious.

The temperature dropped, and Lia shivered. She dug her toes into the gravel. They bit into her skin, and she winced. In the silence of the false scene before her, something tugged at her memory. She had been here before. She looked to the left to the figure struggling in the violent waters. The wind ripped the trees from the roots and toppled them over. In front of her stood the tall blurry man.

Lia glanced furtively at the figure. Catching her breath, she turned and began to run swiftly in the opposite direction. Within seconds, she tripped and fell, tumbling down the bank. She moaned and gripped her arm. Pain ricocheted up her arm, into her shoulder, and through her neck. The river splashed on her, and she turned her head, staring at the figure that struggled unsuccessfully against the deadly waters. For a reason she could not fathom, she wanted to save them.

"Help them," she whispered.

"I cannot," the voices replied, floating towards her.

"Will they die?" She watched as her blood curled slowly into the water.

"That is up to you."

"*You said I could not change the past. How can it be up to me?*"

"*You must surrender to who you are.*"

She moaned with the pain and turned her back to the river, folding into a fetal position. "*I do not want to do this anymore. Please just leave me alone. I am happy where I am.*"

"*How do you know what happiness is?*"

"*I am connecting with people. That is what I am supposed to do to be happy.*"

"*You will never find true happiness until you come to terms with the person that you are. Without that, you will never find peace,*" the voices said.

She turned her head and stared at him. Finally, with her good arm, she reached up and touched him. She welcomed the pain and the darkness, anything to escape the figure that haunted her in the water.

She stood in the middle of a battlefield. The smoke was clearing, and bodies littered the ground. She walked across, trailing their blood across the field. They moaned, reaching up to her for help. For a moment, she wondered if they could see her. She looked at them impassively. She could not help them.

With each step, she moved until she reached the end of the field. There her image stood over a body. He was still alive, missing a leg, bleeding and gasping. Her reflection knelt next to him and cupped his chin. "*You will live,*" she said.

She trailed her hand down his body. With a smile, she pressed against his wound. He screamed. "*I should let you. It could be a wretched life for you. But somehow, I do not think that is the person I am.*" The memory of Lia tilted her head. "*Do you know the person that you are? I do. You are the person who kills your own company. You hide behind the veil of war. It is okay. I hide behind the false lies of justice.*" She whipped out her knife and sunk it into his stomach.

Lia watched as her reflection stood and faced her. The dream began to blur. "*Surrender to who you are,*" the image said in a thousand voices.

Lia shook her head. "*Stop. I just want the truth,*" she said. She looked down at the soldier. His image blurred until he wore Hunter's face.

"*No. No!*" She screamed over and over. Something was wrong. Someone was watching her, manipulating her. Someone else was in her mind. She ran,

searching the faces of the dead, trying to uncover the truth. She tripped and fell.
Down. Down. Down.

Westin pulled her up from the parking lot. Lia steadied herself against him. She blinked and took note of her surroundings. Everything was real.

She looked at Westin. Her voice was clear and calm. "Someone is playing with me."

"What are you talking about?" he asked gruffly.

She took a deep breath trying to collect her thoughts. Even as she attempted to focus on the details, they faded from her memories. "I am not sure. It felt as though someone else was there."

"The killer?" Westin asked, walking her towards the car, one hand gently steadying her as she stumbled.

"No. It was someone with power. It was real. I do not doubt that. It just seemed layered," she finished lamely. The dream was already fading from her mind. She shook her head, frustrated. "I do not know what I mean."

He folded her up into the car, reaching over to buckle her in. She stared at him. "There is more to me that just a killer. You know that, right?"

Westin stared at her for a long moment. He snapped the buckle and pulled away. "I don't know what to think when it comes to you," he finally muttered before closing the door.

She stared out the window as he started the car. There was something she should be remembering. It was right on the edge of her mind but always flitted out of reach when she tried to recall it. It was important, but she couldn't remember why.

With a sigh, she closed her eyes. The gentle rumbling of the car lulled her into a shallow sleep.

The next afternoon, Westin eyed her from the doorframe as Lia stared at herself in the mirror. She ignored him and smoothed her hands down her body, feeling the fabric of her dress under her fingertips. "How do I look?" she asked.

"I don't want you to go on this date," he said for the hundredth time.

"And I don't want to live under your thumb," she pointed out mildly. "I guess neither one of us are getting what we want."

She'd settled on the green cotton sundress dress. While it looked casual on the hanger, it told a different story on her body. It stretched out across her body, wrapped intimately around her figure, rode dangerously up her thigh, and cut low across her chest. There was no denying what she wanted, and she intended to have it. Tonight.

"I could deny you," Westin said roughly.

"Give me one good reason I should not go out today," she challenged him. He made it seem personal, and she wanted to know why. "Do you want me for yourself?"

He chuckled dryly. "No, Lia, I have absolutely no interest in you." She'd already known that, but she was taunting him. She was fired up and wanted him to break.

"Then what? Feeling tense? There are quite a few girls that I work with who would be glad to help you relieve some of that stress," she continued.

"Don't you understand what's at stake here? Do you have feelings for this man? How are you going to feel when he's bleeding to death at your feet? How are you going to feel when you push your blade into his abdomen? Or is that the final goal? You seduce to kill. Do you enjoy it?" His voice was calm, even, but his words were dark.

She trembled under his stare. Was he right? There was no denying that she wanted Hunter, but what exactly did she want him for?

"If you are so worried, then come with us," she said coldly.

Westin raised his eyebrows. "You told me to stay back," he pointed out. "That's why we're having this argument."

"And now I am telling you to do whatever you want," she snapped angrily. She whirled around to face him. "If you do not trust me, then come with me."

He smirked. "You are not dressed for activities that I wish to witness. If you are concerned, you should cancel the date. Tell me, Lia, are you concerned?"

"No, I am not concerned," she muttered.

"So you don't rake your nails across his skin and wonder what it would be like to have his blood under them? You don't feel his pulse and wonder what it would be like if it stilled under your control?" He moved closer to her, brushed his lips over her ears. "You said you crave life. He is life. How much control do you have?"

She swatted him away. "Stop it. Are you trying to lure me into killing him? Would it make your life easier if I went away?"

"Infinitely easier. But I don't even come close to the seduction of your desires. If I make you concerned, how are you going to feel alone with him?" Westin pointed out.

She turned and faced herself in the mirror again. She had this. She was in control. She wasn't going to hide anymore. She needed to experience life, and Westin was right. Hunter was life.

"We will be in public. There is nothing to worry about," she said confidently.

"You've killed in public before. And also," his eyes traveled up and down her body. "I have a feeling you won't be staying in public."

The doorbell rang. He smiled at her in the mirror. "I won't forbid you. This is your decision. But I don't believe for one second that this situation is going to end well for you. Know that." He left the room.

She could hear him opening the door for Hunter. Their voices were low. She crept to the doorframe hoping to catch a bit of their conversation, but their words were muffled.

She bit her lip and closed her eyes. He was right. She had

very little control around Hunter, and the chances were excellent that this wouldn't end up well. But she was drawn to him, and she wanted to know why.

She ran her fingers through her hair and straightened her shoulders. With an air of confidence that she didn't feel, she made her way down the steps.

Hunter shifted from foot to foot as the agent stared at him. The man in front of him eyed him with pity, but the hostility was unmistakable. Hunter couldn't deny the agent was intimidating, but he wasn't about to give up any ground. He wasn't trained that way.

"This is not an ideal situation," the agent said grimly. "There is real danger here."

Hunter nodded. "I'm not a stranger to dangerous situations,"

The agent, Westin, raised his eyebrows. "You've seen violence," he said after appraising him. "I can see it in your eyes."

Hunter clenched his teeth. "I have. I would prefer it if I never saw it again, but I am not walking into this lightly."

The agent laughed. "You have no idea. I thought you were a doctor, but you have soldier written all over you. I should have seen it before. You hide it well."

Who was this guy? "I am a doctor. I have served, but that's all behind me. I'm surprised. I would have thought the bodyguard would have run a background check on me," he said coldly.

The agent smiled. "Dr. Hunter Carter Logan. It must have been interesting growing up with three first names. Served for five years in the army. Discharged honorably after two tours. Suffered from PTSD. Drank too much and got into many fights, but you managed to get your shit together. You were at the hospital during almost every single local attack. You're a workaholic, but you have a strong alibi. If I had thought for a single second that you were a suspect, you would not be standing at this door. So you abhor violence? And yet you want to date the amnesiac target of a serial killer. It sounds complicated."

Hunter cocked his head. "I'm sorry. You speak like a man who has an invested interest in the lady."

The agent nodded. "I take my job seriously." He reached around and pulled out an automatic handgun. "This is to stay with you at all times. Be aware. Do you understand?"

The gun felt heavy in his hands. "I don't have a permit," he said as he gripped the handle. It was familiar, achingly so. He wanted nothing more than to give it back, but he had a feeling that the gun came with the girl. No exceptions.

"You let me worry about that. I like you, Hunter. You better not be the reason I fuck up this job."

"Sorry I'm late," Lia called out from the steps. Hunter moved the gun behind him, but he knew she'd already seen it. Her eyes flickered to Westin. "Is there a reason he's carrying a gun?" she asked lightly as she made her way down.

"It's for protection," he said smoothly.

"For my protection?" she asked mockingly. Hunter frowned. Clearly something was going on here.

"I want everyone to be safe tonight," the agent responded evenly.

Hunter cleared his throat. "You look amazing," he said honestly. She wore a simple green dress that looked tailor made for her body. She'd swept her hair to one side, exposing her neck. Her skin was creamy and flushed with excitement. Desire stirred in him.

She smiled as if she was enjoying the effect she had on him. What happened to the girl who seemed so innocent and fresh? This was a woman who knew what she wanted.

He loved it.

"Thank you. I am not sure what you wear to the fair. You would tell me if I were overdressed, right?" she asked teasingly.

"It's perfect," he said hoarsely. He frowned and cleared his throat. "Sorry."

"You will stay in the public eye. If anything suspicious happens, and I mean anything, you call me right away. I've requested to have the local police patrol the area. You call me when you leave. You come straight home. Questions?" Westin asked.

Lia leaned over and whispered something in his ear. He frowned. "Just call me," he muttered. She smiled.

"I am excited," she said, a bright smile lighting up her face. Hunter couldn't help but smile as well.

He nodded to the agent and reached out to take her hand. He'd been denying himself this moment since he'd first met her. He wanted to enjoy every minute of it. "What did you tell him," he asked curiously as he opened the car door for her.

She shot him a mischievous grin. "I asked if I had to come home alone."

"I see," he murmured. He shut the door and walked around to the other side. "Agent Caxton seems to have an invested interest in you," he commented.

"It is his job," she muttered, snapping her seat belt.

Hunter started the car, and it sat idling in the driveway. She looked at him in puzzlement. "Is there something wrong?"

"You seem to have an invested interest in him as well," he said, without looking at her.

"Oh," she said softly. "I feel, sometimes, that he is my one connection to the world. He provides help and answers. He is the one constant in my life." Her eyes widened a bit as she stumbled over her words. "What I mean to say is he is my new life. I do not have any romantic interest in him nor he with me."

Hunter turned to look at her. "It sounds complicated. I get that I may have competition with someone when your memories return. I need to know that I don't have competition now. If I haven't made myself clear before, let me be clear now. You are not a passing amusement for me. I hope you feel the same way."

"I am taking things one day at a time, but so far, I have

found nothing in this life that serves as a passing amusement," she said quietly. He frowned. Her words were hesitant. Still, he felt that he couldn't ask for too much.

As they drove, he pointed out landmarks and pulled over several times for her to take pictures. The mountains remained a constant companion as they made their way south. At times, she was so absorbed in the scenery that she fell silent. Other times, she was a bundle of questions. He answered all of them patiently. The hour-long drive flew by. He loved every minute of it, but he couldn't shake the feeling that there was this void between them. Maybe it was her amnesia. He tried not to dwell on it.

As they pulled up to the event, he smiled at her. "All right, let's see how you feel about nauseating rides, livestock, and tons of sugar and fried foods."

Her brows knitted in puzzlement, but she jumped out of the car with excitement. Already they could hear music coming from under the tents in the distance. She saw crowds of people milling around, and heard laughter rising from the groups. She followed the sound, a few steps ahead of Hunter.

He quickened his steps and wrapped his arms around her from behind. "Whoa," he said softly. "I know you're excited, but you need to make sure you don't lose me. You're more responsibility than an average date you know."

She stiffened under his touch but relaxed the muscles in her hand as he captured it. It molded softly with his. He ran his thumb across her skin. "I'm not complaining," he whispered.

"I am excited," she said smiling. "I will do better."

He pulled his hand away. "Hang on a second," he muttered, adjusting the gun beneath his shirt. She frowned.

"You seem comfortable with that," she said quietly.

"I wish it were not the case," he said shortly. He didn't like talking about it.

As they closed in on the festivities, he pushed the thought out of his mind. He studied her carefully. She seemed enamored with the colors and the lights, and she laughed at the characters and the children. She ran her fingers along every surface. He touched her waist lightly and whispered in her ear. "Tell me what you see."

"So much joy," she murmured back. "Everything imaginable is thrown together in such a small spot. It is almost nauseating, but do not think I have ever seen anything like it. It is beautiful." A laugh escaped her as Hunter pulled her close for a dance on the lawn. It was one of those synchronized dances and while most of the people were stumbling and playing, Lia found herself picking up on the moves easily. He found himself following her lead.

She spun and twirled and laughed. "You are really good at this," Hunter laughed. "I've always been a terrible dancer," he said even though he had no problems keeping up with her.

She reached over and kissed him. He stilled in the middle of the dance, embracing her and letting the world melt away.

"Come on, the song is not over yet," she said as she broke away and danced around him. He shook his head and took her back into his arms as they flowed into the circles with the other dancers.

The time flew by, and before too long, the sun was setting and the fair was coming alive, bathed in lights and shadows.

Lia was exhausted, but couldn't even begin to make herself leave. It was still strange to her, this weary feeling that overtook her body. Adrenaline kept her going. It wasn't from the thrill of a chase or blood. She couldn't put her finger on it, but it wasn't a singular thing. The feeling coursed through her body, animated her, and kept her alive for the evening.

Everything was easy. It was easy to smile and laugh. It was easy to touch Hunter and let him touch her. She felt, for the first time, that she might have a place here, on this earth. In his arms? She didn't dare entertain that though. One minute, one step at a time. That was all she could do, all she dared to hope for.

When the sun went down, the fair was in full swing. She'd tentatively touched the animals. They hadn't shied away from her or barked violently at her. To them, she was no different than anyone else. She either had food or she didn't. It was refreshing. She'd let the sugary stickiness of cotton candy dance on her tongue and attempted fried Oreos and fried bananas. They nearly came back up again on the spinning contraptions. She'd watched fascinated as people drove dirty, beat-up cars around, crashing into each other. She'd tossed rings onto bowling pins and raced tiny toy cars around a track. She'd let someone paint a butterfly on her cheek, and she danced and danced until she thought for sure she'd never be able to walk again. And then she made Hunter do it all again.

When Hunter left to find them some water, she wandered around the tents and gift shops. She ducked into a yellow and green tent. Many of the tents were open and inviting, but this one was completely closed. She had to search for the opening before she entered. Very little light escaped through the cracks, and candlelight sparkled off racks of jewelry. She caught her breath at the beauty. There was no one in the tent except a young woman. Freckles spotted across her nose, and her red hair fell in curls over her shoulders. She watched Lia intensely with one blue and one green eye.

Lia passed a glance at the woman and shuffled through the racks of pendants. None of them were the same. Odd symbols were painted on the front or imprinted on the back of each charm, and they hung on heavy, dark, iron chains. The lights reflected off the precious metals as she flipped through them until her hand stilled. In the middle of the rack was a small, slender silver chain with a large round metal pendant featuring two halves blending with a scripted symbol on each half. The pendant warmed in her hand.

"It's the symbol for duality: good and evil, mortality and immortality, male and female, night and day, and so forth." The woman moved to her side and stared at her. "Do you like it?"

Lia nodded. She felt a connection to the piece. "What do the symbols mean?" she asked. At first glance, they resembled Chinese lettering, but as she studied it, she thought they resembled a crude drawing of an eye. The bottom symbol was a line intersecting two parallel lines. Two smaller figures stood on each side of the lines, and a V hovered over the symbol.

The woman frowned. "My grandmother used to have these dreams riddled with symbols. I never knew her, and my mother never talked about it, but my grandmother used to sketch them. These are the two dominant ones. She drew them over and over again. I found them pretty." She shrugged nonchalantly, but her eyes were intense as she watched Lia finger the pendant.

"There you are! Are you trying to give me a heart attack?" Hunter approached her, and she dropped the necklace.

"Sorry. I can't stand still for long." She looked up and smiled. "Next tent?"

He nodded. "Fine, but no more wandering away."

The woman's eyes widened. "You don't wish to purchase the necklace?"

Lia smiled. "It is beautiful, but I think I will pass." The words were difficult to say, but she had no money with her. The woman nodded and drew back into the shadows, letting Lia and Hunter exit the tent.

Hunter passed her the water bottle. "You ready for the Ferris wheel? You're going to love looking at all the lights."

She nodded eagerly. He smiled. "Okay, the line seems pretty long. Go ahead and grab a spot. I've got a craving for some nachos. Are you hungry?"

Hungry? Her eyes widened. "I do not think I will be able to eat anything ever again," she said truthfully.

He laughed and kissed her on her forehead. "I'll be right back," he promised. "The line is right over there, so I'll have my eyes on you the whole time. Do not leave it."

She shook her head. He had taken Westin's warning about leaving her alone very seriously. "I am fine. Go on."

She took her place in line and wrapped her arms around herself. There was a chill in the air, but it wasn't like across the veil. She welcomed the chill. It made her feel breathless and alive all at the same time.

Hunter had joined her just moments before they climbed into the cart. He dipped a chip into the nacho cheese and held it in front of her. Laughing, she reached over and bit the chip. The spicy cheese slid down her tongue, but it tasted artificial and thick. She scrunched up her nose, and he laughed. "Fair food is something that can only be enjoyed once a year."

The wheel started, and she slipped her hand on his leg as she looked out over the edge. He had been right. The lights were breathtaking. They surrounded all the rides and lined the fair in multiple colors. For a moment, they looked like small souls dotting the silhouette of the festivities. She caught her breath.

He leaned over and nuzzled her ear. "Was it worth the wait?" he asked. She'd been begging to go on the Ferris wheel all night.

She nodded. He had no idea how long she had waited for something like this. She swallowed hard. Deep down, she wondered if she would even remember this moment.

By the end of the day she was both exhausted and renewed with energy. They left the festival hand in hand. "Did you like it?" Hunter asked.

She leaned against him while they walked to the car. "I think it is the best day I have had so far," she said honestly.

She napped during most of the ride back, her energy sapped. He nudged her gently when they pulled into the driveway, and she woke instantly. Hunter walked her to the door.

"I got something for you," Hunter said in a low voice. He stood behind her and draped something across her neck. She could see the reflection in the windows, but from the weight of the pendant against her cleavage and the warmth of the metal as it hit her skin, she knew it was the yin-yang charm from the tent. "I saw you eyeing it in the tent. I thought you might like it."

She didn't say anything as she turned and pressed her lips to his. She slipped her hand under his shirt, making her intentions know as she trailed her fingers along his skin. His muscles trembled under her touch.

"Lia," he whispered reaching up to capture her hands. "I can't even begin to tell you how badly I want to come inside, but I can't tonight."

Startled, she stepped back. Was he rejecting her?

He followed her step and pulled her back close to him. "Don't pull away. Just listen. I need more time. I need to know that I've given you more time. There is so much going on, and I need to know that you are sure about being with me. Okay?"

She rested her head on his chest. He was sweet. It almost made her angry. Taking a deep breath, she nodded. "I understand."

He lifted her face to his and kissed her gently. "I will see you soon. Now get inside before I change my mind, and before Agent Caxton comes out and shoots me." He reached around and removed the gun, pressing it into her hands.

It was heavy. She had no doubt that Westin had given it to Hunter to protect him from her. It was unnatural in her hands, but power coursed through her as she held it.

Trembling, she shoved the key into the door and pushed through the doorway, shakily placing the gun on the side table. It almost mocked her.

Turning her back, she flew up the stairs and closed as many doors as she could along the way, trying to create as many boundaries as possible between herself and the instrument of death.

Chapter Seventeen

Luke glanced up from the kitchen to see that the hostesses were seating another table. He frowned. It was late, and he was hoping he'd be cut soon so that he could go home, but he needed the money. Once the guests sat, he made his way over to the table.

"Good evening, folks. My name is Luke. Welcome to West Philadelphia's Grill. Can I get you something to drink?" he asked.

He'd only been working at the grill for a few months. Before this job, he'd worked behind the scenes at a local pizza place. The economy was difficult for a literature major. The flow of cash was okay, but it was hardly the intellectually stimulating job he'd hoped for.

He went through the motions as the night winded down. The biggest problem he had with waiting tables was the monotony. Although they occasionally cracked jokes, few guests were funny. His life had become boring. And fuck was he poor.

He finished up his side-work as his guests finished their food. While he waited for them to cash out, he helped his friend wipe down the server alley.

"So table ninety-seven is weird," Jeff commented.

Table ninety-seven was next to Luke's section. He glanced around the corner and saw the man Jeff was discussing. He looked like he was staring at Luke, but with his baseball cap pulled so low over his face, Luke couldn't be sure.

"Why do you say that?" Luke asked.

"He ordered a plate of fries and didn't eat them. He paid out nearly two hours ago, but he won't leave. He hasn't even touched his water."

"Dude, that is strange," Luke agreed.

"You coming out tonight to watch the band play?"

"If I ever get out of here," Luke responded wryly. "Are you leaving now? You still have a table."

"The closer agreed to clean it for me. I've got to shower and change. I smell like fried onion rings and scotch."

"I didn't want to say anything, but you really do," Luke said, scrunching up his nose. He pushed his black-framed glasses higher up on his nose.

"Fuck you. I'll see you in a bit?"

"I'll call you when I get out."

He only had to wait a few more minutes before his table finally paid out. After picking up his tips, he tossed on his brightly colored knit beanie and pulled the hood of his gray sweatshirt over it, and left the monotony behind. Outside, he took a deep breath of the slightly chilled air. For a brief moment, he felt alive. As he pulled out his phone to text Jeff, he noticed the customer from ninety-seven bent over the opened hood of his Jeep.

"Sir? Sir? Do you have any jumper cables?"

Luke looked around him at first before ambling his way over to the man. "Sorry bro, I don't."

The man nodded. "It was worth a shot. Any chance the restaurant would let me borrow a phone?"

Luke held out his cell phone. "I'm not sure. Just use mine," he volunteered.

The man took it and walked over to the hood of the car, and Luke followed, unwilling to lose sight of his phone. "Thanks. You know anything about cars?" He gestured to the engine. "It just sputtered and died. I'm hoping it's the battery. Will tow trucks come out and charge your battery? Or give you a jump?"

Luke didn't know anything about cars, but he moved towards the Jeep. He was so focused on the vehicle that he didn't notice when the man walked behind him and placed a rag over his mouth.

He instinctively gripped the man's wrists, panic washing over him. It was only a moment before the odd aroma overpowered him, and he blacked out.

Charlie dragged the body around and shoved it in the backseat. After wrapping zip ties around the kid's arms and ankles, he threw a blanket over him and quickly shut the door and the hood. He glanced around before sliding in the driver seat.

No one was around. No one saw a thing. Once again, everything was going smoothly.

The boy didn't make a peep as Charlie drove home, but he frowned as he pulled in the drive. Connor's car was in the driveway next to him. The kid was obnoxiously desperate for attention, and Charlie had no way of knowing if the kid was looking out his window, ready to pounce. Of course, he was usually too busy with a girl to notice much.

He stayed in the car and tapped his fingers. The waiter should be out cold for a few more hours, but Charlie didn't want to chance it and have the boy wake up still in the vehicle. He got out the car and slammed the door shut waiting to see if Connor would come out and greet him.

No one came. He walked across the yard and knocked on the door. Connor opened the door in his boxer shorts, his hair rumpled in a mess. The kid looked awful. His usually pale face was splotchy red, and his eyes were watering. Charlie raised his eyebrows. "You okay, Connor?"

The Irishman nodded and wiped his nose. "I think I got a wicked bad dose," he muttered. "I feel awful." Charlie stared at him. "Cold," Connor explained. "I think I've got a cold."

"I'm sorry. I tell you what, I'll come back another time. You should get some sleep."

Connor frowned. "Did ya need somethin'?" he asked nasally.

"Not really. I was going to see if you wanted to go out and watch the Rockies game with me tomorrow," he lied easily.

The kid shook his head. "I have class until eight and then a bunch of homework. I should probably stay in."

Charlie turned to go, but he felt some pity for the kid. "Do you need me to make a run and get your any medicine or soup?" he asked.

"No, I picked some stuff up on the way home today. I already took some Nyquil. I'll probably just finish this movie and hit the scratcher." He smiled. "I appreciate the offer."

"Relax and feel better," Charlie said, his mind working. He could see the television on in the living room. If he moved quickly, he could probably get the body into the house before Connor could make it to his window.

When the door closed, Charlie made his way back to the car. The moon hung low that night, hiding behind a row of trees. With no cars passing by, he worked quickly under the cover of night.

The kid stayed knocked out until Charlie got him into the bedroom and tied him to a chair. He pulled up another chair and relaxed. As much of a nuisance as Connor made of himself, Charlie had to admit that he enjoyed their social gatherings. It had been a long time since Charlie had been able just to talk with someone. Talking to himself made him feel a little mad, and talking to his victims garnered little feedback.

Finally, the kid started muttering, rolled his head around, pulled at the ropes, and instantly came awake.

His eyes widened and rounded while he took in Charlie. "What the hell is going on?"

"Luke, Luke, Luke. You have no idea how perfect you are for the role you are about to play." Charlie jumped up and started to pace. "Normally, I take the scene to the person, but this is special. I mean she walked onto a battlefield. Canons were still exploding, and blood was still spilling, but she braved it all just to take his life. She is so amazing, and that means that this has to be perfect."

He stopped pacing for a moment and patted Luke's head. "I

just don't know how I'm going to do it yet. An explosion calls attention, and I don't need any attention, but a bone saw is simply too mundane. I need to give it some thought. I wasn't ready for you yet, but you just walked into my life, and Luke, you are perfect."

Luke struggled against his restraints. "What are you talking about? Why, exactly, do you need an explosion?"

"Oh," Charlie waved his hand. "I need to blow off your leg before I kill you."

"Would it help at all...," Luke swallowed hard. "Would it help if I asked you not to kill me? I'm attached to my leg, to all my limbs, just to be clear. And for the record, I'm pretty attached to my life as well."

"It's for a purpose. It's for her. She is so special. I need her to understand how special she is. You know how it is."

"I don't think I've ever met a woman that I needed to kill for," Luke said hesitantly.

Charlie smiled. The kid was taking it all in stride. He liked that. "You will! Well, in this case, you won't, but my point is that she out there, and you would do the same in my shoes."

"Oh God," Luke muttered. He pulled harder.

"Relax. I want you to be comfortable while you are here. It may take some time for me to figure this task out." Charlie reached behind him and checked to make sure the knots were sound. So far, they weren't giving an inch.

Having the kid here gave him a sense of excitement. His adrenaline was pumping, and he skipped about the room.

He whirled around, and instantly he felt the room change. "Here we go again," he said, sitting down. The first few dreams and visions had caught him off guard, but now he could feel his body change. It started deep within him, weak at first, but growing stronger. It was a call that he felt compelled to answer.

He assumed a meditation stance and waited.

It was dusk. There were horses and people milling about, laughter as children chased each other. He watched the street ripple, and Lia stumbled through a portal.

She hit the stones laid out across the bank and fell to her knees. The children screamed and ran, the words devil and witch carried in their wake. The adults looked at each other and edged away from her. Charlie smiled.

Lia looked around wildly. "Where am I?" she demanded. "Where am I?"

The shouting began all at once. The words ran into each other, indiscernible but angry. A horde advanced on Lia.

She scrambled back and made it to her feet. "Wait, wait," she said.

One of the men reached her, grabbing at her skirts. It tore, and she fell again. She reached for a rock and turned, hitting him upside the head with it.

The crowd stopped and watched as the man fell to the ground dead. Lia gripped the rock and watched everyone with narrow eyes. "I will spill the blood of everyone here if you do not leave me be," she said quietly.

She got to her feet, still gripping the rock. Holding them all in her trance, she took a few steps back. Then she turned and ran.

The crowd let her go, but Charlie took off after her. Surely this wasn't one of her kills. It was self-defense, wasn't it?

She didn't even make it past the edge of the woods before Westin stepped out. Charlie felt his blood begin to boil.

He watched. Lia didn't even put up a fight. She seemed to want to cross the veil. She didn't even look over her shoulder as Westin drained her.

Charlie began to fall...fall...

Charlie centered himself again. He seethed in silence at first but then remembered that he had an audience. He raised his gaze to Luke, who was anxiously looking about. "They would have killed her. She was alone and defenseless, and they would have tortured her. She defended herself, and that bastard took her anyways."

"What are you talking about? What the hell just happened to you?" Luke demanded, still struggling against the ropes.

Charlie jumped to his feet in one smooth motion. "They love to play God, and we help them! Do you understand that? We believe the system works, but we are just their playthings. We are expendable to their everlasting reign. No more, Luke! No more! She and I, we are going to take them down. I just feel it. Together, we are undefeatable. It is going to be beautiful."

"Who are you talking about?"

He ran over and squeezed Luke's cheeks. "After that vision, she'll be confused, lonely, vulnerable. I don't want her to turn to them for comfort. I want her to know that I'm here for her. No more hiding in the shadows. I think it's time I give her a gift."

Luke stammered. "I think a gift is a fantastic idea. Flowers and jewelry and teddy bears and chocolates and all of those lovely personal gifts are the way to go. In fact, the more you give, the better. Show her you really care."

Charlie smiled. "She is above flowers and such glittery nonsense. I'll need to think about this. I should spend some time with her. I've spent so much time in her past, but she could be different now. She might want different things. I want to make sure it's perfect."

Luke exhaled deeply and nodded. "Yes, take all the time you need to make it perfect. Bounce ideas off me. I'm an excellent listener."

"I'm sure you are," Charlie said, distractedly. "Excuse me, I need to do some thinking. Also, I need to make a bomb."

Connor hummed to the radio as he drove. The middle of the semester was drawing to a close, and he had received high marks in all his classes. His advisor was even discussing an assistantship program for him next semester. He hoped it worked out for him because his part-time job delivering pizzas wasn't cutting it.

He and Charlie were still the only two renters on the street, and while the man had warmed up a bit during their front porch chats, Connor still couldn't figure him out.

Charlie kept odd hours, sometimes not getting back until late at night. He drove an old model Jeep, and since Connor had pulled a few all-nighters, he was no stranger to the loud vibrating hum of its engine in the wee morning hours. Charlie was quiet for the most part, and Connor slept like the dead, so the odd hours didn't bother him.

Sometimes the man was eerily silent while they shared a couple of beers, and other times he was loud and excited. He spoke about his job like it was a labor of love and talked about all the places he had visited. Connor couldn't help but admire the man's intelligence and experience.

As Connor pulled into his driveway, he noticed Charlie dragging a large wooden box down his front steps. "Need a hand?" he called out as he opened the car door.

Charlie grunted and paused waiting for Connor to pick up the end. "Thanks," he muttered, straining a bit.

The gravel crunched under his feet as Connor stumbled backwards to the car. They slid it into the open trunk of the Jeep.

"Bloody hell Charlie. Ya hauling rocks in that thing?"

Charlie chuckled and shut the gate lift. "Not quite. It's the primary piece of a set. It's not quite done yet. I need to move it to my studio while I figure out how to perfect it."

Connor leaned against the truck. "I swear, all ya do is work. Ya need a day off. Ya need a woman."

"I've got one."

"Really?" Connor narrowed his eyes. "I've never seen one around."

Charlie raised his eyebrows. "You spying on me, Connor?"

"Nah. Don't have time for that. Besides, yer so boring!" Connor joked. "Tell me about this woman."

Charlie leaned up against the Jeep next to Connor, still breathing hard. "Technically, she's not mine yet. I'm still trying to figure out how to introduce myself to her."

Connor laughed, wheezing a little. "Ya mean to tell me that

she doesn't know who ya are?" He caught sight of the murderous look on Charlie's face and cleared his throat, straightening up. "Sorry," he said sheepishly.

"I met her some time ago while I was traveling overseas. I was only with her for a moment, so I doubt she remembers me, but she helped me out a great deal. And now she's here."

Connor's eyes widened. "Here in Colorado?"

Charlie nodded. "She's a waitress at a local tavern."

"Right. It is meant to be!" Connor clapped Charlie on the back. "Seriously. That never happens. Ya need to visit her at work."

"I don't know if that's such a good idea."

"Don't be such a jibber, Charlie, it will be okay. Ya don't have to talk to her, but what if she recognizes ya? Then ya don't even have to worry about the awkward introduction!"

It took some cajoling, but eventually Charlie agreed. Connor cast one more look at the odd box in the trunk before saying goodbye and heading back to his house.

He wondered a bit about the woman who had caught the attention of his odd friend. She was probably an oddball herself.

Chapter Eighteen

O'Ryan stood over the body, rubbing his eyes. The victim was dressed in a full civil war costume, a detail that overshadowed the rest of the victims. They were nearly three hours southeast of Denver at a small site erected for the South Creek Massacre, a battle site from the American Indian wars of the 1860s. To his knowledge, South Creek Massacre had nothing to do with the Civil War, but then, there were no battle sites dedicated to the war in the vicinity.

The boy had no identity on him. He was missing a leg, although it was clear that the removal of the leg was deliberate. There were no footsteps or tire tracks in the area, only a bag of ash.

Lichton walked over, his phone in hand. He showed an image to O'Ryan. "Kids name is Luke. He's a server in Denver and a recent graduate of CU. His roommate reported him missing three days ago."

The lead agent clenched his fists. "The bodies are piling up, and we are no closer to catching this son of a bitch. I want this entire area gone over with a fine-toothed comb. We are not dealing with a ghost. There has to be some connection!"

He glanced over at his partner. "Get Caxton on the phone. I want to see if Lia has had any miraculous breakthroughs with her memory. Tell him I want to talk to her myself."

Lichton nodded and moved away to talk to the crime scene unit. O'Ryan stared at the kid on the ground. He had a feeling things were going to get worse before they got better.

Westin stood in the back corner as he watched O'Ryan interview Lia. She sat upright in the chair, but her manner was calm and composed. He'd spent the entire car trip lecturing her before they entered the building.

"Remember, this is not an interrogation. You need to answer their questions as best you can, but you don't need to be nervous. It doesn't need to blow into anything," he had repeated over and over again.

She finally glared at him. "I understand, Westin. I think you are making this a bigger deal than it is," she pointed out.

She may have been right. He wanted to reach out and erase her existence from the minds of the agents, but instead he fidgeted nervously in the corner. He was sure at any point the other agents were going to ask what was wrong with him.

Finally, O'Ryan nodded and escorted her to the door. When she was safely out of the room, he walked over to Westin. "She doesn't recognize anything about the pictures. She doesn't even remember any historical facts about the time period. It's like someone erased her memory of all trivia and dropped her in the town. It doesn't make sense."

"Do you think she still has a connection to the killer?" Westin asked.

"I don't know. I feel like there is something about her, something big and important. I don't think she's lying, but I feel like there is something about her that she doesn't even remember. She's the only new factor in this case. He has to be catering his kills to her," O'Ryan said, frustrated.

"The young girl is new," the collector pointed out.

The agent shook his head. "It doesn't fit the profile. Why would a little girl care about Word War Two or the Civil War? No. This is definitely about Lia. It makes me wonder if he knows that she doesn't have any memories," he said slowly.

Westin raised his eyebrows. O'Ryan was a smart man. "You

think he's trying to trigger memories?"

O'Ryan nodded. "Now that I think about it, it makes sense. I just wish she would get her memories back before the killer decides to create any more scenes." He tapped his foot on the ground. "Okay, if this is true, then there has to be some common thread in these murders. If he knows her memories, and he's trying to trigger them, then he knows her personally. If he knows her, then someone else does as well. I think it's time to get proactive. Rather than waiting for her face to cross our desks, it may be time to put her picture on the news and ask for information."

"What if you're wrong? What if he thinks she's dead?" Westin asked. He didn't want the public to see her face.

"We could double up on her protection."

"You would be using her as bait," Westin said coldly.

O'Ryan ran his hands through his hair. "How long should I keep waiting? How many more people have to die before we're sure there is a connection?" He blew out his breath. "I'll hold off for now, but I need everyone to redouble their efforts. We need to know who she is."

Westin nodded. "She's trying to fit in. I think you're doing the right thing by giving her a chance," he said softly.

"Yea, but Caxton, we may not have a choice," he said seriously. "I think she's the key."

Lia shuffled around in her chair. She'd just left the agency, and now she had to answer more questions from the therapist. This part was much more difficult. She could lie to the agents until she was blue in the face, but she couldn't lie to Dr. Teston. She wanted to know what everything meant. She wanted to tell the doctor her life story, but she didn't know how to formulate it so that the doctor didn't have her committed to an insane asylum.

Dr. Teston looked up from her notes when Lia remained silent for too long. "Lia? I asked you about your relationship with

Hunter. You were going on a trip with him, correct?"

Lia sank back into the cushions. "That is correct."

"And how did it go?"

"It went well. He bought me this," her hands went up to touch the yin-yang symbol. She hadn't taken it off since the weekend. There was a connection that she just couldn't explain.

"It's lovely. And how did the night go?"

"I enjoyed myself."

"Lia, have you felt attached to anything since the incident?"

"What do you mean? Westin is constantly watching me, so I feel very attached to him. The girls at work try to make me feel included, so I feel attached to them. I have spent many consecutive hours with Hunter, so I feel attached to him as well." She frowned as she tried to think of more things to add to her list.

"I don't mean physically attached. I mean emotionally attached. If your memories came back and you moved home, is there anything in your life right now that you would miss?"

All of the memories of her physical life blurred together. The memories of blood and death intermingled, and she shook her head to clear her thoughts. "I guess I still do not know what I am supposed to find important and what I am supposed to find temporary. A new life exists just beyond the brink of my memories. I am not sure if I should find myself attached to anything."

"And what if that other life never presents itself? What if this life is all you have?"

"I feel," Lia began slowly, "that these moments are the most content I have ever been, but I do not know if I could ever make it work. There is this shadow lurking over me, yet I am still here. I am meeting people and learning things and developing relationships. It seems foreign to me, like this moment is my first attempt at life."

"I think that is the most conclusive thing you have said to me. This is progress," the doctor said, putting down her notepad.

Lia nodded. A weight seemed to be gently lifting off her shoulders. She wanted to make this life work. She wasn't going to wait for the judges to make a decision for her. The veil would have to wait. She was going to stay.

Even if it meant that the Phoenix would have to live.

The therapist pulled out her tape recorder when Lia left. "Patient continues to suffer from retrograde amnesia. She seems less detached from life and is making connections. I think the job and the social engagements are helping her feel as though she belongs. I have noted that, in past sessions, the patient views her attack with cold and clinical judgment rather than fear. I would like to bring it up in the next session and see if her view is any different. I am concerned that her amnesia does not stem from a coping mechanism. She does not seem to suffer from depression or anxiety. Furthermore, her curiosity about the life around her has only grown in strength. She is eager to try new experiences. Normally, I would encourage such activities, but her lust for life seems almost desperate. I have no doubt that she lies in her answers."

Dr. Teston paused while she gathered her thoughts. Lia was a mystery. Dr. Teston had never encountered a patient quite like her. She seemed to touch on many sociological and psychological dysfunctions, but her answers always seemed rehearsed. Many times, Dr. Teston wondered if the amnesia was real, but she couldn't imagine why Lia would be faking it.

"She presents a case that certainly needs a more in-depth study. I can't help but feel that she may be presenting something that has never been seen before. If she continues to show such abnormal behavior, I may need a consult."

The doctor clicked the recorder off and stared at her notes. If she didn't know better, she would have guessed that Lia was something entirely different and only playing at being human.

When Lia slipped into Westin's car later, she was practically floating. There was a jaunty tune in her head, and she hummed it merrily all the way home.

Home. This wouldn't be her permanent home. She couldn't live under the shadow of the FBI forever. She would have to find some place small. Perhaps the agents could give her some ideas and some references.

"What the hell is wrong with you?" Westin growled as they entered the house. Lia twirled a bit.

"I am in a good mood. Is that not allowed?"

"For most people, yes, it's preferred. On you, it's creepy. What's up?"

Lia stopped moving about. She was a little breathless. Clearly she would need to work out. Perhaps she would start running. "I think I'll start now," she mused.

"Start what?"

"Running. I did it all the time as a reaper. I should try it now that I am alive. Excuse me. I need to change." She brushed past Westin on the way up the stairs. He grabbed her arm.

"What is going on with you?"

The last dream still lingered in her mind. It was clearer than all the other dreams. "I was in the middle of an angry horde," she said, her voice going flat. "He was going to kill me. It was self-defense. I wasn't even there long enough to feel anything, let alone a lust for blood. It was him or me. I was quicker. You collected me for that." She pulled her arm out of his grasp. "I am done, Westin. I do not know what they want from me. I am not waiting any longer. You want me to feel sympathy for humanity. I have chosen them. You should be happy. I am going to live this life, and no one is going to take it away from me."

A few minutes later Lia was hitting the sidewalk hard, her tennis shoes pounding against the concrete. She could feel the life coursing through her, the adrenaline that kept her moving. It was exhilarating how her lungs fought for air and yet her legs didn't stop.

Each step seemed to take her farther and farther away from the reach of the judges. In her mind, she could see Hunter and the employees at the tavern. She thought about her future. Perhaps she should go to school. Maybe she could be a useful part of society.

She waved as she passed neighbors in the yards and cars along the road. She wondered what good neighbors did. She would need to know so that she could be the best neighbor possible.

A bright yellow Volkswagen Beetle passed her, and she nodded in approval. She still needed to learn how to drive. Then she would also get a brightly colored car.

Lia had barely made it a mile before she thought her lungs and her legs were going to give out. She slowed to a stop and rested against a tree, gasping for breath. Her normally pale skin was flushed, and for a brief moment, she thought about the blood that was pumping under her skin.

It gave her life.

She turned and walked slowly back to the house. From her calculations, she only had a few kills left to endure. Whether a memory or vision, several minutes were all that remained that plagued her. She thought hard, trying to will the vision to her and get it over with.

She thought about the connection she had with the killer. That too would pass. Connections to souls never lasted long. Maybe if she moved, the connection would fade quicker. Of course, that meant moving away from Hunter.

Hunter. Lia mulled his name over in her head. Had she ever had a relationship before? She couldn't deny that he made her happy, but could she make it work? Could she be a girlfriend?

She grimaced. That was a thought for another time. One major life altering decision at a time.

Westin was waiting for her when she made it back. He lifted

an eyebrow at her. "Out of shape?"

She nodded. "Running seems to be more difficult when you need to breathe," she muttered.

"For what it's worth, I stand behind your decision. It's complicated, and the decision straddles a moral fence, but if you can make it work, you should try."

Lia paused, her hand on the doorknob. "It may be far from what I deserve, but the opposite is to kill and be judged all over again." She looked at Westin. "I know they want me to kill him. There is no other reason for me to be here, but I am not a weapon to be used lightly. As I believe you have said before, I am also not a judge of souls. If they want him so badly, they can just collect him."

She left Westin silent on the porch while she went to shower.

Westin watched her go up the stairs with a small smile on his face. Maybe it was him and maybe it was Hunter, and maybe it was something else entirely, but the idea that Lia felt she had a chance gave him certain peace of mind. He could move on with the plan that had been developing in his mind.

Charlie would have to show his face sooner or later. He would soon feel Lia's disinterest in him, feel her pulling away, and would take action. Westin could only hope that he was ready. It had been a long time since he had collected a soul this way, but collecting Charlie was the only viable option. He couldn't be killed, and he couldn't be stopped.

It wasn't even the collection of Charlie that bothered Westin. It was what happened next. The moments after the collection were critical. Lia would have to be present, and even she wouldn't go away unscathed. The truth would be revealed, and Westin would have to face the consequences.

Lia would face the damage. Maybe she would bounce back. The judges would do the most damage, probably retiring him and sending him on his way.

But Westin had lived a long time. Perhaps it was time for him to finally die.

He would most certainly be taking Charlie with him.

Hunter smiled into the phone. His mother demanded to know why he hadn't called immediately after his date with Lia. He was throwing the ball out in the yard to Jacks, wasting a little bit of time before he picked Lia up for dinner.

"I'm sorry I didn't call, but I'm an adult now. I don't need to call my mom every time I go on a date," he said teasingly.

"You know damn well it's more than just a date. Aaron has told me that you've been spending more time at Owen's Tavern. I thought you'd started back your drinking again, but he says you're there several times a week to see a girl. I want to know who this girl is and why it is that you are taking her on an out of town trip without telling your mother anything about her!"

Jacks dropped the slobbery ball at his feet, and Hunter bent down and chucked it across the yard. Grass flew up beneath the golden retriever's feet as he raced to the other end. "I didn't want to tell you because I don't know what to say. It's complicated, and it may not turn out to be anything."

"I know you, Hunter. You wouldn't be spending so much time in a bar if you didn't think she was special. After what happened to you..." her voice caught in her throat as it trailed off.

Hunter sighed. His mother meant well. "Okay, maybe I think she is special, but that doesn't make it any less complicated."

"Complicated as in she has amnesia and could have a husband waiting for her somewhere?"

Aaron had been running his mouth a bit too much. "Yes, complicated like that. Not that I think she has a husband, but she does have a past that could make being with her very difficult. No one has come looking for her, and it's not from lack of trying on the agency's part."

Hunter could hear his mom clanging pots and pans in the

kitchen. "Are you cooking again? Don't you remember what happened last time you were on the phone and cooking?"

"Don't you change the subject young man. Trent gave me this blue tooth thing that makes me look like some fancy corporate businesswoman. It's supposed to keep me from boiling any more phones. Anyhow, are you sure this woman isn't just some project for you?"

Hunter frowned. "Project?"

"I know it must pull at your heart strings that no one has come looking for her, but sometimes you open your heart up to too many people. She could be trouble."

"It's not like that Mom. She has this passion for learning everything she can about life. It's like she has never lived before, and it's so amazing to see everything through her eyes. She's blunt and open about everything. I think there's been so much loss in her life, and she's guarded in a way that even she can't explain, but she is embracing this new life and giving it her all. It's beautiful. She's beautiful."

There was a moment of silence on the other end of the phone. "Mom?"

"I'm sorry, darling, I just haven't heard you talk about anyone like this since that tramp you brought home a few years ago."

"Carol wasn't a tramp," Hunter began, still trying to defend his ex-fiancée.

"Excuse me? She slept with half the town and then had the nerve to try to sleep with Aaron. If it weren't for Aaron, you'd have married that little slut."

Hunter winced. His mother rarely used language like this, and when she did, it was always about Carol. "Lia isn't Carol. She feels honest and genuine to me. It's hard to explain."

"Well, that settles it. I want to meet this Lia. You will bring her to the barbecue next weekend."

"I don't know Mom, I think springing the whole family on

her at once could frighten her," Hunter said frowning.

"Nonsense. She needs to know that you have strong family bonds. And I need to lay eyes on this woman you have fallen so quickly for. If you don't bring her, I will stalk her at that restaurant."

"Oh God, Mom, please don't do that. I'll ask her tonight if she feels comfortable enough meeting you. If she says no, you won't push the issue. I think she's still a little raw from the weekend, and I want to give her some time to adjust to the idea of a new relationship."

"Fine. Promise me that you'll remember the risks of getting involved with this girl. I'm sure she's lovely, but it's always the beautiful that make the best bait."

"I get it, Mom. I have to go inside and get ready. Give Dad my love."

"Good night, darling."

"Bye." Hunter hung up the phone and tossed the ball one more time to Jacks. He thought over what his mother had said. He knew she didn't mean it. He didn't think Lia had it in her to put anyone in significant danger, but he couldn't ignore the way she had ended up in his hospital or the fact that no one had come to claim her. Whatever was in her past, it couldn't be good.

Lia smiled at Hunter over her wine glass. He had been staring at her for most of the night, marveling at how beautiful she could look in a simple pair of shorts and a t-shirt. He imagined there was very little that she could put on that wasn't stunning. It was unnatural the way she glowed.

"What is it?" she finally asked.

"I'm sorry?" he said, startled out of his thoughts.

"You have been staring at me all night. I am starting to think that there is something hideous on my face," she said seriously.

"Not at all. God, you look beautiful. Something seems different about you tonight. I didn't mean to stare. Actually, that's a lie. I totally meant to stare. I may stare at you all night."

She blushed. "Actually, there is something different about tonight. I have made an important decision, and it concerns you. Does that scare you?"

He raised his eyebrows. "I think that depends on the decision. If you have decided to join a nunnery, then yes, I am very frightened."

"No, not at all. My therapist has been helping me see the present a little more clearly. I have been obsessed with the past lately. I wonder what happened to me, and the person that I must have been to end up like this."

Hunter reached over and grabbed her hand. "Hey, you can't think like that."

Lia shook her head. "No one has come to claim me, and if my memories return, they may not be pleasant." She took a deep breath. "I have always known that I would eventually have to choose which life I belonged to. I am not saying this because I have not gotten any of my memories back, but rather what I have learned about life now. No matter what happens, I choose to continue this life. I choose to be in the present."

Hunter squeezed her hand. A weight over his shoulders lifted. She hasn't come out and said that she chose him, and he wasn't sure she ever would, but this was good enough for him. "There is no need to be scared of that. I think you have carved out a nice little life for yourself here. I know it hasn't been very long, but I can only imagine that things will get even better for you. Having said that though, you may find your past life hard to give up, even if your memories return. I don't think anyone can fault you if you change your mind."

Lia exhaled and smiled. "I am not trying to look too hard at the future either. I hope that is okay with you."

"If you could look as far as a week into the future, I'd be happy."

"What happens in a week?" Lia asked.

224

"I have dinner with my family every month. It's my mom, dad, two younger brothers, and my younger sister. I know it's a lot of people, but my mother has asked that you join us this weekend."

"Meet your family?" Lia asked slowly.

"Yes."

She bit her lip. "I will think about it."

Hunter asked, searched her face. "It's okay if you say no. I realize that you have a lot on your plate." He switched subjects. "How is the wine?"

"It is tart. It makes my face want to go like this," she scrunched up her face. "But then, for some reason, I like it, and I keep going back for more. It makes me feel very pleasant."

Hunter laughed. "I think it's the skin of the grape that makes the wine tart. They call it tannins."

"Would you like to try it?" she asked, offering her glass to him.

"No, no, no. It makes my face want to scrunch up like that too, and that makes me feel very emasculated."

Lia chuckled and ran her eyes up and down him slyly. "I do not believe anyone questions your masculinity," she said with a wry smile.

He felt a little jolt in his system and raised his eyebrows. "My masculinity huh? Are you trying to make things difficult for me?"

"I am trying to respect your decision," she sighed, clearly frustrated.

"I appreciate that," he said softy. "Maybe, after we leave the restaurant, you'd like a tour of my house this evening before I take you back? It's just down the street."

He watched her eyes light up. "I would like that very much."

Hunter raised his glass again and found that he couldn't keep his eyes off her for the rest of the evening.

The dog met them at the door with an excited wag of his tail.

Lia eyed him warily, but the dog seemed to want nothing more than to sniff her and lick her all over. She ran her hands through his warm fur with a sense of wonderment. He was a creature who accepted her unconditionally, and he was soft and furry. She loved him instantly.

"Jacks, get down," Hunter commanded. The dog ignored him, and Hunter rolled his eyes. "I'm sorry. He loves meeting new people."

"It is okay," she said softly. "I think he is wonderful." She suddenly felt very shy and unsure of herself. She looked around the house nervously. This wasn't just a house. It was a home. It was a permanent part of someone's life, and it seemed to represent the absolute opposite of her.

"I live with my brother Aaron and his girlfriend, but they're out of town for the week. I think he might be proposing to her," Hunter said idly. "Would you like a tour?"

She shook her head vehemently. She did not want a tour. She only wanted him. He seemed to mistake her answer for second thoughts, and he took her hand. "Hey, it's okay. I can take you home," he started.

She didn't say anything as she turned and pressed her lips to his. She slipped her hand under his shirt and trailed her fingers along his skin. His muscles trembled under her touch, and she broke the kiss. "I am not interested in your house. I do not believe you are all that interested in giving me the tour," she said, gazing steadily at him.

He inhaled sharply. "You're not wrong," he whispered.

"Where is your bedroom?"

He took her by the hand and led her up the stairs and through the darkened hallways into his room. He went to flip on the lights, but she stilled his hand. She'd never had the lights on before, and she didn't want to start now.

She pushed him to the bed. Releasing him, she removed her shirt and shorts, letting them slip to the floor. He lifted her, placing her on the bed as if she were light as a feather. She closed her eyes as he stared at her. Without a word, he trailed his fingers and then his lips over her scars. She gasped and lifted her hips as he moved lower.

Sex was a casual entertainment for her, but as a reaper, the feelings were muted, a break against the mundane. Here, as his tongue touched her, the feelings were intense, streaking through all parts of her body. She trembled, losing control.

"So beautiful," he said in the darkness and he lifted himself up to her mouth. She listened in the dark as he removed the rest of his clothes. She cried out as he entered her and gripped his hips. In and out. She gripped the bed, pushing herself up. He let her flip them over until she straddled him. The cool air rushed over her skin as she sat up.

As she pulled him deeper, she moaned, feeling herself lose control. He moved again, lifting up his torso, and moving up to meet her mouth. She placed her hands on his chest, but he had already grabbed her waist, pulling her closer as she sat up. She looked into his eyes and felt herself surrender.

Lia pulled the sheets up over her as she curled around his body. Her skin was sticky, but the air chilled her. He was already asleep and unaware that she was staring at him.

Her hands trembled as she trailed a finger over his skin. She felt so different with him, so torn about herself and her life.

The necklace warmed against her skin. She reached back to unclasp it and put it on the table.

She laid her head on his chest, and even as she drifted into sleep, the dream overcame her.

The temperature dropped, and Lia shivered. She dug her toes into the gravel. They bit into her skin, and she winced. In the silence of the false scene before her, something tugged at her memory. She had been here before. She looked to the left at the figure struggling in the violent waters. The wind ripped the trees from the roots and toppled them over. In front of her stood the tall blurred man.

The memories blasted into her mind, and she gasped. She sat slowly on the ground, careful to avoid hurting herself. After a moment, she picked up the rocks and tossed them into the river. They splashed into the violent waters soundlessly.

"You are spending quite a bit of time and trouble on my account. Why do you want me to know who I am?" she asked.

"It could be crucial. It could also be unimportant."

Lia rolled her eyes. "That is hardly an answer," she pointed out. "Can you see me? When I am awake, I mean."

"I cannot see anything while I stand in this place," the voices echoed.

She juggled a few rocks in her hands. "How do you know when I have committed a crime?"

The wind began to gust. While he never wavered in his steps towards her, she fell over, scraping her knuckles along the rocks as she rolled.

"Stop," she cried out in pain when the wind died. She dug her fingers into the ground trying to still her body.

"This is not my doing," the voices responded. "I have no powers over this place."

Lia arched her body against the rocks and struggled to get up. "You have not answered my question. How do you know when I kill?"

He held his hand out to her. "Your blood, your tears, your screams, even your heartbeat vibrate the earth.

"You can feel it when we cry?" she asked.

"We can feel it when you cry." He reached out and touched her forehead.

"It hurts so much," she whispered, and for a moment, the pain took her breath away. She fell into her memories.

"Surrender to who you are."

She stood in the middle of someone's yard. There was a table set with delicate china and silver utensils. A platter of cakes decorated the center and next to it, a pot of tea steamed. As she walked around the table, figures began to materialize. A young woman dressed in an ornate white dress with gold trim reached for the pot and poured three cups. Two men stood a few feet away, watching her.

"A fall wedding would do nicely," the younger man said, nodding to the older gentleman. There was a disturbing gleam in his eye as he stared at his future bride.

"Excellent. We'll get plans underway immediately."

Lia watched as the woman's hands shook. The cup rattled against the plate as she picked it up. Her face grew paler by the minute. She put the cup down and reached into her pocket. Lia's eye widened as she saw the butt of a revolver. The young lady gripped it for a moment before sliding it back into place. Touching the weapon seemed to steady her. She returned to her cup and served the men.

Lia could see another figure out of the corner of her eye. A woman darted out of the trees. Lia stood, frozen, as her own reflection passed through her. The chill of a reaper rattled her bones, and she gasped. The pocket of cold air faded as quickly as it had appeared. The others didn't know until it was too late. Lia watched as the blade slid into the older gentleman first. It was quick.

As the blood ran, Lia shared the emotion of her memory. The lust was rising inside her. The crazed feeling gripped her, and the reflection turned to the young man. He was shouting now at the young lady. She had pulled out her gun and raised it, but already the reflection of Lia slashed the throat of the young man. The reflection turned now. The woman fired, but missed. The memory advanced quickly, knocking her hand away.

"You were going to kill them anyways. I saw you barter your goods for that gun. You feared for your life, and now it is yours," the memory stated softly.

The young lady shook, raised her gun again. The reflection sprang into action, knocking the gun out of the hand. Even as the gray portal opened, and Westin stepped through, the memory had her hands on the gun. She locked eyes with Westin, who was raising his hand. Before he could take control, she fired, planting a bullet into the head of the young lady.

"I was saving her life," she said as Westin gripped her.

He cast the gun aside and pulled her closer. "You don't save lives. You only take them."

Lia's head whipped around and stared at Westin as he removed the memories of her reflection. The dream suddenly seemed less real. The voice was not his own. It was close, but Lia began to detect a lie. She turned her head away from the collection and studied the landscape. She could see the edges of the dream were altering, shifting.

Something wasn't right.

She turned again to watch him remove her soul, but the scene was blurry. Lia took a step forward, and she was falling.

Her eyes flew open, and she saw the rise and fall of Hunters chest. His heavy breathing cut through the silence and for a moment, every nerve in her body screamed for life, his life.

She scrambled away from him, closed her eyes, and focused on her breathing. As the dream blurred in her memory, Hunter's face filtered out, and her body returned to normal. She opened her eyes, and all she could see was him, peaceful and calm.

Lia settled against him again. The river and Hunter's face faded from memory, and all she could hear as she fell asleep were words echoing in her mind.

Surrender to who you are.

Chapter Nineteen

Connor popped a jalapeño in his mouth and grinned. "Fried jalapeños and cream cheese wrapped in bacon," he moaned before taking a swig of his beer. "I love this country."

The tavern was dark with a mixture of dark green and blue booths. Dusty colored lamps swung over their tables, reflecting light on the sturdy oak tables. Connor fingered at the small tear at the seam of his booth, pulled at the fuzz absently and stared at his friend.

Charlie's mouth was slightly opened, and he was breathing deeply. There was intensity in his eyes that Connor had never seen before. "If ya start drooling, people are going to notice," Connor said wryly. He craned his neck to see behind them over the tall booth. Across the restaurant, a slender woman with dark hair pulled back in soft curls was talking to a customer. "She's a sniper's nightmare, but hardly a minger," he said with a grin.

"Stop staring at her. And what the hell does that mean?" Charlie asked coldly.

Connor swiveled his head back around. "She's a bit thin, but she's pretty. And she can't see us considering that we are on the opposite end of the restaurant. Now, if we had sat in her section..."

"Do you ever stop talking?"

Connor just shrugged and dove back into their food. The restaurant was buzzing with business, but Charlie barely took his eyes off the server. His beer was untouched, and he didn't even notice when Connor polished off the jalapeño poppers.

"My professor was talking about the Phoenix killer yesterday. He said the city should enforce a curfew until the man is caught. They've got seventeen bodies in eight months. The crime scenes are just getting more and more bizarre. My mum even wants me to come home," Connor said.

Charlie's gaze shifted and settled on Connor. "Bizarre?"

"People in costumes positioned in some strange places. One of them was even missing a leg. The guy must be insane."

"Quite the contrary," Charlie said slowly. "He is deliberate and methodical. The scenes that he creates are beautiful and clearly meant for a specific audience."

Connor's jaw dropped. "Beautiful? Are ya mad? People are dead."

"People die all the time in bizarre and idiotic ways." He leaned across the table. "You never think about it until the media gives Death a name. The Phoenix strikes fear in the heart because it can never die. Are you afraid, Connor?"

Connor shook his head. "You are so weird. We need to work on your conversation starters before ya talk to your girl over there."

He reached for his beer, but noises behind him interrupted him. He turned his head. A large man was shouting at the waitress. Connor shook his head. "What a melter. People are so rude. I bartended for a few years in England. That job nearly drove me to murder."

He turned back around, but Charlie didn't seem to be listening. His eyes had darkened, and there was anger on his face.

"Relax, Charlie. I'm sure she's used to it. Ya wouldn't believe the crap servers put up with."

"She deserves better," Charlie said quietly.

Connor shifted uncomfortably in his seat. "Unless ya want to say hello, there isn't a whole lot ya can do about it now. Is that you?"

"Is what me?"

"I mean, are ya done drinking? Rev up or get the fock off," he encouraged.

Charlie shot him another odd look. Connor sat back and stretched. "The semester will be over in a few weeks. I'll be able to enjoy the rest of the summer," he said casually. Charlie didn't answer. Connor blew out his breath and shrugged. "All right, I've got to find the bog. If ya see our waiter, grab the check. Tonight's on me." He looked at Charlie, but there was no answer. He left his silent friend and went to relieve himself.

When he got back, the check was on the table, and Charlie was gone. There was a flurry of commotion among the employees. Connor could hear them whispering to each other and glancing back to the waitress Charlie was so in love with.

Connor grinned as he put some cash on the table. Maybe the sly dog had said hello after all.

Lia whistled softly while she prepared for the dinner shift at the tavern. She had slept peacefully last night. She'd cuddled with Hunter that morning, and he drove her home.

She had spent most of the day straightening up the place, reading, and looking for more permanent places to live on the Internet. There was a pleasant song in her head, and she belted out the lyrics to the empty home, smiling to herself and dancing.

She felt free. It was amazing.

She carried the positive attitude with her to work. "Somebody is in a good mood," Barbie noted laughingly. Lia only smiled and continued her work. Karen and Andy were both there tonight, and everyone took a moment to tease Lia about the good mood, but she kept her thoughts to herself.

She focused on her job, and within a few hours, she was so busy that she didn't even have time to hide away in her mind. Towards the middle of the night, a heavy feeling settled over her, but she dismissed it as stress. As the night got busier, everyone was on edge. Lia struggled to keep up.

She frowned as a single individual was seated at her large corner booth. Alyssa apologized as she came to return the rest of the place settings. "I am so sorry, Lia. He was adamant that he was given a large booth. He said he liked to spread out. He's really rude."

Lia smiled. Alyssa always tended to feel personally responsible for when the servers had a bad night. "It is okay, Alyssa. It is not your fault."

She continued to smile, desperate to hold onto her good mood for the night. She approached the table with a genuine cheery disposition. "Good evening, welcome to Owen's Tavern. My name is..."

"What are your happy hour specials?" the portly man interrupted her.

Lia took a deep breath. She wanted to point out that it was rude to interrupt people, but she had a full section and little time to spend with this man. "Our happy hour ended a few moments ago."

"I came into this restaurant ten minutes before happy hour ended. It is not my fault that it took this long for me to get a table. I'm going to ask you again what the happy hour specials are," he said icily.

Lia narrowed her eyes. "You were free to get a drink at the bar while you waited for your table, sir," she pointed out.

"I didn't realize it would take twenty minutes to get a table on a Wednesday night," he growled.

"You waited twenty minutes because you specifically wanted a large booth. There were plenty of other tables that you could have taken," Lia said, reaching the end of her patience.

He grunted. "I want your house whiskey on the rocks. None of that sissy pour. Make it a healthy pour."

"I would be happy to make it a double for you, sir," Lia said.

"Are you retarded? Did I say I wanted a double? No. I said I wanted a healthy pour."

"Sir, it is a standard pour. If you pay for a single, you are going to get a standard single."

He leaned in close. "Don't give me that bullshit. I come in here so often that I should be getting drinks for free."

Lia bit her tongue and turned to leave. She could feel anger rising within her. She tried to ignore it. She went and talked to Andy about her issue, and he assured her not to worry. He would take care of it.

She returned to the table a few minutes later, and the man eyed her up and down lecherously. "I want a strip cooked medium plus with a baked potato loaded and those little onion rings to start with," he said gruffly.

"So you want that medium well," she asked.

"No. I want it medium plus."

Once again, Lia bit her tongue. "Would you like it red or pink on the inside?"

He cocked his head. "Are you not listening? I want it between red and pink, damn it!"

Lia took a deep breath. She reminded herself that she was trying to be happy, and she would just let it go.

"Keep the bread coming too," he said, shoving the menu in her face.

She silently took the menu and walked to the back. She rang in the order and went to fill a glass of water on the next table.

The man wasn't happy. "Hey!" He grabbed her elbow as she was passing him. "Didn't I say that I wanted bread?"

Lia pulled her arm away. "I will get it to you when I get the chance," she said coldly and moved on. The table next to him smiled sympathetically and thanked her for the water. She could feel tension rising in her chest.

She got the man his bread and tossed it wordlessly on the table. It only took him a few minutes to go through it before he was demanding more.

She was relieved when his appetizer went out without

incident, but the relief was short-lived. He claimed that the next drink they brought him was watered down. When she tried to explain that his drink had been sitting on the table, melting the ice for the past ten minutes, he got red in the face and demanded another on the house.

When his steak came out, he pounded his fist on the table and yelled angrily that it was undercooked. When she brought it back, having put it on the grill for a few more minutes, he threw the plate back at her.

"What the fuck is this? You need to cook me a new steak!"

"Then you will pay for a whole new steak. That strip was perfectly cooked the first time." Lia finally snapped and shoved the plate back on the table. "If you want a new one, you are going to pay for it."

He reached over and grabbed her arm. "You can't talk to me like that."

Enough was enough. She saw red and shoved his arm aside. Andy was already rushing to her side, but Lia couldn't focus on anything but the man in front of her. She could feel her heartbeat speed up. "You do not touch me," she said coldly. "You do not ever touch anyone in this restaurant, do you understand me? If I ever see you again, I swear I will..."

Her vision began to blur before she finished the sentence. Lia swayed a bit. She struggled to keep her focus on the man, but already, she could hear water crashing on the rocks. She frowned, puzzled, and a vision overtook her.

The temperature dropped, and Lia shivered. She dug her toes into the gravel. They bit into her skin, and she winced. In the silence of the false scene before her, something tugged at her memory. She had been here before. She looked to the left at the figure struggling in the violent waters. The wind ripped the trees from the roots and toppled them over. In front of her stood the tall blurry man.

Screams rose from the earth. Lia covered her ears and fell to the ground.

"What is that?" she cried out.

The screams died down. "Your victims, perhaps?" the voices questioned. He remained unaffected by the grotesque horrors that still echoed in her head.

"They never screamed," she breathed.

"That is true," he conceded. He looked up, and the screams rose again.

She struggled to her feet and tried to run and escape. The wind rushed in and knocked her down. She screamed as her skin tore against the rocks. As her blood flowed towards the water, her muscles twitched violently against the pain.

The figure moved to her, casting a new shadow. She whimpered. "Am I being punished?"

"This is not my doing," the voices replied, echoing his past words. "I have no power in this place." He looked around, his eyes roaming over the river. "This place is beyond violent. It has been so for centuries. It sits beyond a small village in modern-day England and has claimed the lives of many. It was, at one time, a peaceful place. We cannot control it. We can only hide it."

Lia dragged her arm over the rocks and pointed. "It is claiming another."

"Not just another victim. She is the first victim." He touched her again, and she fell screaming into her memories.

The darkness receded. She was standing in a doorway. In front of her, her memory stood over a man lying on the floor. In her hands, she held a knife.

"You lied to me. You thought you could control me. You have no idea what I'm capable of." She brought the knife up. The man raised his hand to defend himself, and Lia's memory stabbed him through the hand, burying the blade in his chest, pinning his hand over his heart.

She moved up and put a hand on her abdomen. Lia's eyes widened. Her memory had been stabbed. She moved past Lia, through the doorway and out into the street.

Lia followed her, watching the blood drip down her memory's dress and smear onto the dirt road. Minutes had passed before a portal opened up, and Westin stepped through.

Her reflection stopped and stared at the scene before her. "You," she said, surprise in her voice. "Where did you come from?"

There was nothing but rage in Westin's face. He reached out and grabbed her, forcing his hand to her head. The memory of Lia cried out and struggled.

"I condemn you for crimes against mankind," he whispered hoarsely. "You will be judged for your actions and sentenced to a life of servitude in the world where you will never harm another being."

Lia frowned and searched the shadow that remained of her dreams and visions. That didn't sound right.

The memory of Lia fell to the ground as Westin drew her memories from her. As he placed a hand on her chest for her soul, something triggered in Lia. It was an idea that shook her to the core, but per usual, as she fell out of her vision, everything faded away except the blood on her hands.

"Lia?" Andy was shaking her now. The man was still making demands, and as Lia regained her footing, she felt a rage in her soul. It was strong and staggering, and it did not belong to her.

She gasped and whirled around, falling into Andy.

"What? What is wrong?" he demanded.

"He is here," she whispered, shaking.

The Phoenix was here.

Westin watched as the agents spoke to each other. They were all shaking their heads. He was called to the scene before they were, but he hadn't had a chance to talk to Lia. Instead, he was stuck interviewing the employees who were all wondering what was going on. Lia was still shaking in the office. He moved in closer when O'Ryan approached her.

"Lia," O'Ryan said softly. "Lia, I know that this is difficult for you. We think that you may have had a flashback and it startled you. We're interviewing all the employees, and no one remembers seeing anyone suspicious. How do you know the unsub was here?"

Lia bit her lip. "It was just a feeling that I got," she said quietly.

O'Ryan nodded. "I get it. Let's talk about the flashback that you had. Was it about the attack?"

Lia shook her head. "I do not believe so. That man was yelling at me, and I just...I think I just saw another man yelling at me. It was in bits and pieces. I do not even remember any details now."

Westin could see that O'Ryan was not buying the story. The agent put his hand on her shoulder gently.

"Lia, I want to help you. There is nothing I want more than to put that man behind bars so you can feel safe again, but I need you to be honest with me. What happened tonight?"

Lia glared at him. Westin froze. He could see the old Lia shining through, the Lia who didn't hesitate to spill blood. "I told you the truth," she said coldly. "Maybe he was not here and maybe I was confused, but I am not lying about what I felt and what I feel now."

Westin closed his eyes. Her reaction to the situation was adding to the doubt that already clouded O'Ryan's mind. They would be watching her very closely now.

O'Ryan nodded and moved over to Westin. "We used the sketch that Amanda gave us to question the employees. We don't think the sketch is accurate, but we also don't have any indication that he was here. It's possible that she is lying to us, in which case she does remember what he looks like, and she recognized him. If that's the case, he probably bolted. But why would she continue to lie to us?"

"You don't think she is just confused by the flashback?" Westin questioned.

O'Ryan shook his head. "I don't know. What I do know is that she is hiding something. She isn't to have any more freedom. I want you on her twenty-four seven. I want her protected, and I want to know what is going on. She is key to this investigation, and I want to go home. Do you understand?"

Westin nodded. "Twenty-four-seven," he confirmed.

"Good." He nodded to her. "Take her home. I want to make

sure her cover isn't blown. Tell the owners to spread a story of her abusive husband. Do not let anyone think this is about the killer. Also, Westin, if he was here, he knows about her. We can use that."

Westin turned and stared at O'Ryan. "Her protection is still a priority, right?"

O'Ryan clapped him on the back. "Of course. Her protection is very important. I get the feeling that we aren't going to catch him without her."

He walked over to collect the other agents, and Westin went to retrieve Lia. He had a brief word with Andy and Karen about the cover story and then moved Lia a little forcefully into the car.

Once alone, he turned to her. "What the fuck happened?"

She met his glare. "I messed up. I had a vision, and when I came too, I felt this alien emotion inside me. I mean, I was already angry with that rude customer, but this was unbridled rage. It was not mine. I panicked. He was so close. I could feel it. At the same time, I felt so weak. It just slipped out." She turned the stare out the window. "How bad is it?"

Westin started the car. "It's bad in a lot of ways. He knows where you work now, and that means that he has easy access to you. The agents know that your story doesn't add up. It's not a huge problem, but I'm not allowed to clean it up, so they are going to be a nuisance. What did you see?"

"What?"

"Your vision," Westin said impatiently. "What did you see?"

Lia shook her head. "It's blurry, just like all the others. I just remember a man in a study. I stabbed him through the hand and the heart. I was angry with him, but he was also angry with me."

Westin felt himself grow cold. It was her second kill. She was so close.

He felt as though he had waited a lifetime for this moment, and now that it was almost here, he wondered what it would all mean.

"You are not to go anywhere without me," he muttered. "Until I take care of this, you are not to be alone."

Lia turned her head. "You are going to take care of this?"

Westin didn't take his eyes off the road. "You said you made the decision to live. That leaves it up to me."

"Are you going to kill him? Won't you be collected?"

Westin shook his head. "It takes more than a kill to be collected. It takes a very evil soul. Besides, I'm not sure what I'm going to do yet."

"An evil soul? I guess it is a good thing that I do not have my soul anymore," Lia said quietly.

Westin clenched his jaw. "Yea," he said finally. "Good thing."

Chapter Twenty

The next night, Lia was pacing about her room like a caged animal. Karen and Andy had ordered her not to come in. When she protested, they reminded her that she would be facing a lot of questions from the staff. They needed some time to speak to them about the new cover story. Lia relented.

Westin wasn't letting her out of the house. When she tried to sit on the porch to read, he yanked her back inside. It had only been a day under his supervision, and she was ready to scream. She couldn't even speak to Hunter over the phone without Westin first filling him in on the details. Hunter had, of course, agreed with Westin. She was not to be left alone. That irritated her more than anything else.

At first, she was scared and felt weak. She would never be able to fend off an attack if one came her way, but now, with all the anger building up inside her, she felt strong again. She argued that being scared and vulnerable was a part of life, a part of the life she was trying so desperately to experience. Westin had shut her down, and now she felt as though she was back behind the veil, being controlled by someone else.

She tried to jump around the room to loosen up, but it didn't help. Finally, she opened her door and slipped downstairs to get a glass of water. Westin looked up from the kitchen table.

"Going to bed soon?" he asked, paperwork spread out in front of him.

"Yes. It is not like there is anything else to do," she complained. She moved closer to the table. "What do you have there?"

Westin shuffled the papers into a pile and placed it in a folder. "It's just some information the FBI has on the killer. I don't think it's a good idea if you look at it. It's too violent."

Lia rolled her eyes. "Fine. Good night," she muttered.

She poured her glass of water and slipped back upstairs. A thought occurred to her. The security system beeped every time a door opened, but what about the windows? She slipped one open and listened. The house was silent.

With a smile, Lia completed her nightly activities and acted as though she were getting ready for bed. She slipped on her running shoes and turned off the lights. After a few moments, she climbed out the window, hung for a second by her hands, and launched herself down, landing on her feet but quickly tumbling to the ground. With a frown, she massaged her butt. Getting back up into the window would be impossible. Evidently, she hadn't thought it through.

In any case, she was out now, and that was all she wanted. Westin could yell at her later. She rolled her shoulder and began to jog out on the darkened street. Maybe it was the thrill of courting danger or the thrill of defying Westin, but Lia felt alive and exhilarated. The crisp night air brushed up against her skin, and she shivered as her feet hit the pavement.

The more she ran, the more her worries began to fall away. Her mind was clear and focused, and instantly it zeroed in on troubling thoughts.

Something had been very different from that last memory, but no matter how hard she focused, she couldn't remember what it was. She could hear a distant sound of water rushing, but that didn't make any sense. As far as she could remember, she hadn't killed anyone by the water.

She remembered blood. She remembered the look on her face when the blade broke the skin. After every memory, she remembered the excitement as the light died out in the victim's eyes. But these weren't the parts she wanted to remember. The emotions both shook her and felt so familiar. She wanted to remember the details.

It didn't make sense to be given her memories only to have most of them erased.

To her left, she heard a tree branch break. She stopped suddenly, her heart pounding. Every muscle in her body was tensed. Deep inside, she knew she wasn't ready for a fight, but that didn't mean she was going to back down.

A squirrel scampered across the tree, and she relaxed. As she started to jog again, she wondered if she would always live in fear. Westin said he would take care of it, but Westin wasn't a killer. What if he couldn't follow through? What would she do then?

Gasping and out of breath, she finally stopped and stretched. A car drove by, blinding her with its headlights. She winced and turned her head.

Surrender to yourself.

Lia froze and looked around. No one seemed to be near, certainly no one close enough to whisper in her ear.

Catching her breath, she shook her head and started the jog back to the house. Westin was going to be furious.

As she neared the house, she felt a warming in her chest. She slowed and placed a hand over her heart. An excitement built up inside her, warming her. Lia stumbled, falling to the ground and breathing hard. She tried to fight it, tried to remind herself that it was unwanted emotion, but it was comforting. He was close.

She sprinted into action, springing up from her knees and cutting across people's yards to get to the house. If he was there, she was going to meet him head on.

Once again, she was out of breath and flushed when she made it to the house. She stopped dead in her tracks when she saw the body slumped on the porch. Pooling blood down the steps, it laid unmoving. Trembling, she stared at it.

It was far too big to be Westin. As she moved closer, she

recognized the customer from the other night. His hand had been removed, his lips sewed shut, and his chest stabbed.

The blood was still running out of the body. Visibly shaking, she knelt and dipped her fingers in the blood. It was warm.

He had been killed on her front stoop.

The porch light reflected from the blood, shimmering. Time slowed, and all she could see was him. There was no soul, no life fleeing from his body, but she wanted to touch him and feel his chill on her skin. The blood beckoned to her. It filled her mind with a thousand questions that she couldn't answer.

There was a noise on the other side of the door, and it pulled Lia back into reality. She raised her head over to the video camera that was above the door. She swallowed hard and wiped the blood on his clothes. There was a note pinned to him.

The hand for touching you.

The lips for degrading you.

His life as my present to you.

Tossed, seemingly carelessly to the side, was a bag overflowing with ash.

The door opened, and Westin stepped through. His eyes fell to Lia, who was kneeling by the body. "What the fuck have you done?" he demanded. "Get away from the body."

Lia stumbled back. "I did not do this Westin. I swear." His lack of faith in her shook him.

Westin shook his head. "I was deluding myself, thinking that you could make this work." His eyes moved to the bag of ash and the note on the body.

"This is not me," Lia said quietly.

Westin shook his head. "I see that," he muttered. He glanced up at the camera. "The agents will be here soon. Don't touch anything." He pulled out his phone.

Lia stared at the blood on her skin. Westin thought she would never change. No matter what he said, when he looked at her, he only saw a killer.

When she looked at the blood, she saw the same thing.

Westin swore when he hung up the phone. "They are on the way." He moved away from the cameras, his eyes falling on her hands. "Listen to me, what did you do when you saw the body? I need to know."

She raised her eyes to his. "I touched the blood," she said, her voice flat.

He searched her face. "Hell," he swore again. "They saw you on the camera, or they will see you. You didn't scream or react like a normal person. This message looks suspicious enough, but your reaction is going to raise flags. We need to play it off as shock. When they question you, you need to play the part. You're shocked and scared and don't understand what's going on. Do you understand?" He shook her a little bit. "Lia, do you understand?"

"You see me as a killer. You thought I did this. It never crossed your mind that I did not," she said quietly.

"Do you understand?" he demanded.

She pulled away. "Yes, I understand. Shocked. Deluded. Not a cold-blooded killer. I got it."

He growled a bit and pushed her away. She stumbled. "Why is he leaving me presents? I thought he wanted to kill me," she asked.

Westin ignored her, surveying the body.

"Answer me," she shouted. "Why does he not just kill me?"

"He can't," Westin shouted back. Soon, the agency's car pulled up followed by several police cars and an ambulance.

"What does that mean?" Lia asked, ignoring the cars.

"We don't have time for this," Westin muttered, going out to meet the cars.

Lia grabbed his arm. "Tell me," she pleaded. "I want to understand."

"Shocked and scared, remember?" Westin said through gritted teeth. He glanced at the agents opening the door, and pulled Lia close to his side, restraining her.

She glanced at the agents walking rapidly to meet her. Their eyes weren't on the body but directly on her. She pressed herself against Westin. He was right.

It wasn't good.

Westin gritted his teeth as the agents approached. He felt guilty for thinking that Lia had done the crime.

O'Ryan stopped directly in front of them while the other two and their team of police and investigators swarmed the body. "Agent Caxton," O'Ryan greeted him. "What is going on?"

"I'm not sure. Lia slipped out for a run, and when I found her, there was a body on the porch. I was inside the whole time, but I didn't hear anything." He slid his eyes towards Lia. "She's freezing. Can we get her a blanket?"

O'Ryan nodded and waved over the paramedics. They moved her gently away from under Westin's arm and over to the ambulance for evaluation. O'Ryan's eyes moved sharply over to Westin's. "You let her go out by herself."

Westin pointed to the opened window. "We had an argument earlier. She tried to go outside to read. I may have overreacted. She slipped out the window to go for a run."

O'Ryan nodded sharply and moved over to the body. "The hand for touching you. The lips for degrading you. His life as my present to you," he read out loud. He looked at Westin. "Do you know who this is?"

Westin nodded. "It's the same man who triggered Lia's memory last night."

O'Ryan nodded. "So, the same man who was unpleasant to our girl here is now dead on the front porch. Apparently, he's a gift for Lia." He looked at Westin. "It sounds to me like our killer not only knows that Lia is still alive but is also following her. She recognized him in that restaurant. She slipped, and we've caught her in her lie. Mallich? What do you think?"

The woman surveyed the note. "He's developed a crush on her."

"Lichton?" O'Ryan cocked his head towards the big agent. "Your opinion?"

"This isn't a developed crush. It's a gesture, an apology." They all turned their heads to Lia. "I think she had a personal relationship with our killer."

O'Ryan nodded. "Exactly what I was thinking. Finish up here. I doubt you'll find any evidence, but give it your best shot. Caxton, bring her in for questioning. We're not letting her go until we get some answers."

He strode back to the car. Westin narrowed his eyes. The young agent had found a case that would make a name for himself, and now he was growing a little too big to handle.

"Caxton, we know you've spent a lot of time with the girl. If it's easier, I can bring her in," Lichton offered.

Westin shook his head. "No worries. I got it." He moved over the retrieve Lia.

She was wrapped in a blanket and watched the scene unfold before her with a blank look on her face. He moved her away from the paramedics. "It's not good," he muttered. "You're going in for questioning. Remember what I said. You are a victim. Stick with your story. They think you have a relationship with him. Don't deny it, but tell them you have no memories. They cannot hold you for long if they can't charge you with something."

She looked at him. "You can make this go away," she muttered.

"I have orders not to interfere," he reminded her.

"Fuck your orders," she whispered angrily. "Do something for me."

He gripped her tightly. "I don't owe you anything," he hissed. Anger washed over him. He searched for emotion in her eyes, but they slipped away. She got in the car and stayed silent the whole trip to the police station.

There was so much tension that Westin couldn't think. She was right of course. It would be so simple for him to make it so that she didn't even exist in the FBI's mind, but to blatantly disregard the order of the judges would ruin everything.

He pounded the steering wheel. He didn't owe her. For years, as he watched her struggle, he thought that he did owe her, but it didn't need to be that complicated. She was being punished for her crimes, and that was that.

He would give her Charlie. Charlie was his mistake, and he would make amends for that. He would do that one thing for her, and then he was done. He could finally wash his hands of Lia and be free.

As he drove, he ignored the whisper in the back of his mind, the one that taunted him, asking him if he thought it was going to be that easy.

Raindrops drummed steadily on the roof. Connor sighed and sank on the couch. The summer semester was finally over, and he was drained. He flipped idly through the television stations and paused as an oddly familiar face filled the screen.

"The latest victim of the serial killer people are calling The Phoenix has been identified as real estate mogul Carl Franklin. Franklin was found earlier this week stabbed to death and dumped outside a local residence. His body was mutilated and dismembered. Police are saying this is the most brutal attack so far. They are urging people to use caution when leaving their homes. There is no word as to whether the homeowner where the body was found can provide any new leads."

The anchorwoman launched into a new story, but Connor had tuned out. The picture of Carl Franklin still burned in his memory.

He was the rude customer from the tavern a few nights ago. Connor's body went cold. He tried to dismiss the thoughts that entered his mind, but he couldn't ignore the facts.

He turned off the television and crept quietly to his bedroom. In the dark, he stood at the corner of his window and stared at Charlie's house. His neighbor's words echoed in his ears.

I do set designs for scenes.

Connor tapped his finger on the wall. He should call the police, but it could be a coincidence.

He sighed. Charlie was strange, but surely he wasn't a serial killer. He was a friend. How could he call the police on a friend?

There wasn't a car in the driveway. Connor crossed the house and slipped on his shoes. He needed to be sure.

He jogged out in the rain and crept behind his neighbor's house. Shivering from the weather and nerves, he tried to peer in one of the windows.

He had never been in Charlie's house before. They had never made it past the front door. All the lights were off, so Connor couldn't see very much. It looked as if most of the rooms were empty except for the back bedroom. He thought he saw a faint outline of a chair and a mattress.

Lightning lit up the sky, and Connor's eyes widened. Was that blood on the wall?

Headlights swept in from the front window, and Connor ducked. He could hear the Jeep pull into the gravel. He stepped back, but his foot slipped on the wet grass, and he fell.

He pulled himself up and crept to the corner of the house, his heart pounding. He waited for the sound of the front door opening. When he was sure that Charlie had entered the house, he sprinted for his house.

"Connor?" Connor froze at the sound of his name. He had barely reached his steps. He turned slowly. Charlie was jogging over, beer in hand. "I wanted to thank you for convincing me to go to the restaurant. I think it was exactly what I needed." His eyes swept over Connor, taking in his disheveled shirt and muddy jeans. "Why are you so dirty?"

Connor's eyes widened, and his hands began to shake. "I fell getting out of my car," he burst out loudly.

Charlie's eyes narrowed. "I didn't see you outside when I pulled up."

"I was on the other side of the car. The passenger side," he stuttered. He had never been a good liar.

Charlie knit his eyebrows together. After a moment, he held up his six-pack. "Beer? I love a good thunderstorm." The rain continued, drumming on the sidewalk. It felt, to Connor, like impending doom.

"No." Connor shook his head quickly. "I'm giving up beer!" He cringed inwardly. What the hell was he saying?"

"You're giving up beer," Charlie repeated slowly.

Connor nodded quickly. "Yes. I don't want a beer gut." He could feel the blood draining from his face.

"I've never known an Irishman to give up beer. Let me know when you come to your senses," Charlie said easily.

Connor exhaled slowly. He was afraid to say another word. He watched Charlie until the man turned slowly back to his house. After a beat, he turned and raced up his stairs, desperate to get to the safety of his home. Before he reached the doorknob, he felt something shatter against his head.

With a moan, he fell to the ground. He flipped over and tried to crawl away on his back. The killer stood over him.

Charlie raised another bottle. As he cracked it over his head, Connor could swear the man was apologizing.

Lia waited for what seemed like forever. The chair was hard and uncomfortable. She shifted around a bit before realizing that it was exactly what they wanted. She tried to sit still, but then she realized that it would make her look guilty. Conflicted, she shifted around even more. Above her, the fluorescent lights flickered angrily. She tried to look down at the floor, but the stains on her hand caught her attention. She stared at it a little more before trying to wipe it away on her pants. They had taken the clothes she was wearing, and now she was dressed once again in baggy sweats.

It seemed she had come full circle.

Finally, O'Ryan entered the room. He carried a file folder, and just like in the television shows that she watched, he spread out pictures in front of her. Each of them showed a corpse next to a pile of ash. As she surveyed the photos, she recognized some of the scenes as mimics from her memory. The soldier with a swastika on his shoulder, the bartender, the crime scene with a female and two male victims, all dressed in period clothing, and the soldier.

She looked away. "Why are you showing me these?" she asked.

"It's time to stop lying Lia. You are a striking woman. It's hard to believe that no one, no one, has stepped forward to claim you. We've sent out pictures all over the country, and so far, not one person has reported you missing. There are no co-workers, no family members, no friends, and no angry exes who have come forward to give us a clue as to who you are. It makes me think that you have either hidden yourself very well or the people who do know you aren't ones that are willing to be seen by the police." He tapped his finger on the pictures. "Our unsub's MO was not particularly pattern oriented, but until you showed up, it didn't include dressing up his victims in costumes. What does this mean to you?"

Lia met his eyes. "I do not know. I already told you. I have no idea who he is or why he is doing this. I am a victim!"

"He tried to kill you, Lia," O'Ryan said calmly. "Now, perhaps he's sorry. Perhaps he's infatuated."

"Sorry? You think this is an apology?" Lia asked incredulously. "You are out of your mind!"

O'Ryan leaned back. "You think I'm out of my mind?"

Lia leaned over. "I was stabbed! You do not apologize for that with another body." She glanced over at the pictures. They were distractions. She pushed them away.

"What were you expecting then, Lia? Flowers? Chocolate? How does a serial killer apologize for stabbing someone he loves?"

Lia nearly choked. "Loves? Where are you getting this?"

His voice softened. "He killed someone that was rude to you. It's clearly a gesture. Now, maybe you haven't gone back to him because you are under surveillance, but maybe it's because you are scared. And if you're scared, we can help you," he coaxed. "We just want to help."

Lia spread her hands. "Fine. You know what? Maybe I was his lover. Maybe I am his wife. I do not know. I have no idea who I am, what I did, or who I ran around with! If I could give him to you, I honestly think I would. Then maybe I would have some answers. But I cannot. I do not remember."

O'Ryan bowed his head for a moment. "You said you felt him before, in the restaurant. What does that mean exactly?"

Lia tapped her fingers on the table. "I felt scared. There was something familiar about his presence, and I recognized it. It is hard to explain. I felt that I was being watched, and I felt cold."

"And you don't think that the little memory flash you experienced had anything to do with him?"

Lia bounced impatiently in her chair. "I already told you. I just saw a face yelling at me, like déjà vu."

"Why'd you touch the body, Lia? Why did you dip your fingers in his blood? Were you happy that he was dead on your patio? Did you appreciate the gift?"

"Jesus. I thought maybe he was still alive. I thought I could try and stop the bleeding, but when I touched it, I felt the warmth and heaviness of it. I saw the note, and I knew that he was dead. I do not know what I thought after that. I just froze," she lied. She had practiced that part in her head while she waited in the room. She hoped it was as convincing as it sounded in her head.

"You didn't freeze Lia. You looked at the camera."

Lia shook her head. "I do not remember. Maybe I realized

that it would have captured the murder."

O'Ryan leaned over. "You think he was killed on that porch? You think the killer was brazen enough to do it on camera with an FBI agent a few feet away from him?"

"I do not know," Lia said exhaustedly.

"You would be right. He dragged what looked like an unconscious body on the patio. He'd already had his hand cut off and lips sewed shut, but he was stabbed on camera. He pinned the note to the body, tossed the bag of ash, and waved at the camera." He reached into his folder and pulled out another picture. An image in a black mask stared at the camera with one hand lifted up in a casual wave.

"All we can conclusively say from this picture is that he's average height, Caucasian and has brown eyes. It looks like his clothes are stuffed with something, so we can't even tell weight accurately. He's good, Lia." O'Ryan tapped on the picture. "Help us. If you helped him, if you were his partner, we could help you. Give him to us, and we'll make a deal. I promise you'll serve very limited time."

Lia shook her head. "I cannot help you. I do not know anything." She was starting to sound like a broken record.

O'Ryan slammed his hand down in frustration. "Think about it," he said through gritted teeth. He pushed the pictures back over towards her and stormed out the room.

Lia knew she was being watched. She glanced at the photos again before flipping them over and pushing them away from her. She clutched her arms and began to rock.

It had seemed like forever before O'Ryan returned. "Last chance Lia."

She shook her head. "I do not know anything," she muttered.

He nodded. "You're still under the protection of the FBI. You will be monitored. If you help us, we can help you." He opened the door wider. Westin stepped into view.

"Let's go," he muttered.

She slipped past O'Ryan, careful not to touch him, and followed Westin out. It wasn't until they were out of the building that she dropped her act.

"Nothing is going to take my freedom away," she said coldly. "You will take care of this or so help me God, I will kill everyone who stands in my way."

Westin stared at her. "It's not that easy Lia. You can't just murder your way out of this."

She opened the door. "Watch me. I seem to be very good at it."

Chapter Twenty-One

Lia shook with rage. Her new life was falling apart around her. She slipped off the sweats that she was wearing and stalked around her room naked. There was still blood on her skin, and she trembled every time she looked at it. The anger and lust were taking over.

"No, no, no, no, no," she muttered. She walked over to her mirror and stared at herself. Her skin glowed with a slight tan, her hair was shiny and bouncy around her shoulders, everything about her body screamed life except for her eyes. They were cold and dead. Angry, she grabbed the water glass on the table and threw it against the mirror, watching as her reflection shattered to the floor.

Westin pounded on the door. "What are you doing?"

She opened the door. "What do you want, Westin? Are you afraid that I am killing someone in here? You seem to be so sure that I cannot change. Why is that?"

He shook his head. "Go to bed, Lia."

"I cannot wash the blood off my hands."

"What?"

She lifted her shaking hands. "It is hard to look at it. He is dead because of me, and I was not even the one holding the blade. I cannot look at it long enough to wash it away. It makes me unsure of myself." She dropped her hands, defeated.

"Christ," Westin muttered. He grabbed her by the arm and hauled her into the bathroom. "Why aren't you wearing any clothes?"

"I wanted to see the person I was becoming. I wanted to know if I was starting to look like her again."

"Look like who?"

"The reflection in my memories."

Westin turned on the water and started to rub her hands with soap. She stared at their reflections. Westin looked up and met her gaze. "I don't know the person that you were before, Lia. I don't know what caused you to kill before, and I don't know how you are feeling now. I do know that since you have started killing, this is the longest you have ever gone without taking a life. It's the first time you've tried to be happy without killing. I just don't know if you are going to make it."

For the first time, Lia looked at Westin. His face was drawn, and his eyes were tired. He dried her hands, and his shoulders slumped.

"You asked to cross over to watch me. You claimed you were here to protect people from me. You thought I was a danger, and yet you advocate for my change. Why not just let me kill so that you can collect me and be done with this whole mess?" She looked at her hands. Westin had washed all the blood off.

"It's not that simple. Go to bed," Westin said tiredly. "We'll talk in the morning."

She frowned but did as she was told. She could feel his eyes on her as she walked down the hall and pulled the doors shut. Her anger had washed away with the blood, and all that was left was a tired shell. There were no alien feelings inside her. She was alone with herself.

She pulled on a pair of cotton shorts and a tank-top. Her nakedness was starting to feel like vulnerability. She side-stepped the broken glass and crawled into bed and prayed that, for tonight, there would be no dreams.

She dreamed.

In the early hours of the morning, she began tossing and turning into her sleep. Even in her sleep she tried to deny it entry, but she was weak. Something pulled her kicking and screaming through a portal, and shoved her into a violent storm.

The temperature dropped, and Lia shivered. She dug her toes into the gravel. They bit into her skin, and she winced. In the silence of the false scene before her, something tugged at her memory. She had been here before. She looked to the left at the figure struggling in the violent waters. The wind ripped the trees from the roots and toppled them over. In front of her stood the tall blurry man.

The screams rose, but she only stared at the water. "Last victim," she said tonelessly.

"Yes," the voices replied. "Your first."

"I suppose it is the girl in the water," Lia said unmoving. There was no reply. She turned her head to stare at the blurry figure before her. He had not moved. "Get on with it," she said through clenched teeth.

"Save her, Annalia. Overcome the power of this place. Save her," the voices commanded.

Lia stared at the figure and then the woman dying in the water. "I have already tried. I cannot."

"Do you want to save her?"

Lia stared at the water. She remembered her blood dancing in the waves. "I do not want to die."

"It is a dream, Annalia. You cannot die."

"Tell me who I am," she demanded.

"Annalia Sophia Asim."

Anger washed over, and the earth trembled. "There is more to me than a name," she said through clenched teeth. She raced to the water, fighting against the wind, fighting against the screams.

Lia dove head first into the water, and she felt a ripple of power flow through her. She moved through the water, but it pulled against her. It began to drag her down, slamming her against the bottom. She smashed her head against something sharp. The water around her turned red, and she began to drown in her blood.

Her lungs screamed for oxygen, and darkness claimed her.

Then she was standing in front of a door, dry and far away from the river. In her hand, she gripped a blade. She tried to look around, but her body betrayed her. Her eyes focused straight ahead, and her hand reached up and opened the door.

She struggled for control over her body, but it was useless. While an alien part of her felt cold, controlled, and focused, another part struggled to surface, to understand what was happening.

She moved quietly through the hallway. In the end, she could see the flickering light from the fire. She could smell a mix of smoke and brandy. There was laughter floating from the room. She paused.

Part of her knew something wasn't right. She understood that she was there for a specific reason, but something wasn't going as planned. Still, she began moving forward again.

She stopped at the doorway and peered into the room. A man sat on the floor, wrapped in a blanket in front of the fire drinking. "Hurry up, will you? My glass is empty, and my body is cold," he called out.

A woman's laughter rang out from the other side of the room, and she walked through placing the bottle on the floor. "Just a moment my love," she said sweetly and, within a second, she was standing in the doorway in front of Lia.

"What are you doing here?" she cried. Lia looked past her, to the man who was struggling to get up. A certain understanding flashed in the woman's eyes. "No, you will not take him," she said and pushed Lia.

The two women fell to the floor, and it was instinct that raised Lia's arm and brought her knife down into the chest of the woman.

Lia struggled to her feet and moved away just as the man reached them. His eyes fell to the fallen woman, and he fell to his knees. Lia raised the knife again.

He gathered the woman into his arms and rocked back and forth. "I am so sorry, my love. I should have listened to you. I am so sorry. Please, please don't leave me. Help! Someone help me!"

He never even looked up at Lia again, and her hand shook. Her will faltered, and she ran for the door out to the street. Finally, Lia pushed herself out of her body, stumbling. She turned and watched her reflection flee down the street, dropping the knife along the way.

Lia walked over slowly and stared at the knife. Slowly, she turned back and stared at the doorway. She waited for the man to come out and pursue her, to avenge the death of his beloved.

But Westin stayed inside, holding the corpse of his wife, and slowly, Lia faded away.

Lia awoke, struggling for air. In a flurry, she shoved the blankets off her and struggled off the bed. Even as her feet hit the floor, she knew she wasn't alone. The smell of brandy mingled in the air. She didn't even turn around.

"Her name was Caroline. I married her for duty, but she was my love. We were happy. We lived in bliss for five years. Then everything changed. Earlier that week, she went to my brother's to deliver a letter from me. My brother and I were not close. I didn't want to see him, so Caroline offered to deliver the letter for me. I don't even remember what was in it. When she got back, she was terrified. She said she had overheard plans that my brother was going to have me killed. I told her it was nonsense. I loved my wife dearly, but I had notions that women could be frivolous and dramatic. I brushed it aside."

Lia rose to her feet and turned to Westin. "And then I killed your wife," she finished.

Westin drained his glass. "And then you killed my wife. Oddly enough, I think it was the only time you had failed to kill the one you wanted. You left me alive. I always thought maybe you found it a crueler fate."

He weaved slightly as he stepped forward. She frowned. "You are drunk," she observed.

Westin nodded. "Caroline was your first kill. I knew you'd dream about her tonight." He tilted his glass at her. "I wanted to be prepared."

He took a deep breath and looked around, his gaze resting on the broken glass still on the floor. "I find it odd that you're so quiet. You normally have so many questions."

Lia trembled and stepped back. "Do you want to kill me?"

Westin popped his head back up. "Kill you? No, it was a long time ago. I remember almost nothing about my life then, except that night. And I've had plenty of chances to kill you. Why would I start now?"

"Then what do you want?"

He stared at her. "I suppose I want to know why."

She shook her head. "I think she got in the way. I was there for you."

"Why were you there for me? Why would my brother want my life? She died to save me, and I never knew why."

"You took my memories. I do not know why," Lia said quietly.

Westin blew out his breath and nodded. "I did that. I did take your memories, and then I took your soul. It's ironic that she would die to save me, and just a few weeks later, I bound myself to you. I certainly didn't know at the time that I would be chasing you all over the world." He rubbed his hand over his face. The more he drank, the thicker his British accent became. "Of course, I didn't know they would give you your soul back. I didn't know that Charlie would steal it. Oh, it's all such a big mess now."

Lia backed up. "What did you just say?"

Westin looked up. "They gave you your soul back. Did you think that you could survive on this side of the veil without a soul? It can't be done. You have to have at least a part of your soul to survive on this side of the veil. Of course, until Charlie, I didn't even know that souls could be broken."

Lia felt a blow to her chest. She gasped for air and clutched her chest. "That is not possible. I would feel differently if I had my soul."

Westin toppled over, drunk, and slid to the floor. He waved his hand about. "Yes, you would probably feel differently if you had your whole soul. You probably would have killed someone by now. God knows it turned Charlie evil."

Lia rushed over, crossing the broken glass. She didn't even flinch as it bit into her foot. She reached Westin and kneeled down. "You are not making any sense. Where is the rest of my soul? Who is Charlie?"

Westin looked up and touched her face. "You killed my wife, and now I am obligated to save you."

"Save me from what?"

"Save you from yourself."

Lia slapped him. "What the hell are you talking about?"

Westin grunted and rubbed his face. "I did something dangerous. In return, the judges decided that volunteered collectors were a bad idea and couldn't be trusted. Charlie arrived on my doorstep as the new generation of collectors. He was a reaper who had proven himself to be obedient. In return, he was given a minuscule part of his soul to train with me."

He laughed. "You know, I liked him. He made me laugh. I thought he had faith in the system, you know?"

Frustrated, Lia snapped her fingers in front of him. "I do not care about that. Get back to the point. You were training Charlie?"

"Hmm? Yes, I was training Charlie. You weren't the only soul I had to collect. I don't know what his plan was. I don't know if he knew about you, the reaper who was allowed to keep her soul, or if it was a momentary decision." He laughed. "You stabbed me you know. I think that partly makes it your fault."

"What happened when I stabbed you?"

Westin scratched his head. "You killed a guard at Auschwitz. You know, I think I was proud of you for that one. They were all a bunch of assholes. I wanted to collect the whole lot of them."

Lia shook her head. "Focus."

"It was odd. You knew I was coming. I think a part of you even recognized me. You were ready. You already know that part. I started the collection, you stabbed me, and as I staggered, Charlie jumped in and grabbed your soul. Now, I wasn't that incompetent. I did manage to hold on to a piece of it. The larger chunk, if it makes you feel any better. And the judges never knew. I thought Charlie was just going to live out his life peacefully and die of old age. As long as you stayed behind the veil, you would have been fine."

A realization was dawning on her. Lia stepped back slowly, blood seeping into the carpet. Westin pointed to it. "What is it with you and blood?"

Lia shook her head. "It is not possible," she whispered.

Westin struggled to his feet. "Charlie didn't live out his life peacefully. He started to slowly die. I guess a soul cannot exist in distant pieces for too long. It must be close to its other half. He started ducking back into the veil to try and gain strength. I guess he knew it wouldn't last. He started to kill. He could see reapers. I guess that's a side effect of your soul. He started looking for you. I thought he was trying to reap the rest of your soul, but as it turns out, he was just trying to kill you. I think he wanted to break the bond. It wasn't his brightest idea."

Lia stumbled back on the bed and grabbed her chest. "Please stop," she whispered.

"No, you wanted the whole story. It's a good plan, you know? The judges can't identify a soul and body that don't match. They were confused by the fact that they couldn't identify this new evil. I knew what was going on though. I tried hunting for your soul, but I kept getting drawn back to the bigger half, your half. Finally, my only option was a demotion. I became your Master to keep you on this side of the veil."

Westin started to hiccup. "Whoops, I think I drank too much. My efforts were for naught. It wasn't an accident that you were there. As it turns out, the judges had been placing you at certain sites for years hoping that you would catch up with him. And then you did. They ripped you out of one world and put you in another in hopes that you would kill Charlie."

Lia nodded. "If I kill Charlie, I go back," she muttered.

Westin burst out laughing. "Lia, if you kill Charlie, you'll die. Your soul cannot live without that half. Soon you'll start feeling the effects of it. You'll start to wither and die just as Charlie discovered."

Lia shook her head. "How could you keep this from me? You have known all along, and you did not say anything."

Westin stopped and stared. "You haven't even said that you were sorry. You murdered my wife. Before you didn't know, but now you do. And you have not once said you were sorry."

Lia stared at him. "This whole time I have been blaming those kills on a soulless creature who was not me. And I was wrong. She is me, she always is me, and she always will be me. An apology is not going to change that."

She pushed past him and rushed down the stairs, grabbing the keys on the way out. She trailed blood all the way to the car. Westin didn't follow her. With some difficulty, she managed to back the car down the drive-way. Once in gear, she sped through the night trying desperately to remember the way to Hunter's house.

Chapter Twenty-Two

Hunter watched Lia silently as he bandaged up her feet. She was staring off listlessly and hadn't said a word since he'd found her on his front porch. He didn't even know how long she'd been waiting. He'd returned from a twenty-hour shift to find her bleeding on the concrete.

When he was finished, he rose and kissed her on the forehead. "Lia, it looks like you've been through quite an ordeal. Do you want to talk about it?" he asked quietly.

She crossed her arms over her stomach and shook her head.

"Okay, you don't have to if you don't want to. I'm going to call Agent Caxton to let him know that you're here."

She grabbed his arms. "No," she said urgently. "You cannot do that."

He covered her hand with his. "Lia, I don't know what's going on, but I want you to be safe. You're bleeding. I need to notify the police. You shouldn't be without an escort."

"You do not have to worry about me. I am currently the most well-protected soul in the universe," she said dryly.

A confused look passed over his face. "What do you mean?

She sighed and stared at the floor. "Nothing."

He touched her feet once more. "Lia, what happened to your feet?"

She shrugged. "I stepped on some glass."

He raised his eyebrows, hoping for a better explanation. There was none. He kissed her again and helped her off the sink. As he walked her out to the living room, he wondered how it was that she wasn't even limping in pain.

"How did you get here?"

"I drove," she answered listlessly. She laid down on the couch and closed her eyes.

"Do you even have a license?" he asked, but she'd already fallen asleep.

He sat down in the chair opposite of her and wondered what he was going to do.

Lia awoke with a start. For a moment, she stared at the walls disoriented. Where was she? She sat up and saw Hunter dozing in the chair with Jacks nestled at his feet. Her heart ached.

She tiptoed quietly across the room, folding her arms across her body and hugging herself. Why had she come here? Now that she knew what she was, what she had done, why hadn't she run far away?

The windows were big and open, allowing the sun to stream freely into the house. It was cozy and inviting. She studied the pictures on the wall and the side tables. They were all of Hunter's family. She could see the similar features in all of them, from the aging parents to the purple haired younger sister. In each picture, Hunter had his arm protectively around someone.

They were a beautiful family.

She wandered out into the hall and found pictures of Hunter joking around with his co-workers. Everyone in the photos looked exhausted, but there was a sense of pride and companionship in their eyes. The work they did was important to them. They were saving lives.

Lia clutched at her chest once more. She closed her eyes and saw the blood flowing from all her victims. She saw the pain in Westin's eyes as he held his dead wife. She saw the smile on her reflection as she pushed the blade into her skin.

She doubled over and dry heaved. Hunter came flying into the hall. "Lia?"

Lia backed up. "This is a mistake. I should not have come

here."

"Lia, stop. Whatever is going on, I can be there for you. Tell me what is scaring you so I can protect you."

She shook her head wildly. "It was just supposed to be sex. I just felt different with you, different than what I felt with Paul, different than what I felt then, but you deserve so much more. After the fair, I thought I would fit in, but I do not think that will ever happen. I am different. I see that now."

Hunter was staring at her strangely. "It was just supposed to be sex? What do you mean? Who is Paul," he asked slowly.

"Before I met you, I had another life," Lia began weakly. Her error hadn't gone unnoticed.

"So you remember your life." His eyes hardened. "You've known who you were before we had sex? Before the fair? How long have you been lying?"

Lia looked down at her hands. They were shaking. Her heart was beating harder, and she just didn't feel right. "Not lying. I mean not lying on purpose. If I could tell you, if I thought you'd believe me, I would. I did not lie to hurt you," she protested weakly.

He ran his hands through his hair and shook his head. "Jesus. I waited because I wanted to give you time, but you've always known. I must have looked like an idiot. I feel like an idiot. So what? What was worth hiding?"

She shook her head. "You could never understand."

He nodded. "No, it's okay. I'm used to dealing with women who lie. Does the FBI know? Are you scamming them too? Or is your precious Agent Caxton in on it? I never even checked his credentials."

"Hunter wait, it is not like that," Lia said. She reached out for him. A few moments ago, she was ready to walk out of his life, but now that she was losing him, she wanted desperately to hold him.

"Did you ever have amnesia? I mean, you acted oddly. It never occurred to me that it would be anything else, but there were no signs. So have you been faking it this whole time?"

The lie caught in her throat, and she couldn't force it out. "It is complicated. I have always known who I am, but there were missing memories," she said finally.

He stepped away. "Get out, Lia, or whatever your name. Just get the fuck out."

"Wait, you do not mean that. Please, I will tell you everything. I will explain."

His face darkened. "I don't think you understand. I don't care. I don't care about your past or why you lied. I'm done. Leave. Now." His words were cold and final.

Her hands dropped to her side, helpless. She knew it was for the best, but pain pierced her chest.

Her face hardened, and she turned to the door. As she walked, the pain flew up her leg, and it was no longer a reminder that she was alive. It was a reminder that she was weak. She stumbled, and Hunter moved to catch her. Instead, she caught herself on the wall and pushed herself off, half running half limping down the hall to the door.

Outside, the trees and the wind screamed at her.

Surrender to who you are.

She climbed into the car. As she sped away, the voice followed her.

Surrender to who you are.

She gripped the steering wheel and let out a scream. "Fine," she said. Her voice died down, and she took a deep breath. "You win," she whispered.

Chapter Twenty-Three

Hunter sat in his parent's kitchen, running his fingers across the condensation of his beer bottle. He was falling off the wagon, hard. His siblings had left a few moments before, and his mother sat across from him, waiting for him to tell her what was wrong. He gripped his glass tightly. Lia had been gone for hours now, but he knew as soon as the door slammed behind her. He knew he'd made a mistake.

"She admitted that she lied to me," he said hoarsely, still trying to make sense of the odd conversation that Lia had with him.

"Lied about what?" his mother asked.

"She said she never had amnesia. I don't know why though. When she offered to tell me the truth, I pushed her away." Hunter saw Lia's face in his mind. There was anguish in her eyes as she backed away from him. He reached into his pocket and pulled out the necklace that he had given her. It must have come undone when she was sleeping and fallen in the couch cushions. Just seeing it there, against the fabric instead of around her neck, had forced him to see the reality of the situation. She was gone. It was cold against his skin. No matter how long he held it, it never warmed. He rubbed his thumb along the divide in the middle.

Deep down, he knew something was wrong. "I don't know what she's done in the past, but I don't think it's who she is now. I think she's in trouble."

His mother reached out and stroked his hair. "Maybe you should have listened to what she had to say."

"How can I trust someone who lied to me?"

"Do you look at her and see Carol?"

No, he didn't see his ex when he looked at her. He saw pain, violence, and sadness. He saw all the things that had once rested inside of him. He shook his head. "What do I do, Mom?"

Tears welled up in his mother's eyes. "Hunter. I have always taught you to follow your instincts. Maybe she is dangerous. She is certainly in a dangerous situation. Is that something you want to be involved in?"

Hunter stood, pocketing the necklace. "I've never felt with anyone the way I feel when I'm with her. She makes the earth move under my feet. She has this power I've never seen in anyone."

"In that case, you owe it to her to listen to her side of the story. You'll never know what to do until you know what motivates her," his mother said finally.

He nodded, knowing his mother was right. He kissed her on the forehead and made up his mind. He needed to find Lia.

As Hunter left the house, he was so focused that he didn't even notice the figure hunched over in the back seat. It wasn't until he drove home that he realized he wasn't alone.

Charlie reached up behind the driver's seat and covered the man's mouth with a cloth. It only took a moment for Hunter to pass out.

Lia awoke in a hotel room. The sun had long past set, and the rain had started to pour in what seemed like a desperate attempt to wash the day away. Lia shivered. She was still wearing the pajamas from the night before.

She inspected the bandages around her feet. The bleeding had stopped, but the wrappings were soaked. Without shoes, the wounds would continue to reopen.

"Damn it," she whispered.

She couldn't continue to walk around barefoot. She ran out into the rain and drove to the nearest convenient store. Under the watchful eye of the curious employee, she purchased new bandages and a pair of flip-flops.

"You're bleeding," he pointed out.

She glared at him. "I know that," she said coldly.

"Maybe you should go to the hospital."

She leaned across the counter. "Maybe you should mind your own business," she threatened in a low voice. He took a step back and stared until she finished paying and left.

Back in the car, she dried her feet the best she could and rewrapped them. She leaned against the seat and thought about what she would do next.

Her relationship with Westin was torn to shreds. She murdered his wife, and he had lied to her about her soul. That was hard to repair. Hunter had rejected her. That pain was something she wasn't ready to deal with yet.

As she drove back to the hotel, she passed a bar. Intrigued, she made a u-turn, tires squealing and pulled into the parking lot. She stared at the large neon sign above her.

Terrible, miserable, karaoke music was spilling out from the door. Scantily clad women and men with hungry eyes loitered outside the door. It called to her. She tapped her finger against the steering wheel.

She stepped out of the car, still dressed in her soaking wet cotton shorts and tank-top. The men outside immediately responded in whistles and cat-calls. She glared at them. Staying could mean trouble, but she didn't have the willpower to turn and walk away. She needed to release some energy.

Inside, she slid onto the bar stool. When the bartender asked her what she wanted, she had flashbacks of two bartenders, the one she had killed, and the one Charlie had killed. She shivered. "Whatever will get me drunk for cheap," she muttered.

The bartender nodded and poured her a shot from a bottle. Lia tried to drink it, but she immediately started to cough. The liquid went down burning the lining out of her throat. The bartender wordlessly poured her a soda. Once she properly washed the liquid down, he poured her another. As she lifted it to her lips, a man slipped onto the barstool next to her.

"Can I buy a pretty woman a drink?" he asked, his voice slurring.

Lia turned to examine him. He was slender with pale skin and bloodshot eyes. He was young, barely old enough to drink, and clearly strung out. The kid had demons pouring out of him, and Lia felt a kinship with him. Under the rough exterior, she found him attractive. It occurred to her that the best way to drive away the image of Hunter was with another man.

"Yes, please," she responded. He bought her two more rounds of shots while he consumed half a bottle.

"What brings a pretty girl like yourself to a place like this?" he muttered, trying to maintain eye contact.

"I needed a place to think."

He laughed, spitting a little of his drink out. She straightened up and frowned while he wiped his mouth. "What do you need to think about?" he asked finally.

"My place in this world."

A twisted grip spread across his face. "I know a good place for that pretty mouth of yours."

The obscene comment struck a cord, and she narrowed her eyes. "I would be careful if I were you," she said coldly.

A shameful looked crossed his face. "I'm sorry. Sometimes, when I drink, I sort of turn into someone else," he said quietly.

Lia looked at him thoughtfully. Under the rough exterior, she thought she would see a wounded soul. For an instant, she saw the scars behind his eyes, and she thought of her own. Perhaps they were not so different.

A few hours later he was so drunk he couldn't stand. She was disappointed that she didn't even feel a buzz. Still, she wanted a few moments of escape, so she hauled him into her car and drove him to her motel room.

He stumbled inside and turned to kiss her. As soon as his lips touched hers, she felt dirty and cheap. Hunter's face rose in her mind, and she pushed the boy away. "Stop," she muttered.

"What? C'mon girl. It's gonna be so good," he slurred. He moved again for a kiss.

"I said no," she said strongly. She pushed him again, and this time he fell to the floor, striking his head on the bed. The light caught something metal as it fell out of his pocket.

Lia leaned over to check his pulse. The kid was knocked out cold, but he was still alive. Lia felt her throat tighten as the blood trickled out of his wound.

She pushed herself away, her hand brushing on something metallic. Immediately, her hand closed around it. It was a large pocketknife. She gripped the hilt tightly as she flipped the blade open. Wordlessly, she stared at it.

The blood from his head wound was roaring in her ears. Her heart beat loudly, and she leaned over his body. Trembling, she touched the blade to the skin on his neck. He was just a junkie. What did his life matter? This is what she did. This is what she was born to do.

The blood slowly reached her hand, and she watched as it created a tiny pool in the crevice of her fingers. It called to her, taunted her. It wanted to flow freely. It begged to be released.

With a cry, she stumbled away from the body. She felt tears well up behind her eyes. Lia crawled out of the hotel room and stumbled back into the car. She tossed the knife onto the passenger seat. Away from temptation, she sobbed freely. Once started, it seemed the tears would never end. Her chest heaved up and down as she gasped for breath.

For the first time that she could remember, Lia felt broken and wrong.

Westin awoke from his drunken stupor. He glanced about confused. Why was he in Lia's room? After a moment, all the words that had poured out of his mouth in his drunken misery rushed back into his memories.

He ran a hand over his face. "Shit," he muttered. "Lia?" he called out. The house was silent. "Shit, shit, shit. What have I done?"

He pulled himself to his feet and cried out as his temples pounded. He grabbed his head and banged it lightly a few times against the wall. It had been a long time since he had to deal with a hangover.

He stumbled out of her room. "Lia? Lia!" He stumbled down the stairs. He reached for his keys on the counter, but they weren't there. "No," he muttered to himself. "She wouldn't."

Westin moved to the window and pushed the curtains aside. The rain was pouring outside. He squinted, but there was no car outside.

He growled, and as his eyes focused on his reflection, he saw another come up behind him.

"Charlie," he muttered, but the rag was already over his mouth. Within seconds, Westin slumped back against the wall, unconscious for the second time that day.

The pain in his head broke through the darkness, and Connor moaned. He tried to grab his head, but he couldn't move his hands. After a moment of struggling, Connor opened his eyes. Before him stood a large antique mirror on a swivel stand. He stared at himself.

He was tied to a chair with his hands behind his back. Blood trickled from his head and down his collar bone. Behind him were streaks of blood. Connor felt his stomach roll.

"Thirsty?"

Connor's head snapped up. He watched Charlie from the mirror. "Haven't killed me yet?" he asked weakly.

Charlie stepped forward, a cup of water in his hand. He offered it up to Connor's lips who, after a moment, leaned his head down and drank from the cup. "Do you know how old I am

Connor?"

Connor licked his lips and shook his head. If Charlie wanted to talk, Connor would let him talk. "No. I don't think we ever got that far."

"I don't know either." Charlie walked to the opposite wall and slid down it. "I remember World War Two. That was fun."

Connor let out a wry laugh and nodded his head. "Right. Well, ya look good for an oul lad. Ya must be past seventy."

"Oh, I am far older than that. That just happens to be as far back as I can remember. In all those years though, I never had a friend until you." He cocked his head. "How did you find me out? It was the prick from the restaurant, right?"

Connor didn't say anything. Charlie continued. "He was the perfect gift for her. Why didn't you call the police?"

"I did not want to falsely accuse a friend to the peelers," Connor said. He stared at the blood on his shirt. "Believe me, I see the irony in that."

"She is a part of me now Connor. I need you to understand that. I have killed randomly before, but now I do everything for her. I can't get her out of my head. I need her just to keep breathing. You understand right?"

"Who was in the box?"

Charlie stared past him. Connor narrowed his eyes. "Who was in the box that I helped you carry into your Jeep?" he repeated.

"A server named Luke." Charlie smiled. "Luke was the perfect prop. It's hard enough setting up a scene, but to find a character that so perfectly matched the description? It was too good to be true."

He pulled himself up and began to pace. "I'm so close. She knows me now! Westin will have to tell her the truth, and when he does, she will come running to me, and we will be together forever."

Connor pulled at his ropes. "Let me go, Charlie. I'm not

going to tell anyone, I swear," he pleaded.

"I can't do that Connor. I wish I could."

He turned his back and turned to the hallway. "Charlie, don't do this," Connor called out. Charlie shut the door behind him. "Charlie!"

He pulled at his ropes, but they only bit into his skin. Finally, he relaxed and stared at himself in the mirror. "Move to America. Check. Ace your first semester. Check. Befriend a serial killer. Check. Get yourself killed. Check."

The pain worsened in his head. He could feel his body weaken. After a few hours, he slumped against his chair and lost consciousness.

When he came to again, he was in another room entirely. He was propped against the wall on the floor, his hands bound in front of him. There was a sandwich on a plate in front of him. His stomach growled, and he gobbled it down before he realized that he had an audience.

He raised his head slowly and stared at the men in front of him. They were both bound to chairs, staring at him.

Connor froze. "Who the bloody hell are ya?"

Westin struggled for a moment against his ropes. "I could ask you the same question." He looked at Hunter. "Are you all right?"

Hunter nodded. "Where is Lia?"

Westin shook his head. "I don't know. We got into a fight, and she left."

"Same here." Hunter shook his head. "She admitted she never had amnesia." He looked at Westin. "You knew all along, didn't you? You know who she is?"

Connor waved his hands. "Excuse me? I'd like to know who ya are."

"My name is Westin. Can you untie us?"

Connor shuffled around. "Do you know Charlie?"

Westin craned his neck and stared at him. "Do you know Charlie?"

Connor tried to work on the ropes. His fingers were numb. "I live next door." He stopped and stared at the room. "At least, I think I'm still next door."

The two new men stared at each other. "Tell me," Hunter said.

Westin shrugged. He watched as Connor struggled with the ropes. "It doesn't matter. You won't remember. Lia is, first and foremost, a murderer. Up until recently, she was a reaper of souls. Now she's fully human armed with dangerous knowledge and stuffed in a powder keg of emotions."

Connor stopped. "You sound just like Charlie," he said quietly.

The man shrugged. "I should. At one time, we filled the same position."

The door slammed open, and Connor backed up. Carrying a third chair, Charlie entered the room. Seeing Connor, he dropped the chair and pulled out a gun. "Don't make me use it, Connor. Back in your corner," he said, waving the gun.

"Do as he says," Westin said quietly. Connor backed into his corner, and Charlie glared at Westin.

"Don't talk to my friend," he said threateningly.

He pulled the chair over, scraping it against the hardwood. "Sit," he ordered. With the gun pointed at him, Connor obeyed. His body tightened as Charlie wrapped some ropes around his chest and stomach. Secured to the chair, he relaxed, helpless.

Charlie stepped back and surveyed the scene in front of him. "Not quite what I was expecting," he muttered, glaring at Connor.

Connor shrugged. "When I pictured my summer, this wasn't really what I had in mind either," he said wryly.

"This is your fault," Charlie cried out, his voice rising in pitch.

"My fault? I didn't go around killing a bunch of people!" Connor said defensively.

"This is ridiculous," Westin finally broke out. He glared at Charlie. "What are you doing, Charlie?"

The man known as the Phoenix fell silent, visibly trying to calm himself. After a moment, he holstered the gun. "Connor, meet Hunter. Hunter is a surgeon at Saint Antony Hospital. He's a bit of a kink in my plan."

Connor looked over at the silent man. There was fear in his eyes, but his face remained calm and cold.

"Westin," Charlie continued, "is masquerading as an FBI agent. He has a unique talent of making people think whatever they want. He can also make people forget." He leaned over, putting his face in Westin's, and smiled. "Hello, old friend. I honestly did not expect to see you."

"What did you expect? You can't continue killing people."

"I fully expected you to kill me. But you've grown fond of her, haven't you? It's a bit twisted, don't you think?"

Westin fell silent, and Charlie backed away, positioned himself in front of Connor. "I'm going to tell you a story, Connor. It's going to help you understand. You see, the world is not just made up of things you can see. In a parallel world, there is a group of things, individuals, species of some sort, which monitor you. They sense your motivations, they see your soul, and on occasion, they step in and interfere with human affairs. They call themselves judges."

Connor's eyes widened. His neighbor was further around the bend than he originally expected. Charlie continued. "Westin is not an FBI agent. He was born in the seventeenth century. I don't know all the details, but I expect that he was an outstanding citizen. He always played by the rules. Of course, that was before his wife was murdered by a young woman with lovely porcelain skin, raven black hair, and eyes that could see right through you."

To his left, Connor heard the doctor inhale sharply. Charlie smiled. "Yes. I am afraid that your new girlfriend isn't as innocent as she would seem." He focused back on Connor. "Heartbroken, our young Westin found himself fading away from reality." He glanced at Westin. "Is that right? I must admit, I'm making this part up as I go."

Westin kept quiet. "Long story short, the judges offered Westin opportunity to make the world a better place. He became a collector. He has spent centuries collecting the souls of evil doers, erasing their memories, and forcing them to serve sentences as grim reapers, collecting the souls of the dying. He's quite the hero, isn't he?"

Charlie smiled. "Only he's not. Our soldier in white has a blood-stained hat. He made one mistake, and now here we are, all facing a future that even the judges could not foresee." He stared at Connor. "The cycle has to end, Connor. Do you understand?"

"I think yer mad," Connor said.

"He's not denying it," Charlie said, pointing at Westin.

Connor looked at the stranger on his right. "I think yer both mad," he said finally.

Charlie frowned, pulling away. "You'll see. When you see her, you'll understand," he said finally.

"She won't come to you," Westin said quietly.

"She will come. Whether she comes for you or me makes no difference. I will give her the choice of making her whole. You know her better than anyone, Westin. She'd never pass up such an opportunity. Nobody would."

Lia pulled up to the house. Driving was getting easier and easier with each destination. She would get Westin to help her. After facing the prospect of killing the stranger from the bar, she realized that she needed Westin. If nothing else, she would get him to collect her again.

She ran through the rain and slipped the keys in the door. To her surprise, the door was already opened. She pushed it the rest of the way. "Westin?"

The room was dark. She reached over and flipped on the switch. The room was empty, "Westin?" she called out again. As she moved through the living room, her eyes caught something unusual. A post-it-note was stuck to the opposite wall. She moved closer.

They abandoned you. Let me make you whole again.

Lia stared at the note. Charlie. "No, no, no," she muttered. She ran through the house, but, except for the glass that still scattered the floor of her bedroom, she found no blood and no sign of a struggle. Maybe Westin was still alive. A chill went through her. If Charlie had Westin, he probably had Hunter as well. Where would he take them?

Lia closed her eyes and searched through her memories. If this was a game to Charlie, then she had the answer. All she had to do was find it.

It would be a local place, but Lia hadn't killed anyone in the area. She wasn't looking for some place that was special to her. She was looking for a place that was special to him. She switched settings and grabbed the file Westin had kept on Charlie. There had to be something local that somehow pertained to her.

None of the pictures shocked her. She flipped through them with ease, numb to the violence and blood before her. The number of kills he made didn't even give her pause, yet her hands were shaking, just a little, as she flipped through the pages.

She'd only made it halfway through the file when she found it. With long dark hair, creamy complexion, well-defined features, the woman could have passed for her sister. Lia ran a finger over the picture, lingering over the blood splatter. Most of Charlie's kills were messy, quick, and then ignored, yet this woman was cleaned and posed. The words "break the chains" were painted in her blood.

It was what Charlie had said to Amanda. He needed to break the chains.

She ripped out the page with the address and grabbed

Westin's keys.

Her hand trembled as she set her GPS. Her eye dropping to the knife that was still in the seat, she started the car once again. Westin's words echoed in her mind. She couldn't kill Charlie, but Westin could collect his soul. She only hoped Westin was still alive.

Forty-five minutes and three near accidents later, Lia pulled up to what appeared to be an abandoned cabin. She could feel Charlie, feel his excitement at her approach, feel the adrenaline pulsing through his veins, and feel his lust for blood.

And she was sure he could feel her own lust as well.

There would be no surprise attack. He knew that she was here. She walked up to the front and opened the door, ignoring its creaking hinges.

It was a small cabin, probably only contained three rooms, but there was no need to search. Everyone was in the front room. Westin and Hunter were both tied up to the chairs, awake, but unable to move. They had identical blood tracks down their heads, and fear seemed to wash over them as she entered. They tried to warn her about what she already knew. Behind them, also tied to a chair, was a young man. He struggled against his bonds but stopped when Lia's eyes washed over him. He was not gagged.

Charlie was behind the door, watching her. "Annalia. I knew you wouldn't be able to stay away."

The use of her full name gave her pause, and she drew herself up to her full height before turning to face the man who had almost killed her. "There seems to be more guests here than I would like," she said quietly.

"Yes, well, I've been searching for you for so long! I wanted to make sure this moment was well worth the wait. I have no doubt that you will please me." He bowed to her, and Lia saw the flash of the gun in his pocket. He couldn't kill her. What was the point of the gun?

"Annalia Sophia Asim," he murmured lovingly as he untied the gags around Westin and Hunter's mouth. "Shhhh," he crooned to them. "This is our moment now. You'll have your chance." He turned to Lia. "You are my soul mate!"

"So I have heard," she said, her voice steady. "Why did you do it?"

"That part should be obvious. I needed a soul to survive this side of the veil. The pitiful piece they gave me would hardly last a day. It wasn't planned. I had no idea I would be facing the only reaper with a soul that day. The chance, however, was too good to pass up. I didn't even know it would work."

Lia started to shake. The closer she was to Charlie, the more whole she felt. The connection was strong, and it vibrated within her. Charlie smiled and moved closer to her. "It is not right," she said, trying to gain control of her voice.

"I would never abandon you. For so long, I hated you." He pulled up his shirt, showing the identical scar that ran along his abdomen. "But trying to kill you nearly killed me. It was then that I knew. We are meant to be together. Our lives are tangled up in each other."

She reached her hand up, and Charlie came to her. "I can feel you. You are part of me," she whispered, stroking his chest.

"I feel your desire for life. To live it. To take it. There is something so different about you. I knew it from the moment I saw your soul," he crooned. "We could be together, and no one could stop us."

Lia caught Hunter's eyes. He'd been so quiet through the whole exchange. After his reaction to the truth, Lia could only imagine that he thought himself in the middle of a madhouse. He watched her now, his expression asking for something that she did not understand. She pushed away from Charlie.

"I would just be collected again if I killed," she said, her eyes on Hunter.

Charlie saw her gaze, and his face darkened. He stepped between her and Hunter. "I wouldn't let them. I can see them coming, and, after all this time, I have learned a thing or two. I can open portals, not just to the realm but also to other parts of the realm. We could run, hide, and be together forever. You would be free."

Lia stared at Westin. "No collectors?"

"No collectors. No judges. No reapers. No fear. Isn't that what you've always wanted?"

"Yes," Lia admitted. She closed her eyes. It was everything she wanted. Charlie was the first person who seemed to accept her. Of course, it was probably just her other half of the soul accepting her, but it made no difference. He was offering her everything she had ever wanted.

"There's just one thing."

Lia heard the cock of the gun and her eyes flew open. Charlie was pointing the gun at her. "I need to know you're on board, hook, line and sinker. You've grown soft since these past couple of months. I need to know that you're still the woman who can be my other half." He moved the gun, pointing it at Hunter.

"You will choose. Kill one, or I'll kill them both."

The world slowed down for Lia. She could feel every heartbeat, hear every breath, as her eyes slid from Charlie to Hunter to Westin. She imagined Hunter's blood on her hands, and Westin's blood weighing down on her. She saw their expressions of betrayal. She felt the satisfaction of slating her desire to kill. It was her choice.

She pointed to the kid in the back. "Can I kill him?"

"What?" The kid squeaked.

"No," Charlie said mildly. "He's my friend."

Lia stared at him. She cocked her head. "You have a friend?"

Charlie nodded his head. "Yes. It's a bit odd, I know."

"And you're going to keep your friend bound?"

Charlie shrugged. "I haven't thought that far in advance

yet?"

Lia turned and smiled at the kid. "You're his friend?"

"I'm his friend," the kid repeated.

Lia fell silent, and Charlie waved his gun around. "Who will it be? The lover who denied you? No one would blame you. Westin has been with you for years, but this man has only known you for months.

"Or maybe it's the collector. He has lied to you from the start. He's over four hundred years old, and this man is still so young. It would be coming full circle. You were supposed to kill Westin all those years ago, in your first life."

Charlie moved the gun back and forth as if mimicking her decision. "Decisions, decisions. I feel the stress in your soul. Let me make it easy for you. One last bit of truth." He smiled at Westin, as he leaned forward, brushing his lips over Lia's ears. "You were not on the list."

Lia snapped her head around, giving Charlie a quizzical look. "What list?"

A smile crossed his face. "The list. The list the judges maintain on who gets collected. You were never on it."

Lia searched Westin's face. The look of shame he wore was too much to bear. She chose, instead, to stare into Hunters eyes. She found comfort there as her chest squeezed tight. "That is not possible," she whispered.

"Adrenaline, anger, it can give a person so much strength. After all, you almost reaped my soul when we first met. What makes you think that a man, given the power to destroy, wouldn't go after the woman who killed his wife? What makes you think that he didn't have the power to collect a soul that was never meant to be collected?"

"I'm sorry, Lia," Westin whispered. "I'm so sorry."

His words fell on deaf ears. Lia wasn't even paying attention to Westin. She was still staring at Hunter. Reality had finally hit home, and the truth was dawning on him. He knew that she was a killer. He knew the truth about her.

"I was not supposed to be collected," she echoed, still staring at Hunter.

"No, you could have lived a long and murderous life had it not been for a vengeful collector. Why do you think you kept your soul? The judges saw an opportunity to experiment. She's not supposed to be here. Let's use her! What happens if reapers keep their souls? Let's find out. Not to mention that your soul was deliciously tempting," Charlie said softly.

Lia nodded. Her decision had been made. "That does make it easy," she whispered. She walked over to Hunter and reached out, touching his face. "I know you hate me. I know this is so hard for you to understand. I scare you. You do not even know who I am anymore." She laughed a little. "I heard that line in a movie somewhere, but I think now it is very true. I want nothing more than to prove you wrong. Being with you made me think that I could change, and I want you to remember that as you watch me do this. Remember that I wanted to change for you. And..." she swallowed. The words were difficult to say. "Forgive me for this."

"Lia," Hunter said softly. He had watched everything silently, not knowing what to say. The situation was beyond comprehension, and he saw no way out. He wanted her safe, and he saw that this was the only way.

She smiled and leaned over to kiss him one last time. "You save lives. And you have your whole life ahead of you, and I know you will continue to save lives. Charlie is right. We are very old. It is time to do what should have been done a very long time ago."

She moved from Hunter to Westin.

"It's okay," Westin said.

"It has to be immediately fatal or else he'll heal. He still has a lot of reaper realm remnants on him," Charlie warned.

Lia nodded. "We are very old," she said to Westin. "Even with all those memories back, I probably still do not feel as old as you do, but I know it. I feel it in my bones." She smiled. "I find it ironic that you have taught me so much about life. Perhaps it is guilt from taking my first from me."

She rolled her head back, attempting to relieve the tension in her shoulders. She raised the blade. "All those corpses you saw. All those kills, and yet you said you believed I could change. But you lied to me. You kept so many secrets from me. Maybe, if I had known, things could have been different. I could have been different." There was a harsh truth behind her words, but no malice.

Her eyes fluttered towards Charlie's gun. "Put it away. I have made my choice. I will be very upset if you kill Hunter after I kill Westin."

Charlie lowered the gun. The words finally came to Lia, the ones she'd struggled with for so long. She looked at Hunter. "I am sorry you have to see this," she whispered. She moved her attention to Westin. His eyes widened in surprise. "I am sorry for everything. Goodbye."

She plunged the knife. Westin realized too late what she was doing. "No," He shouted, even as the blade tipped into her chest, sliding in, straight into her heart.

Time slowed. Everything happened simultaneously. A portal opened, and Paul and Allen stepped through. Charlie, still connected with Lia, began to bleed from his chest. Allen caught Charlie as he fell, raising the soul inside him as he died, blood pouring out of his chest. Paul caught Lia and pulled the knife out. It clattered to the floor. He placed a hand over her chest, slowing the blood.

The kid in the back stared at the scene, a look of horror on his face. Hunter held the same expression. They could see the portal and the two reapers. "Who the hell are you?" the Irish boy sputtered.

Nobody answered him. Allen held the soul he'd pulled out of Charlie with an odd look on his face. "What the hell is this?" he asked Paul.

Paul reached over and took it. "Orders are orders," he said. He reached over Lia, half her soul in one hand, the other over her heart. Time slowed. "Hello, lover. Time to fix you," he muttered. She could feel him calling for her soul. She struggled against it, but she wasn't anywhere near strong enough to stop him.

"No. I did not kill anyone," she managed.

"Well, that's not technically true. You nearly killed yourself," Paul pointed out. Lia arched in pain as her soul slid out of her body. The whole room fell silent. Paul stopped a moment to stare at the two halves of her soul, each in separate hands.

The soul that slid out of Charlie was solid and black. The soul he slid out of Lia was also solid, but white. It pulsed in pure light and beauty.

Paul looked at Westin, but Westin was used to the sight of Lia's soul. He smiled.

"This should be interesting," Paul muttered, and then he closed his hands, melting the two together. They all watched in silent anticipation.

Lia was freezing into a shell, but she forced herself to view her memories, to stay human. She wanted to see. She wanted to remember.

The two sides fused together to form one. After a moment, Paul shrugged then reached over and hovered the soul over Lia.

Even as she was dying, she struggled. "No," she cried out. "I do not want it," she managed, but Paul was already pushing the soul against her chest, melting it into her. He put one hand on her head.

"Good luck," he said, and her vision faded to black.

Attempting to process the scene around him, Hunter stared. "Oh my god," he whispered. Then it dawned on him. She was gone. He'd watched her shimmer out of the man's arms into nothingness.

"What did you do to her? Who the hell are you?" Hunter

demanded.

Allen walked over and undid the ropes on Hunter and Westin. Hunter immediately launched himself at Paul. "You could have saved her. I could have saved her. Where the hell is she?" He punched Paul before Westin pulled him away.

Paul rubbed his chin and glanced at Westin. "Really? She picked this guy?"

"What is going on, Paul?"

"Special reap," Paul said. He wiggled his fingers. "Special abilities, and a new promotion!" He reached over, touching Hunter's head.

"No, don't take his memories," Westin objected.

"Relax. I'm under strict orders to plant new ones."

Hunter cried out at Paul's touch. "Oh god," he muttered, shaking his head in confusion.

"Dual memories. It's difficult to get used to, but when the police ask what happened here, you are now programmed to give them a different scenario, one that does not involve Lia. She no longer exists in anyone's mind but yours and Westin's."

Westin understood. "You are collecting her."

Paul shook his head. "I don't know what I'm doing. I was told to send her some place special. I think..." he hesitated. "I think she has to face a judge."

"What? What the hell does that mean?" Hunter demanded. He thought he was taking all of this in stride, but he wanted answers.

"Why?" Westin asked, ignoring Hunter.

"What the hell is going on?" Connor asked frantically. "Can someone untie me, please?"

Everyone turned and stared at him. Paul reacted first. "Who the hell is this kid? He's not supposed to be here."

Westin stared at Connor. "I'm not sure who he is exactly," he muttered.

"No worries," Paul said. He reached out to touch Connor.

The man jerked away, pushing his chair over, landing on the floor.

"Don't touch me," he hissed.

Paul shook his head. "Sorry, kid." He reached over and touched the kids head again, frowning. "I can't take his memories. What the hell is this?"

Westin whirled around. Of all the strange occurrences of the day, this was the least of his worries. "I will deal with him."

The portal was opening again. Hunter looked around, realizing they were leaving. "You never answered my question. What does it mean that Lia needs to face the judges?"

Allen stepped through, melting into the gray. "I don't know, man. It can't be good," Paul answered before backing in through the portal, also disappearing.

Westin and Hunter and Connor were alone with Charlie's dead body. Westin walked over, untying Connor. "He was telling the truth," Connor whispered.

"Yes," Westin said quietly. The man didn't put up a fight as Westin reached over and planted the new memories. "Anytime anyone asks about what happened, you will lie. Lia no longer exists. Reapers don't exist. Is that understood?"

Connor stared at him. "No one would believe me."

Hunter's head hurt. He felt powerless after everything he had heard, everything he had witnessed. "She's gone," he whispered.

Lia was gone.

Chapter Twenty-Four

Water rushed somewhere off in the distance, and a constant breeze was assaulting her body. Lia shivered as a cold chill wreaked havoc on her body, bringing her to her senses. She opened her eyes and stared at the blue sky above her. Gravel dug into her back.

She pushed herself up and found herself staring at the blue waters of a rushing river through the green of the rustling leaves of a tree. She was not in the reaper realm.

Flashes entered her mind. Pain ripped through her head, and she cried out. It seemed as though an eternity of time marched through her head. She saw the dead, those that she had killed and those that she had reaped, scream in agony, trapped in her mind. She saw the living, all that she had known, staring accusingly.

Memories. She held her head silently, rocking back and forth until the pain subsided.

"Not so fun, is it?"

She looked up. Standing over her was a man, tall and slender. She recognized him. He held his hand out to her. "I imagine that mashing in centuries of memories would cause a bit of a headache."

Tired, Lia reached up and took his hand. As she straightened, she felt a sharp pull of her chest. Ignoring modesty, she lifted her shirt. Mirroring each other were her two old scars on each side of her abdomen. High on her chest, in the very middle, were the stitches holding her skin together. She tried to remember how they got there.

"It took a lot of energy to keep you from dying. Odd, that those stitches are the only thing holding you together." Lia looked up at the man sharply.

"It's only been a week, I believe. I would leave them alone. We are equipped to do an extraordinary amount of things, but stitching up people does not seem to be a talent of mine," the voices said wryly.

She moved her hand down, touching the scars. Memories rushed at her, and she ran her hand over the mysterious left scar. She smiled.

"Name me." His voice commanded her attention, and she obeyed.

"Judge," she muttered. He finally came into focus, and she stared. He was no one, nothing stood out, nothing to describe him, nothing to remember him by, and yet he seemed to demand her attention.

"Very good."

"Are you the only judge?" she asked.

"No. I am the undecided."

Lia waited for an explanation, but it never came. She looked around. "Why do you keep bringing me to this place? Where are we?"

"Oh, you know that better than I do. Tell me where we are."

She focused on several points of her setting. To her left was a smooth rock, perfectly round, blending in with the others but grabbing her attention. Above her were towering trees that whistled angrily in the wind. The water was crashing against the riverbanks violently, far more violently than the wind allowed. Instinctively she knew that this was normally a calm place. Something had upset this spot. Something violent.

She focused her memories. It came to her, buried deep. Further down, to her right, a woman materialized.

Lia gasped. The waves were crashing to shore, and they brought with them the body of a young woman. As soon as the river had pushed her out, the waters calmed, and the wind died down. The young woman coughed violently, expelling water. Her long dark hair hung down her shoulders, weighing her down. Her flimsy dress had turned transparent, pressing against her skin. She looked over, staring right through Lia, not realizing that her future self, centuries old, was watching her.

"I remember this." She turned to the judge. "Why have you brought me here?"

He was staring at her memory as she struggled to pick herself up. "We want to know why you were in the river."

It was an odd question. She opened her mouth before realizing that she didn't have an answer. "I do not know. I guess you did not give me that memory," she said a little angrily.

"We brought you here to walk you through your first memory," he said, now turning his attention on her.

"My first memory? That is not possible. I look no younger here than I do now."

He started to walk towards her memory, and Lia followed, stumbling over the rocks. He seemed to float over them. They stopped short of the younger Lia, who was oblivious to them.

"Did you see it?" he asked abruptly.

Instinctively, Lia knew what he was talking about. Her soul. "Yes," she said guardedly.

"Do you know who carries white souls?"

Lia shook her head. "No. I have never seen one before."

"White souls are found in newborns and infants. They are the purest of souls, occurring only in those who have not been tainted by the human experience. By the time you humans become toddlers, you begin to learn, to puzzle out strategies, and to retain memories. You mimic what is around you, and you begin to look out for yourself. By doing so, the soul becomes colored with desires, dreams, and lies. Experience strips it, and the result ends in common colored and transparent souls, and far darker black and opaque souls." He searched her face for answers. "So why was your soul so pure?"

Lia was uncomfortable with the question. "The obvious

answer is that it is not. You know the life that I lead. How can I have a pure soul? Maybe it is just another level of evil."

"Where were you born?"

Lia opened her mouth, but no answer came out. She closed it.

"What is your birthday?

Silence.

"Who are your parents?"

Silence.

"Who taught you to skip pebbles across the water? Who was your first best friend? What was your first injury? When did you first lie?" He fired the questions at her, one after another and seemed to loom larger with each word. "These shape you as a person. Answer me!"

"I do not know!" she shouted finally

The judge exhaled, becoming normal again, and cocked his head. He seemed to search her for an answer. Finally, he turned his head to the memory of Lia, who had now pulled herself up and was stumbling slowly down the bank.

"We do not judge actions. We judge intentions. We know when humans are going to kill long before they kill. We don't judge the actual action of murder. That is why some murder and go uncollected. Instead, we judge the whole life. We see the experiences leading up to the kill, the circumstances surrounding the kill, and finally, the consequences of the kill. We know the color of your soul long before we send a reaper or a collector for you.

"You can understand our surprise when the collector's wife was murdered without our knowledge." He looked at Lia for comprehension. "The killing of Westin's wife is the first time we'd ever laid eyes on you, and even then, we could not see your intentions or your soul. We could only see your body, a shell, which housed a memory bank that was far too short for your age."

"What do you want from me?"

The judge drew himself up, seeming to grow another couple of feet. "We want to know where you came from. We want to know who you are. We want to know what to do with you."

Lia squinted her eyes to focus on the judge, but the river was disappearing, and the judge was fading away.

O'Ryan found Agent Westin waiting outside a cabin with the doctor and a stranger. He stared at the three men as the conversation with Westin over the phone echoed in his head.

The Phoenix was dead.

He looked around, looking at the woman. "Where is Lia?" O'Ryan demanded.

Westin stared at him, and O'Ryan could hear an odd whine in his head. He put his finger up to his temple, massaging it. In an instant, the odd pain and whine were gone. He shook his head, trying to refocus on the agent. What was he saying? He stared at Westin.

"Are you all right?" he asked.

"I'm fine. You remember Dr. Logan?"

O'Ryan searched his memories. "Yes. You treated Amanda," he said, shaking the man's hand.

The doctor nodded. Westin pointed to the stranger. "This is Connor. He was Charlie's neighbor. He made the original call to 911. He witnessed his neighbor dragging Hunter's body inside. When he went inside to try and help. Charlie drugged him."

The agent turned to the young man. "You're a hero," he said, shaking his hand. The boy looked dazed.

Westin motioned for him, and O'Ryan, with the other agents, followed him inside. O'Ryan winced. There was something he wanted to say, something on the tip of his tongue, but he couldn't quite make it out.

Inside, they found Charlie's body. "He pulled a gun on Logan. I snuck up from behind, but he heard me coming. There was a struggle. Charlie pulled a knife, and I overpowered him. I'm sorry, O'Ryan, I know you wanted to question him."

O'Ryan waved his hand. "I just wanted it to be over. Are you sure we have the right guy?"

"There are piles of ash upstairs. That, and a verbal confession to me and Logan and Connor are all we have."

O'Ryan nodded. "Why didn't you follow protocol and wait for backup?"

The other agent shook his head. "I was afraid there wouldn't be enough time."

O'Ryan turned to the officers. "Detail the area. I want as much evidence as possible. Caxton, you've got some paperwork to fill out."

Westin nodded. "Connor needs to be looked over by a paramedic. I think he's dehydrated, and he may still have some lingering substance from whatever Charlie subdued him with."

Lichton stepped forward. "Come on, kid, I'll take your statement while the paramedics look you over."

"I'll head back to the station and start on that paperwork," Westin said quietly. O'Ryan barely heard him. As the man walked away, another sharp tone sounded in his head. He exhaled sharply and rubbed his temple. His vision was blurring a bit.

"Are you all right?" Hunter asked.

O'Ryan stared at the doctor. "I just keep getting these headaches," he muttered. "I'd like to take your statement back at the station if you are all right with that."

The doctor nodded. "Sure. I'll hitch a ride back with Agent Caxton."

O'Ryan looked up. "You mean Agent Lichton?"

Confusion crossed the doctor's face. "No, I mean Caxton."

O'Ryan narrowed his eyes. "Doctor, we don't have any agents named Caxton. Maybe you should go to the hospital with the kid just to be on the safe side. I think you might have taken a harder hit in the head than you realize?"

The doctor looked around. "Right," he muttered. He followed Mallich to the car.

The agent stared at the body of the man before him. He'd been the stuff of nightmares, but now, lying still on the ground, he looked like an ordinary man incapable of evil.

Eager to wrap up the loose ends and head home to fix his marriage, he turned and left the nightmare behind him.

The bank disappeared. Lia found herself standing in a large seemingly endless room. A spotlight surrounded her and the judge as they stared at each other. She closed her eyes against the dizzying effects of the jump. "Take a moment to steady yourself. Walking through a memory is not easy."

Lia swallowed hard, trying to ease her turning stomach. "Where are we?"

He ignored her. "We could not list you for a collector because we could not identify you. After the kill, we lost sight of you. How Westin ever found you is nothing short of luck. We thought perhaps the holes in your memory bank were simply because we hadn't had enough time to analyze you. When Westin pulled out a pure white soul, we knew that we were wrong."

"Maybe I had a head injury and forgot who I was," Lia tossed out, her senses returning to normal.

"Amnesia is merely suppressing a memory. If it exists, we can access it. That is not the answer."

Lia started to pace in frustration. "What do you want from me? I do not have the answers you are looking for."

Suddenly, the room lit up. Television screens lined the walls, displaying her most prominent memories. Her kills, her collections, the girls from the restaurant, and her moments with Hunter played silently. Lia caught her breath. It was one thing to remember them. It was something entirely different to see them in front of her.

"You are very technologically advanced," she muttered.

"You do not have the answers for us. Although you display the stark duality of good and evil, you are human through and through. As a collective, we are split. Half of us believe you belong to us, the other half believe we have wronged you. I stand here, before you, as the only undecided."

Lia did not like the sound of that. "What do you think you need to decide?"

"Are you in love with him?"

Lia's eyes immediately focused on Hunter's face on the screen. He was laughing at her as they danced in the crowd at the fair. Her face was lit with delight, and his with love.

"What does that matter?"

"I am the undecided. Please answer the question."

Lia rolled her eyes. "I do not think I know what love is."

The judge raised his hands, and a different screen grew larger and came into focus. It was of Westin, standing over his wife's body while Lia stood over him with the knife. "Why did you not finish the contract?"

Lia closed her eyes. She didn't want to relive these moments. "Why are you asking me?"

"I am the undecided. Please, the answer the question."

She looked at Westin again, crying over his wife's bloody body. "The contract was to release a woman from an abusive and unloving relationship. I knew the brother wanted her for himself, but I thought his love was genuine. Rather than an abusive husband, I instead found that Westin was ready to die rather than face the pain of being without his wife. That is a moment I had never thought possible. The brother lied, and I had already taken enough away from Westin. I spared his life."

"Do you forgive Westin?"

Lia turned to the judge. "For what?"

"For his deceit. For his collection."

Lia laughed. "He may have collected me, but you kept me."

"Do you regret your kills?"

"No."

"Why not?"

She closed her eyes for a moment. "I do not think I am capable of regret." There was silence. Lia watched the judge look at her in puzzlement. "Have you decided what kind of person I am?"

"Are you aware that your soul is whole?"

Lia's eyes flitted over the screen where Paul was merging her souls. "Yes," she whispered.

"How do you feel?"

"Weighed down."

"We believe the soul to be the very core of your desire to kill. You are a danger to the whole system."

Lia rubbed her temples. "I think it does not matter. My future is based only on your curiosity. And on that, I believe, you have already decided to recycle me into the system."

"You are wrong."

His voice was monotone. No excited or accusations. Lia watched him closely. "What does that mean?"

"I want to give you a choice. As undecided as I am about you, I do believe that your present state is the direct consequence of us choosing your path for you. That does not mean that the blood on your hands is not solely your own, but I do believe, had we left you alone, your path could have been different. That does not mean that I believe it would have been different. I am merely accepting the possibility."

She puzzled through the silence. "Are you going to tell me what my choices are?"

"I am waiting for you to ask."

She exhaled irritated. "What are my choices?"

"You did try to kill yourself. We are offering you a chance to cross over and die."

Again silence. "I believe there is supposed to be another

option," she pointed out.

"You could be a master. You would run a unit of reapers until you decided to move on. It will free you from the burden of your past."

"Die or be a master," she mused. She blew out her breath. "How long do I have to decide?"

"Immediately would be preferable."

"You want me to make a decision about my future now?"

"Yes. And by preferable, I mean that you have no choice. Choose, or I choose for you."

"That request seems familiar," Lia muttered. Was she ready for death? Was she willing to be back under the control of the judges?

"Would you like to hear your third option?"

Lia stared at the judge. "Yes, yes I would. And any other options that come after that!"

"There are no other options after the third. You only have three."

Lia threw her hands up in the air. "What is my third option?"

"Life."

Lia froze. "What?"

"Assuming you don't kill anyone, you can live the rest of your natural life in this time period. You retain all of your soul and all of your memories. You can have your life back, and you can spend it with him."

Lia's breath caught in her throat. A life. A life with Hunter. She closed her eyes to imagine it. She could hide in his arms whenever she felt scared; she could kiss his lips whenever she needed to remember that she was real.

Assuming you don't kill anyone. Her eyes flew open, and she stared at his face on the television screen. The judge waved his hand, and the screens shifted. Each of them showed Hunter, slumped over in the chair, his head in his hands. "He is mourning you. He does not know if you will return."

She could feel the war inside her. She felt the chains of her soul wrapping around her, struggling for control.

And then she knew. "Death," she whispered. "I choose death."

The judge's eyes widened. It was the first expression he had given. "I give you a choice of master and death and you cannot choose. I offer you life, what you desire most, and you choose death. Why?"

She looked at him sharply. "That is not your concern. I made a choice. I expect you to honor it."

He turned his gaze to the screens. They flickered and changed again. As he focused on a screen, it grew. One by one, they projected snapshots of her life. The night she spared Westin. The night she received her first stab wound. The day her soul was first revealed. They went on and one until he focused on the moment Lia tried to kill herself.

Suddenly he was standing right in front of her. She stumbled back, but he gripped her tight. "You made your choice. I will honor it."

Pain ripped through her. She blacked out before she could open her mouth to scream.

Chapter Twenty-Five

Exhausted from the night's events, Hunter dragged himself to the sofa in the living room. After the hospital, he had found Westin waiting for him in his house. He dropped next to him, putting a hand on Jacks for comfort.

"Everything was true. I saw you erase that agent's memories. You do have that power," he said quietly. "Tell me about her," he asked quietly.

The collector sat next to him on the sofa. "I was born in 1627. When I first encountered Lia, we were both human. She was a killer for hire. She had a contract on my life from my brother, but she ended up killing my wife instead. I was grief stricken. Within days, I was offered a chance, by a voice in the wind, to help cleanse the world of evil. It was convincing, and I agreed. That was how I first learned of judges and reapers and collectors.

"It's a flawed system but still decent. The judges monitor humanity. When evil becomes too unmanageable, they step in. They send collectors. I erase their memories, collect their souls for the judges, and they are reprogrammed in an alternate plane. They carry out their sentences reaping souls and helping them pass on.

"Souls are complicated but beautiful. Most of them are translucent, swirling about in colors, much like auras. They are forever changing by outside influence and human will. Unfortunately, there are also opaque, black souls. They are unaffected by the world, bogged down in evil.

"When I was first given the powers of a collector, I was still enraged by the death of Caroline. It gave me unimaginable power. I did the unthinkable and went after Lia. In my mind, she was evil, but to the judges, she was a mystery. When I handed Lia over to the judges, they found their first adult with a white soul. White souls are unaffected by the environment. They're found mostly in infants. Also, her soul was solid. It couldn't be changed by will. It is constant. It's the first I have ever seen. The judges didn't want to give her back. She was a puzzle to them, but they had no place for her soul. She was allowed to keep it, but she had no idea. Housing a soul gave her the ability to move through the veil that separates the reaper realm from this world. She didn't do it on purpose, but there were accidental slips. At least, it seemed accidental."

He turned and looked at Hunter. "Are you sure you want to hear this?"

Hunter swallowed and nodded. "Yes."

"Every time she slipped though, she killed someone. She totaled nineteen deaths. They were almost all instant. It usually only took days for her to kill."

He went on the explain Charlie, and how the partial soul weakened Lia. "I think, for the first time, she was susceptible to humanity. She tried so hard to be good. Her will might be stronger than her soul if she just gave it a chance."

"Will she come back?" Hunter asked.

Westin shook his head. "I don't know. Do you want her too?"

Hunter nodded. "Yes."

"Even after everything you know about her?"

"You have witnessed her actions, and you still stand by her side," Hunter pointed out.

Westin paused. "I want to believe there is something more to her."

Hunter exhaled slowly. "I don't want to believe it. I already know it," he saw quietly.

Lia opened her eyes. She was relieved to find that death was warm and comfortable. She burrowed deeper into the soft materials beneath her.

A mattress.

She frowned. Someone was panting.

Jacks.

She bolted up to find herself in Hunter's room with the golden retriever staring at her from the floor. He looked around for his master and, not finding him, jumped up on the bed to give Lia a slobbering kiss on the cheek.

Lia ran her hands over everything to confirm that it was real. It felt real.

"Why?" she whispered.

The judge's voice whipped through her mind. *His safety was more important than your life.*

"What does that have to do with anything?" she asked.

Maybe everything. Maybe nothing. You are unknown. But knowing love could save you.

"I made a choice."

I honored the decision in your heart.

"You believe I'm good?"

Undecided.

She closed her eyes and searched for her soul. It still felt heavy and solid, like it could destroy her.

Tell Westin we will be seeing him soon.

Lia was alone once again. Listening for sounds of Hunter, she slid off the bed and made her way through the house. She found him in the kitchen, staring absentmindedly at an untouched plate of food.

She knocked softly. He looked up and stared for a moment. "Are you real?"

She nodded. "Yes."

"Are you staying?"

She shook her head. "No. It's too dangerous," she said, her heart breaking.

"I don't care what you've done. I don't care what you feel like you might do. I won't let you go again," he said softly.

She leaned against the doorframe. "If you knew," she muttered.

"I do know. Westin told me everything, and it makes no difference. You are not the person you once were." He stood and walked over to her.

"Death speaks to me. It's stronger than me," she whispered.

He wrapped her in his arms. "It's not stronger than you. I promise you I won't let anything happen to you. Stay with me."

He held her tighter, and she finally surrendered.

He kissed her on the top of her head. "Stay with me."

Westin found himself on the edge of a river. The trees swayed dangerously in the violent wind. The waters rose in waves, tossing Lia's body around like a ragdoll.

"Hello, Westin."

He turned and faced the judge. "Why have you brought me here?"

"Twice you have disobeyed us. You have kept a dangerous secret," the voices accused. The man floated his way, his eyes boring into Westin's. "You do not deserve another chance."

Westin tensed, waiting for his inevitable execution. "The world is not as black and white as you would have us believe," he said coldly.

"We know that better than anyone," the judge said softly. He faced the river. "Do you know who she is?"

"Lia."

"Do you know who Lia is? Do you know what she is capable of?"

Westin followed his gaze. "She's capable of murder," he said, puzzled at the turn in conversation.

The judge moved suddenly, so quickly that Westin nearly fell over. He stood close to the entity, and for the first time, he could see the differences between them.

The blurred figure was focused, his eyes completely black, his cheekbones jutting outwards, stretching the skin so taught that it was nearly translucent.

On the side of his neck was a tattoo, a symbol similar to one Westin had seen before. He stared at it.

"We are not of this world, Westin. We stay here to protect you from the dangers you could not possibly comprehend. She is like us, but she is not one of us. She is dangerous."

Westin stepped back. "What are you talking about? Yes, she's a murderer. That's well established."

"She is more than that. She is dangerous."

"If she is so dangerous, why don't you recycle her?"

"We cannot. She resists. She is dangerous."

"I don't understand," he breathed heavily. "She's just a woman."

The judge turned and stared at the figure crawling up on the shore. "She is a key. You must find the door. If she opens it, we are all lost."

The scene was fading. "What?" Westin called out. "What the hell are you talking about? How can she be a key?"

"Find the door. Find the door, and we will give you a second chance."

"The door to what?"

"The door to worlds."

Lia stared at herself in the mirror of Hunter's bathroom. She was fully human, with a full soul, albeit one half dark and the other half white. She had a boyfriend. She was capable of feeling something for that boyfriend. She was able to forgive Westin, and Westin was able to forgive her.

She frowned. Westin. She was concerned for his future. She was concerned for her future. How long would this last? How long until she felt the urge to kill? How long until the judges realized that they had made a mistake.

Who was she? She looked normal enough. She looked human. She felt human. How could the judges not know where she came from? What could she have possibly done to make her erase her memories? To make the judges forget her?

"One day at a time," she whispered to herself. Hunter was downstairs making dinner. She made her way out of the bathroom to join him.

She could hear him clanking around the kitchen and singing to himself. He had a terrible singing voice. It made her smile.

"Can I help?" she asked tentatively.

He whirled around and stared at her. "What?" he asked.

"Can I help you?" she repeated.

A strange look crossed his face. "What are you doing here?"

She took a step back. There was a blank look in his eyes that she didn't like. "What do you mean? We were just talking," she said confused.

"Excuse me? Who the hell are you? What are you doing in my house?"

Acknowledgements

This book has been several years in the making, and it would not have been possible without the help of several amazing people.

To my mother who always supported my writing endeavors, and to my brother, Taylor, and my sister-in-law Tamara, who thought my book was awesome before they even read it.

To Allison, who helped with the last-minute copy. You're awesome.

To Katie, who suffered through some awful first drafts. I'm sorry.

To Kira, Shayla, Amber, Robin, Luke, Meredith, Beth, Cam-Van, Danielle, Jeremy, Kristina, and Maggie for all their opinions on content and book covers.

And lastly, to the crewmembers of Firebirds for putting up with my constant conversations about my book. I'm sure it got annoying. I'm sorry.

You have all been amazing. Thank you.

About the author

Abbie lives in central Virginia with her two dogs and cat. She has a M.A. in English Literature from Mercy College and loves all things mysterious and fantastical. When she's not writing, she's usually obsessing about her favorite television shows Charmed, Merlin, and Once Upon a Time.

This is her debut novel.

CPSIA information can be obtained at www.ICGtesting.com
Printed in the USA
BVOW06s0907300916

463786BV00037B/174/P